PRAISE FOR SARAH A. BAILEY

"Bailey's prose is so achingly romantic..."
-*Kirkus Reviews*

"**Lush, sensual**, and **entirely fresh**,
Sarah A. Bailey's writing is certain to be a **new favorite!**"
- *USA Today* Bestselling Author Tarah DeWitt

"*Heathen & Honeysuckle* is a second-chance masterpiece.
An absolute must-read."
- *USA Today* Bestselling Author Cali Melle

"*Wicked & Wildflower* is romance at its most breathtaking–emotion-packed and **brimming with delicious tension.** Sarah always creates a world you can get lost in, with characters so real it feels like they're sitting next to you, and *Wicked & Wildflower* is no exception.
Simply unputdownable."
- *USA Today* Bestselling Author Bailey Hannah

"A perfect blend of **carefully crafted plot** and **irresistible heat**. Sarah is a master at creating relatable characters that you can't help but fall in love with...Her writing is both passionately sexy and **deeply heartfelt**, and *Wicked & Wildflower* is no exception. **Pure perfection.**"
- Ambar Cordova, author of the *Baker Oaks Series*

TATTERED TIDES

TATTERED TIDES

SARAH A. BAILEY

PAGE
&
VINE

Page & Vine
An Imprint of Meredith Wild LLC

This is a work of fiction. Names, characters, places, and incidents either are the product of the author's imagination or are used fictitiously, and any resemblance to actual persons, living or dead, business establishments, events, or locales is entirely coincidental. The publisher does not assume any responsibility for third-party websites or their content.

The author acknowledges the trademarked status and trademark owners of various products referenced in this work, which have been used without permission. The publication/use of these trademarks is not authorized, associated with, or sponsored by the trademark owners.

Paperback ISBN: 978-1-964264-42-4

For the tender-hearted girls who carry it on their sleeve:
May you wear it proudly, and never forget the
quiet courage found in a soft soul.

& for Jenna, because there wouldn't be this
if there hadn't been you.

CONTENT WARNING

Tattered Tides is intended for readers 18+ and includes heavy emotional and explicit content.

Detailed warnings can be found at:
www.sarahabaileyauthor.com

CHAPTER ONE

WESTON

I WONDER IF I'm an adversary or a welcomed friend to the water that laps at my fingers, splitting around the atoms of my flesh and bone before rejoining behind my palm, continuing its tidal journey toward the shore.

I wonder if it's all connected, each droplet aware of the others. I wonder if they're aware of me, and if I'm a disruption to their peaceful way of life. Or maybe, I'm connected to them too. Sitting atop ocean waves is the closest I've ever been to peace. Perhaps it's simply the water sharing its tranquility with me. Maybe it knows I won't find it elsewhere.

If the moon can connect with the tides, who's to say the tides can't connect with me too?

Penelope believes in shit like that, I think. That we're all just pieces of stardust stuck together in human form, and the true purpose of life is our search for other pieces of stardust that feel like home.

But maybe I was never stardust. Maybe I was an ocean wave.

"Wes? You good? Want to head back?" The sound of Carter's voice floats to my ears from behind, and I turn to find him watching me curiously, head tilted. His hands curl around the edges of his board as a swell rolls beneath him.

It looked like a nice one, and I realize now, I let it coast past me as I'd been staring at the water, lost in thought. I turn back around, lifting my head toward the horizon. It's early, so the sun rise is behind us, casting light over the Pacific. I inhale the fresh salt air, remembering a time when the concept of deep breath, seawater, and a surfboard were all but foreign to me. An unreachable desire, an undiminishable craving. There weren't even pockets of peace in those years. The day I stepped out of those thick steel doors and tasted that ocean breeze again for the first time in too long, I swore to myself that I'd never take it for granted.

"I'm good!" I call behind me. "You can head back if you want, though."

He doesn't respond immediately, but after a moment, I hear the precise rhythm of paddling before the tip of his board floats past me, and Carter appears at my side. His black wetsuit is zipped to his neck, just like mine. He runs a hand through the dark curls tousled on the top of his head, the slivers of silver at his temples glistening in the early morning light. "Nah, I'm here with you. Unless you want me to leave?"

I wish he'd stop treating me with kid gloves. When I was in my teens, he was adamant I never be out on the water on my own. He'd spend hours—entire days—out here with me, no matter how much I'd bitch and moan about wanting to be left alone. Now, I never have to fight for space. I never have to fight at all. Every meal I eat, every place I want to go, everything I want to do—it's like my former foster parents are at my beck and call.

It's never what I wanted from them.

I just wanted to be treated like any other kid, and I know there can't be any other unemployed, fresh-out-the-slammer, no-future-to-speak-of twenty-year-old out there who is as fucking spoiled as I am.

"What do *you* want to do right now, Carter?" I ask, though it comes out snappier than I intend. I take a breath before continuing. "Do you actually want to be out here surfing, or would you rather go back to bed with your wife?"

"Pep doesn't let me back in bed after I've been covered in salt water." He flashes me a grin, then frowns, jaw tightening. "Do you know what I actually want, Weston?" When I don't answer, he continues, "I want you to recover from this in whatever way you can. I don't know what that looks like, and I don't know how to make it work for you, but I want—desperately—for you to be better."

I shrug, unsure how to respond or comfort him. I don't have the answers either.

In the past six months since being released from jail, I've tried individual and group therapy, living on my own in one of the apartments Carter and Penelope own above their art gallery, living with Carter and Penelope themselves, and I've tried community college. None of it panned out. The only thing that makes me feel okay is sitting out here on a surfboard. It's the only time my past feels escapable. It's the only time I'm not eaten alive by the reminder of the future I gave up in a regrettable act of revenge.

"When you were placed with us, you were this broken, mute fourteen-year-old kid who'd gone through something fucking unspeakable." Carter sighs. "We thought we might have nothing more to offer you than a bed and a roof, but over the years . . . you bloomed into this funny, smart, driven young man. A good student. An incredible athlete. A champion. You're kind and caring and thoughtful. Then . . ."

I look down at my board, unwilling to make eye contact. I know what he means. I know I threw it all away too. I know I'm a different person now than I was before it happened.

"Now, we've got you back, but it feels like you're that broken boy again, and what put you back together last time doesn't seem to work now. The wounds cut deeper, and I'm not sure I have the equipment to stitch you up. I need you to help me out."

I shake my head, watching again as the water splits and glides around my legs where they dangle off my board. If I thought I might be a friend earlier, I certainly feel like an adversary now.

"Surfing is the only thing that makes me feel okay. I know I threw away any future I had in the sport. I know my title was stripped, and it can be nothing more than a hobby to me now . . ." I lift my head, meeting his hazel-eyed gaze. "But out here is the only time I feel like I might be healing—like I could be capable of it."

He studies me for a moment, a deep furrow setting in his thick brows before he nods curtly. As if my explanation were enough. At least for now.

I've been working as an assistant to Carter, picking up shifts in his and Penelope's art gallery, Muse, but I know it's not enough. I can't keep living with them and offering nothing more than a bit of half-assed free labor.

I need to get a real job, which isn't easy with my record and lack of work experience.

I turn toward the horizon, studying the oncoming swells, assuming our conversation is over and hoping that Carter might save the heavy shit for when we return home.

But just as I lower to my board, his voice rings out among the waves, "What if I told you this didn't have to only be a hobby? What if I told you that you could still have a future in surfing?"

CHAPTER TWO

WILLOW

I LOWER MY window as I stop at the first four-way intersection in town. My tires grind against the pavement as I press the accelerator again, making a right turn onto Oceanside Boulevard. The sun is just beginning to kiss the horizon to my left, a direct ray of light blasting my cheek as seagulls sing and wind whips through my hair.

I breathe deeply, centering myself in the sights and sounds of home—my favorite place in the world—though the nerves in my gut continue the familiar somersaults I've been experiencing for the duration of my seven-hour drive.

Since I got off the Interstate 5 exit ramp, I've been running on pure instinct. I don't need to make a conscious thought about the first left turn or the three stoplights I pass through before I reach the four-way intersection at the center of Pacific Shores. Just as I don't need to pay attention to where I'm going before my car is suddenly parked in front of the pale yellow, two-story Craftsman-style home with honeysuckle vines framing the front bay window, the white wraparound porch, and the twin rocking chairs beside the front door.

They repainted the house a few years ago, and my mom picked the color. Her favorite.

I know this town well enough to find my way home without much thought, which allows all that extra brain function to filter right to those pent-up nerves inside my stomach and shove them up my throat. I inhale again, giving myself three deep breaths before I'll force myself out of the car. The cameras out front would've already sent an alert about my presence in the driveway, and both cars are here which means they're home. They'll be expecting me now.

I take those three breaths, counting with each one, and on the final exhale, I throw open my door. Stepping out into the California sun, my legs wobble as I stretch. I tremble with each step I take up the path that leads to the front door, past the hydrangeas and wildflowers. I climb the three porch stairs, passing the hanging baskets of violets and calliopes, until I reach the front door.

I lift my fist to knock, but the handle turns before I have the chance to make contact with the door. As it creaks open, I see her hair first—shoulder length and golden, the same color as mine besides the few silver highlights within her strands. I meet my mother's kind hazel eyes and freckled cheeks. She lights up with the warm, familiar smile that feels like home, but the expression on my face must hold something different because her grin quickly fades, replaced by knit brows and a worried frown.

"Willow?" she asks, and I don't know what it is about the sound of her voice that does it to me, but I break down.

The nerves in my throat wrench free in a sob, my trembling limbs finally give out, and my eyes flood with all the emotion I've been holding back. I crumble, collapsing in on myself like a demolished building—breaking from the inside out.

My mother catches me, hooking her arms beneath my shoulders and stopping me from falling to the ground. "Willow," she gasps. "Baby."

I realize she's struggling to hold me up, and I summon all of the strength I can muster to step into the house. Mom helps, hauling me in before slamming the door with her foot.

"Come on, baby," she whispers, keeping her grip on me as she leads me through the foyer and around the staircase into the living room. "Leo!"

It's bright, the sun glittering off the Pacific beyond the paneled windows that line the far wall, and the double doors that lead to the back porch and the cliffside beyond. She helps me onto the plush, cream-colored couch before laying a navy throw blanket over my lap and sitting down beside me, taking me into her arms.

She smells like floral and vanilla, the same body lotion she's worn my entire life.

Footsteps echo from the hallway past the kitchen—the direction of my parents' bedroom. "He'll do great here, don't worry. And bring Penelope down with you, we'll make a night out of it." My dad laughs, the sound a familiar song. "Okay, see you in the—" The moment he enters the room, the words die on his tongue, and I look up to find him frozen, blinking at me.

It only takes a moment for him to scan my face—my tears and my presence, because I'm not supposed to be here to begin with—before he launches into hyperdrive, hanging up his phone and tossing it onto a side table before reaching me in two quick strides and kneeling in front of the couch, leveling our faces.

"Sugar?" he asks, strain in his tone.

I open my mouth, but only another sob bubbles out the moment the nickname leaves his lips. His eyes dart to my mom's, etched with confusion and concern. He rises on his knees, grabbing my face as he brings me into his chest before wrapping one arm around my back and the other around my mother's, cocooning us in a three-way hug that smells like my entire childhood.

"It's okay, Willow," he whispers against my temple. "You're home."

I don't know how long we stay like that, but I'm grateful. Grateful they don't press me immediately for information, grateful I have a place to run—a place to call home. My parents give me time to calm myself and collect my thoughts, because it took all my energy and strength to keep myself going this morning—to hold myself back until he left for class, to pack as much as I could fit into one duffel bag, and sneak out of our apartment before he returned. The composure it took to make the drive, to get back home, exhausted me.

The moment my mother said my name, it hit me like a freight train. Not only the fact that I made it here—that I could finally take a breath, that I could uncoil the knot of anxiety at the center of my being and let my emotions run free—but also what I had escaped. What I had endured that led me here, and the fact that I have no fucking clue what I'm going to do about it.

Once my breathing evens out, my father finally pulls away. He tilts his head, studying me with piercing blue eyes that match my own, keeping a steady hand on my cheek. "What happened, Sugar? Tell me so I can fix it."

My mom grabs my hand where it rests at my side, squeezing it four times. "You're safe, Willow. You can tell us anything."

My eyes sting, and the composure I just spent our long embrace regaining crumbles as tears spill freely down my cheeks. Though I try to swallow the emotion clogging my throat, the words that leave my mouth are nothing more than a fractured whisper.

"He hurt me."

CHAPTER THREE

WILLOW

Five Weeks Later

"Hey," I say to my mom as I round the doorway that leads from the dining room to the kitchen.

She's standing over the island, the counter littered with stems and petals as she trims a massive bundle of flowers. Irises, roses, and peonies burst with bright shades of lavender, yellow, and pink, accented with baby's breath and white foxglove. All spring blooms from her garden out back.

"Morning," she chimes, focused on the flowers in front of her.

When I was younger, my parents were surprised by my engrossment in the arts—painting, specifically. They claimed they didn't know where it came from, but I think they're artists too. I use a brush and a canvas, but my mom uses the earth and my dad the ocean. We're all artists in our own way.

"Allie is back for the summer and had her first shift at the bakery today, so I'm going to see her and we might go out on the water afterward."

Mom pauses, raising her eyes to study me curiously. "Okay. Have fun. Be safe."

"I will." I smile, hoping it reaches my eyes the way I intend.

I spin, stepping toward the front of the house as I grab my purse off the hook behind the door before my mom calls out,

"Willow?"

"Yeah?"

"We've only got a few weeks until the registration deadline for the fall semester, so . . . we should sit down and talk about that here soon."

I sigh, reaching for the door handle. "Yep. Got it. We can talk this weekend."

I don't wait for her response before slipping out of the house. I know there was a deeper message behind her casual observation, but my parents have been trying not to push me on it. I've been home just over a month now, and I've yet to disclose the details of my abrupt breakup with Parker, or my plans for returning to Berkeley—mostly because I don't know them myself.

When I admitted that he'd hurt me, my parents immediately jumped to the conclusion that I'd meant that in a physical way, and even now . . . I'm not sure how I meant it myself. I still don't know how to make sense of what happened, or why it made me feel the way it did. Why it activated my fight-or-flight, or why I ran away. When I rationalize it, I realize I must sound incredibly silly, but when I think about returning to that apartment and back into his arms, bile rises in my throat and my entire body trembles.

The messages he began sending me when he discovered I'd left didn't help the anguish swirling in my bones. At first they were concerned and confused, asking me where I was and when I'd be back, but slowly they turned demanding and harsh when he must've realized I'd packed enough things to signal my intention of never returning. They escalated into phone calls and voicemails where his tone was so curt and cold my spine went rigid with fear.

That's when I knew my instincts had been correct, and I couldn't go back to him. So I sent him one text saying I was moving out and ending things, then promptly blocked his number and all his social accounts. I wanted to cut off all his access to me.

Though, that didn't stop him from finding Allie on social media and reaching out to her too. I hadn't gotten around to explaining the situation to her yet, I'd only told her that I returned home for the summer. Parker was much kinder to her than he was to me, lacing his words with worry and softness—though it was just fake enough to raise Allie's red flags.

I had her and the twins block him too.

I told my parents I wasn't happy, that I thought he might be cheating on me, and I needed time to sort through my feelings and figure out what to do next. I dropped the summer classes I was supposed to take and quit the job I had lined up at a children's art camp in Orinda. My summer courses would've put me on track to graduate a semester early, now that's down the drain. I'm not even sure I want to continue attending Berkeley, and I don't know how to explain to my family that I may be throwing away my entire fucking future over one small instance with my boyfriend that made me feel . . . uncomfortable? Violated? Truthfully, it made me fucking sick, but I can't make sense of my own response to the situation, or whether I'm overreacting.

Sure, Parker's reaction to my leaving was all the confirmation I needed that our relationship should end for good, but I don't think he'd *physically* hurt me. Eventually, he'll get over it, and I'm sure I'd be safe to return to Berkeley, yet some deep unease in the pits of my body surges at the thought of that—the thought of ever being near him again.

Pushing those thoughts and inevitable family conversations to the back of my mind—they're Future Willow's issue—I take a right toward downtown. It's about a ten-minute walk from my parents' house to the boardwalk—which they also own. Five businesses make up the Pacific Shores boardwalk, and each one is operated by a member of our family.

It's become somewhat famous over the years, from the surf shop run by my dad and uncle that's been featured in everything from articles and travel guides to movies and television shows. My aunt's bakery has been highlighted by the Food Network numerous times, her specialized pastry and coffee pairings becoming a Southern California staple. My mom is the most sought-after florist in the region and currently has a wedding waitlist of two years.

My dad's sister, Elena, is better known as an author than a bookshop owner. She's an international bestseller so the store is more of a passion project. Her partner, August, owns the tattoo shop at the end of the boardwalk. He's an award-winning artist and runs a prestigious apprenticeship program for up-and-comers in the industry.

Ultraviolet Tattoo was where I spent most of my boardwalk time in high school. It felt edgy and different from the rest of the businesses. It made me feel cool. August would let me come in after school and mock up digital drawings on his iPad, some of which he's even added to his premade design collection. He still pays me a commission when they get used. Since he's an artist too, when I was young and tumultuous and always mad at my parents over something, Ultraviolet felt like a safe place to escape.

Though, now I prefer Honeysuckle, the flower shop, most of all. It's always bright and colorful. Fragrant in a way that smells like my mom. Since moving to Berkeley for college three years ago, it's Honeysuckle that always brings me back to the peaceful feeling of home when I return.

Now that I plan on staying in Pacific Shores for the remainder of my summer, I'm probably going to need to pick up a few shifts around the boardwalk to pass the time. I make a mental note to ask my mom if she needs any help, because I'd rather work there than Heathen's, my dad's surf shop, and I think my aunt Elena is now fully staffed in the bookstore.

I'm not allowed to work at the bakery after my cousin Zander and I started one accidental, very small kitchen fire when we were seventeen.

When I make it to the intersection of Oceanside and Pacific, I cross the street before making another right turn, which places me directly in front of the boardwalk.

It's a lively, sunny morning. The pier is littered with fishermen, the whitecaps below them dotted with surfers. The Pacific stretches on forever past the carnival rides at the end of the pier, the entire scene nestled picturesquely behind our family's shops.

My mom maintains the rosebushes planted between each of the doors, with baskets of various spring flowers beneath all the windowsills. There are surfboards lined up in front of Heathen's, and buckets of fresh blooms line the sidewalk outside Honeysuckle. Beside it is The Wicked Wildflower, my aunt's cafe and bakery.

Six tables sit to the right of its front door, each one occupied. The sounds of conversation and laughter mingle with the seagulls overhead and the crashing waves in the distance. A few of the cafe's local patrons sitting out front greet me as I pass by, welcoming me home.

"I'll be right with you!" Allie's familiar sing-song voice chimes when I enter.

Her back is turned, facing the espresso maker, so she must not realize it's me. Inside the bakery is much more vacant than outside, but it appears she's running the coffee bar by herself, so I'm sure she's busy. Allie thrives in this, though.

We've been best friends our entire lives, a relationship practically engineered by our parents. Allie grew up in Los Angeles, so we were more like pen pals in our youth and only saw each other a few times a year. By the time we reached our teens, we realized we didn't like any of our other friends quite as much as we liked each other, so during the summers we began begging our parents to let us stay together—either me with her in Pacific Palisades, or her here with me in Pacific Shores.

We convinced our parents to agree to a trade-off that first summer when we were fifteen. Two weeks with Allie's parents, and two weeks down here with mine. Then we repeated it for another month before we had to go back to school. The next summer we did the same thing, except our parents' new stipulation had been we had to work too. Shifts at the boardwalk when we were staying here, and shifts at the art gallery Allie's mom helps run for her best friend up north.

Allie liked being here in Pacific Shores more, not just because she got to work at the bakery, but because of my cousins too. The twins, Archer and Zander, are only a few months younger than us, and Allie's exceptionally close with Archer. She never liked being away from him for long.

I preferred working at the gallery, though. It never felt like work for me. I'd loved art for as long as I could remember, and Allie's aunt, Penelope—another good friend of my parents—is a professor of ancient art and the gallery's owner. Working around her quickly morphed my hobby-like interest into a full-blown obsession, and an artist is all I've wanted to be ever since. I interned with Penelope every summer before I was accepted to Berkeley, and luckily for Allie, she found the same kind of passion in the kitchen at The Wicked Wildflower.

She's attending Golden State University's prestigious culinary program. She tells everyone she wants to be a pastry chef, but I know secretly, her dream is to take over my aunt's bakery someday. She's afraid to voice the desire, assuming the business will go to one of Dahlia's three kids, but honestly, I don't think any of us could imagine my cousins running it better than Allie would.

"No problem." I smile as my best friend freezes at the sound of my voice. "I've got all day."

She immediately drops the portafilter she's holding and whips around. The dark curls framing her face bounce as she spins, and I can't help but laugh when her chocolate eyes go animatedly wide, jaw dropping before a piercing shriek leaves her lips.

She's a flash of movement, running around the counter and into my arms like we're two long-lost lovers that have been searching a lifetime for the other. It feels like that sometimes with her. I've never quite fit with any other person the way I do Allie Evans.

She jumps into me, and I stumble back at the force of it, wrapping my arms around her back as she locks her legs at my waist and forces me to hold her.

"I missed you," I murmur.

"I can't believe you're here all summer," she says into my

shoulder before dropping her legs and stepping out of the embrace. She grabs my face, studying me like she's not sure I'm real. Her entire body vibrates with an aura of excitement that is wholly her before she squeals. "I'm so excited!"

She jumps up and down a few times before pulling me into another hug, and I can't help but laugh, squeezing her extra tight. I'm hoping I can absorb her energy, let some of her zest rub off on me. I need it right now. Everything in life has felt upside down lately. I've been exhausted and drained and sad. Confused and lost.

Allie hasn't been far, not physically. It only takes about a half hour to get to Golden State from Pacific Shores, but in the midst of her finals, I didn't want to add my issues to her already full plate, so I down played the situation with Parker after he reached out to her. Plus, she has a new boyfriend, and I didn't want to take her away from him on top of everything else.

But now she's back here for the summer and has a break from her classes, and I've missed her desperately. "Please tell me you don't have plans today and you're off soon."

She smiles. "I just moved my crap into the studio upstairs last night, so my only plan was to unpack. If you can come help me, I'm all yours, baby."

"I'm all yours too." I squeeze her hand, realizing just how much we look, act, and sound like we truly are long-lost lovers. We're both straight, though, which certainly feels unfortunate at times.

"Do you want something to eat in the meantime? I've got about twenty minutes left."

I shake my head. "I'm not hungry."

I've been feeling nauseous lately. I think it's a side effect of all the stress and gnawing anxiety.

Allie's lips cluster at the corner of her mouth, eyes etched in concern, but she only nods.

I find a table at the back of the cafe and pull out my e-reader, returning to the deliciously angsty small town romance I've been reading while I wait for Allie to finish her shift.

ALLIE AND I exit the bakery out the back before slipping through a second door that takes us up a narrow stairwell, and to the locked door at the top. Allie presses her code into the pad, and I already know what it is without having to look. One-one-two-three. My cousin's birthday. Just the same way his passcodes—and his ATM PIN—have always been hers: zero-seven-zero-six.

After punching in the code, the door clicks, and she pushes it open. All the boardwalk suites have studios above them, but our family has renovated them over the years. There are offices above the surf shop and storage spaces above the flower shop and bookstore. This studio and the one above the tattoo parlor were made into apartments. They're only ever rented out to trusted friends or family.

Directly to my left is a tiny kitchen along the wall, with enough counter space for a sink, stove, coffee maker, and microwave. At the end is a fridge, with cupboard space above and dishwasher beside it. To my right is a small round dining table that only fits two chairs, stacked high with unopened boxes. Past the kitchen is an open room with a queen-size bed beneath a large window spanning the far wall. A pale pink couch sits in front of it, and a TV is mounted on the opposite wall. Beside it is an alcove that houses a clothing rack and a dresser, with a door leading to the bathroom.

"God, it's somehow smaller than I remember," I say.

"I know." She sighs. "It'll work for the summer though. Plus, I don't have to pay rent."

She tosses her keys onto the table, slipping off her shoes by the door before padding to the couch and throwing herself onto it. I do the same, sitting down beside her.

"It's cute, though." Her curtains match the couch, and the embroidery on her comforter is the same color. Boxes line the floor, overflowing with trinkets and decor. I see cream with pops of blue. Inviting and bursting with color, which is the embodiment of Allie. "How did you get the furniture up here?"

"Oh my God." She laughs, hugging a throw pillow to her chest. "My dad and Everett had to do it, and I swear it almost gave them both an aneurysm."

I force a giggle from my lips before crossing my legs beneath me, head swivcling around the room. "Well . . . what should we start unpack—"

"What's going on, Willow?" Allie asks, and when I turn to face her, she's studying me with a hard expression.

I cock my head. "What do you mean?"

"Nope." She shakes hers. "We're not doing that. You knew I'd ask. You were supposed to stay in Berkeley this summer. You broke off your relationship of two years, and prior to you doing so, I'd never heard a lick of concern about Parker from you. It was nauseating, in fact. How perfect you made him out to be. Now, he's messaging me about your whereabouts, and you're back home, pretending like you're fine, when I know there is no way you can be. Spill."

She's right. I knew she'd immediately see right through me, and maybe I need her to.

I was nauseating about Parker. I did think he was perfect. At first. He swept me off my feet from the moment I met him—kind, attentive, driven. He made me laugh, he surprised me with flowers, and planned dates. He looked at me like I was the reason the world spun, and I thought all of those things meant we were something special.

I've grown up around a pretty perfect example of what love is supposed to look like, so when Parker offered me a painted picture of that, I thought I got lucky. I thought I found my person at eighteen, just like my parents had.

Maybe that's why I still can't process the way I feel. Maybe that's why, after our first few months together, when he became paranoid about who I was speaking to or spending my time with, when he started policing how I looked and what I wore, I let it slide. It was infrequent and vague, most of the time. Tiny digs that shouldn't have made an impact. I told myself it was just who he was, that he had no filter, and his words were always laced with care, even when they were harsh. Comments that hurt in the moment, but he chalked up to being concern over my well-being. He was outgoing and funny and boisterous—brutally honest, sometimes, but people loved that about him. He was supposed to be perfect. We were perfect together.

Still, I try to convince myself that what he did—what he said that night—was merely a misunderstanding or a mistake. I tell myself I should call him, go back, hear him out. I ponder how awful I must be for leaving the way I did, for not offering an explanation. I wonder if I broke his heart, if I tore him open, if he's bleeding out without me. But, when I imagine seeing him again, touching him . . . his laugh and smile—I feel sick. He feels like a mirage that's been wiped away, and all I can see now is the truth. It feels like I'm broken. I'm torn open. I'm bleeding out, but I'm the only one who can see the color red.

"Willow." Allie gasps, and I realize I'm crying. She tosses the pillow in her lap to the floor and crawls across the couch, wrapping me in her arms. "What the hell happened?"

My tears drip off my cheeks and into her neck, but she pretends not to notice, only squeezing me tighter. I want to tell her so badly, but I can't escape this feeling of oversensitivity.

I must not remember it correctly.

I must be overreacting.

It must be my fault, just like he said.

It could've been so much worse. I should feel lucky.

Either I tell Allie this, and she agrees I'm being ridiculous—or she validates my feelings and . . . what then? How do I move past it? How do I make these feelings go away and what if they never do?

I pull back from her quickly, wiping my eyes. "I'm being silly." I attempt to laugh through a sob. "It's nothing. Really. We just broke up, and it's been tough."

She studies me, her eyes deep and assessing. Her full lips twitch with a frown, jaw tight and tense. She's waiting for me to say more, but I don't. *I can't.* I cast my gaze downward.

"I don't believe you, Willow, but if you're not comfortable sharing with me, I understand."

The broken tone in her voice, the clear indication of a lack of trust. She thinks I don't trust her, when in reality, it's myself I hold no faith in. The defeated sigh that leaves her lips may be the only thing to pull me out of the selfish stupor I've found myself trapped inside.

"I feel like I was raped," I whisper, so low it's hardly audible. Only her choked gasp tells me she heard. "But I wasn't." I raise my eyes to hers. "I wasn't. And I don't know why I feel this way."

She pulls my hands from my lap, wrapping her fingers in mine and squeezing. "Tell me everything."

And I do. Every detail. All of the confusing and chaotic thoughts raging in my head.

By the time I'm done, Allie's crying too. Silent tears drip off her chin and into her lap. She's still holding my hands when she says, "Willow, have you seen a doctor?"

"Like a therapist?" I ask.

She lets out a rough laugh. "Well . . . yeah. But I meant a gynecologist. You should get checked. An STI panel and probably a Pap smear too. Just to be sure."

"I honestly hadn't thought about any of that." I swallow. "Parker would never have cheated on me, I couldn't imagine . . ."

"You probably couldn't have imagined this either. That's why you're so unsure of your feelings around it." She lets go of my hands, wrapping me in another hug. "But your body doesn't lie to you. This is real, and I'm so sorry it happened. I'm sorry if the confirmation hurts to hear, but you need to know that the way you feel is valid, and I'm happy you ran away."

I'm crying again. Locking my arms around her lower back, hugging her tighter. Like she's anchoring me to a reality I really fucking wish I wasn't living in, but one I need to confront.

"Will you come with me?" I whisper. "To the doctor."

"Always. I've got you."

CHAPTER FOUR

WESTON

"YOU'LL CALL AS soon as you get settled in, right?"

"I'll call, I promise," I say, setting the last bag of my things in the back of my truck. Not that I had many to begin with. Only three duffle bags and a suitcase. The guesthouse I'll be living in comes fully furnished, so all I needed to bring were my clothes and my board, really.

"You sure you don't want us to come with you?" Carter asks.

"Nah. I think I'll probably be pretty tired tonight, so I'll want to unpack and chill."

Penelope offers me a closed-lip smile as she presses off my tailgate and throws her arms around my neck. "I'm proud of you," she whispers.

I return the embrace, squeezing her lightly. "Thank you."

Neither Penelope nor I am particularly affectionate people. I don't like to talk about my feelings, and she can always tell when it's not a good time to ask. I think she understands me a little better than Carter does, and I appreciate that. He's an open book, eager to voice any thought running through his mind and pull all of mine from me too.

Penelope helps rein that in a little. She gets it—the desire to process things alone—so she didn't push me when I told them I wanted space to myself tonight, and I'd prefer they wait until next weekend to drive out to Pacific Shores—my new home.

"I do think it's a little odd that we haven't been able to get ahold of him all day, though. What if he forgot I was coming? I don't want to show up unannounced."

Carter spoke to Leo over a month ago about my training with him for the summer. It was a long shot, but Leo was able to make time for me in his training schedule and offered to mentor me in exchange for my working in his family's surf shop through August.

Leo and his wife, Darby, offered to let me stay in the guesthouse on their property, with the stipulation that if I fucked up, if I didn't do my job well, or didn't take training seriously, he'd send me packing.

I think they checked in a couple of times since we decided on today's move-in date, but when Carter called to confirm this morning, there was no answer, and we haven't heard back yet.

Carter rubs his neck. "It's not like Leo to avoid a phone call, but it's also not like him to forget something like this, either. He may just be busy today." He shrugs. "I gave you his number, I'd try him again when you're closer to town. I told him you'd be arriving around four so he should be keeping an eye out."

"All right." I sigh. "Feels odd to be showing up at the house of someone I've never met before and just suddenly . . . move in."

"Well, technically you're living in their guesthouse, so it's not like you're living *with* them," Carter begins.

"And you've met them before," Penelope adds, pulling back from me. Her auburn hair is slicked back into a low bun, emerald eyes squinting in the sunlight as she peers up at me, crossing her arms at her chest and stepping up the curb and onto the sidewalk.

I cock my head at them, trying to think back to when I could've met Leo Graham.

I think I would've fucking remembered. He's *Leo Graham*. He was the face of American Surfing for years, and his training program is one of the most prestigious in the world. Multiple Olympians credit him with their medals.

Of course, I'd heard of Leo Graham—anyone who follows the sport of surfing has. I called it fate when my life fell apart and

I was placed into a foster family who just happened to be friends with the man himself. The one silver lining in my life at that time was convincing myself I was destined to be a surfer. I *had* to be. It was the only way I could make sense of all the bad shit, I took it as a sign that something good could come out of it.

I could train with Leo Graham. I could be a world champion. An Olympian.

I dreamed of working with him, but I was too young then. I never got the chance to train beneath him, but I was confident he'd take me under his wing after I won Worlds when I was seventeen. I planned on joining one of his camps that following summer . . . until my entire life fell apart again. Though, that time it was my fault, and I sure as fuck paid the price.

"We went to Disneyland on Christmas that first year you lived here. You met everyone," Penelope says before sighing. "Though, I suppose it all ended up being a bit much that day, it's okay if it's fuzzy."

Flashes of it filter across my memory. There were so many people I didn't know. Too many names to remember. Too much noise. I was still too raw. Scared. Broken.

It was my first Christmas without my mother. They were all family, and I didn't belong.

We ended up leaving before anyone else because I was struggling, and I felt guilty about it the entire drive home, even though Carter and Penelope tried to reassure me it was okay. I know they felt guilty for putting me in the position to begin with.

The first six months were hard. They'd never had kids. I'd never had a safe place to live. None of us knew what we were doing or what our family dynamic was supposed to look like. There were a lot of things I blocked out, things I can't remember even if I wanted to, because my life felt like too much at the time.

What I still recall, though, is the devastation that flashed across Carter's eyes the first time he tried to touch me and I thought he might hit me. Or the way I made Penelope cry when I cried because she dropped a ceramic plate in the kitchen and it shattered. I thought we'd both get in trouble. It felt like reality was short-circuiting when Carter simply grabbed a broom and a dustpan, sweeping up the broken shards before kissing his wife on the mouth and promising me it was okay.

Nothing in my life had ever been okay before.

So, I honestly can't remember that first Christmas at Disneyland. I can't remember much from that first year. I can vaguely visualize flashes of holiday lights, the sound of too-cheerful music, the smell of the theme-park food. I don't remember the people I met, though. Not even Leo Graham.

Except . . . there is still a lingering glimpse of *her.*

The sound of her laugh. The smell of the churro in her hand. Her face. Hair split at the center of her forehead, twisted into braids that hung over her shoulders, the blue Mickey Mouse ears on top of her head. The denim overalls that stopped mid-thigh, the cut-off tee beneath that displayed hints of her waist on the sides. Her matching baby-blue high-top Converse that were custom-painted in a *Lilo & Stitch* theme. Ones she painted herself, according to Penelope.

"What was her name?" I ask, suddenly desperate to remember. "The blond around the same age as me."

"Willow," Carter says. "Leo's daughter."

Willow.

"Is it the loud noises? Or the music?"

"What?" I asked.

"You seem like you're experiencing sensory overload." She chuckled. "It's the music for me. Is it the same for you?"

She tilted her head while she waited for me to answer, but the only word in my mind was blue. *Her ears and her shirt and her shoes—most of all, her eyes. Blue. So much blue.*

"It's everything, I think," I finally responded.

She smiled, and suddenly my stomach was caught in my throat.

"Theme parks are a little overwhelming for me too. I get it." She nudged my shoulder with hers, and I don't think I've welcomed

a touch so much since my mom was still breathing. "But you get used to it. I promise."

"Wes?" Carter's voice pulls me from my thoughts.

"What?"

"I said you probably won't see Willow much this summer, if at all. She's living in Berkeley now."

I nod, confused by the sting of disappointment that pinches my gut. It's a good thing. I've never been distracted by girls before. Not when I was a teenager, not that I had the opportunity to be when I was on trial, and I'm certainly not in a place to start now.

Surfing is my only focus. My only purpose.

This is my last chance.

"Right." I clear my throat. "I just forgot her name. Figured that might set me off on the wrong foot with her dad, y'know?"

Penelope gives me an unconvinced look, her lips clustering in the corner of her mouth like she's fighting back a smile. Whatever she's thinking, she doesn't voice, throwing her arms out wide once more. "Give me another hug before you go."

She says she lacks motherly instincts, and it's why she never had kids. I don't know if I believe that though, because as much as I loved my mom, Penelope is the most nurturing woman I've ever met.

I embrace her one more time as Carter steps beside her and pulls me in himself.

"We'll come visit next week," he says.

"And I'm offering a summer course at Golden State next month, so I'll be stopping by for lunch after my classes every Wednesday!" Penelope chimes.

"If I'm not working." I laugh.

She deadpans, "I'll ensure our schedules align, don't worry."

A smile springs to my cheeks, the expression something foreign enough to me that when it happens, I find my brain wanting to catalog the reason why. In the past three years, the two people standing in front of me are the only reason for any rare smile I've worn.

My throat is thick when I step off the curb and toward the driver's side door of my truck. "I'll call you tonight!" I call as I slip inside, taking a last glance at the two of them.

They're waving, the white stucco town house with the terracotta roofing beneath a piercing blue sky as the backdrop behind them—the only place that's ever felt like home to me.

I wave back before slipping my key into the ignition, my old Ford sputtering to life. I watch my foster parents in my rearview mirror until I take a left toward the interstate, and they disappear from sight.

CHAPTER FIVE

WILLOW

"Did you decide whether you want to register for fall courses?" Mom asks, assuming the impending deadline is the reason I've asked to talk to them this afternoon.

We're knee-to-knee, she and my dad on the couch, while I'm on the ottoman between it and the TV against the wall. Allie sits quietly in the oversized chair in the corner. My dad catches on first, eyes narrowing as his gaze darts between Allie and me.

He knows I wouldn't have her here for something unimportant, and he knows Allie wouldn't be the silent, trembling, wide-eyed mess she is right now unless the news was dire. Allie has never been afraid to wear her emotions on her sleeve, and normally I admire her for it, but right now her fear is written all over her damn face.

"No." I run my palms up and down my thighs. *God, I'm sweating.* "I actually . . . I'm not sure if I want to return to Berkeley in the fall."

I bite my lip, cutting my gaze to Allie, afraid to look at my parents. I know they'll be upset, and the worst part is that this is the *least* devastating news I have to share with them today.

I gave myself a full forty-eight hours to grieve my past life, all the versions of myself I'll never become. I gave myself two days to figure out a plan, so that I could have a clear head going into this conversation. I gave myself two days to prepare for the look of disappointment on their faces when they found out the perfect ray of sunshine they raised is not at all who they hoped she'd be.

"Because of Parker?" my mom asks.

I'm still looking at Allie, and she nods, as if to say, *Go on*.

I turn to face my parents again, and the moment my eyes meet my dad's, they begin to feel heavy. I don't want to look at him when I say this. I don't want him to know, because I know it's going to hurt him as bad as it hurts me.

"Yes," I murmur, dropping my gaze.

"What happened, Willow?" There is a curt, clipped tone to Dad's voice that slices right through me.

"I lied." I link my hands together at the center of my lap, keeping my eyes fixed there. I can face them when I say the words, but I don't have to look them in the eye. The sorrow within them can continue belonging wholly to me. "He didn't cheat on me. He . . ."

"Call it what it is," Allie whispers, cutting through the tension that's hazed this room to the point of near blindness. As if I can't see anything but my own self-doubt.

"He sexually assaulted me." I trade the words in my mouth with the air in front of me, inhaling sharply enough that I'm damn near choking on it.

I'm still staring at my hands, and I hadn't realized I was crying until a drop lands on my thumb, cascading down my knuckle and over my wrist. There is a gasp, and a muttered *fuck* before a shuffling in my periphery tells me that my dad has risen from the couch, his footsteps now pacing back and forth between it and the ottoman I'm sitting on.

"Oh, Willow." My mother's hand lands on top of mine, and I finally lift my head, meeting her face. There are tears shimmering in her hazel eyes and raw devastation in her features. "Can you tell us what happened, baby?"

I nod, taking a shaky breath before I say, "The sex was consensual." I wince, hating that they're hearing this. "It wasn't until afterward I . . . I went to the bathroom and thought the condom broke. He said that was what must've happened, but . . ." Parker had a habit of lying to me. Always small incidents, things that were easy to brush off and overlook, but I could tell when he wasn't being truthful. He'd spin the situation and make it my fault, call me paranoid, or quickly change the topic and force us to talk about something else. When I asked him about the condom, he asked me when I planned on getting back on birth control, because he hated condoms, anyway. So . . . "I fished it out of the trash can, and found that it wasn't broken . . ." I sigh, shuddering with tears. "After pressing him about it, he admitted he hadn't been wearing one when he . . . He'd taken it off at some point, and I . . . I didn't notice." My voice breaks, "He never told me. He never asked."

"Baby." Suddenly, I'm pulled into the space my dad vacated and wrapped in my mother's arms. Her chest expands rapidly against my ear, her body shaking with sobs, though I can feel the restraint of her attempt to keep them under control. "I'm so sorry."

I lift my head, and through tear-blurred vision, I find my dad standing in front of us, utter desolation on his face.

"I told him I wasn't okay with that. I told him I hadn't consented. I asked if he had planned to tell me about it." I wipe beneath my eyes and clear my throat. "I got angry. I felt . . . I felt violated. Disrespected. Like my body didn't matter beyond a means of him finding pleasure. Like *I* didn't matter." I swallow, and it feels like my insides are filled with cement. "He got defensive. He told me . . ." I shake my head.

I don't want to share what he said back to me. I don't want to admit to my parents—to anyone—that another person could think such a thing about me. I'm terrified of the words sticking in their heads, that they'll never be able to see me as anything different ever again.

I'm still looking at my dad, watching the slow fall of one tear down his cheek.

"I'm sorry," I whisper.

That desolation morphs into indignation as he rapidly shakes his head, forcing the ottoman out of his way with his foot before dropping to the floor in front of me. He grabs my face with both hands, lifting my head from Mom's chest and leveling me with his gaze.

"Do not ever apologize for his actions. For anyone's. This is not your fault."

"I'm pregnant," I blurt.

It rushes out before I can catch it. I don't know why I say it. I didn't plan to share it this way. I'd planned to give them time to process what happened with Parker first. I didn't want to bombard them with the news, and the way my dad's frozen face stares back at me now tells me I absolutely fucked this up.

His hands remain on my cheeks, stiff and hard. He's blinking, staring back at me like he's trying to figure out if he's even conscious—I wonder if he thinks he's inside his own worst nightmare. I turn within his palms, facing my mother, who's giving me the same expression.

My eyes flutter to Allie. She's folded over her knees with a hand covering her mouth, brown eyes wide with a *what-the-fuck* look.

Allie and I went to the local clinic a few days ago after I broke down in her apartment. I had an exam, a full STI panel, and they took a urine sample too. I hadn't even thought about pregnancy—a fact I'm ashamed of now. It never crossed my mind until I received a call from the clinic yesterday afternoon: all clear of infections, not cleared for a bun-less oven.

I don't know how I hadn't considered it sooner. I don't know why it wasn't my first thought that night.

Maybe it flashed through my mind, but I was too afraid to address it. I can't remember now.

I'd been on birth control for years. I stopped taking my pills just a couple months ago because I was having side effects that I didn't like. Honestly, I should've seen the signs then. Parker wasn't happy when I stopped taking them and told him we had to use condoms. He was okay with my constant headaches, mood swings, and nonexistent libido if it meant he could explore his breeding kink without repercussions.

It was a point of contention for us, but I promised him I'd make an appointment to have an IUD inserted by my primary doctor here in Pacific Shores this summer during a visit to my parents. I didn't want to have something like that done at a clinic I was unfamiliar with, and knew I'd be more comfortable doing it here at home. He was frustrated at having to use condoms for a period of time, but I thought he'd accepted it. I also thought it was unlikely I could get pregnant so soon after stopping birth control. I've heard it takes some women years, so I easily pushed any fears to the back of my mind.

I'm so fucking stupid.

Dad's hands fall from my cheeks, and I look at my mom again. Her eyes are on him, some unspoken communication written on her face. She blinks rapidly, sighing before directing her gaze to me.

"Okay," she breathes. "Okay. That's . . ." She shakes her head, clearing her throat. "Okay."

I turn to my father. His eyes are fixed on the floor as he runs a hand through his hair.

"I didn't mean to say it like that," I whisper.

A strained laugh leaves my mom's lips. "Is there a better way to say it?"

Suddenly, a chuckle escapes me too. I shake my head. "Guess not."

She cups my face, smiling gently before pulling me back into her arms. A moment later, a second strong pair of arms wraps around me. Emotion pricks my nose once again, and suddenly tears are spilling over, soaking the fabric of my mother's shirt.

She hushes me, running a hand over the back of my head, whispering reassurances like, *We've got you, you're all right, we'll be okay, you're safe.*

My parents say that often. The reminder that I'm safe with them, we're safe with each other. My dad once told me he couldn't guarantee a life free from pain, but he could promise me a safe place with him. That there would never be anything I'd need to hide, nothing I could do beyond forgiveness—that I could always come back home and find acceptance.

I sure am testing those promises now.

Pulling back, I turn my head to face him. He's still sitting on the floor in front of me and my mom. His hand rests on my shoulder, and he gives it a reassuring squeeze, offering a wistful smile.

"Do you want to talk about what comes next?" my mom asks quietly. "Or have you already explored your options?"

I sit up, wiping my eyes. "Oh. Well . . ."

"We don't have to talk about it today," Dad says. "If you need time, if you're too tired, we can wait."

"No. I've decided," I say, looking at Allie.

Another moment I'm not sure I want to face my parents for. I know they'll support me through any decision, but I don't know that they'll agree with it. I don't know if it'll disappoint them or make them sad, especially considering my mom's history with infertility.

"I'm going to proceed with termination. I have an appointment with a doctor early next week. They'll do an ultrasound to confirm, but it sounds like I'm early enough that I can do a medical abortion here at home." I swallow, looking at them again. "If you're not comfortable with that, I can stay with Allie instead."

She nods in my periphery but doesn't say anything.

"Of course we want you here at home, Sugar," my dad says, the words falling from his lips immediate and rushed. "We'll take care of you. That should never be a question."

"I'd like to go with you to the doctor, if that's all right," Mom adds.

I nod, my throat heavy once again. "Thank you."

It's Dad hushing me now, and they both pull me in for another hug. Allie quietly excuses herself, murmuring something about using the restroom, but I know it's to give us a moment alone. She'll wait for me upstairs in my bedroom. She was confident my parents would be understanding and unquestioningly supportive, but offered to be here anyway, just in case.

A buzzing erupts from beside my mom, and she pulls back to glance down at her phone on the table beside the couch. Her nose scrunches, eyes narrowing as she grabs it and opens the notification. "Leo," she says, turning toward my dad. "A car just pulled into the driveway. Some kind of old truck. There is a board in the back. Are you expecting someone?"

My father scrambles back from us, standing abruptly as his eyes go wide. "Fuck. Shit."

He walks into the dining room, pulling the curtains aside to look out the large bay window at the front of the house before returning. "It's Weston."

"Oh?" Mom asks. "*Oh*. Shit. That was today, wasn't it?"

"Fucking apparently," he mutters. Pulling his phone from his pocket, he nods as his thumb scrolls over the screen. "Yep. Yep. I have about seven fucking missed calls from Carter. I can't believe I forgot to turn my phone off silent when I woke up this morning."

Mom shrugs. "You were preoccupied."

I don't even want to know what she means by that.

Dad bends over the couch, pressing his lips against my forehead. "I'm so sorry, Sugar. Let me go take care of this. I'll get him a hotel for the weekend, and we can figure the rest out on Monday. I'll be right back."

"No, wait . . ." I grab his arm before he can walk away. "What's going on? Who's Weston?"

The name sounds so familiar, like someone I *should* know, but I can't place a face in my mind.

"Carter and Penelope's foster son," Mom says quietly. "I think you only met him once, years ago."

"The kid who went to prison?" I rear back, head swiveling between my parents.

"He never went to prison," Dad counters. "County jail. He's out now."

"Still . . ." I swallow, forcing the accusation out of my voice. I am not in a position to be doling out judgment right now. "What did he do?"

"We don't know. The court records are sealed because he was a minor, and Carter and Penelope aren't comfortable sharing details on his behalf. All we know is his charges were lowered to a misdemeanor, and he was released with time served."

Dad nods, but the way he's chewing on his inner cheek makes me question if he does know more.

"He was on the fast track to professional surfing before everything went down, and he's been struggling since. I agreed to mentor him for the summer and see if I can get him back to a competitive level. I offered up the guesthouse." He nods toward our back property. "And he's going to be working at Heathen's. But I agreed to all of this before I knew you were coming home, so . . ."

So I came along and wrecked everyone's plans.

I don't know this kid, but regardless of what he did, he was a minor when it happened. I know he ended up with Carter and Penelope after being removed from an abusive home. I know he lost his mother when he was a teen. If he was truly as dedicated to surfing as my father made it sound, this opportunity is probably life-changing for him.

Who the hell am I to take it away?

"It's okay," I say. "Let him stay. I don't want to be the reason you send him packing before he's even had a chance."

"Sugar, after what's happened . . ." He squeezes my hand. "I understand if you're not comfortable having a stranger around the house. At the very least, I can find someplace else for him to stay."

"You wouldn't have offered the guesthouse if you didn't trust him. You wouldn't let anyone that close to Mom unless you thought she'd be safe. Plus, Carter and Penelope wouldn't still be taking care of him if they didn't love him. I trust their judgment. I trust yours. I'll be fine."

"Fine isn't good enough, Willow," he counters. "I want you happy."

I shrug. "I think it might be a while before I'm happy again, but that doesn't have anything to do with you or the surfer you're mentoring."

He lets out a defeated sigh.

I know that's a terrible thing to hear, but it's the truth.

Dad looks at my mom, question written in his gaze. She nods, and he returns it with his own. A resigned, heavy understanding settles over the three of us. They know the truth, I've made my decision, and now all we're faced with is the courses of action that follow.

There isn't anything left to say, but my dad hovers in the center of the room because I'm sure he's feeling the same way I am. Nothing feels resolved. Nothing feels better. The bulk of the pain is yet to come, but there's nothing that can be done about it now.

"You should probably go greet him." I nod toward the front of the house. "Help him get settled in."

"Yeah." He drags a hand down his face. "You're right."

"I'll still be here when you get done." I try to smile reassuringly, but my dad doesn't look any less concerned.

"Do you want me to have your aunts come over? We can make cake and listen to Shania Twain." Mom kisses my temple.

"I'd love that."

"In that case, I'll take my time." Dad winks, squeezing my hand once more before he leaves the room. The opening and closing of the front door echoes behind him.

CHAPTER SIX

WESTON

"THE CODE TO unlock the front door is zero-five-two-eight," Leo fucking Graham says as he punches it in, and the gear-sound of the lock follows.

He'd appeared in the driveway not long after I pulled in, barefoot and wearing sweatpants. He looked disheveled, honestly. His expression fell somewhere between I-just-woke-from-a-nap and I-just-found-out-my-cat-went-missing. The smile on his face when he greeted me was incredibly forced. I'd know—I'm an expert in them myself.

Leo helped me grab my things before leading me through a gate that bridged the main house and the detached garage, down a concrete walkway and to the guesthouse that sits directly behind the garage, a smaller-scale replica of the main house. A small front porch faces the cliffside, offering a perfect view of the Pacific in the distance.

I'm watching sunlight dance across the whitecaps when I hear Leo open the door behind me. I follow him as he takes a few steps inside, turning to face me before extending an arm to his right. "My wife stocked the fridge for you in accordance with the meal plan I'll be putting you on. She checked with Penelope that you don't have any food sensitivities." There is a small kitchen tucked into the corner by the front door. An island counter, with a range, sink, and fridge across from it. "Make sure you thank her when I officially introduce you next week."

"Of course." I nod.

Leo sighs, and it sounds almost defeated. I have no idea what I'm doing wrong.

"Anyway," he continues, spinning again and pointing to the closed door beside the kitchen. "The bedroom is through there. Bathroom too. All of the linens are clean, and we have a washer and dryer in the garage you can use." He motions toward the space opposite the kitchen, where a long couch is spread out beneath a window, and a television is mounted on the wall. "This is the living room, obviously. The place is small, but it should do."

"It's great. I really appreciate it."

He faces me, eyes sunken and exhausted, and though he's looking at me, it almost feels as if I'm not here at all. He blinks, shaking his head quickly, as if ridding himself of some haunted thought, before he nods and steps past me. "Let's get the rest of your things so you can settle in."

I wordlessly turn to follow him when he stops with his hand on the doorknob. "Oh, and I should let you know, something came up, and I'm not going to be available to begin training this week. I'm sorry." Leo steps onto the porch, and I shut the door behind me. "I should've called earlier and given you the option to delay your move by a week, but I didn't have the chance." He runs a hand through his hair, leaning against the porch railing. "I do have an alternate coach who can start working with you Monday, and you and I will begin together the week after."

Well, that confirms it. I really am a nuisance.

What the fuck am I actually doing here? I want to ask, but I keep my mouth closed, offering a simple nod.

"This weekend you can work in the garage. All my boards need to be cleaned and waxed."

"Oh, is this like a Mr. Miyagi kind of thing?" I grin, attempting to pull a smile from him too.

"No." He tilts his head, giving me a once-over with an unamused expression. "It's a boards-need-maintenance-or-you-can't-surf kind of thing."

Cool. I'll go fuck myself, then.

Leo pushes off the railing and descends the three porch steps, heading down the path that leads back to my truck and the front of the main house.

"Are there any rules I need to keep in mind while I'm staying here?" I call out, trailing behind him. "I don't want to fuck up this opportunity, and I don't want to impose on your life any more than I already am, but I *need* to be here. I need this. I'll earn it."

Thus far, being kind, quiet, and funny—and that Mr. Miyagi joke *was* funny, especially to an older person like him—hasn't worked. I guess I'll try being straightforward instead.

He stops so abruptly I nearly walk into him. I stumble back as Leo spins to face me. For the first time since I met him a half hour ago, some kind of spark lights in his eyes. He's finally looking at me like I might hold some sort of value, like I'm actually a person standing in front of him, and not an apparition he's trying to get away from.

"I watched your film. Watched the competition where you won your Youth Worlds title. You weren't privy to it back then, but Carter and I had been in talks about you for a while. I had plans for you before . . ." He swallows. "I know you count swell periods. I know you have an eye for barrels, and you almost always choose the right one. I know you sure as fuck get up every time a wave knocks you down. You have the kind of born talent that can't be taught, though you'll be rusty. Your form already needed work, your balance was off, and your agility is shit."

Ouch. But okay, at least we're getting somewhere.

"Luckily for you, these are all buildable skills. What I need you to bring to the table is focus, determination, and patience. It's going to take time to get where you want to be, and you're only going to reach it if you're giving this one hundred percent, okay?"

I nod rapidly.

"I need you to not fuck up again, either. No reckless, impulsive decisions."

"Okay, so . . . rules are: show up and don't fuck up?"

Leo lets out a rough laugh, shaking his head, but movement in my periphery catches my gaze and pulls my eyes from him. Something flashes across one of the upstairs windows in the main house.

Her silhouette fills the window, long hair swaying past her shoulders as her head is cast down, stacking a pile of books on the sill. The late afternoon sun filters over her, casting her in gold.

She lifts her head, and her eyes immediately fall on mine.

Blue. She's all blue.

Even from this distance, even behind the window, they're a blazing aquamarine, searing right through the center of my chest. I feel her gaze in my ribcage—warming me from the inside out.

I don't know what it means.

"Actually, I have three other rules . . ." Leo continues, but I only half hear him, I can't look away from her. The girl in the window. "Be on time, and I don't just mean for training. Your shifts at the shop too. Even if I'm asking you to wax boards in the garage or help my wife bring in groceries. My time is valuable, and I'm spending a lot of it on you."

I nod absently.

Punctuality. Check.

I'm still watching her, because she's watching me. Her hair drapes over her shoulder as she tilts her head, eyes narrowing as if she's challenging me to look away first. I can't, and I don't know why. It's fucking infuriating.

"Speaking of my wife—do not disrespect her. Ever. If she asks you for help with something, you do it. If you see her in the garden, you tell her that her flowers are pretty. If she offers you a meal, you eat it. I don't care how bad it tastes."

Nice to wife. I can do that.

Her lips tilt at the side before her tongue slips between them, swiping over her fuller bottom lip before they part slightly and her shoulders shake. She rolls her eyes playfully, and I swear to God I can hear her laughing. The sound doesn't float through the closed window, but my ribcage echoes with it all the same.

"Weston." The tone in his voice is stern enough to pull my gaze from the window. His head had turned too, looking in the same direction before he faced me again. "My third rule," he continues, slowly raising one brow at me.

"Your third rule." My eyes flash to her window again, but the curtains are now closed.

Something pinches the pit of my stomach. An unfamiliar and unwelcome feeling.

"My daughter is home for the summer. I wasn't expecting her to be." His voice is low and rough, pulling my focus back to him as Leo Graham looks in my eyes and says, "So, third rule: I need you to stay away from her."

"Uh—" The word lodges in my throat. I open my mouth wider, attempting to say *understood.* But it's just stuck there, refusing to leave my lips. Refusing to comply.

I swallow down my response, only capable of offering a nod.

CHAPTER SEVEN

WILLOW

My mom gifted me an easel for Christmas, but I forgot it when I returned to Berkeley in January. I'm thankful for that now. I left so much behind in that old apartment with Parker, I think I would've left this easel too.

My dad called the manager of the building I was living in and bought me out of my portion of our lease. He offered to drive up to Berkeley and recover the rest of my things, but I assumed Parker had already tossed them out by then.

I've been meaning to check in with my friend Chelsea to see if she might have intercepted anything after I left. Her boyfriend, Hayden, is Parker's best friend, so they spent a lot of time at our place. She's called a few times since I left, and I was intending to call her back once I figured out how to explain my situation to her.

She and Parker have always been close.

Though, I'm more lost about what to say to her now than I was a few weeks ago. Back when I convinced myself this was nothing more than an uncomfortable situation that obliterated my attraction to my boyfriend and made me want to leave him.

It's so much worse now.

Parker assaulted me. He put me at risk without thought for my well-being. Without my consent.

Now I'm the one facing the consequences of his actions.

After today, I will never be the same, and he'll never even

know it.

The shades of indigo, lavender, and soft orange across my canvas blur behind my tears, matching the sky in front of me. I was painting the sunrise, but all I see now is my own pain.

I didn't sleep last night at all. Not a single minute. The moment daybreak lightened the sky just enough for it to fade from black to blue, I crawled out of bed and walked down to the cove. I like the West Coast sunrise. It's less dramatic than sunset. People don't flock to the beach for it. Nobody notices except those of us who wake before dawn to appreciate its quiet beauty.

Soft and pastel—the slow awakening of a new day.

I haven't painted in the month and a half since I've been home, and this morning was the first time I felt the urge. I think part of me is afraid that after today, I'll never want to paint again.

I don't know how to feel about any of it, so I find myself anticipating every emotion possible: fear and relief, freedom and shame.

I channel my emotions through my art—it's how I express them. It's the path I planned to explore for the rest of my life. The name I aimed to create for myself. I've been double majoring in art design and psychology, hoping to someday help others as an art therapist, treating patients through the guise of their creativity, teaching them how we can heal ourselves through the act of art.

But after what happens today, I don't know what emotions will pour out of me, or how they'll alter the way I create. If I don't know what comes next, at least I knew the sun would rise this morning, and that was something I could paint. A Celestia Cove sunrise is as familiar to me as my own breath. I could paint it with my eyes closed.

So, even through the tears, I swipe my brush across the canvas.

I wipe my eyes with my forearm before I swap the feather brush in my hand with a mop brush and mix pink and white before swirling the sky's wispy clouds, softening the edges with a brighter shade of fuchsia.

My breathing is choked, tears cascade down my cheeks and drip off my chin, but I keep going. I lose myself in the blur of colors and the brightening sky. The movement of my arm swiping across the canvas is a feeling akin to floating weightlessly in the cove when it's calm.

Just flowing. No direction, but not directionless, either. The purpose finds you.

My emotions even out, and the rocks rattling around my chest cavity settle. I'm entirely focused on the current moment, my existence centered on the painting in front of me.

Until the clearing of a throat nearby breaks my concentration.

I whip around, finding *him* standing on the bottom step of the staircase that leads from the house and down to the cove. "Sorry," he says gruffly. "I didn't think anyone else would be down here."

I turn away, wiping beneath my eyes and willing the tears to stop flowing.

"It's fine." I laugh, but it comes out in broken pieces. "It's your beach now too."

Weston is undeniably handsome, standing in front of me with his wetsuit folded at the waist, his toned and tapered chest on display. His skin is smooth and sun-kissed, hard jawline clean-shaven. All of his features are hard. Broad nose, wide mouth, deep-set brows over stormy-blue eyes.

He doesn't have the kind of eyes that reflect the sun or portray the shades of the sky. No, his eyes are the kind of blue that absorb light and create shadow—as if they're hiding whatever lies behind them. A raging sea and thunderous clouds.

He blinks at me, descending the final step and propping his board into the sand beside him. "Am I . . . Should I come back?"

Somehow, a laugh bubbles out of me. I don't even know why. I know he's not trying to be funny. It's just . . . for how different he looks now than the day I met him when we were young, he seems just as lost as he did back then. A little overwhelmed by the world around him, like he's searching for his place within it.

Back then, I just wanted to help a kid who looked a bit scared feel better.

Now, I wonder why the hell I relate to the feeling so deeply when I'm standing on the same foundation that's held me up my entire life.

"No, you're fine. I was just about to leave." My painting isn't finished, but that honestly feels like the most accurate representation of my current emotions anyway. "But, uh, just so you know, my dad is going to be pissed if you go out in the water before he gets down here."

Weston sighs, placing his hands on his hips as he lifts his head to the sky defeatedly. "I was attempting to be proactive."

I smile, gathering my brushes off the tray attached to my easel and slipping them into the pouch of the smock tied around my waist. "He's strict about surfing alone—especially for amateurs who are a bit too fearless. The person most at risk of being caught in a riptide is always the one who thinks they can outswim it."

"It's a cove. There aren't any riptides here."

I lift my head, raising a brow as I give him a once-over.

He stands in front of me like he has no fucking clue what he looks like. The backward baseball cap atop his head has a lock of his dark hair peeking out over his forehead, and the way he's now crossing his arms as he leans against his surfboard makes his biceps flex and bulge. He's obnoxiously attractive, without any ounce of the arrogant aura most men who look like him would possess, which almost makes him more annoying.

"If there is water, there is a chance of drowning. Always. You should never go out alone." I shrug. "But feel free to test his temper about it if you'd prefer."

He huffs, frustrated, and I want to laugh at that too.

I haven't spoken to Weston directly since he moved in Friday. I've mostly stuck to my room. But I saw him through my window after he arrived, so I knew he'd know I was home too.

"I'm not meeting with your dad, though. I'm meeting some other coach," he says incredulously. "I guess your dad is preoccupied this week."

Yeah, sorry. Hate to be inconvenient, but I've got a pregnancy to terminate.

I roll my eyes, capping each of my paints and adding them to my smock before I untie it from my waist and roll it up.

"Would the other coach even care?" he asks.

I stuff my smock into my tote bag before folding up my easel. "I mean . . . yeah. It's a rule my dad set for anyone surfing in the cove. Plus, Liv is going to report back everything you do toda—"

"Liv?" he asks.

I pause, lifting my head, and suddenly, Weston is a step closer. Close enough that I can smell whatever aftershave he used this morning. Something like lemons and sandalwood. My breath catches at the proximity, and I lean back.

He clocks the movement, keeping his eyes on mine as he gently takes one of the legs of my easel from my hand, pulling it toward him. His lips tilt at the corner, and I wonder if it's supposed to be a comforting smile. I let it go, and he steps away, continuing to fold my easel for me.

"Yeah," I breathe. "Liv Costa-Ramos. Please don't tell me you're attempting to be a professional surfer and you don't know who she is."

His head snaps up as he pauses, jaw dropping. "I'm . . . I'm being trained by Livia Costa-Ramos today?"

"Yeah? Dad didn't tell you? Liv is family."

"What?" he gasps, staring after me in astonishment as my easel hangs limply from his hands. "I . . . I knew your dad trained her before her first Olympics, but I hadn't realized—"

"She's married to my cousin, Lou." I point to my easel. "Are you going . . . What are you doing with that?"

He blinks rapidly, dropping his head and inspecting his hands as if realizing for the first time that he's holding something. "Sorry. I was trying to help and then you . . ." He sighs as he drops to his knees in the sand and continues folding the legs together.

"Thanks," I say, tucking my unfinished painting beneath my

arm as I swing my bag over my shoulder. "And Liv is great, by the way. Don't be nervous. She's . . . intense. But great."

He nods, standing and holding my compacted easel that was definitely folded incorrectly.

I bite my lip to hide my smile, taking it from him. "Thanks."

"No problem." Weston is so stoic, it's as if his skin is made of something impenetrable, and I'm frustrated by how frustrating I find it.

"Well, I'll see you around, Weston." I pass him, and he anchors his eyes to mine—just as he did the other night through my window—watching with rapt focus until I reach the stairs.

His stare is steel, impassible and impossible to comprehend, though he doesn't look away.

"Sure, Willow," he says, his voice a rough caress. The sound of my name from his mouth feels intentional, brushing over the back of my neck as I turn and begin ascending the cliffside.

His gaze brands me with every step I take.

The house is still quiet when I slip through the back door and sneak into the kitchen, assuming my parents are still in bed. It's just before six a.m. Neither of my parents are particularly early risers, and Allie will be sleeping until at least eleven, as she often does when she doesn't have a morning shift at the bakery.

I open the fridge, staring blankly at the shelves. I'm sure I should eat something before my appointment today, but what I thought was stress-induced nausea is actually morning sickness, and my appetite is nonexistent.

The front door creaks from the front of the house, and the sound of two hushed voices filter through. I shut the fridge and turn around just in time to find my cousin and her wife entering the kitchen through the dining room.

Lou pauses, eyes widening as she notices me. "Willow," she breathes, before a bright smile takes over her face and she closes the distance between us, wrapping me in her arms. "I didn't think you'd be awake already. I missed you."

Lou is my aunt Dahlia and uncle Everett's eldest daughter.

She's twelve years older than her brothers and myself, so she always felt more like a big sister than a cousin. Fierce, confident, and incredibly intelligent, she's been a role model to all of us our entire lives, and the embrace she's giving me now is a comfort I didn't know I so desperately needed.

"Didn't sleep well," I murmur. "But I missed you too."

She squeezes me tightly before pulling back. "How are you feeling?"

"Honestly? I don't know."

Lou smiles softly as Liv steps up beside her and hugs me too. "That's okay. You can feel however you need to feel to get through it."

"All feelings are valid. Not feeling is also valid." Lou nods. "Since Liv had to drive down today to work with your dad's new surfer, I figured I'd tag along. We're staying with my parents for the week, but I thought I'd stop by and have breakfast with you."

"Don't you have to work?" I ask.

Lou is a senior agent at one of the top sports talent agencies in the country. Liv is an Olympic surfer and travels all over the world during competition season, but they're settled in Los Angeles in her downtime.

"I can work remotely most of the time." She shrugs.

"Thought I heard voices out here." My dad rounds the corner from the hall that leads to my parents' room. "Hey, Lulu. I'm glad you came." He hugs my cousin, then her wife, and as he pulls back he says, "Thank you for helping out this week."

"Oh, yeah." She claps her hands, rubbing her palms together. "I love breaking a man down to nothing but sweat and tears."

"Well, he's eager and waiting for you," I say. "He's already down at the beach, suited up and ready to go."

Liv checks her smartwatch, brow raising with a nod of her head as she realizes the time.

"You were in the cove this morning?" Dad asks, leaning a hip against the counter.

"Wanted to watch the sunrise."

He inhales deeply, a contemplative look crossing his face. Whatever the thought is, he shakes his head—like he's ridding his mind of it. "I'm going to go down with Liv to check in with Weston before they get started, but I'll be back in a little bit. I'm going to get some of your favorite things—food, snacks. I think I'll grab a new heated blanket and body pillow for you too." He steps into me, kissing the top of my head. "When you get back from your appointment with your mom, I'll have a whole nest set up for you in the living room. We'll watch your favorite movies, and you'll have everything you need. Okay?"

"Thanks, Dad." My voice is cracked and strained, emotion pricking the back of my throat.

"Love you, Sugar," he says as he and Liv head out the back door.

"Love you!" I call back.

Lou does the same to her wife before leaning across the island on her elbows and resting her head in her palms, smiling at me. "Penelope is teaching a class on Wednesdays at Golden State this summer, so we thought if you're feeling up to it, we could have everyone come over Wednesday night for book club instead of waiting until the end of the month?"

"Has everyone read the book, though?"

"Who cares?" She shrugs. "We can just talk about other books instead."

I laugh. "That sounds fun."

My mom, both of my aunts, Allie, her mom, Penelope, Lou, my grandmother, and I have had a book club since Allie and I turned eighteen and could openly admit to reading steamy romance novels. Every month we rotate who chooses the book, and we do our best to meet up once a month to talk about it over dinner or dessert. It's harder during the school year when I'm in Berkeley, or when Lou and Liv are traveling, so it's been three months since our last meeting—when I was home for spring break.

"Good." She jumps up, spinning toward the pantry. "Now, what do you want for breakfast?"

"I haven't had much of an appetite."

She chews her cheek, peeking at me over her shoulder. "You know, I make strawberry French toast almost as well as my mom."

"Listen, totally sympathize with the tummy issues, Low, but I'm going to need some of that French toast." Allie's voice has me jumping, startled. Lou and I both whip to the side, watching as she enters the kitchen in her pajamas, wild dark curls sprouting in a thousand directions, yawning as she smiles at me.

Lou laughs, pulling Allie in for a hug before they begin rummaging through the pantry for supplies.

CHAPTER EIGHT

WILLOW

I'M WOKEN BY the sound of my own groan, and a sharp pain in my abdomen follows. It's jarring and jolting—like the twist of a flaming knife stabbing me from the inside out.

I question it at first, for one brief moment. A flash of panic crossing my mind because I don't know why it's happening, why it hurts so bad, why I feel so much pain.

Then consciousness takes over. I'm awake, and I remember why I've been in fight-or-flight since the morning I left Berkeley. That was the flight. The running and coping and vowing to start over.

Now, I'm fighting. Fighting consequences I didn't cause, harboring pain I didn't ask for, facing guilt I don't think I deserve.

I don't want to be awake yet. I don't want to feel this pain or think about what's happening in my body. I don't want to remember what Parker did, or what I had to do because of it. I don't want to think about dropping out of college or what my future will look like now.

I don't want to feel so fucking lost.

My eyes flutter open, daylight blurring my vision. I blink, and as I adjust to the brightness, I realize I'm in my bedroom. Morning sun filters through the sage-green curtains over my window, and my bed is covered with my new pink heated blanket. My water bottle and a mug sit on the table beside me.

Movement across the room catches my eye, and I lift my head to find my dad curled up in the oversized chair. He shifts, turning sideways and laying his head on the armrest.

"Dad?"

His eyes fly open, and he sits up abruptly, a knit blanket dropping off his chest and pooling in his lap. "Willow?" he asks on a sharp breath. "Are you okay?"

"Ye—" I sigh. "Well, no. But I'm fine? I don't know. Why are you sleeping in that chair? I thought I fell asleep on the couch?"

He raises his arms, yawning with a stretch. "Don't tell your mother this, but she's old. You were both sleeping in the living room last night, and the way she was lying was going to kill her neck today. So I carried her to bed, and then I came back and carried you to bed too. Thought you'd be more comfortable here." He stands, running his hands through his blond hair before sitting down at the edge of my bed. "I wanted to be nearby in case you needed me, though."

For what feels like the millionth time in the last week, I begin crying again. My nose stings with the burn of emotion as my tears spill over. I'm incredibly aware of how lucky I am to have the family I do. I didn't have to hide my choice from anybody in my life. Not only my parents, but my best friend, my extended family, have all dropped what they're doing to support me—no questions asked.

I decided I didn't want anyone outside my parents and Allie to know about what happened with Parker. It almost felt too intimate, the details of the violation on my body. Somehow, telling my family that I came home with an unwanted pregnancy was easier. It made the unconditional acceptance I've received from every one of them mean even more.

"C'mere, Sugar," Dad whispers, sitting back against my headboard and wrapping his arm around my shoulder. "How're you feeling?"

"So exhausted. I think if I slept for three days I'd still wake up tired." I sit up, adjusting the heating pad against my stomach as he fluffs my pillows. "Uncomfortable and crampy. A little sad,

I think."

"That all sounds about right." He kisses the top of my head. "It's okay to feel sad. It's okay to feel like you lost something. It's even okay to grieve."

"It feels more like I had something stolen from me," I whisper. The sentence crumbles from my lips, fractured.

"You did. Pregnancy can be a joyful thing, but when your first experience with it becomes tainted by something tragic, it's hard to get past when it happens again later." I know my dad is speaking from experience. My mom had a miscarriage when my parents got together as teenagers. Years later, after they were married, she struggled with fertility before having me. "You had your first experience stripped from you. It wasn't your turn, Sugar." He smiles softly, wiping my tears with his thumb. "Someday, if you want to, you'll get to try again, with your person. You'll look back on this. It'll still hurt, even then, but you'll know you made the right choice for yourself."

I sniffle, pulling my legs to my chest. "It was the right choice. I know that. Plenty of people in this world would want me to be ashamed, but I refuse to placate them. I guess I just feel sad it's happening at all, if that makes sense."

"It makes sense. All of it makes sense. It's not fair, and it's okay to be frustrated by it. It's okay to be sad and angry and hurt. You're being plummeted by a tidal wave right now, and you're wading through it, treading water until your feet hit the sand again. You make me so fucking proud, Willow."

Well, that does it.

My face falls into my hands because it all hits me at once. I'm sick—aching in my body and my soul. I'm bleeding out, literally and figuratively. It's overwhelming, and I've saddled myself with the immense responsibility of being able to handle it when I *can't*.

Despite the promises that it's not my fault, that my feelings over what Parker did to me are valid, and I should call the assault what it is, I still question it. Every time I close my eyes, the night replays inside my head, and I find myself searching for the words

I didn't hear or the regret I never saw in his eyes. I still gaslight myself into believing it wasn't as terrible as I thought, that what he said wasn't as awful as it feels.

That I'm overreacting and overdramatic.

Though, what I see now when I close my eyes are all the signs that had been there from the start—the signs I was too stupid, too lovestruck, to acknowledge until he went too far.

Some moments I even want to call him. I want to hear his voice because I think it'd be filled with reassurances—confirmations that I'm remembering incorrectly, that what's existing in my brain isn't the reality. That he didn't break me the way it feels like he did, because that's what he used to say to me when I questioned his comments on my body, or expressed concern for his paranoia, and refused to comply to his demands.

I'd never hurt you, Willow.

Nobody will ever love you like I do, I'm looking out for you.

Those memories send a jolt of ice through my veins, because Parker never loved me. He owned me, and I had been convinced that I enjoyed being property.

Yesterday, during my ultrasound—as much as it meant to have my mom with me—I wished he'd been the one holding my hand. When I came home and took the pills, when I began to bleed, when my body felt like it was being ripped apart from the inside out, I wished he'd been holding me. After all, this was half of him too.

I long for his support, even after everything.

I feel like a disappointment, even after all the love I've received from everyone else.

"Willow." Strong hands grip my wrists, but the force is feather light as he lowers them from my face. My dad must've gotten off my bed, because he's standing in front of me now. "What do you need? How can I help?"

"I . . . I think I just want to take a shower," I say shakily.

"Okay, Sugar."

He places one hand at my back as he helps me sit up and turn, gently swinging my legs over the bed before holding my elbows as I stand. Every movement is like the stab of a thousand knives at once. I hiss at the pain as I put weight on my feet and lift out of bed.

"Do you want me to get Allie or Mom for you?"

I shake my head. "No, I'll be fine. Let them sleep, but when Allie wakes up, will you tell her to come upstairs? I think I want to be in bed today."

"Okay. Do you want breakfast?"

"No," I groan as he helps me into the bathroom, keeping a steady hand at my back.

"All right." He kisses my head again. "I'll come check in a little later. I love you."

"Love you too," I say. As he walks out of the bathroom and begins to shut the door, I add, "Thank you for taking care of me. For supporting me instead of hating me."

He pauses, turning back to me. "Taking care of you and your mother is the greatest joy of my life, Willow. Supporting you is the best job I've ever had. And you are impossible for anyone to hate, but least of all me. You are the sum of all our best parts."

He doesn't wait for me to respond before he quietly leaves the room.

I spend the next two days primarily in my room with Allie, who took the week off from the bakery to help me recover. We watch every favorite movie from our childhood and bedazzle the covers of our favorite books. We laugh, and I cry. A lot. By Wednesday evening, my appetite returns enough for me to eat the lasagna my grandma, Monica, brings over for book club, and the lemon bars that Dahlia made for me. The house is full and lively, and while the discomfort lingers, it dulls when I'm surrounded by so much light.

It's all I can do to hope the emotional turmoil will follow a similar path. Scars will stay behind. They'll linger, but the open wound I'm faced with now will clot and scab and eventually heal. Soon enough, I'll stop seeing it all when I close my eyes.

The dull ache will go away, and I'll be light again.

CHAPTER NINE

WESTON

"I THINK YOUR bottom turn needs work," Liv says, wringing out her dark, wet curls once we're back on shore. "That's the culprit for pacing issues and why you're about half a second behind the barrels."

"How can I be behind the barrels when there are no barrels? We're in a cove. I'd hardly call them waves," I grumble, unzipping my wetsuit and peeling it off my arms.

"We utilize the cove to build your endurance—to make you faster, swifter. Hyperfocus on your form and the basics. You don't need a barrel if you're too slow to reach it."

When all I respond with is a huff, she laughs.

I understand the vision of using this cove to train amateur surfers before taking them out to the real breaks, but I haven't considered myself an amateur in a while. I've been surfing since I could walk, and I won a fucking World Championship at the age of seventeen. I would've been an Olympian by now if not for my involuntary three-year hiatus.

I knew I'd be rusty. I couldn't even stand up the first time I got back on a board last year after I was released, but I've been practicing on my own and with Carter for the past six months. I'm not completely fucking hopeless, and I'd expected to be doing a hell of a lot more when I was offered the opportunity to train with Leo Graham.

Including *actually* being mentored by Leo Graham—whom I haven't seen since Monday morning.

"You'll find yourself appreciative of the cove as time goes on," Liv promises. "I thought there was nothing I could be taught when I moved here from Costa Rica. I thought the cove was a waste of my time too." She shrugs, slipping out of her wetsuit, leaving behind only the skimpy red bikini she's wearing underneath.

In addition to being a gold medalist, Liv is also a model, and a total heartthrob of a professional athlete. I'm sure there are countless young men and women all over the world with her Sports Illustrated cover taped to their wall.

Objectively, she's stunning—long dark hair, golden sun-kissed skin, hazel eyes that shift between green and brown—but I never understood it. How people could fawn and obsess over someone they didn't even know. When I was on trial, other inmates would fixate on magazines—models and actresses.

I'd never felt anything when I looked at photos of those women, never felt anything when I looked at men either.

Even standing in front of me now, she doesn't cause my heart rate to pick up. I don't feel anything—outside my frustration with this current training regimen.

"Being here centers me now. It brings me back to myself and the reason I do this, the reason I love to surf. I'm not focused on the waves or what performance I'm going to pull from them. I'm focused on myself. Tricks and shock aren't the reason we train in Celestia Cove. It's purpose you need to find here before you go anywhere else."

Surfing *is* my purpose.

I thought that was made clear before I arrived here. What else is there for me to discover?

It's not worth arguing with her, though. She's tough as fucking nails, and she has two Olympic medals to toss in my face if I want to try telling her I think she's wrong. Plus, she'll make me do push-ups until I'm crying, which was what most of my Tuesday morning looked like.

I like Liv, though. We've developed a camaraderie over the past week, and I find myself secretly hoping she'll continue to train with us this summer, even after Leo returns. She says she sees something in me, and she doesn't peg me as the type of person who says things she doesn't mean. It's been motivating.

"I know what you mean," I murmur.

Her lips tilt up. "I'm sure."

I head over to the cooler we bring down every morning, filled with electrolyte drinks and water. I pull one out and guzzle it down when I notice three figures descending the stairs from the top of the cliff.

Leo is unmistakable, leading them with some kind of huge backpack strapped to his shoulders. I assume the woman behind him is his wife, Darby, because the person trailing her is also unmistakable.

Willow.

I haven't seen her since Monday morning. She'd clearly been crying and tried to hide it as soon as she realized I'd joined her. I hadn't intended to impose, I just didn't expect to see anyone else at the beach so early. She was painting, and though clearly incomplete, her canvas was beautiful. I don't hold a particular interest in art, but I've spent enough time in the gallery to know something good when I see it, and Willow's painting was great.

I wondered if I'd find her working on it again Tuesday, but she wasn't there. Not any other day this week, either. I never saw her around the boardwalk, or even on her parents' property. I almost wondered if she'd disappeared, if maybe she was something I'd imagined, but now that she's in front of me again, I'm reminded she is very, very real.

Her tear-stained cheeks and red-rimmed eyes haunted me all week. I wanted to ask her what was wrong, and then I'd question why I cared to begin with. The longer I went without seeing her, the more curious I became—and I don't have time to be curious.

I'm supposed to be focused, and I'm supposed to stay away from her.

I should be annoyed, because I'm certain her presence is why her father has been unavailable. I was angry about it, about what he said to me on Friday evening—telling me to stay away from her like I'm some kind of fucking pariah. I mean, sure, I had a felony charge on my record. Knowing the background I came from, I'd wouldn't want my daughter going anywhere near a guy like me either, but it wasn't as if I'd been planning to pursue her. If he's so confident I'm a threat, why did he allow me here to begin with?

After I found Willow crying, I started putting two and two together. Something happened to her, and Leo needed the week off to take care of it. I thought it would bother me, but instead I've found myself longing to ask them what happened, ask where Willow is, and if I'd see her again.

Now, instead of being angry with Leo, I'm upset with myself for being so goddamn curious about his daughter.

When the Graham family reaches the beach and I get a clearer view of Willow's face, she appears completely fine. All evidence of Monday's tears is gone. They stop first at Liv, each hugging her. Liv holds Willow's face, and whatever conversation they're having seems serious. It's hushed, Willow's eyebrows are drawn, her lips twisted as she listens intently. The only thing I'm able to make out is a quiet, "I'm not going in the water, and I'm just going to sit." Liv responds, but I can't hear it, and after a moment, Willow nods before they hug again.

I pull my gaze away and find Leo's fixed on me. His face is stern, but as he closes the distance between us, a smile spreads over his mouth. "Hey, Weston. How has the week been?"

"Good." I place the cap back on my drink.

"Liv said you've been doing well, and she has notes for me. I'll evaluate those over the weekend, and we'll develop a real regimen for you on Monday."

"So you'll be back Monday, then?"

He nods. "I will. This week has been…" He sighs. "Unexpected. But we'll be able to really get started Monday. Liv also mentioned you have an attitude problem, but she has the worst attitude of anyone I've ever met, so I take that feedback with a grain of salt." He grins. "Everett said you've been doing well at the shop."

"*Puedo escucharte, idiota,*" Liv mutters.

"And I can understand you, Livia," he teases.

My eyes flit to Liv, but more so to Willow standing beside her, laughing quietly. She turns her gaze to me, her eyes flaring before she slowly lifts her hand, offering me a wave. I wave back.

"Are you working today?" Leo asks.

"Yeah, but not until two."

"All right. Help me carry these bags to the far end of the beach." He nods south, where one of the cliff's rock faces juts into the ocean, rounding out the cove. "My girls are going to paddleboard for a while, and you and I can work on that god-awful bottom turn of yours."

Fuck. I really don't feel like getting critiqued by Leo Graham *and* Livia Costa-Ramos when there are other people around. "I don't think—"

"Oh, so you do have an attitude problem, then?" He raises a brow. "You're going to let a seven-time World Champion and an Olympic gold medalist critique you—and then argue with them about their notes?"

"Nope." I pop the end of the word as I grab the bag at his feet and toss it over my shoulder.

I assist him in blowing up the inflatable paddleboards and putting together the oars as the girls continue their conversation with Liv. Once we're finished and they meet us at the end of the cove, Leo kisses his wife before turning to me. "You met her briefly when you were younger, but this is Darby."

"Nice to meet you." I extend my arm to shake her hand, and she returns it.

It's fucking uncanny how much Willow looks like her mom. Aside from the difference in eye color, and some aging around her eyes and mouth—smile lines, mostly—every other feature could have me confusing them for sisters. Their hair and lips. The way their noses crinkle when they smile.

"I'm so happy to have you staying here, Weston," she says softly, and I wonder if she's ever considered voice acting for Disney princesses. "If you ever need anything, don't hesitate to ask, okay?"

I nod, but the look her husband flashes me tells me I should avoid inconveniencing this woman at all costs.

"And I know you've met Willow already." There is an edge to his voice that slithers down my spine in an uncomfortable way.

"Yeah," I breathe, but it kind of gets stuck in my throat—because when I look at her, she's pulling the white dress she wore down to the beach over her head, and I'm greeted with miles upon miles of fair, exposed skin. She's covered by a total of three pink triangles—one at the center of her thighs, and two over her chest. All of which could fit into the palm of my hand. I never noticed how athletic she was before, but she's outrageously toned. I assumed she wasn't an athlete because it doesn't seem like she surfs competitively, but there is no way that body isn't the product of some kind of intense training. I rarely notice anyone's body, but I'm afraid I'll never *not* notice hers again.

"You look good."

The dress falls at her feet, and when my eyes track back up her body to her face, hers are wide—horrified, in fact—darting back and forth between her father and me.

Fuck. Did I say that out loud?

The aggressive clearing of Leo's throat answers me, and I'm terrified to look at him.

"I just meant . . ." I stumble over my words, backtracking. "Because Monday you . . ." I don't know if her parents know she was crying on the beach at six in the morning.

"I'm feeling better. Thank you." She smiles, and her cheeks are as red as I imagine mine are right now.

"Great." Leo claps me on the back harder than necessary, spinning me in the opposite direction. "Let's get to work, kid."

"DO YOU THINK you're comfortable enough to be here alone for a little while? My daughter is only in town for one more night, and I want to see her before she leaves."

I glance up from where I'm folding T-shirts at the register, finding Everett peering down at me over his sunglasses, hands on his hips. He's a menacingly large man—broad chest and wide shoulders, tattoos running from his neck to his hands, the faded ink only making them look cooler and more intimidating. His salt-and-pepper hair is grown out and feathered behind his ears, his short beard the same color.

When his lips form a flat line, he appears well and truly frightening, but I've heard him laugh before. I've seen him interact with his wife. I think he's soft-hearted, but he does kind of look like he could kick my ass if he wanted to.

"I think I'll be fine," I say.

Working at Heathen's is easy enough. All their merchandise is pre-populated in the register, which is simple to operate. When it's slow, I fold clothing or dust shelves. When people come with questions about surfing or boards, I'm expected to be an expert—and that's not a problem for me either. Plus, it's four o'clock on a Friday afternoon, so it's slow as hell.

I'm just lucky to have an official job. I'm on payroll, I pay taxes. It's something I can put on my resume, in addition to assisting Carter, that will help overlook my record. It's something I can show for myself other than being a failed surfer, in the event I end up failing again.

"Great." Before I can register the movement of his hand dipping into his pocket, a bundle of keys is in the air, flying at me. When I reach out and catch them, Everett smiles. "Good reflexes."

I shrug, slipping the key ring into my back pocket.

"Close down around seven. Make sure you lock both the back and front doors, and the office upstairs. If you need anything, text me."

"Have a good night." I wave him off, turning back to the T-shirts on the counter.

His footsteps shuffle over the tile when the bells on the front door chime. "Hey, kid."

I perk up, turning around in time to see Willow gliding through the double glass doors at the front of the store. Her smile beams as she rises onto her toes and hugs Everett. "Hi."

"Are you coming over for dinner later?" he asks as he pulls away.

"Yeah." She nods. "But I'm closing up Honeysuckle for my mom tonight, so I'll be a little late."

Everett's wife, Dahlia, is Darby's sister. Their daughter, Lucille, is Livia's wife. The entire dynamic of this family and the people I'm working for is confusing as hell to me, but I can at least make out that much.

"How are you . . ." Everett's words dissipate as his eyes dart to me. I immediately lower mine to the register in an attempt to not make it obvious my attention isn't on the two of them. "Okay?"

Willow takes a beat to respond, but a soft, "Yeah. Okay," leaves her mouth.

"Good." His voice turns low, and I keep my gaze down, fiddling with the cash register.

I don't know what to do with my hands. I press the button for the cash drawer, and it opens with a deafening pop. I jump back, startled. *Why did I do that? I knew it'd make that noise.*

I lift my head and find them both watching me. Everett's brows are furrowed, lip slightly curled like he's fighting the urge to ask if I'm stupid. Willow's head is cocked, and she's blinking at me with a bemused smile. *At least someone finds me entertaining, I guess.*

"Okay . . ." Everett drawls. "I'll see you tonight, kid. Love you."

"Love you!" she calls back as Everett leaves.

My mind has been stuck on Willow all week. Fixated on her bare skin since this morning. Reeling over the fact she wasn't okay on Monday, but she seems better now. Everett all but confirmed my suspicions. Something happened to Willow, and I'm so damn curious to know what it was. If someone hurt her. If she's truly okay now, or if that's a mask she's putting on to placate those she cares about. The same mask I wear around my foster parents.

Though I imagine the job is much tougher for her. She has so many people who love her.

I've never known what that feels like.

I told myself earlier, after making a complete fool of myself during my first training opportunity with Leo, that I'd stop thinking about her. I'd stop the curiosity from roaming free in my mind. There is absolutely no reason for me to be concerned about this girl I hardly know.

Our interaction this morning threw me off, and I was already tired from my practice with Livia. As soon as I got into the water with Leo, it was like I'd forgotten every basic aspect of surfing I've known all my life. I was way too aware of her. My eyes kept drifting to the far side of the cove where she paddleboarded in the calmer waters with her mom.

I lost focus. I looked awful. Leo was short and impatient. Frustrated with me, I think. I should be much better than the way I performed today. I am better than that. Today I was not the surfer he agreed to train. Today I wasted his time.

I can't do that again.

So I vowed to stop thinking about her. To stop theorizing about what happened to her or who she is. I'm in Pacific Shores to get my life back on track. To be the surfer I was destined to become. It's the only way to make sense of my life—and every terrible thing that happened to me and led me here. Every good thing too.

I can't allow it to be all for nothing.

Plus, regardless of my curiosity—possible interest, even—she's off-limits. Her father has already drawn a hard line—I'm not to entertain his daughter more than a passing greeting. Not that I needed the confirmation from him, anyway. I know I'd never be good enough for a girl like Willow.

"Hey, Wes—"

"Do you need something?" I ask, my tone coming out far more accusatory than I intended. I meant to sound distant, uninterested, yet polite. Because I need to be distant. I need to be uninterested. But fuck—I'm not rude.

Willow rears back, pink lips pouting, blue eyes wide and blinking. "Oh. Um . . ." She crosses her arms, kicking out a hip defensively from the other side of the counter. She's wearing a yellow tee and a pair of denim shorts beneath a white Honeysuckle Florals apron, and another pair of hand-painted sneakers. These are sage green, with multicolored flowers dotting the sides. "I just came by because . . ." She shakes her head, appearing flustered. "I normally close Honeysuckle around the same time as the surf shop, and I noticed your truck wasn't in the lot when I pulled in earlier. I thought you may have walked here? Figured I'd ask if you wanted a ride."

"That's okay," I say gruffly, but the words get trapped in my throat. Clearing it, I add, "I like walking."

Which isn't a lie. It's also true that my truck sometimes refuses to start, and I'm too embarrassed of that happening in Darby and Leo's driveway, so I haven't even tried since I've been here.

"Are you sure? We're actually all having dinner at Everett and Dahlia's tonight . . . although it sounds like you heard that." She laughs quietly, and I drop my head, heat creeping up my neck. "You know you're more than welcome, right? We can go together after work."

More than welcome? I hardly know these people. I'm certainly not family to them. I imagine being at that dinner party would feel a lot like looking at a completed puzzle and realizing you're a piece of something else that got stuck inside the box.

"That's all right. I've been up since five this morning, so I'm pretty tired."

She sighs, and the sound pulls my gaze back to her. Her eyes narrow, studying me in quiet agitation. "Are you always so . . .

aloof?"

"Are you always so forward?"

Her hands fall to her hips, and I notice the way her nails are painted, each a different shade of pastel. "Doesn't seem like beating around the bush works with you, so I suppose I must be blunt."

I really fucking wish she'd stop intriguing me, but since she doesn't seem to have any interest in leaving me alone at the moment, I'll bite.

"Well, I suppose growing up in an abusive household gave me poor social skills. My apologies."

I expect her to gasp and step back. Clutch her metaphorical pearls the way most pretty, wealthy daddy's girls would. It's a terrible reality to admit. Those who've never understood the harshness of the world often hate to be reminded of it. Like the presence of traumatized people is an inconvenience to their privilege.

Willow doesn't do that, though. Maybe it's because she could've guessed it. It's not like I ended up in foster care with Carter and Penelope for no reason, and she at least knows that much about me.

Willow's features soften, and she puts those huge, light-blue eyes directly on me. They remind me of the sky opening up after days of rain.

"I'm sorry that happened to you, Weston." She smiles gently, but it's not pitiful or apologetic. "But . . ." She flips her hair over her shoulder, spinning on her heel. "You should probably get out more. Work on those social graces. They're shit."

An unexpected laugh bursts out of me, and she peeks over her shoulder, a surprised smile on her face. She shakes her head, lips pursing with an exhale as she reaches the front doors.

"If you change your mind, meet me at my car after you're done closing up. It's the white Mercedes parked out back," she calls as she pushes them open.

Oh, I know. All three members of the Graham family drive incredibly nice cars, and my old beater looks like utter shit in the gravel beside the driveway next to theirs.

"Daddy buy you that?"

"Yeah." She tsks, zero shame in her voice. "As a graduation present after I was accepted into fucking Berkeley, asshole."

She doesn't wait for me to respond, but another laugh bubbles out of me as I watch her walk away through the windows, my chest seeming to expand with each sound that leaves my lips.

Fuck. This is not good.

CHAPTER TEN
WILLOW

"Honeysuckle Florals, how can I help you?" Mom's pristine voice singsongs as she presses the shop's phone to her ear while simultaneously flipping through order slips for today's pick-ups. It's an especially busy Wednesday afternoon.

I normally answer the phone and run the register, but she beat me to it since I'm elbow deep in a bucket of hydrangeas right now, trimming stems at the counter before I place these with the rest of the buckets on the floor.

"Oh . . ." Her voice drops, laced with a tone I can't quite read, but doesn't seem right. I glance at her from the corner of my eye just as she turns to face me, throat working with a swallow. She taps the phone screen before whispering, "It's Parker."

Every atom in my body twists itself in knots, my insides sticking together in a nauseating funnel that seems to want to crawl right out my throat. "Why?"

I know the word came from my mouth, but it didn't sound like me. It sounded foreign—like the haunted gasp you'd hear from a character in a horror movie just as they realize they've been caught by the killer.

He knows about the abortion is the first thought that rattles my mind, but I know that can't be true. Nobody in my family would disclose that to him—would contact him at all.

Guilt sluices through me. I've battled with thoughts of

whether to call him, to tell him about the decision I made. Part of me believes he deserves to know, another part reminds me that he took away my consent to the risk of pregnancy, so I owe him nothing.

Knowing now that he's on the other side of the phone line, that his voice is filtering through my mom's ear, has my skin prickling with unease. I don't ever want to hear that voice again. I don't think I could bear it.

Mom chews on her cheek, watching me with wide, somber eyes. "I'm going to tell him you're not here, okay? It'll be all right, baby." Her eyes drift toward the front of the flower shop as the chime on the door rings. Nodding behind me, she plasters a soft smile on her mouth that I know isn't meant for me before going back to the phone.

I turn around to find Weston striding up to the counter, eyeing me curiously.

"Hi," I say, voice cracking, all that anxiety I attempted to fight back funneling up my throat anyway.

"Um . . . I need a bouquet." Weston rubs the back of his neck awkwardly, like purchasing flowers from me is the most painful thing he's ever endured.

Apparently, it's been decided we can't stand each other, as he's been avoiding me like the plague since Friday.

I'd be more pressed about it, but as I hear my mom say, "Willow isn't here, Parker," from behind me, I can't find the capacity to care at the moment.

Wes's gaze darts from me to my mother, narrowing with confusion as he assesses the situation at hand. She's turned her back to us, speaking quietly, but there is no doubt Weston's hearing every word.

"She's okay, I promise," Mom continues.

I shoot Weston a sickly-sweet smile. "A bouquet of what?"

"I understand you're concerned, but if she wanted to reach out to you she would—"

Weston frowns, brow furrowing as he overhears what my

mother is saying.

I loudly clear my throat, drawing his attention back to me.

His eyes flash to mine. "Uh . . . flowers?"

I can't tell if his aversion to this interaction is because he's trying so hard to eavesdrop on my mother, or if it's just because he can't stand me.

"Please don't call again, Parker." Mom sighs from behind me, and a small portion of the anguish bubbling inside my veins settles itself.

"What *kind* of flowers?" I ask Weston.

He's still watching my mother as she slides the phone into her pocket, facing the two of us with a placating smile before excusing herself to her office, and promising me she and I will talk at home.

Weston drags his eyes back to me. A long second ripples between us as he studies me for some sort of reaction to the conversation he's just overheard, and I've tried my hardest to pretend wasn't happening at all.

His gaze searches my face for something, and I'm not sure what he finds within it, but finally, he mutters, "Honestly . . . I don't know. They're for Penelope. I'm meeting her for lunch next door. I thought it would be nice to surprise her with . . ." He runs a hand through his hair.

I'm just grateful he chose not to press me for more information regarding the situation he walked in to.

I've seen Weston twice since Friday. I ran into him one morning while he was leaving the beach and I was heading down to it. He gave me one of those closed-lip smiles and curt nods that you offer strangers who pass you on a hiking trail.

Then I ran into him outside my parent's garage one morning when I was returning one of the paddleboards. Sometimes I go out to the harbor on the north end of Pacific Shores for a change of scenery. When I got back, Weston was stepping out of the shower my dad built outside the back door of the garage.

That interaction was definitely awkward for both of us. He was shirtless. I was drooling. I was exiting the back door as he was leaving the shower stall, and we caught each other off guard. He startled, inhaling so sharply he began coughing. My mouth dried out at the sight of him wearing nothing but a towel, slung so low over his hips I could make out the V that led from his stomach and down to his . . .

I shake off the thought.

"That is nice. It's thoughtful," I say softly, forcing my brain to find some other plane of existence outside fear over Parker's unwelcome resurfacing, and curiosity over Weston's sculpted body. "Here . . ." I walk around the counter to the buckets of flowers that line the floor beneath the front windows. "Penelope loves daisies." I grab a handful. "Sunflowers." I pluck two of those from their bucket. "Her favorite color is green," I add, pulling a stem of eucalyptus from a bundle. "Maybe . . . a few pink cosmos for a pop of brightness?" I hold the bundle out to him. "What do you think?"

He tilts his head, studying them intently. "Looks good."

I nod, walking back to the counter, laying them out and trimming the stems before wrapping the bouquet in construction paper and tying it together with white twine.

"How do you know what her favorite flowers are?"

"I've known Penelope my whole life," I say, turning around. "I guess we just absorb information about people we care for over the years."

He chews on the inside of his cheek as he pulls his wallet from the back pocket of his worn jeans. They fit him too well. "Is it bad that I don't know what her favorite flowers are?"

"I don't know. Do you know other things about her?"

I trade his card for the flowers, entering the price for a standard arrangement and subtracting the employee discount before running it.

"I know how she takes her coffee, and I know she doesn't like to eat breakfast but likes eating breakfast food for lunch. Her favorite artist is Georgia O'Keeffe, and the Hanging Gardens of Babylon are her favorite Wonder of the Ancient World."

"See? I didn't know any of those things about her. We all absorb different information."

Although, I did know her favorite artist was O'Keeffe, she helped me write an essay for my advanced art history course after my professor told me I needed to study someone other than Monet—who is my favorite.

He smiles, and by instinct, I return it.

No. Dammit. We're not supposed to smile at each other.

"What time are you meeting her?" I ask.

"Right now."

"Great. I'll walk you over." I need the distraction. I need to leave this space, even if only briefly. I can feel Parker's presence all around me in here, and I'm desperate to run away from it.

Weston frowns. *Back on track.* "I don't need an escort, Willow."

"I'd sure hope not, considering you're a grown-ass man, Weston." I close the register and hand him back his card before calling in the direction of the back office, "Mom, I'm going to take a break and see Penelope for a second. I'll be right back!"

"Okay! Tell her hi for me." Her voice floats softly from the hallway behind me. There is relief in her tone, like she too knows how badly I need to step away.

I begin walking toward the doors, but Weston makes no move to follow. "Are you coming or . . .?"

"Yeah." He huffs, stepping up behind me. I reach for the handle, but his arm shoots out before I can, and he leans around me, holding the door open. "I've got it."

He's close enough that his breath fans against my neck, and I'm shadowed by the hovering of his body. I inhale swiftly, met with the scent of his cologne—something clean and woodsy.

"Thanks," I murmur, slipping into the afternoon sun.

"What do you need to see Penelope about?" he asks gruffly, walking a beat behind me as we cross the ten feet that separates Honeysuckle from The Wicked Wildflower.

"I can't just say hi?" I shoot back.

He brushes past me, grabbing the bakery's door before I reach it and holding that open too. For how reticent he is, he at least has manners. "Of course you can, but it feels a little like you're tryna follow me, Willow."

I let out a low whistle as I sidle up to the counter. "That ego sure is something."

He leans against the register, tossing me a grin before his face straightens again and he turns to Allie, who is now standing in front of us on the other side. Her brown eyes are wide, darting between Weston and me.

I desperately want to pull her aside and tell her what just happened with Parker, but I know now isn't the time, so I push that despair further down—into the very pits of me, until I'm convinced I'll forget it happened at all.

"Hey, Allie," he says casually. I forget they're familiar with each other. When Weston lived with Carter and Penelope as a teen, he and Allie worked together at the art gallery, since her parents help run it too. When I asked her about him last week, she said she didn't know much. He kept to himself, was quiet and shy. I suppose it hasn't changed. "Can I get a hot Americano and an iced almond milk latte with three pumps of hazelnut and two pumps of vanilla?"

"Sure." She turns to me, asking, "Do you want your regular?" before glancing back at Weston. "I assume you'll be paying for Willow's as well."

His brows pop, like he's not sure how to respond, but he wordlessly pulls out his wallet and hands her his card. Allie beams while she runs it before giving it back.

"Is the latte for you or Penelope?"

"Penelope." He yawns and stretches while we walk to a table in the corner of the cafe, and I don't miss the way his Heathen's sweatshirt rides up, offering a glimpse of his stomach. "I don't do sugar while I'm training."

"Bummer," I mutter, sinking into one of the wicker chairs.

Weston places a hand on the back of it, and I'm overcome

by his presence again, breath catching in my throat as he gently pushes me forward, scooting me closer to the table.

"Mm-hmm." He takes the seat across from me, eyes roaming my face. "I have a lot of restrictions I'm becoming less than thrilled about."

His tongue slips between his lips before he pulls his bottom one beneath his teeth, slowly letting it go while his gaze remains on me. He exhales deeply, closing his eyes and shaking his head before turning toward the front of the bakery. I want nothing more than to pick apart his brain and rummage through every thought floating inside of it.

He doesn't say more, and all my words unravel in my throat and become lost on my tongue, so I only study him instead. His eyes are turbulent, jaw tight, mouth tense as he looks beyond the windows and out toward the beach.

After a moment, that rigidity in his features softens, lips spreading into a smile, and as I follow his gaze, I find Penelope pulling open the door and stepping inside.

Weston raises his arm, waving, and it only takes her a second of scanning the semi-busy cafe to spot us. Her face brightens as she waves back and heads to our table.

Weston stands, and when Penelope wraps her arms around his neck, his eyes close and his entire body relaxes. His lips shudder with an exhale, and it's as if the tension he seems to be carrying at all times rolls off him in waves.

I can't help but wonder what Weston's life looked like before he moved in with Carter and Penelope—and I'm curious what it must've been like to be in jail and on trial for the amount of time he was. What he must've done to get himself placed there.

It's clear now that he must rarely feel safe, and perhaps that's why he's so guarded. Penelope must be a place of safety for him, and maybe I am intruding on something much deeper than I realized.

Penelope pulls back before facing me, smiling and hugging me too. "Hi, pretty girl. I wasn't expecting to see you today."

"Weston stopped in to get you those." I nod to the flowers in his hand as I step out of her embrace. "So I thought I'd come say hello when he told me he was meeting with you for lunch."

Weston's gaze pins me from my periphery, and I wonder if he's thinking back on the conversation he overheard, pondering if a simple hello was the only reason I followed him here, or if he too can read the desperation radiating off me to get away from the flower shop. He sighs before handing Penelope the flowers and pulling out her chair. She kisses his cheek, thanking him before she drops into it. Allie calls out that our drinks are ready.

While he's grabbing them, Penelope turns to me. "How are you doing?"

"Better." I smile, and it's only partially a lie. I am better than I was a week ago when Penelope and the rest of my friends and family came over for book club. Physically, I am doing much better, but mentally—emotionally—I'm just as lost.

I'm so grateful I wasn't the person to answer the phone at Honeysuckle earlier, and yet I still find myself wishing I'd heard his voice. If only just to know how genuine his tone may have been, if he may truly miss me. I still miss Parker at times, and I fucking hate myself for that.

I have brief moments where I wake up in the morning and I'm not even sure what I'm doing it for. I had a panic attack in the middle of the night this past weekend, because transfer application deadlines for the fall semester at most universities are at the end of this month, and I have no idea what the hell I'm doing with my life.

Berkeley had been my dream school since I was a child. I honestly don't know why, maybe because of my *High School Musical* phase and the belief the entire campus was crawling with the Troy Boltons of the world.

Maybe that's why I fell for Parker so quickly too.

He was perfect, and I can't seem to come to terms with the fact that all of it was merely a mirage.

I worked so hard to be accepted there. The idea of throwing it away because of him slashes through my gut, and I hate the feeling of walking around with my organs exposed. Part of me wants to be a stronger woman. Wants to face him and take back what's mine—my education, my apartment, my fucking body.

I don't think I'm that girl, though. I don't think I can handle that. And for all the times Allie has told me that's okay, that sometimes simply healing is the strongest thing we can do, it doesn't feel like enough.

I don't feel like enough, and I fear I'll never feel like enough for anyone ever again.

"Better?" Penelope asks, pulling me from my thoughts with a raised brow. She looks so regal with her auburn hair slicked back into a low bun, lips painted a shade of berry that makes her green eyes glitter. She clasps her manicured hands on the table between us, then leans back in her chair as she crosses one leg over the other, causing her beige trousers to sway at the ankles, where her red-bottomed heel plays peekaboo as she shakes her foot. "Are you really?"

Penelope is the most educated person I know. A doctor. An archaeologist and professor. An artist too. She has degrees from UCLA and fucking Oxford. She's a gallery owner who somehow found balance between academia, business, and creativity, honing all of it together to serve her perfectly.

I bet she's never made a mistake in her entire life.

I kind of want to ask her about every decision she's ever made so that I can mimic them, and maybe someday I'll be more like her, and less like me.

"I guess I . . . feel a little lost?"

She smiles softly. "That's okay. You've gone through something that threw you off the road you were on, and you might wander for a while until you find it again. Or . . ." She shrugs. "You might stumble onto a completely new path, and suddenly everything will make sense."

"Actually . . . speaking of that." I swallow. "I know you're teaching that ancient art course at Golden State this summer, and classes have already started, so it's too late to register, but . . . do you think it would be possible for me to—"

Weston slides my s'mores latte across the table, setting Penelope's drink in front of her before he sits down across from me and pops the lid off his coffee. His eyes lift as he brings it to his mouth, locking on mine while he blows over the top of the cup, snuffing out the billowing steam.

His lips look plush—soft when they're pursed like that, and I'm suddenly very aware of the way breath feels when it skates over my skin. Goosebumps rise on the back of my neck as if that's the place he's blowing instead.

A chill bites my spine, and I'm forced to shake my head and look away.

"It would be possible for you to . . .?" Penelope drawls.

"What?" I ask, whipping in her direction.

Weston lets out a soft chuckle.

"You were asking about the course I'm teaching."

Right. Christ.

"Do you think it would be possible for me to sit in? Just so I have . . . something to do this summer that doesn't make me feel terribly useless."

I keep my eyes fixed on Penelope, but I clock the tilt of Weston's head in my periphery, the way he leans onto the table, becoming more invested in the conversation. His gaze sears the side of my face so intensely I wonder if he may leave me burned.

I wonder if I wouldn't hate it if he did.

"You are not useless, Willow," Penelope says quickly, placing her hand over mine before sighing deeply. "But yes, of course you can sit in on the class. In fact . . ." She smiles. "I actually need a T.A. Would you be interested?"

"Really?"

She nods. "The drive from Santa Monica is a long one, and it cuts into my grading time.

The university already approved me for a student assistant position. You'd earn a couple of credits toward your degree as well, and—"

"Yes." The word leaves my mouth so fast I'm gasping for air. "Yes, absolutely. I'd be honored."

"Class is every Wednesday at two, and I'll likely keep you a few hours after each week as well. Is that going to work for your schedule?" Penelope asks.

"Oh, I'll make it work." Mom makes my schedule anyway, and I know she'll be as thrilled about this opportunity as I am.

My parents understand now why I left Berkeley, and they've been patient while I figure out where I want to go and what I want to do next, but of course, I know they're still disappointed about my dropping out of school for the time being. I know assisting Penelope this summer will be a way for me to show them I'm still serious about my education.

A way for me to take it back for myself.

"Okay, we'll plan to start next week then, since it appears you're busy today." She nods to the Honeysuckle Florals apron I'm wearing.

"Thank you, Penelope." I place my hand over hers and squeeze gently. "You don't know what this means to me."

She squeezes back. "Trust me, I do."

Weston steals my attention when he leans back in his chair, crossing his arms. The brewing storms in his eyes cast over me as his lips turn downward in a frown.

Right. I'm intruding.

"I'll leave you two for your visit." I smile at Penelope before pushing back my seat.

"Stay," she pleads. "I imagine you get a full lunch break? Eat with us."

"Oh, no. I—"

"Stay, Willow." Weston's tone invites no argument, and the glare Penelope shoots him must make him realize it, because he softly adds, "Please."

I toss him a closed-lip smile, pulling back to the table as Penelope turns to Weston. "So, tell me all about your training so far. Have you learned anything?"

He huffs a laugh, taking a sip of his coffee. "I've learned I suck, apparently."

"That's not what Dad said." I roll my eyes. "You need to revisit your bottom turn and your cutbacks, while focusing on your endurance and agility so that you can meet large breaks with more head-on precision."

His brows lift. "Is that so? I didn't realize you were also coaching me, Willow."

I can't tell if he's trying to flirt with me or if I pissed him off, and the way Penelope's eyes dart between us tells me she may be thinking the same thing.

I shrug. "I know a thing or two. Maybe you could use the extra help."

"I thought you didn't surf." He tilts his head, appearing genuinely curious now.

"I could surf before I could walk." I sip from my drink. "I don't surf competitively due to a lack of interest, not skill or knowledge. I'm better than most."

He snorts into his cup. "I'd like to see that."

"Maybe if you're lucky."

He hums contemplatively, eyes searing through me, but doesn't respond.

"Okay . . ." Penelope drawls. "Anyway, Wes, tell me how work is going."

His eyes narrow as he takes another sip, swallowing slowly with his gaze on mine, before he finally turns to his foster mother. A warm smile that I've yet to see him offer me spreads over his mouth before he begins telling her about his new life in Pacific Shores.

My phone vibrates in my pocket, and when I pull it out I find a message:

Chelsea

Going to be in your area next month.
Can we meet up?

CHAPTER ELEVEN
WESTON

I REACH THE bottom step of the cliffside stairs, finding Willow's ass right in front of me, high in the air as she pedals her heels in downward dog, the sky dotted with candy-colored clouds beyond her.

She's wearing a lavender bikini this morning, and as she hikes her hips higher, crawling her hands up the mat, her bottoms ride farther between her cheeks, and I'm blushing more deeply than I thought could be possible before this moment.

In what feels like an act of mercy, she stands straight, bringing her arms above her head before dropping into a warrior one pose.

I know I should say something—anything—to make my presence known, but I'm completely fucking frozen. She's no longer bent over, but the memory of her ass and her bare back covered only by the thinnest strap tied at the center of her spine remains vivid—planting itself firmly at the forefront of my mind. All words and language and sound are stuck behind my teeth. I can't decide if my body is refusing to let them out so I can continue watching her, or if I've just forgotten how to open my mouth at all.

A throat clears behind me, and my stomach drops to my ass.

"Sugar, you have company, it appears."

Willow doesn't startle, she simply sinks into warrior two, extending her knee over her ankle and spreading her arms out wide as she turns to face the south end of the beach. She cranes her neck in our direction, smiling. "I know."

Leo takes an exasperated breath, clapping my back as he passes me. "Gonna assume your eyes were on the horizon out there, measuring the swell period."

"Absolutely." I nod.

He steps into the sand, pressing a kiss to his daughter's head as she continues her flow, then drops his board to the ground before pulling up the sleeves of his wetsuit.

"How many seconds?" he asks, facing me, blue eyes narrowed.

"Oh. Um . . ." I stammer. "Six."

Willow snorts, finishing what appears to be a sunrise salutation. My eyes flick to her as she steps off her mat and bends over again to roll it up. *Goddamn.* It's a challenge to pull my gaze from her, but when I do, it unfortunately lands on her dad who's studying me with an unconvinced and unrestrained expression.

I gulp like a fucking cartoon character.

Why the hell is she down here, and why is she so goddamn distracting?

"Well, we'd better get started," Leo says nonchalantly. "See if you're right about that measurement."

I definitely wasn't counting the swell period. I was counting the number of freckles that dot Willow's spine, and the answer is infinite.

"I'm going to join you today," Willow chimes.

"You sure you're up for that?" Leo asks, and I find the question odd, but I'm not about to question him.

"Water's pretty calm today, and I'm only going to take one swell." Willow shrugs, pulling a wetsuit from the bag at her feet and tugging it up her legs and around her muscular thighs and ample hips. "Weston said he wanted to see me surf."

"Oh, no." I shake my head between her and Leo, holding my hands up in surrender. "I didn't mean . . . I trust your skills, Willow. You don't need to prove anything to me."

"I know," she huffs, scrunching her nose at me. "But you said you wanted to watch me, so . . ."

"Sounds like a recipe for distraction," Leo mutters.

"Of course not." Willow bumps into my shoulder with hers as she steps up beside me. It's the first time we've touched, and it feels like I've been branded somehow. I don't like touch. I don't touch anyone outside of professional handshakes and brief hugs from Penelope. "Weston is completely focused, right?"

I frown at her. She smiles back.

Why are you fucking with me? I want to scream.

Is it because I insinuated she must not be good at surfing if she doesn't do it competitively? Maybe that was a dick move. But fuck—having her here absolutely steals my focus. She is the utter definition of distracting. I've never been so frustratingly intrigued by another person before in my life, and I don't know how to make sense of it. She takes up every ounce of free space in my head, and then some.

Especially since whatever weirdness went down in her mom's flower shop. I don't know who Parker is or what he was to Willow, but he must've done a number on her based on the way color drained from her face when Darby said his name on the phone, and how Willow's eyes glazed over with unshed tears when Darby advised him not to call again.

She's clearly been through something with the way everyone in her life treats her like she's shattered glass. Even without Leo's hard-pressed rules in place, a guy with a past like mine would be a sure deterrent for a girl like Willow. I have no business thinking about her so often, studying her so intensely, allowing her to take up every inch of space inside my mind.

The only time I seem to be able to push her from my mind is when I'm on the water—and I can't have her taking that from me now. Not when so much is on the line.

Telling her to leave would probably make things worse, though.

I decide I'll push through today, and afterward I'll pull her aside and ask her not to do this again. I know Willow is being playful, and at moments, I can't help but toss it back. Maybe it's a welcome distraction from whatever she's going through, but I don't think I can play that role for her. I think she thinks we might be flirting at times, and sometimes I wonder the same—but I've never flirted before. I've never been interested in it. In anyone.

I don't know how to tell if that's what is happening with Willow. If the allure is only because she's my mentor's daughter, because I'm always caught in her proximity, or if it is something more. What I do know is that it doesn't matter. I can't be around her—both to stay on track and because it's one of her father's rules.

She's trying to have fun for the summer, rebel with what she thinks is some kind of bad-boy underdog before she goes back to college and continues constructing her perfect future with the blocks she's been gently handed. I'm trying to save my own life. I'm holding piles of ash from my world that burned, and attempting to rebuild a house of stone.

I *have* to stay away from her, and I'll tell her that as soon as today's session is over.

For now, though, I clear my throat and turn to Leo. "I'm good. Let's get started."

I STARE DUMBFOUNDED, slack-jawed, in disbelief as Willow pops up gracefully, falling into an effortless rhythm—legs pumping the board in one fluid movement as her body rises. She presses her weight down and forward, then flexes upward, carving along the face of the wave with perfect fucking precision.

There is no flaw to her form, no misstep in her balance as she completes a cutback before snapping into a floater until the wave is nothing but foam. She hops off the board, skipping through the ankle-deep water until she regains enough control to balance herself on the sand. Her board skims over the shallow water beside her, attached to her ankle.

"Your turn!" she calls, shading her eyes with a hand.

"Why the fuck doesn't she compete?" I ask Leo, breathless

with astonishment.

"It's not her calling, and that's okay." I turn to face him, expecting the same hard expression he's often offering me.

Instead, Leo's beaming at her, pride shining brightly on his face. I can't imagine how challenging it must be to give your genes to someone, crafting a human built for something incredible, and having them not take advantage.

My mom used to look at me like that on the rare occasion she could get me into a competition without my dad finding out about it.

My dad thought surfing was a waste of time—and believed his fist was the best tool for driving the point home to both of us.

Carter and Penelope look at me like that too, I suppose, though it's not the same. It can't be. I'm not truly theirs to be proud of, and I'll never see that look of pride on my mother's face again.

"If she were competing, and you were judging, what score would you award her?"

"Eight-point-five," I say immediately. "Perfect form, basic technique was flawless, but . . . I still think a more advanced maneuver was possible, even with a swell like this." Like Livia said last week, the cove is great for developing foundational skill, but waves this small aren't ideal for competitive tricks. Regardless . . . "An off-the-lip would've been doable there if she'd taken the risk. I'd reward a risk-taker."

"Good." Leo nods. "I agree." He juts his chin toward the waves. "So, go repeat it, and convince Willow to give you a ten."

Fuck.

My gaze finds Willow as she unstraps her board from her ankle before making her way back to us, breathing heavily. She catches her long blond hair in her hands, wringing out the saltwater.

"Weston gave you an eight-point-five. Said you could be riskier," Leo says.

She huffs, rolling her eyes before fixing them on me, giving me a judgmental once-over.

"I told him to repeat it and make you give him a ten," he continues.

Her lips twitch playfully. "Let's see it, Wes. You get exactly one try, because I've got a breakfast date this morning."

"A date?" her dad and I ask in unison, both heads whipping in her direction.

Leo's eyes are narrowed, nose scrunched, lip curled—but it's not directed at her. It's directed at me, I'm sure he's likely wondering why I'm giving Willow a mirrored expression.

I don't know why I care, either.

"With Elena," she explains, eyeing me curiously. "We're paddleboarding in the harbor today."

My gaze flits to Leo, who relaxes, taking a breath of relief. It's odd because, despite how strict and demanding he is with me, it's not how I'd expect him to act with his daughter. Even now, it was concern etched across his face, not control. I know the difference well.

He nods before turning to me. "Well, get the hell out there, kid."

I grab my board—white with a blue stripe down the middle. Carter bought it for me just before I competed at Junior Worlds. It's a high-quality brand that forges their boards with recycled materials, which is important to him. They're expensive as hell, but worth it.

My heart beats wildly as I secure my ankle strap and wade into the waves—deep enough to lay down and paddle toward the break. I fight against the whitecaps until I make it past them, floating between uncrested swells. The swell period is nine seconds—not perfect conditions, but not terrible, either.

I let two troughs pass, hoping to snag a more powerful wave, but also to gather my nerves and swallow them down. Every lip of water that drifts beneath me feels less like floating and more like dropping down a roller coaster—every organ in my stomach lifting into my chest before being tossed around and clattering off my ribcage. My pulse pounds in my ears, and zaps of apprehension surge through my veins and gather in my feet where they dangle beneath the surface.

I know it's because she's watching.

One of the reasons I'm so fucking good at this sport is because it never made me feel this way. I'm relaxed and at ease when I'm out here. Being on the water, facing the horizon, creates this endless vastness of the world, while offering me the solace of being the only person in it. I can't find that feeling anywhere else.

Right now, knowing not only my mentor is watching—judging—but Willow too? I give myself one final swell period, counting eight seconds this time, flipping my board just as the water begins to lift.

I paddle with every ounce of energy I hold, forcing all nerves into my arms as I push through the wave before planting my palms on the front of my board and leaping forward—visualizing the fluidity of the movement in my head as I pop up.

A whistle pierces my ears—so loud and commanding it cuts through the roaring of the waves all around me. A high-pitched cheer follows, and I know it can only belong to her.

A grin splits my face—so swift and fierce it causes my cheeks to ache.

I pump my board, carving along the face of the wave until it begins to crest, the sapphire blue water turning white and foamy. I rock back on my heels, swiveling my hips and bending my knees, snapping my board toward the lip. I press forward, cutting back sharply as I ride over the crashing of the wave, letting its current lead me to shore.

It's been a long while since I felt that connected to the water. I can't remember the last time I wasn't competing—whether it was fighting me or fixing me. Before that day—the day I almost killed someone—it always felt like healing. Like as long as I was out there, I was okay. I'd be safer in the waves than I would at home, because the waves let me in. Let me become one of them for those brief periods of time that I was riding within them.

Ever since, I've questioned whether I'm worthy of being

welcomed back.

Just now, I was completely fluid. I wasn't even inside my body. I wasn't a solid mass. I was wind and water—floating and weightless and unworried. I was free. I've felt comfort and home and healing with surfing since the day I was released from lockup, but I haven't yet felt *free.*

It was as if the sound of Willow's voice shot through the air between us. A tether—a life preserver—lassoing me out here in the open water, keeping me upright. It was support, and for all the encouragement I receive from my foster parents, from Leo now too, it's never felt like that. Pure excitement and true joy—giddy. That's how my mother used to describe it, the way she felt when she watched me surf.

I jump off my board, sprinting through the foam, vision blurred by the swiftness of my movement. I scan the shore for Willow, wanting to tell her that I heard her yell and whistle. I want to tell her how it made me feel—though I know I won't voice that part.

All I find is her dad, eyeing me with his hands on his hips. In the distance behind him, Willow's figure ascends the cliffside toward the house, the sight causing my stomach to descend into the depths of my body, disappointment taking its place.

I jog up to Leo, and he hands me a water bottle. "She had to go get ready," he says. "But . . . she gave you a ten."

That aching grin spreads over my cheeks again. Pride blooms inside me, expanding to the point that my head is floating.

"I gave you a six," he continues. My coach's words pierce the balloon in my chest, and I'm deflating. "So, what's the real lesson of the morning, Weston?"

"I don't know." I sigh. "What is it?"

He smiles, dimples appearing on either side of his mouth. "The only opinion that truly matters is mine. So why don't you get back out there and do it again—until I think you're as great as my daughter does."

"Yes, sir." I toss him a mock salute, but when I turn my back to him and head toward the water, I'm grinning like a goddamn fool.

Willow Graham might be the most alluring person I've ever met. Her ability to take up every crevice inside my mind is maddening, and I'm terrified of it.

But *fuck*. She thinks I'm great.

I ride that high for the rest of the morning.

CHAPTER TWELVE

WILLOW

I WIPE SWEAT off my brow as I step into the late-morning sun and shut the garage door behind me. It's kind of a nightmare lugging in the inflatable paddleboards from the back of my dad's truck, but he wasn't around when I returned home from the harbor. A drop of moisture slips down my spine, and I decide I'll rinse off in the outdoor shower before heading inside to get ready for work.

A soft, melodic folk song flows through my earbuds as I push through the swinging door and step into the stall my dad built behind the garage. Lined with bamboo paneling, it's closed off from the outside world but has an open top that allows a view of the sky overhead. A divider separates the changing area from the shower itself, and the entire stall is lined with planted ferns and calatheas, creating a private paradise. I slip out of my wetsuit and throw it over the bamboo wall before rounding the divider.

Until I smack face-first into something that should not be there.

It takes a moment to regain my bearings, my focus settling on the broad, toned, wet chest level with my eyesight. I run my gaze up that chest, pulse pounding in my ears as I lift my head to find Weston blinking down at me.

His eyes are shadowed, jaw set, brows furrowed beneath the dripping hair hanging on his forehead. The eye contact is too intense, so I drop my gaze—and I can't decide if I'm thankful or disappointed when I notice he's wearing shorts.

His stomach brushes against my waist, and I realize how close our bodies are. I inhale sharply, jumping back to create enough space for the drumming in my chest—but one of my heels clips my ankle, and I stumble backward.

His arm shoots out, gripping my waist and curling around the small of my back, keeping me steady. I wobble slightly before finding my balance again, my mind reeling at the warmth of his palm, the way his fingers curl into my flesh to grip me—keep me upright.

His hold on me is solid and strong, tender when he squeezes slightly, as if reassuring himself he's still holding me. I haven't been touched like this in a long time. I haven't been touched by a man at all. Not since . . .

The memory slams into my consciousness. Parker's hands on my hips, his thighs rubbing against the backs of mine, my hair wrapped around his fist. Everything he was stealing from me in that moment, and the way I hadn't even been aware. How I'd mistaken it for love and care and pleasure.

A nauseating chill rolls down my spine, and a shiver bites my flesh.

Weston rears back, clearing his throat. "So—Sorry. I thought you might fall."

"Oh," I breathe, realizing he must think I'm flinching at his touch. "No. It wasn't . . ." I bite my lip, shaking my head. "I'm sorry. I was listening to music and didn't hear the shower running. I should've knocked."

"You don't have to apologize. I get it." He takes another step back, creating more space.

"It's not you, Wes," I murmur before bursting out an incredulous laugh. "I'm just traumatized."

His brows shoot up, eyes flaring with concern. He rubs a hand across his jaw, lips parting like he may say something before they close again, and he shakes his head.

Parker had opinions about my body, ones he rarely kept to

himself. He'd comment every time I gained or lost a few pounds, and regardless of which direction the scale went, it was negative. I lost weight in the wrong places, and gained it in the wrong places, too. He'd tell me my breasts were too small, but my ass had too much cellulite, and my torso was too wide. I was too athletic but not lean enough, too round but not curvy enough.

Then he'd follow up every comment with *but I love your body anyway, and that's all that matters.*

Then, that night happened and he told me I was—

"Me too," Wes responds, pulling me from my thoughts. "I struggle with touch. I understand."

My nose begins to sting, emotion building behind my eyes, and I can't decide if it's for myself or for him. He's so tall, strong and guarded. Impenetrable. I couldn't imagine anyone being able to hurt him now, but I'm suddenly all too aware he was once a vulnerable young boy living inside a nightmare.

"I'm sorry." I swallow, beginning to walk backward. "I'll go—"

"Willow," he rasps quietly, and I halt. His eyes are pinned to me, unraveling all my composure as they hungrily soak in every inch of my exposed skin. Lips parted, chest heaving, he studies me like a painting he may never see again. "I planned on talking to you after my training session. I was going to ask you to give me space."

"Oh." *What the hell?* How does he expect me to respond to that?

The whiplash between the language of his body and the words from his mouth knocks the wind from my lungs.

"That's not . . . fuck." He sighs, running a hand through his wet hair.

"Why do you want me to stay away from you so badly?"

I've volleyed between whether Weston genuinely doesn't like me, or if he's just terrible at flirting. He looks at me with interest, but speaks to me with disdain. I've considered he might be jealous, assuming I was born with a silver spoon in my mouth and have never wanted for anything, while he's struggled for everything—and he wouldn't necessarily be wrong about that. But I'm not a spoiled brat. I'm not mean or shallow or vain, and I've done my best to prove that, because it's an assumption that's followed me most of my life.

It makes my skin itch—the thought of Weston thinking those things of me, not liking me. It's as if part of me wants to tell him off, tell him I'd like distance from him too, because I refuse to tolerate yet another man who resents me. Yet, part of me wants to fight to prove him otherwise, show him I'm none of those things—that I could be his friend. I think, perhaps, it's because *I* am growing to like Weston. I think I'd like him to be my friend too.

A third part of me is a little afraid that this is his version of flirting, because I find him beautiful, and I *cannot* allow my head to go down that rabbit hole.

"Do you remember when we met at Disneyland? It was Christmas, like . . . six or seven years ago?" he asks.

"Yes," I whisper.

"You knew I was overstimulated." When I only blink, he raises his head toward the sky as if searching for what to say next. "Nobody else noticed. I thought I was hiding it well, but I was having the hardest fucking time. Not just that day, but with *everything* back then. You saw it. I don't even know how. And you didn't make me feel embarrassed or ashamed of the box I hid inside. You were kind. I felt . . . seen." He looks at me again, blue eyes blazing through me. "I never forgot it, Willow. I blocked a lot of shit out, but I remembered you."

My mouth parts with a ragged gasp, desperate to swallow the oxygen laced with his words.

"Since moving in here a few weeks ago, you've been . . . distracting," he continues softly. "Even more so after I found you crying that morning, and how you disappeared for days afterward, and . . . whatever happened at the flower shop."

"Nothing—"

"I don't believe that." He inches forward, like he may step

toward me, before rearing back, as if he thought better of it. "I'm aware of you at all times, and it's completely eclipsed my focus. I can't lose sight of the reason I came here. My entire life hangs in the balance, and I thought you might jeopardize that, even if through no fault of your own."

My heart seems to have sprouted wings, and in an attempt to fly out my mouth, it's been lodged in my throat.

"I wasn't lying when I said I lack social skills." He huffs a laugh. "I grew up around poor communication styles and, according to my many therapists, I isolated myself socially, likely as a way to hide the abuse that was going on at home." He shrugs. "It's why I struggle with touch. I wasn't touched gently as a child. I don't trust the hands of others."

That stinging erupts behind my eyes again.

"Why are you telling me all of this, Wes?"

He bites his lip, lashes fluttering as his gaze falls to the ground. "You make me feel like I can, I guess. Like my truth is safe with you."

"And yet you want me to stay away?"

He shakes his head without raising it—without looking at me. "Not after today." He finally lifts his eyes, and the raging storm inside them seems to have settled. "I heard you out there, cheering for me. It lit a fire inside me. Reminded me what it feels like to surf for someone other than myself. I'm grateful for that now."

I don't know how to respond, still choking on my feathered heart.

I breathe deeply before whispering, "Your truth is safe with me."

Weston licks his lips, nodding before his gaze falls from me again.

"My boyfriend sexually assaulted me," I blurt so quickly I'm not even sure I've spoken until I hear the words leave my mouth and land in the space between us. "That's why I moved home. That's who you heard my mother talking to. He called looking for me."

Weston's head snaps up, eyes widening before narrowing slowly, nostrils flaring, jaw tensing. His breathing picks up, and I imagine if Parker were standing beside me right now, he'd be in grave danger. Though I don't feel threatened at all.

"I thought he was the love of my life." I swallow, emotion surging behind my eyes. "I thought I'd marry him someday. I still miss him all the time, and I hate myself for it." I quickly turn my head, wiping the tears dripping down my cheeks, as if I can hide them from him. "I haven't said that out loud before. Not to anyone."

"But you're telling me," he says softly.

We keep our distance, Weston at one end of the stall, beneath the shower head that's no longer running. I'm pressed against the divider. Plush greenery surrounds us, enclosing us inside some kind of quiet solace. As if everything laid bare in here will stay exactly where it is.

"We're trading truths, aren't we?"

His lips tick up in a smile before his expression falls again. "It's okay to miss him. You're still grieving a future you'll never get to have. It takes time." He speaks as if he has authority on the matter. "More than half of women who find themselves in an abusive relationship return to their partner at least once. You are brave to have found the courage to leave at all, and it's okay to sometimes want to go back."

Tears fall once again, and I don't hide them this time.

I wrap my arms around myself, blinking at Weston through my blurred sight, because I don't know what else to say. I don't know how to explain how badly I needed to hear that.

I wipe my eyes, vision clearing in time to see him moving toward me, a soothing smile on his lips. He passes me slowly, running his fingers along my forearm, tender and featherlight, as if stealing one touch for himself. "I'll give you some space. See you soon, Willow."

Sparks ignite over my flesh at the feel of his skin on mine and the invigorating timber of his deep voice. They spread all throughout my being, wrapping me in warmth as he leaves me alone with the ferns.

"I THINK YOU may actually be a genius," I huff, dropping into the chair beside Penelope's desk.

I just finished my first lecture as her assistant, and listening to her speak about art—its influence on humankind, and the way we're still impacted by the artists of the past—is inspiring. There is nothing boring about the way she lectures. She doesn't drone on as if she'd rather be anywhere else. Every word she speaks is purposeful and filled with passion.

She laughs, shuffling through a pile of papers. "I just love what I do."

"What made you want to be an artist?" I ask.

"I never wanted to be an artist," she says quietly, beginning to pack her bag. "I was good at drawing, and I've always enjoyed doing things I'm good at, so it kind of became like a therapy to me. Reminded me I was capable of having value without earning it. There was a skill I was simply just . . . born with, and I didn't have to question whether I deserved it." She shrugs, glancing at me. "I wouldn't say I wanted to be an artist, though. That would mean accepting the risk of failure—and losing the love and enjoyment of it. I focused on history academically because I also enjoyed that. Studying the past—the mistakes of humankind and how we healed ourselves. Archaeology felt like a way of blending the two together. Even now, despite the number of my paintings my husband hangs in that gallery, I don't consider myself an artist. At least, not in the sense of my career or accomplishments. I think that would negate the identity of it—the piece entwined in my soul." She scrunches her nose before a laugh bursts from her lips. "Does any of that make sense?"

"It does." I nod. "Absolutely. I think that's why I want to study art therapy. I want to paint for myself before I paint for anyone else, and I want to help other people learn to create for themselves—to heal themselves through art."

I've begun painting again this week. I was afraid after everything with Parker, after terminating the pregnancy, I'd never pick up a brush again. I had no idea how it would affect me, and while each day is still a struggle, art has helped.

I woke a couple mornings ago to find I was bleeding. I've been spotting on and off since I took the medication, and each time, I sink to the bathroom floor and cry until I can't breathe. It's like being blanketed in a dull sadness—like the guilt and fear and rage all roll themselves together into one heavy sensation that envelops every inch of my skin, and no matter how violently I thrash beneath it, I can't get it off. The blood is a reminder of the inescapable decision I made.

That morning, though, I forced myself to my feet once the tears dried up, and I stumbled down the hall to the spare bedroom my parents allowed me to convert into an art studio. I fell into some sort of trance, sinking deeper into my feelings than I typically allow myself to, until my canvas was streaked in color—abstract and messy but somehow beautiful.

I felt lighter after that. I shed part of that weight, realized that I'm still me. I can still create—I can keep those parts of me intact, even if I've lost other pieces of myself.

Penelope smiles, squeezing my hand once before tossing her bag over her shoulder. "All right, I need to head back to Santa Monica. Last week I assigned the class an essay on their current favorite piece of ancient art. My goal is to expand their knowledge enough by the end of the summer that they'll each discover something new they love even more. Before you leave, would you mind checking the submission portal, mark those who did not complete the assignment, and then forward the rest of the essays to me so I can look them over this weekend?"

"Of course," I say. Penelope nods, but as she turns toward the door, I blurt out the question I've been wanting to ask her all afternoon. "Can you give me Weston's phone number?"

She cocks her head, raising a brow. "You can't ask your dad for that?"

"Dad's been weird since the whole . . ." I trail off, fluttering my hand in reference to the past eight weeks of my life.

"It's understandable. He's protective." She sighs, already pulling out her phone, and a moment later mine buzzes with a forwarded contact. It's a photo of Weston, more boyish than he is now, smiling wider than I've ever seen as he holds up a gold medal, dark hair wet and dripping over his forehead. The same way it looked when I ran into him in the shower last week. "I'm glad you and Weston have connected. He has trouble with that, but I think he could use a friend." She smiles softly. "You're a good one to have, Willow."

"Thanks," I whisper. "I think I need a friend too."

Her smile fades, brows pinching. "Have you considered talking to someone about . . . everything?"

"Yeah, I know I need to find myself a therapist." I laugh awkwardly, fiddling with the ends of my hair. "I'm just not sure I'm there yet."

"I get it." She nods. "Sometimes abuse doesn't look the way we expect, and that can make it harder to accept. Harder to process. Just remember that everything you feel is valid, and healing looks different for every person, but I've found that sharing the burden with others can help."

"What . . ."

I never told Penelope about what Parker did. She knows I had an abortion, but nothing about the event that caused it. Even if I had told her, I wouldn't have called it abuse—even the patterns of his behavior that only became clear in the aftermath of my assault. I'd never heard of it referred to that way until Weston used the word last week.

I don't know at what point actions turn from incidents to abuse, and I'm not sure what his would've become if I had stayed, but it's still not a word I would've chosen.

I don't know why Penelope would be under that impression.

Unless . . . "Did Weston . . .?"

"No." Penelope shakes her head rapidly. "It's just . . . there are more of us out there than you may realize, and sometimes we see the signs in each other. That's all." She holds her hands up in surrender. "And I don't need to be the person you talk to about any of it, Willow. I'm not trying to pressure you—I just want you to know that you're not alone."

I'm still twirling my hair around my finger, dropping my gaze as I ask, "Do you think you're healed?"

"Healing isn't linear. We carry our baggage our entire life, and sometimes it weighs. But I'm a very happy person, and I have been for a long time."

"What helped you?" I whisper.

"I stopped keeping my hurt to myself. I found someone to share my baggage with, and he's made sure I've never carried it alone." With one last smile, she softly says goodbye before slipping out the door that leads to the lecture hall's exit.

Later that evening, I sit cross-legged on my bed, chewing my lip as I decide whether to press send on the text I have typed out.

"Fuck it." The swoosh echoes through my silent room as the message flies from my hand and across my parents' property to the guesthouse outside.

Trading another truth. I tell everyone I'm allergic to tomatoes, but I actually just hate them.

Weston

Why don't you just trade truths with the people you're lying to about your tomato hatred?

Because tomato enthusiasts peer-pressure me into eating them. Saying I'm allergic shuts 'em up.

Weston

Tomato enthusiasts. Terrible people.

Is that your truth?

Weston

I don't know. Depends on who I'm talking to.

I smack my forehead. *Fucking idiot.* Why did I assume he'd know it's me?

Weston

I'm kidding, Willow.

Weston

My truth is that I say I don't eat sugar when I'm training, but truthfully, I don't like sweets.

You're a monster.

Weston

Ouch.

Kidding...kind of. Definitely going to make you try my aunt's lemon bars, though. They'll change your mind.

I got your number from Penelope, by the way. I guess I figured I'd text you so you have mine too. In case you ever need something.

In case you ever need something? I roll my eyes at myself.

Weston

Thanks. Same to you.

Goodnight, Wes.

Weston

Goodnight, Wills.

Wills. I sigh, flopping back on my pillows to stare at the ceiling, alarmed by the butterflies fighting to break free inside my chest.

CHAPTER THIRTEEN

WESTON

If not me, if not therapy, someone else. Please.

I'm thinking back on Penelope's big, begging green eyes after I'd told her I didn't want to go back to therapy. We met for breakfast this morning before her lecture at Golden State, and she's been pestering me to continue my sessions since I stopped attending upon my move to Pacific Shores. My therapist was never a good fit for me, anyway. I know I could find someone here, but I don't think I'm ready yet.

I've had countless counselors over the years. Dead mom, abusive dad, attempted murder charge, and a stint in county lockup. My rap sheet is longer than any twenty-year-old's should be, and I have more reasons than most to seek help. Despite that, I haven't yet met someone I feel *gets* it, and I'm too burned out to continue trying.

Penelope worries that turning to surfing is merely a way of covering my pain, and that I'll never truly heal if I can't face my past. I'd argue I won't ever heal at all, so what does it matter? Except, Penelope's mom also died. She never knew her dad. She was adopted and can relate to the feeling of being completely alone in the world. So, she's difficult to argue with.

I also realize Penelope, like Willow, is a victim of sexual abuse. I wonder if Willow knows, and if she's ever considered talking to Penelope about what she's gone through. Though, I know it's not my place to be involved. Willow likely disclosed that bit of information with me out of pity, or by a slip of the tongue.

Yet, it's clouded my head since the moment the words left her mouth. I found myself grateful I don't know who her ex is, it made it harder to visualize harming him—but I can't pretend the thought hasn't crossed my mind several times since.

I know it's not healthy—especially with my past—to have a reaction like that. Truth be told, I haven't wanted to lay a hand on any person since the day I almost killed one—until Willow told me she'd been sexually assaulted. The way her golden face lost its color, her bright blue eyes turned almost gray, her sing-song voice cracked and broke . . . Someone who could take a woman like Willow—gentle and lively and soft—and shatter her doesn't deserve to walk free.

And yet, so many men do.

I think that's what triggers me. The unfairness of it. I've been struggling to come to terms with the fact that my mother wasn't the world's only victim of it. A fact that I am aware of, but feels much more real when I see it up close with Willow.

I wonder if perhaps she could understand me. The choice I made and the way I acted. If she came face-to-face with her monster again, if every instinct screamed at her to slay him, would she do it? Maybe she has more control—she's well-adjusted, raised in a stable household with patience and love. She'd never harm anyone, I'm sure, but maybe she'd understand why I did. Perhaps we could be a comfort to each other. A friend. Companions living in darkness together. Though, mine is dark and turbulent and violent. Sure, that violence has only ever been aimed at the abuser, never the abused, but I can't deny that my father's blood still runs through my veins, and it's no good.

Yet, my mind wandered to Willow when Penelope pleaded with me to find someone to share my trauma with.

I crane my head toward her dad, who straddles his board about fifteen yards away, paying me no mind as he laughs with Carter beside him. I trained hard this morning, and Carter made the trip out with Penelope today so he could join Leo and me. They both took a break about ten minutes ago, opting to float out on the waves instead of riding them. I kept going, but now realize I've been so lost in thought I don't know how many minutes have passed since I paid attention to the swells in front of me.

Only Penelope, Carter, and Carter's dad—a lawyer who significantly assisted us in navigating my charges—know the true depths of my case. They had to disclose the basic details to Leo and Darby before I came to stay with them, but otherwise, my past has stayed between us. I'm not fond of others knowing my trauma if it's not coming from my mouth, and I don't like talking about it either.

My initial arrest warrant was public record, and while the court documents have since been sealed, it's not difficult for someone to search my arrest online and find the information they're looking for. The gist of it is there: I was charged with attempted murder and eventually convicted for only misdemeanor assault. The fact I sat in a cell for nearly two years awaiting trial without bail makes me a villain in the eyes of most. Many believe that I got off on technicalities—I committed the crime two weeks short of my eighteenth birthday and had a damn good lawyer—but I'm still a monster nonetheless.

I'm not even sure I mind that narrative. I think the alternative might be worse. Being pitied, seen as a victim. The idea that I somehow had no other choice, or that my actions were a trauma response, a form of self-defense. That was my team's entire argument. I was a child of abuse, so I turned to violence when I felt threatened. That I wasn't able to register the extent of the injuries I caused because I was so used to being harmed myself, I had no threshold for the damage that could be done to another person. While all that may be true, there was one aspect of the defense that wasn't—the narrative that I never intended to murder him, I was only protecting myself.

I had every intention of killing my father that day.

If I hadn't approached him, he'd never have bothered to

look my direction. I wasn't threatened, never in danger. I was no longer a boy he preyed upon. I became a fucking predator. I'm every bit the criminal the prosecution and the media made me out to be.

A good law team and a warranted motive certainly don't make me a victim in the situation, but in my experience, most people can only see me as one or the other. I don't want to be viewed as another result of my father's wrath, as a consequence to his actions. That's a burden my mother already carried to her grave, and I'd rather be remembered as the person who tried to enact revenge than as another victim of domestic violence.

I don't know how to explain the complexities of these thoughts, and every time I've tried in therapy, it feels as if I'm doing it wrong. Rather than constantly venting to others and watching them fail to understand, I find myself holding it all in and living with the fact that some will think lowly of me because of my past.

There is no reason to believe Willow would be understanding of my baggage, or that she'd be willing to help carry it like Penelope suggested I find someone to do. It's a ridiculous burden to place upon her—hell, I don't even know her, really. I don't trust her. She's so far removed from the reality I've lived . . . I don't understand why any part of me believes she'd be the one to actually understand me.

And yet . . . she remains right there, nestled in the center of my mind.

"Wes!" Leo calls over the roaring waves. When I turn toward him and Carter, he hitches his thumb. "Dinner at the big house tonight around seven."

I toss him a thumbs-up, and before I can allow nerves to knot inside my stomach, I lay flat and begin paddling toward the swell in front of me instead.

"Thanks for letting me use your shower," Carter says as he follows me down the steps of the guesthouse and across the yard to the back porch of Leo and Darby's.

"I mean . . . it's not my shower, but also, it's literally not a big deal."

He chuffs, nudging me with his shoulder. "I'm being polite, you menace."

As we reach the deck, I find Penelope and Darby, rocking on the porch swing facing the horizon, a bottle of wine on the table between them. Darby says something under her breath, and Penelope bursts with a cackle I've never heard before.

It's loud enough that I rear back, blinking in surprise.

"She's so pretty when she laughs like that." Carter sighs, abandoning me in the grass and heading toward his wife. He grabs her hand and pulls her to her feet before twirling her around, making her laugh harder.

I've always liked watching them like this. It tears me up inside, slashes through my chest when I think about the fact my mom never experienced that—she was never cherished. But for all the aching it causes, it makes me smile in equal measure—because at least love like that exists for others. Maybe not for my mom, and likely not for me—I'm too damaged—but Carter and Penelope are no less deserving.

I laugh to myself, shaking my head as I pass them and throw open the back door, pondering Carter's comment. I've never thought of laughter as *pretty*.

Though, as I enter the house and soft, wistful chiming giggles envelop me—wrapping around my body like some kind of incandescent mist, akin to that of a long lost favorite song—I realize that perhaps laughter *can* be pretty after all. Beautiful, in fact.

I follow the music of her laugh down the hall, and Willow comes into view as I round the kitchen doorway. She's standing against the counter rolling meatballs. A green apron covers the yellow sundress she's wearing, and a high ponytail swings between her shoulder blades as she sways with laughter.

Leo stands over the stove, stirring a steaming pot of what I assume must be marinara sauce based on the garlic and oregano smell in the room and the box of spaghetti beside him on the counter. "I offered up the bottle because I knew once she finished her first glass, there'd be no chance she'd try to take over dinner prep."

"Mom *knows* she's a terrible cook at this point. Why does she keep trying?" Willow asks, smiling as she shakes her head.

"People-pleasing tendencies. I've been trying to break them for about thirty years—" Leo turns, startling when he catches me in the doorway.

I realize I've been standing here, staring at them, with no attempt at making my presence known.

"Fuck, Wes. You scared me."

"Sorry." I wince.

Willow lifts her head, smiling wider when she spots me. "Hey."

"Hey." I wave awkwardly. "Sorry. I know you said seven, but Carter wanted to come by early, so . . ."

"Not a problem." Leo grins, dimples appearing on either side of his cheeks. A perfect match to Willow's. "I'll put you right to work." He nods toward a bundle of lettuce on a cutting board beside Willow. "Can you make Caesar salad?"

I nod, stepping up beside her. There is a bottle of pre-made dressing beside the lettuce, but when I check over the ingredients, I frown. "Uh . . . would you mind if I took a shot at making my own dressing?"

Willow pauses, holding a ball of ground meat in her hand as she lifts her head and raises a brow at me. "You can make homemade salad dressing?"

"My mom was a cook." I shrug. "I'm not terrible, I suppose."

"Well, we sure as fuck can't cook in this house, so I'm sure whatever you come up with won't be worse than this sauce I just made," Leo says, and as I glance at him over my shoulder, he tastes the marinara, wincing when it hits his tongue.

"I could probably help with that too." I laugh. "If you'd like."

"Have at it, kid." He tosses the wooden spoon on the rest. "I'm going to get wine-drunk with my wife."

"Oh! I have something for you." After her dad leaves the kitchen, Willow leaps over to the sink, washing her hands before opening the fridge and pulling out a small, white paper box. "They're fresh. Dahlia made them this morning."

She extends the box toward me, popping open the lid to reveal four square pieces of bright yellow lemon bars, finely dusted with powdered sugar.

"Oh. I . . ."

Willow pouts, plucking a square from the box and nudging it at my lips. "Please, Wes."

I could be deathly allergic to lemon, and even then, those wide blue eyes and puffy pink lips would convince me to risk it all. *Dammit.* I open my mouth slightly, just enough for her to slide half the dessert inside, allowing me to take a bite.

It's flavorful and soft and crumbly. The perfect balance of sour lemon and sugar.

She grins when a moan slips past my lips. "See? I knew I'd convince you that you like sweets."

"It's not sweet. It's tart." I wink, tossing her a closed lip smile as I finish chewing.

She pouts again, brows knitting. "Whatever," she huffs. "You still like it."

A laugh escapes me, and she takes the opportunity to shove the remainder of the lemon bar into my mouth. She pushes a little too far, the tip of her finger hooking behind my bottom teeth. Willow gasps as I close my lips around it, licking the sugary residue from her skin. Her blue eyes flare, and if I'm not mistaken, her pupils expand as I pull back and her finger pops out of my mouth.

She stares at me with her full lips parted, rapid breath bursting out of them in sync with her expanding chest. I drag my gaze up the column of her throat, watching it move as she swallows hard before I reach her eyes again.

"You're right, Wills. I do like them. Thanks for thinking of me."

She blinks, dumbfounded, and a surge of pride floods my chest.

This is flirting. I'm definitely flirting.

I don't flirt. I've never wanted to. I've never cared. I've never had to bite my lip to stop a smile after watching a woman's eyes widen at my touch. I've never felt the urge to jump up and down after making someone blush the way Willow is right now. I've never had my insides twist and lock and expand at the sound of a laugh the way they do when I hear Willow's. Like the very tides themselves are cresting and breaking and crashing inside my body at her command.

Like she's the moon.

And fuck. I should not be feeling this way. I shouldn't be acting like this. I don't know what came over me just then, and I'm sure all the playful courage I'm feeling right now will fade any second. Maybe it's the fact she thought of me enough to buy me pastries, that she was comfortable enough to shove them directly into my mouth.

I don't stand this close to people. I don't hold casual conversations about my truths and my fears. I don't look forward to seeing anyone the way I do when I run into Willow. I anticipate her presence everywhere, all the time.

She's off-limits, and it can't ever go further than this. I'm painfully aware of that, but I guess for one brief moment, I wanted to pretend I could be playful and flirty and charming with a pretty girl whom I somehow make laugh, who somehow makes me feel like I matter.

Though, the longer Willow goes without responding, the more fleeting this newfound courage seems to be.

Shit. Maybe I crossed a line.

You sucked on her finger.

Yeah. I definitely crossed a line.

"I'm sorry," I rush out. "Was that—"

Willow grabs my arm, using both hands to guide mine into the box of lemon bars. She grasps my finger, swiping it through custard before lifting it to her mouth. She flicks a brow at me, running her tongue up the length of my finger before wrapping her lips around it and sucking the lemon filling away.

And I'm hard.

"Ah," I whimper. *Whimper.* Because she's still touching me. She's still smiling at me. Licking her lips with the same tongue that was just on my skin. Batting those unbelievably massive blue eyes with an innocence that's somehow the most erotic thing I've ever seen.

"I can play too, Wes."

Now I'm dumbfounded. Slack-jawed and staring.

Willow's sultry blue eyes scan my body, and I curse the thin shorts I'm wearing as her gaze glides down my face and over my chest. I spin around, bracing my arms on the counter, turning my back to her.

"Yeah," I say through gritted teeth. "Well, good game."

Her laugh rakes along my bones, and I wonder if it's possible for a simple sound to set one's blood aflame.

"WESTON, WOULD IT be inappropriate for me to ask you to make dinner every night?" Darby asks, twirling spaghetti around her fork.

"It's what I miss most about having him at home. That's for sure." Carter nods.

"Rude." I laugh, pointing my fork at him before turning to Darby. "And of course. I'm here to help with whatever you need."

"Correct answer," Leo responds. "But we won't be asking you to do that. Weston's here to surf." He eyes me. "Right?"

I nod rapidly, going back to my food.

The remainder of the meal passes with comfortable conversation, and far too many stolen glances at Willow, who blushes every time she lifts her head and finds our gazes clashing. As if the room is in orbit, and we're each the other's center.

I can still taste her skin on my tongue. Still feel her tongue on my skin.

It was so simple—innocent, really. Yet I fear I may spend the rest of my life playing that interaction on a loop.

"Wes, I need to clear the table and do the dishes, but when I'm finished, why don't we chat in the office?" Leo says, sliding out of his chair and nodding toward the kitchen. "Down the hallway, you'll see it to your left just before you reach the back door."

Willow's head snaps up, eyes meeting mine before drifting to her dad's. His gaze is pinned on her before it slides back to me, and though he offers me a smile, it feels laced with something harsher.

Fuck.

He saw us in the kitchen earlier. Heard us. Maybe he noticed my hard-on.

Are there cameras in here? I swivel my head, searching the room. I don't see anything, but there is no way to be sure. When my eyes find Willow again, she only shrugs, smiling softly before excusing herself from the table.

I rise from my seat, slowly making my way down the hall. My footsteps echo with every stride, sounding like a squealed *fuck, fuck, fuck* with each press my heel makes into the floorboards.

I find the door Leo spoke of, and if I hadn't been searching for it, I'm not sure I ever would've. I slide open the barn-style door, painted the same shade of cream as the wall, revealing a small corner room. Built-in, ceiling-high bookshelves line the entire space, with a corner nook beneath one window and a small desk between the shelves under the other. The room is painted sage green, with accent wallpaper dotted with yellow flowers. A small couch sits on the one bare wall beside the door.

I slip into the room and shut the door behind me, leaving it cracked just a sliver. Circling the space, I think it almost more resembles a reading nook or home library than an office. There must be hundreds of books, the entire room is lined with them.

Almost every space on every shelf is taken up by spines, with the exception of a few knickknacks and framed photos.

One picture in particular pulls my attention. Leo and Darby ankle-deep in the waves, younger than they are now, on the beach I recognize as Celestia Cove. They're both crouched over a baby Willow as she sits cross-legged on a green surfboard. She can't be more than a year or so old. Pudgy fingers wrap around each of her parents' pointer fingers, and she's laughing with her eyes closed.

I guess she wasn't lying when she said she'd been surfing longer than she'd been walking.

I study more photos, each one a bright memory of a happy life. Willow grows throughout the room, from chubby baby to young girl to awkward teenager. She's always smiling, though.

I'm not sure a single photo of me exists where I'm smiling outside the ones snapped by photographers after I won Junior Worlds years ago.

I grab a frame off one of the shelves—a photo of Willow holding up a painting of a wave from the perspective of being inside the barrel. The crest arches over the top of the canvas with a multi-colored sunset behind it. The water reflects every color in the sky, sparkling with sunlight, somehow creating the essence that you're right there in the ocean itself. As if you can taste the salt on your skin, hear the waves crash, feel the heat of the sinking sun.

A gold first place ribbon is pinned in the top corner of the painting, and Willow beams into the camera as she holds it out in front of her.

"What're you lookin' at?" Leo drawls, startling me enough that I damn near toss the frame back onto the bookshelf, making the whole thing shake.

"I was . . ." I spin clumsily, knowing my cheeks are flushing at what I've been caught staring at. Leo cocks his head, focusing on the photo behind me. "Honestly . . . I'm not used to seeing family pictures." I laugh awkwardly, rubbing the back of my neck. *Might as well be somewhat honest.* "I don't even think I have any from my own childhood. Caught my attention. That's all."

To my surprise, Leo smiles wistfully. "I didn't either. At least, not until I was brought in by my best friend's parents. My mom for all intents and purposes—Monica—made sure to take a lot of photos after they began looking after me. But before then . . ." He circles the room in search of something before he pauses, plucking a photo off a shelf behind the desk. "This is the only photo I have left of my real mom and me."

I step closer, narrowing my eyes to make out the faded image. A young towheaded blond boy, who must be Leo, sits on a surfboard as a brunette woman in a red swimsuit stands behind him, the grandest grin on her cheeks as she holds his hand the same way Leo holds Willow's in the first photo I grabbed.

I knew the folks Leo called his parents weren't his real parents. I know he refers to Everett as his brother even though they're not related by blood, but I suppose I never questioned what must've happened to his birth family.

"She died when I was eleven. I was with her when it happened. My dad abandoned me about a year later."

My eyes snap to his, and there is too much familiarity swirling in his gaze. The same perpetual pain I've seen in the mirror every day for the last seven years.

He was eleven, I was thirteen. I was with my mom too, and I couldn't save her. My dad gave me up to the state, not that I would've preferred to stay with him anyway. Not after I watched him kill her.

"I'm sorry," I say.

"I'm sorry too," he responds before turning to place the photo of his mother back on the shelf. "Do you know why I asked to speak to you here, Weston?"

Because I can't stay away from your daughter like I promised I would.

I only shake my head.

"Because it's time for you to make a choice." He crosses his arms, facing me again. *Fuck*. "You know I told you before that you have raw skill—God-given talent that can't be taught. I still think that's true. I think you've been focused and determined. You've applied the corrections I've given you, even if you've had a bad attitude about it at times." He pauses, eyes meeting mine. I swallow. "You're learning. You're getting better. And now . . . you need to decide what you want to do with it."

"What do you mean?" I ask.

"Well . . ." He flops onto the couch, getting comfortable. "Your career can go two ways. We can start entering you into some competitions, work on landing you an agent. Sponsorships and championship titles. You'll likely do well. You could make decent money. A comfortable living." He shrugs. "Or you can buckle down and get serious. You could be an Olympian."

My brows shoot up. *Olympian.*

I mean . . . of course I've dreamed about the Olympics. I think every athlete imagines themselves standing on a podium holding a gold medal. For a little while after winning my championship, I almost felt I could even see that future on the horizon.

Then I was charged and committed, and I was sure I'd thrown it all away.

Junior Worlds held a morality clause, and after my arrest, they took the title away from me and barred me from future competitions. While I'm now eligible to compete in the World Surf League as an adult, I never thought I'd find a trainer who would be willing to work with me after the nightmare that is my past.

Sure, my charges were lowered to a misdemeanor, and the court records were sealed, but my initial arrest was public. Losing my title was a newsworthy scandal in the surfing world.

Training with Leo this summer, the picture he'd painted for me—an agent, sponsors, and a few decent titles—was more than I could've hoped for at this point. I thought I'd lost the Olympics long ago, if I'd ever had a chance to begin with.

"If that's the route you want to pursue . . . I talked to Liv, and she's willing to step in and help with your training. Put you on a regimen more catered to the Games. She'd be training with you, since she's preparing for next summer in Tahiti."

"You think there is actually a chance I could be in Tahiti next year with Liv?" I run a hand through my hair, astonished. My body sways as I suddenly become lightheaded, leaning against the desk for support.

"If not next summer, then in five years."

I shake my head, all language stuck to the roof of my mouth. It's been so long since I believed in any kind of potential for myself that hearing not only Leo Graham, but Livia Costa-Ramos see a future for me in Olympic surfing has me floating.

The question dawns on me then: "Why didn't you ever compete in the Olympics?"

Leo huffs a laugh, rubbing his jaw. "I'd been in survival mode my entire life, and all I wanted to do was break the cycles. I wanted to make money, make a name for myself. I was running from heartbreak, and I wanted the route that would help me forget as quickly as possible. I landed modeling jobs just about as easily as I won competitions, and it felt simpler." He sighs, deep in thought. "I trained, I worked hard, but I knew that even a gold medal wouldn't give me the fame or the paycheck a cover would. Surfing for me was always about escape and belonging and finding myself. The harder I competed, the more I felt I was losing that sense of belonging—losing myself. I never would've made it as an Olympian. I wasn't in it for the reasons an Olympian should be."

Leo's eyes drift to a photo on the shelf behind me. I follow his gaze to a wedding photo of him and Darby.

"As soon as I found the only thing I'd ever really been chasing, competing didn't feel like a priority. Plus, I enjoyed training more than I ever did competing." He smiles to himself. "I like being a teacher. And I'm not saying you can't find a balance in it all, but for me . . . I was never going to work hard enough to be an Olympian, and deep down I always knew it. You can't just be good. You can't just show up. You need to be exceptional. You need to be one-of-a-kind." He looks at me again. "I think *you* could be all those things, but you have to choose them too."

My gaze lands on another photo of Willow. She's sitting on

the beach in a blue bathing suit, facing the horizon, looking at the camera over her shoulder, grinning.

Leo said he didn't want to work hard enough to be an Olympian, and I can't help but wonder again about his rule that I stay away from Willow. If it was merely for her benefit—because I have a criminal history and violent past, because I'm simply not good enough. Or if it was for me too, because he thinks I have what it takes. That I have what he didn't, and he doesn't want me to become distracted. A mixture of the two, I'm sure.

I wonder if he'd want Willow to end up with someone who can do it all. Not just to be an Olympian, per se, but someone who's not afraid to show up. To be exceptional and one-of-a-kind, not just for themselves, but for her too.

Despite all he's said about himself, I know the rest of the world finds Leo Graham to be exceptional. But no matter how impressive others find him, he'd want Willow with someone even better.

"I want to be an Olympian," I say, looking at him again.

He smirks, as if he already knew my answer, before standing from the couch. "Good. I'll see you tomorrow morning at six, then." I nod, stepping toward the door, but the moment I begin to slide it open, Leo continues, "And Weston, I know you didn't forget rule number three."

I halt, a shuddering breath exiting my lips.

"I don't want you to think I'm some controlling, overbearing father. That's not me. My daughter has the freedom to make whatever choices she wants, as do you. I asked you to keep your distance because . . ." He sighs. "I have my reasons, and they're not because I'm crazy or because I think you're a bad guy. I'm just trying to protect her. So . . . friendship is one thing, but I'd prefer you two not be alone together."

That's a fucking sucker punch.

But I nod. "I understand."

"Good. Oh, and one more thing."

"Yeah?" I glance back at him.

"Keep your fingers out of each other's mouths in my kitchen."

Oh my fuck.

I swallow. Hard. "Technically she's the one who . . ." The slow raise of Leo's brow tells me to stop talking. "Understood. Won't happen again."

I don't wait for his response as I slip into the hall and beeline for the guesthouse.

CHAPTER FOURTEEN

WILLOW

Weston

I don't like sleeping in the dark.

My phone chimes with a text from Weston just a moment before two more follow it.

Weston

That's my truth. Now I need one from you.

Weston

Do your parents keep cameras in their kitchen?

Um...yeah?

There are cameras in all the common areas.

We've had break-ins over the years.

Weston

Your dad asked me not to suck on your fingers in his home.

Oh my God. My teeth grind as I throw the comforter off my legs and bound out of my bedroom, barreling toward the stairs. I'm ready to rain hell upon that man when my phone vibrates in my hand again.

Weston

Please don't tell him I told you.

I'm on my way to kick his ass, Weston.

Weston

I don't doubt you could, Wills.

But honestly, it would just make things more awkward for me.

I roll my eyes, typing back.

He's a stalker weirdo freak.

I'm sorry.

Weston

I just figured I should let you know so the next time you're planning on getting tongue-y with me you can do so in a camera-less location.

A snort rips through my throat. *Tongue-y*? He's so bad at flirting, and it may just be the hottest thing I've ever experienced. The words *next time* set a fire deep inside my belly, and the thought of tasting his skin—touching him—again is so enticing I don't even care that he's a dork.

Still...I can't believe he spied on us.

Weston

Honestly...your parents and mine were probably watching us together.

Weston

Fucking weirdos. It's like they're obsessed with us.

I laugh, shaking my head, feeling like a child—in the best way. In a way I haven't felt in a long, long while. It feels as if I've aged ten years in the past two months. I'm not even sure the last time I giggled before I met Weston.

We need to get back at them somehow.

I'll begin brainstorming.

Also...you call Carter and Penelope your parents?

I don't know why the reference caught me off guard. I suppose because I'm desperate to know every single detail about him. Every fragment that makes up who he is.

Weston

They're the closest thing I have to parents now.

I'm happy they found you.

So...why are you afraid of the dark?

Weston

I'm happy they found me too.

Weston

And I'd tell you, but then you might become afraid of the dark too.

I scramble back into my bedroom, stopping at the lamp on my windowsill and flicking it on. I toss open my curtains before texting him back.

Look outside.

It's difficult to see across the lawn, but I can just make out a dim light from the guesthouse bedroom behind its shut blinds. They flick open, and the light becomes brighter, Weston's silhouette visible through the slits.

Hopefully it feels a little less dark now.

If you ever want to talk about it, I don't scare easily.

If not, I'll still leave the light on for you.

Weston

Thanks, Wills.

Weston

Another truth: I misjudged you, and I'm sorry.

How so?

Weston

I assumed you were spoiled and bratty. Maybe selfish.

Weston

I think you're selfless instead.

I smile at my screen, biting my lip to hold back a schoolgirl laugh.

Lol. Truth: I am spoiled, and I can be bratty when the situation calls.

Weston

Truth: Maybe you deserve to be spoiled so it's okay.

Weston

And maybe I like a brat.

Damn. The fire he started in my belly spreads to my core.

Truth: Maybe I like broody surfers after all.

My dad always told me to stay away from them.

Weston

Truth: Your dad told me to stay away from you.

Truth: Maybe I like a rule breaker. Maybe I want to be one.

Good night, Wes.

I end the conversation before it can go any further, because truthfully, I have no idea what the hell he and I are doing right now. I don't know if this is good for either of us. I don't even really know if Weston likes me, or if he's just bored and I'm the only girl around. I'm easy access, and I'm giving in far too quickly.

I trust easily, I always have. I've got to stop falling in too deep and too fast because a boy is pretty and has the ability to make me giggle. My bar has been on the fucking floor.

I lock my phone and place it on the charger beside my bed, vowing not to wait for Weston's response. *Boundaries, Willow.* A little casual flirting with the boy next door never hurt anyone, but that's where it needs to end.

God, I can't believe I put his finger in my mouth.

Though in all fairness, he started it.

When his tongue made contact with my skin, some kind of dormant spark reignited inside me. His mouth was the soft blow on cindering embers, warmth suddenly flaring in my being again. That familiar ache and gnaw of desire, what I'd been so sure I'd lost and never feel again.

I sigh deeply, pressing my head back against my pillows and closing my eyes as I slide my hand beneath the comforter and over my chest. Dipping into the band of my pajama shorts, I brush the tip of my finger through my slit.

"Weston," I breathe, reminding myself who has me feeling this way.

Parker's gone. I'll never see him again. Weston.

I'm absolutely crossing a line, but if there is any place to push boundaries, I think my own mind is the most appropriate.

I think back on the way it felt when his tongue wrapped around my finger, and I make the same motion with it now over my clit. I replay his soft moan when I did the same to him, the way he tasted in my mouth, the flare in his eyes at my boldness. Like that spark of desire was ignited inside him too.

A small moan claws at my throat, and I curl my wrist, slipping inside myself, adding a second finger. Pushing in, I fill myself, coating my hand with my arousal.

It's not my fault, Willow.

I can hardly feel a goddamn thing. You're too—

His words barrel through my mind a fraction of a second before Parker's disappointed face flashes behind my closed lids. My hand flies out from between my legs, and I'm filled with disgust.

Rolling over with a groan, I curl my legs into a ball and pull a pillow to my chest as tears prick my eyes. Like every time I've attempted this in the past three months, I talk myself away from the tidal wave of hatred that crashes over me. Hatred for him. Hatred for myself. My body. I count my laughter for the day. I visualize the finished painting I've been working on.

I also think about Weston. The way he makes me feel. The comfort in his gaze.

I toss and turn most of the night, sick to my stomach yet choking on butterflies. When the sky finally begins to brighten my window as dawn rises, I give myself permission to check my messages. One notification blinks back at me. A response from Weston.

Weston
You're trouble.

Weston
Good night, Wills.

CHAPTER FIFTEEN

WESTON

It's 6:03 a.m., and the sky is just bright enough to see my way down the stairs to the cove. I have a yoga mat I found in the garage beneath my arm, and when my toes sink into the sand I'm grateful the tide remains low enough to lay the mat out on a flat, compact area closer to the water.

I pop earbuds in, setting my playlist to something called "Vibey Yoga" before stepping onto the center of my mat and beginning my breath work. I started practicing yoga while I was incarcerated, after the therapist I was seeing in jail recommended it as a way to split up my recreation time each day. I lifted a lot too, and we had a track around the courtyard I ran on. Moving my body was the only thing that quieted my brain, but my counselor urged me to focus on my mind equally. Find a way to balance the two.

I often find myself wrapped in spells of insomnia, my anxiety reaching a peak that doesn't allow me to eat or rest or even breathe. I've been prescribed medication that I take on an as-needed basis when I'm having a particularly rough phase. I didn't experience attacks growing up, though I've been told it might be because my body was in a constant state of adrenaline and fear I never recognized what it felt like to relax. That I'd spent my entire life anxious and thought it was a default setting.

After I moved in with Carter and Penelope, began processing

my grief, and stopped living in constant fear, my nervous system regulated. My anxiety came in temporary waves, typically triggered by a resurfaced memory I'd been suppressing. Like my mom's birthday or death date, or when I cross paths with someone who has the same name as my father. If I see someone who looks like him.

After I was arrested, the spells of anxiety became more frequent, sometimes even leading to full-blown panic attacks. That's when I was prescribed medication.

It started Friday night, though I don't know what the reason was this time around. I wasn't triggered last week. At least, not any instance I can remember.

Yet, I woke up around three in the morning on Friday, and it was as if no matter how many gulps of air I swallowed down, I couldn't breathe at all. Like tendrils of dark matter had risen up from beneath the bed, slithering viciously toward my throat, wrapping around it and pulling tight. Like the tentacles of some kind of sea monster only I could see.

I'd forced myself out of bed and into the bathroom, finding my pills buried deep in the medicine cabinet—I haven't needed them since being here—and began working on some deep breathing exercises. After that, I put on a comfort movie, and though I settled, I never fell back asleep.

The sudden switch from rest to fighting for survival was brutal. I've had trouble sleeping in the days since, afraid it'll happen again. I've been tossing and turning through most nights, rising the moment dawn crests. Every morning when I'm waiting for daylight, watching through the window beside my bed, warmth floods me when I find the lamp in Willow's window still lit. She flips it on every evening after dark, and it's still illuminated when I rise in the morning, though she hasn't mentioned it again. Hasn't asked for details or pressed me to talk to her about my issues.

In fact, outside a few brief run-ins around the boardwalk to and from work, I've hardly seen her at all. I've wanted to text her every single day, but she didn't text me back last week, and now I don't know what to say to start a conversation.

I inhale deeply, raising my arms over my head before bending at the waist on an exhale and planting my palms at the top of my mat. I walk my feet into a downward dog, flexing my heels and pedaling my legs to loosen my limbs.

I've been running a lot too. In addition to the lifting sessions Leo requires of me, and all the on-water training. I feel good for the most part, but it's possible the added stress to my body is contributing to the anxiety, and I'm hoping a switch into something more moderate will help. Fresh air and fluid movement have always been therapeutic for me, even before I was capable of understanding it.

I keep the music low enough that I can still hear the roar of the crashing waves—the tides my welcoming friends, the ocean a calming force. I close my eyes, lifting into upward dog before completing a cycle of vinyasa. I work through it twice more before I hear my name called faintly over the mixture of soft electronic sound waves and the crashing ocean.

My eyes flutter open, focusing on the purple-painted toes dug into the sand in front of my mat. I crane my neck upward, gaze following endless inches of sun-kissed legs before reaching a flare of hips only covered by a pair of athletic shorts. Teased by a glimpse of midriff, I continue my ascent along her body and over her cropped hoodie until I reach Willow's freckled face. Her golden hair is braided down one side, a few loose strands wisping in the breeze. The rising sun behind me casts her face in gold, setting her blue eyes on fire. They're depthless—like staring into the sea on a clear day.

She's transcendent, and I'm so struck by her that it takes me far too long to realize her lips are moving. I scramble back on my knees, pulling a bud from my ear and sounding stupid when I mutter, "Huh?"

"Sorry." She pouts. "I just wanted to let you know I came down here to paint. I didn't think anyone else would be out this early. Wanted to make sure it was okay with you."

"Of course it's okay with me, Willow. I'd never ask you to leave your own beach."

She laughs softly. "Well, just because you wouldn't ask me to leave doesn't mean you want me around, either."

"I always want you around," I say way too quickly. A truth I hadn't intended to trade.

Though the way she blushes makes me feel less embarrassed.

"Okay." She smiles, nodding toward a piece of driftwood a few feet away. "I'll be over there."

"You haven't painted down here in a while," I call, shifting from a flow into a slow stretch. Leo will be down soon to begin surfing anyway.

"I'm up most mornings, but I paint from the back porch or inside the house. Sometimes I'm more inspired down here, though," she says, spreading out a blanket before pulling a tabletop easel and small canvas out of her backpack. She digs the easel into the sand deep enough for it to stay steady before setting the canvas on it. Next, she pulls out a bundled-up piece of pale yellow fabric, unrolling it on the blanket, revealing a pouch of brushes and numerous tubes of paint. "I didn't know you yoga."

"Yeah, I yoga." My lips pull into a smile. "Sometimes. A therapist recommended it a few years ago while I was in . . ." I shrug. "It helps when I'm having trouble sleeping."

She nods, unfolding an apron that she tosses over her neck and wraps around her waist. Sitting on her knees, Willow squeezes a dollop of paint onto her palette. "Do you still attend therapy?" she asks, dipping a brush into the white paint and swiping it across the canvas.

"I'm uh . . . between counselors right now."

She pauses, glancing at me with a smirk. "Have you ever tried art therapy?"

"Definitely not." I laugh. "I don't think that's for me. I'm not artistic."

"Don't have to be." She shrugs. "That's what I'm going to school for. It's about processing our thoughts and trauma and feelings through creative avenues. It's not a skill one is required to possess to benefit from it."

"Really?" I ask. "You want to be a therapist?" She nods. "I'm—I was—double-majoring in psychology and art theory."

"That's incredible, Wills."

"Thanks." She sighs, turning back to her painting. "Although, who knows if I'll get to stay in school at this point."

"So you're not returning to Berkeley?"

"Every time I think about it, I feel sick. So, no. At least not any time soon." She tilts her head, studying the canvas before grabbing another tube of paint and squeezing out a light pink shade. "Penelope wrote me a stunning letter of recommendation, and I submitted transfer applications to a few schools closer to home, but who knows."

"They'd be fucking stupid not to accept you," I say, meaning every word. The conviction in my voice is so raw it nearly breaks.

Willow takes notice too, because she pauses, dropping her brush and glancing at me, brows knit as if she's surprised, before an awed smile spreads over her cheeks. "Thank you."

I nod, smiling back. "So, is this your therapy, then? The painting?"

She chuckles. "I don't know, honestly. It feels different when you know the intricacies of the way it affects the brain. It's comforting. I love it and it makes me happy, but I'm not sure it's therapeutic for me."

Somehow, watching her paint feels therapeutic to me. I could study her all day. The way she scrunches her nose in concentration, or when she wipes hair from her forehead when she's thinking through a specific stroke. How she regards the sky, the water, the sand, before mixing colors to match the environment around her. Listening to her soft sighs of contentment, her mewls of frustration, or the hum of focus when she's zoned in is like listening to rain sounds. I could fucking meditate to the noise.

"So what do you do?" I ask. "For therapy? For release?"

She pins her eyes on me, raising a brow.

"Oh, no," I backtrack, shaking my head rapidly. "I didn't mean . . ."

Knots form in my stomach, only loosening at the sound of her laughter. "Well, I don't do *that*."

I wonder what *that* must be like. What *that* must mean. Especially with her.

The curiosity, the thought, the *vision* floats across my mind, and I could almost choke on it. The roof of my mouth goes dry, and my skin feels tight. Like I need to shed it, cover myself with hers instead. I've never experienced a sensation like that before. A raw, consuming *need*.

It makes me afraid to look at Willow, fearful she'll see all my thoughts written on my face.

"And that's probably why I need a therapist." She laughs, and I want so badly to ask her what she means by it. "I'll gain the courage at some point, but in the meantime, I just . . ." She settles, and when I hear the shuffle of her brushes, I finally glance at her again, finding her eyes fixed on her canvas. "I try to laugh every day," she continues. "Sometimes, on really bad ones, I even count my laughter. It helps me feel like the day wasn't wasted when I go to bed at night. Sometimes I run. I like to swim. I really enjoy paddleboarding, either out on the cove"—she nods toward the rock face to the south—"or at the harbor on the other side of town. It's peaceful there."

"I like that. The counting laughter. Maybe I should pick up that habit," I muse.

She nods without looking at me. "You should."

"I've never been to the harbor."

"Really?" She pauses her brushstrokes. "Well, you have to. You need to paddle down there. The water is like glass early in the morning. It's a great core workout, and it'll help your balance too."

"My balance has gotten better." I roll my eyes, huffing a laugh. "But yeah, that sounds fun. I'll have to go out sometime."

"What about Friday? You don't train on Friday mornings

until nine, right?"

"Oh. Well . . . yeah." *But your dad told me not to be alone with you, a rule I'm actively breaking right now.*

"What, Wes?" she asks, pursing her lips in a pout. "You don't want to go with me?"

Her tone is playful, but sincerity brews behind her blue eyes when she turns toward me. She's anticipating the rejection on the tip of my tongue, and though she doesn't understand the reason for it, I know it'd sting her all the same.

When her gaze bores through mine, pillowy lips pouted, sun-kissed cheeks flushed pink, I realize that I don't think there is a damn thing on this planet Willow Graham couldn't make me do if she asked.

"Nothing, Wills. Let's do it. That sounds fun."

When she grins, warmth floods my entire body.

I am so fucked.

CHAPTER SIXTEEN

WILLOW

I DON'T KNOW why Weston is so hellbent on the idea that his balance isn't utter shit when he tumbles off his board and into the water for the *third* time this morning.

"Goddammit," he mutters when his head pops above the surface a moment later, shaking the water out of his hair.

Even through his wetsuit, his muscles bulge as he tosses his paddle onto the board and braces his arms on the center, hoisting himself up. He sits on his knees, wobbling as he slowly rises into a standing position.

"Your legs are spread too far. They should be aligned with your shoulders." I nod toward his feet, which continue to navigate toward a surfing stance. "Paddle with your arms and keep your hips and legs sturdy. You don't need to move your entire body. Engage your core."

"Willow, you've seen my abs. I have a great core."

I have seen his abs, and he's not wrong, but . . . "Your balance still sucks. You can't be cocky when you're dripping wet and I'm entirely dry."

He pokes the corner of my board with his oar. "I'll make you wet."

"*Weston.*" My breath hitches with a gasp as I gape at him.

"What?" His brows furrow before the realization hits him and his gray-blue eyes bulge. "Oh, fuck." He rapidly shakes his head. "I didn't mean it like that, I swear."

Unfortunately, I know.

I burst with laughter, and he follows it a moment later. He throws his head back, momentarily losing his stance before throwing his arms out, balancing himself again. The movement only makes me laugh harder, enough so that I have to squat down on my board to avoid tumbling off.

I glance up at him, shading my eyes with my hand, watching as his go wide with surprise. Weston looks around, ensuring our place in the harbor is free of any passing boats before he slowly lowers himself on his board, straddling it and letting his feet dangle off each edge.

We migrated to a shallow enclave at the farthest corner of the harbor where the water is ultra calm, but I grab the clip strapped to the front of my board and attach it to the clip on Weston's so we can relax without worrying about floating away from each other.

"So, did yoga help? With your trouble sleeping?" I ask once we've caught our breath.

"Yeah, a little." He smiles softly to himself, running his fingers through the clear water. "It comes in spells. The insomnia and anxiety, I mostly wait it out. Medicate and cope best I can until it passes."

"Are you ever going to trade that truth with me?" I ask. "The time you spent in jail?"

Weston lifts his head, and those storm clouds are back in his eyes, guarding all his thoughts. I understand him better now than I did a few weeks ago. I think I get why he keeps it boxed in, why he's afraid to show his mind to another person, but I wish he'd show it to me.

Partially because I think he needs that. Someone to trust. Someone to rely on. A friend.

The other part of me thinks it's because I need the same thing. I have Allie, of course, but Weston seems to see me differently. See *through* me. As if he reads the thoughts I haven't yet learned how to voice, and it's a relief to spend time around someone who can hear me even when I don't have the energy to speak.

Yet, I don't want to open up until he does. I can't have the bearing of my soul be a one-sided event.

Weston hasn't answered, still staring at me—studying me—and I wonder if he's processing the same thoughts I am. Like we're two wounded animals who can no longer tell enemy from ally.

"Sorry if that was too forward." I smirk playfully, hoping to ease the tension. "You're being aloof again, so I defaulted to bluntness."

That seems to snap him out of whatever trance he was stuck inside, his nostrils flare as he huffs a laugh, shaking his head. His gaze drops again, eyes on the surface of the water as he says, "The truth is exactly that. My charges, what I'm sure you've already read. You already know."

"I don't know a single detail of what you did, Weston," I say softly, hardly audible over the sound of seabirds flying overhead.

His eyes snap to mine, wide and searching—shell-shocked. "What?"

"It was clear you weren't comfortable sharing those details, and it felt like an invasion of your privacy to research them. I figured if you ever became comfortable enough with me to tell me, I'd wait until I could hear it from your own mouth." I shrug, offering a consoling smile.

He shudders at the sentiment, like the concept of security over his past is foreign to him. I lean over my board, grabbing the edge of his and pulling it closer. I wrap my fingers around his, where they rest on his knee.

I squeeze them four times.

"What does that mean?" he asks, voice rough and gravelly.

"You're. Safe. With. Me," I whisper, repeating the gesture. "Whatever you want to share, and whatever you don't. It's all safe with me because . . . Because you make me feel safe too."

"I do?" The question releases from his mouth fractured and raw, the expression on his face utterly gutted.

I wonder if anyone has ever told him that before.

"Yeah, Wes." I smile. "You do."

He swallows hard, gaze distant and hazed as he stares toward the horizon. "I was first charged as an adult with attempted murder, because the altercation happened two weeks before my eighteenth birthday," he says, emotionless. "I was held without bail, and it took nearly six months for me to reach trial. My lawyers worked their asses off, and eventually, a mistrial was called. I was recharged as a minor. It took several more months for a new trial date to be set, during which time I remained in jail. When I was tried again, the charge was lowered to attempted manslaughter, though I was eventually only convicted of misdemeanor assault. I was released on a six-month probation, which ended about a week before I moved to Pacific Shores."

"Who did you assault?" I ask, hollow, terrified of the answer.

I believe to the depths of my bones that whoever he harmed wasn't blameless, even if violence is never the answer. Not only because I believe I now know Weston well enough to see he's not an evil person, but because I don't think there is any way my father would've invited him into our lives without the certainty he wasn't a threat to my mother or me. Despite that knowledge, I had no idea his charges were as severe as they are, and I'm dripping with trepidation.

"My father." He bites his lip, gaze so distant I wonder if he's even here with me. I squeeze his hand again. "He . . . She died because of him, and he didn't even care. After years of hurting her, hurting us both, killing her slowly—he went on with his life without an ounce of guilt. During the investigation into my mother's death, I was put into foster care by the state, but my dad never attempted to regain custody of me. I thought he was out of my life for good after the dust settled and I didn't hear from him. I never expected to run into him, but sure enough, one afternoon while walking home from school I saw him stumbling out of a bar." He runs a trembling hand through his hair. "It wasn't premeditated, it wasn't planned, but . . . He noticed me, and flashed me this look, a smirk that said, *we both know she didn't fall.* I lost it."

His eyes drift to mine, and they're filled with so much shame it rattles me.

"She didn't fall?" I ask.

He shakes his head. "That was the official cause of death. That she fell down the stairs of our apartment building. I know he pushed her—he knows it too—but the . . ." He pauses, swallowing hard, as if the pain is choking him. "The autopsy couldn't prove foul play, and they never even opened an investigation. Despite numerous domestic dispute reports filed by neighbors, coworkers, even teachers of mine over the years—it wasn't even enough for the authorities to ask questions."

"If someone hurt my mom, I think I'd snap too, Wes. I'd want to hurt them."

He nods, but says, "I . . . I went too far, though. I became the monster that he is."

"Or . . ." I sit up on my hands and knees, extending my upper body over his board before slowly dragging each knee over, until I'm in front of him, straddling his board in the same position he is, mine now floating empty beside us. "You had a moment of weakness, and you acted on instinct because it was the only thing you'd ever known. Have you ever laid your hands on someone else? Even had the urge to?"

"No," he rushes out. "Never."

"Exactly. I'm not going to judge you for the worst day of your life, Wes. I'm going to judge the twenty years that have made up who you are. I'm going to judge the experience *I've* had with you myself, and I'm not afraid of you. Not even a little. Not even if you want me to be."

His lips tilt slightly. "I don't want you to be afraid of me."

"Good." I smile reassuringly. "Thank you for sharing that with me."

He squeezes my hand this time. "Now I want a truth, Willow. Are you still missing him?"

Parker.

"Not as much as before. I'm mostly missing who I was with

him. Who I was before . . ." I've told Weston what Parker did, I haven't told him what *I* did as a consequence of it. "I ran away."

"You did the right thing. Running." He sighs solemnly. "There is no fixing men like that. The ones that decide you're a possession for them to control and alter at their will. If he couldn't fundamentally understand consent and safety, if a man can't control his rage, it's not likely they'll ever learn how. The best thing a person can do is get away. I'm glad you did."

"Me too." I nod. "I'm glad we both did."

Weston doesn't respond. Instead, he untangles our fingers, sliding his hand from his knee to my own, gripping it gently. We sit in silence, focused on the sound of the other's breathing, the gentle lapping of water against the docks, the distant noise of bustling businesses around the perimeter of the harbor, and the cries of seagulls circling overhead.

Eventually, I move back to my board, and we both stand, paddling back to the dock in peaceful quiet. It's comfortable and familiar. That language of understanding that doesn't need to be spoken aloud. Still, I can't shake the feeling we're both only telling half-truths.

As we drive back to my parents' house with the windows of my car rolled down, I glance at Weston. He appears surprisingly relaxed. Beautiful, even. Head back against the seat, eyes closed, elbow propped on the window as the sun shines down on his sun-kissed skin.

I like him like this. Those storm clouds lifted and cleared, only light left in their place.

"Are you coming to the Fourth of July party next weekend?" I ask.

His eyes flutter open. "Your mom told me about it, but then your father quickly followed

up with a reminder that I'm not exempt from training the

next morning, so probably not."

"Oh, come on. It's not like you're going to sleep anyway. The party will be right outside your window. Plus, it's Allie's birthday, so Carter and Penelope will be there, and Allie's parents too."

He only shrugs. "I don't really party. I don't thrive in social situations like that. I didn't have much experience with them when I was younger. In fact, this might be my first ever birthday party invite." Weston laughs, but I frown.

"You know, I suffer a bit from social anxiety, too. Even around my own family. It's particularly difficult when my best friend is such a social butterfly," I murmur. Allie is the life of every party, the star of every room she enters. I wouldn't change her for the world, but I don't always operate well when I'm pulled into her orbit of attention. "You and I could stick together?"

He cracks open one eye, glancing at me. I bat the biggest puppy-dog eyes I can muster, dramatically pouting my lips.

He groans, hiding a laugh as he runs a hand down his face. "Fine, Wills. You twisted my leg."

I clap my hands together, grinning in triumph. "It's *twist my arm*, by the way."

CHAPTER SEVENTEEN

WESTON

I DON'T KNOW what throwback lo-fi indie rock song is blasting through the backyard stereos right now, but it kind of sucks.

"God, Wills. Who made this playlist?"

She gasps, turning around to face me. "Weston, you cannot talk shit about Surf Curse around here. My dad is *very* passionate about his music tastes." She swivels her head around the backyard, even though nobody is out here but us. "You'd better hope he didn't hear you."

I can only smile at her, bemused. She's still glancing around dramatically, before her gaze snags mine and she freezes. She tilts her head, the freckles on her nose dance when she grins, perplexed. "Why are you looking at me like that?"

"You're dorky." I smirk, and when her mouth drops open, I add, "In a funny way. A good way."

"*Me*?" she claims, placing a hand on her hip. "I'm *dorky*? You're the biggest dork I've ever met in my entire life." She flails her arms in the air, and the theatrical display of her reaction only proves my point further, causing me to laugh harder.

"I guess we're in good company then," I say, because I don't think she's wrong about me either. I also don't think any other person I've known my entire life would describe me as dorky, and yet with Willow, it makes perfect sense.

I've never had the opportunity to be myself like this before knowing Willow—maybe I've been an undercover dork this whole time.

Her features relax, though her pert nose remains scrunched, dimples on display, and blue eyes blazing in the early afternoon sun. She tosses her long, loose braids over her shoulders, revealing the writing on her cut-off white tee: *Baby, I'm your national anthem*. Two red-and-blue fireworks are stitched into the fabric, right over where I imagine her nipples would be. My gaze glides down her body, over her high-waisted denim cut-offs, her hand still placed firmly on her hip, nails painted red, white, and blue. She's wearing high-top red Converse painted with multicolored fireworks and . . . hot dogs?

The look is vintage and entirely Willow. She pulls it off flawlessly.

As I lift my eyes, they get stuck again on those two fireworks. Almost as if the shirt is taunting me, forcing me to ponder whether they're strategically placed, and what may be underneath them.

Willow clears her throat, and my gaze snaps to her face. She smirks at me knowingly, then tosses her head in the direction of the big house's porch. I follow the movement, gut plummeting when I find Leo leaning over the railing, watching me with a frown.

"Well?" he calls.

"What?" I ask, realizing if he'd been talking I certainly did not hear him.

He scoffs, rolling his eyes so dramatically I can see it from where I stand at the center of the yard. Willow giggles, slipping past me. My skin lights on fire when her shoulder brushes my arm. "I have to go pick up Allie. I'll come find you when I get back."

I can't help myself from peeking over my shoulder to watch her walk away.

"Weston," Leo snaps, pulling me back to him. "Can you help me with these ice chests?"

"Absolutely." I salute him lamely, immediately regretting it when he only responds with a bewildered crinkle in his eyes and curl of his lip before beckoning me to follow him inside the house.

THE ENTIRE PROPERTY is teeming with people. From the back deck, it's almost like a sea of them expands below me, all the movement like rippling water. I stick to Willow's side like she's a fucking buoy and I'm desperately holding on, waiting for the storm to pass.

She doesn't seem to mind, though. She's velcroed herself to me too.

We spent the first hour chatting with Carter and Penelope while most of the other guests arrived, and after briefly greeting Macie and Dom, Allie's parents, Willow whisked me away. She turns from the drink table set up against the side of the house, extending a cup to me.

"Oh, I don't drink alcohol—"

"I know." She snorts. "You're a child. It's soda. Sugar-free or whatever."

"I turn twenty-one in three months, Willow," I deadpan. "I don't drink because I come from a family with alcoholism. I plan on never starting to begin with. But thank you for the soda. Sugar-free or whatever." I wink.

Her eyes flicker with understanding, features turning from playful to solemn. "I respect that." She lifts her cup to her mouth, before pausing. "Does it bother you if I drink alcohol?"

"No, but I do have a criminal record, so I can't be seen with delinquents. Are you twenty-one yet?"

Her lips quirk. "I turned twenty-one on May twenty-eighth."

Damn. That was just over a month ago. I was already living here at the time, and I had no idea. "Sorry I missed it. I didn't know."

She shrugs, taking a sip of her drink. "It wasn't a memorable birthday, anyway. Allie made me a cake and we ate it in bed. It's um . . . It's been a rough couple of months." She huffs an exasperated laugh. "But according to Taylor Swift, twenty-two is the year that really counts."

"Well, that's good, because I've heard nobody likes you when you're twenty-three," I say, referencing the old blink-182 song.

She chokes on her drink, coughing with laughter. I can't stop the proud smile that springs to my lips at her reaction. I know this summer hasn't been easy on her, battling with her feelings regarding her assault and the heartbreak that fell out from it, but right now isn't the time to dwell on it.

"Wait . . ." I grip her forearm as the realization dawns on me. "Zero-five-two-eight is the code to the guesthouse. I've been typing in your birthday every day for weeks to unlock my door and I had no idea."

She snorts, placing her hand over mine where it holds her. "My dad changed the code before you moved in—for your privacy. It used to be my mom's birthday. Eleven-eleven."

She laughs again. "You should be careful, Weston. I could break in and watch you sleep now."

I bite my inner cheek, raising a brow. "Maybe you should."

She rolls her eyes, but I don't miss the flush to her cheeks before she grabs my hand, twining her fingers through my own. If it were any other person, I'd pull away, but with Willow, the gesture is comfort in a distressing environment. "C'mon," she says. "I want to introduce you to Zander."

She drags me down the porch steps, weaving us through the crowd. The air is thick with the smell of the grill and the sound of mingling laughter, mixed with Leo's shitty music drumming in the background of it all. The sun sinks low on the horizon, blinding everything in gold. The way Willow's hair catches the light almost makes it glow, and I'm sure if I saw her eyes right now, they'd be a blazing aquamarine.

"Did you meet August and Elena yet?" she asks, stopping at the edge of the property. I follow her gaze to the couple sitting together on a lounge chair facing the cliffside.

Both dark-haired and heavily tattooed, she sits between his legs as he props himself on the chair, his arms wrapped around her shoulders. She laughs into his neck as they watch the sunset, as if the raging party going on just a few feet behind them doesn't exist at all.

"Yeah, I met them briefly when Everett showed me around the boardwalk and introduced me to everyone on my first day." Elena, Willow's aunt, owns the bookstore two doors down from Heathen's, and August, her partner, owns the tattoo shop beside it.

"Okay, great." She continues on in search of her cousin, Zander, I assume. "She's the person to go to if you need a good romance book recommendation. You should definitely let August tattoo you before the summer is over too."

"I don't read romance, and I'm afraid of needles."

She halts, whipping around. Stray strands of her hair blow in the breeze as she scowls in my direction. "You should absolutely read romance. Everyone should read romance."

I pop a brow. "And why is that?"

"All women should read romance so they have a bar to set their standards, all men should read romance so they can learn how to properly please a woman. That's what Elena says."

"Hmm," I muse. "Maybe you can give me a list of your favorites?"

Her eyes flare, cheeks turning the sweetest shade of pink.

"Oh?" I draw my bottom lip between my teeth, grinning. "Or are you a little hesitant to let me see what books you enjoy most, Wills? Are they the real filthy ones?"

What the fuck has gotten into me?

When Willow becomes bashful, it spurs me on. Makes me outspoken and . . . allured? I'm not sure. It stirs something in my core that I've never felt before. A warmth. A hunger.

"I don't think we're going to judge my choices in literature when you're afraid of a little tattoo needle, Weston," she snaps back, as if attempting to hide how flustered I've made her. "And if anything, *you* couldn't handle what I read."

She's probably not wrong. I step into her, dropping my head, leaning close enough to whisper against the shell of her ear, "Guess you better get me that list, so we can test the theory, yeah?"

She trembles when I breathe against her skin, and I'm fucking giddy as I brush past her. So much so that I don't even realize I don't know where I'm going or who I'm looking for.

Thankfully, an outrageously tall, broad, olive-toned guy around my age rounds the corner of the garage. He lifts his arm, yelling Willow's name, eyes trained on her behind me, and I assume I'm heading in the right direction.

Willow buzzes past me, walking into his massive open arms. He kisses the top of her head, and my stomach pinches. Suddenly, I'm antsy with the need to confirm this man is, in fact, Willow's cousin. She steps back from him, taking a place beside me as she brushes her hand over mine where they hang between our bodies, linking our fingers together again.

"Z, this is Weston. The surfer my dad is training this summer."

I let out a sigh of relief, extending my hand toward him. "Nice to meet you."

He tosses me a breezy grin, returning the shake. "You too, dude."

Zander is one of Everett and Dahlia's twins, and while his hair is a muted dishwater blond, and his eyes are a light shade of brown, the rest of his features match his dad's with striking resemblance.

"Oh, no," Liv drawls, emerging from the sea of people, her wife at her side. "Not the pornstache."

"I eat pussy better with a mustache." He waggles his eyebrows, smoothing two fingers over the hair on his upper lip, the rest of his face clean shaven.

"No." Lou, Zander's older sister, smacks his arm. "I told you to knock that shit off when I'm in earshot."

"If you actually think that, you're more hopeless than I thought," Liv snipes back nonchalantly. "Facial hair does not make you better at cunnilingus. See my smooth, pretty face?" she asks, rubbing her cheek before she nods toward her wife. "How many times did you come this morning, baby? Three? Or more?"

Zander gapes, horrified. "You are crossing a line, Livia."

"Stop provoking each other," Lou growls, running a hand through her shoulder-length blond hair before turning to me. "I'm sorry, Weston. We're not normally like this."

"She's lying. We're always like this." Liv grins.

I smile awkwardly. I have no idea how to react to this conversation, and now I'm terrified my utter lack of experience is apparent.

"I'm terribly embarrassed." Willow sighs, pulling my gaze to her. Bright blue eyes shine up at me. "Would you believe me if I told you I'm not of relation to any of them?"

"No." I smirk.

"Weston's gonna have to learn to be real chill if he's hanging around this family," Zander says, popping a brow as his eyes flick to our joined hands.

My stomach flips, and I quickly glance around the party for any sign her dad might be watching us. I've been somewhat aware of the risk holding her hand in public provides, but I honestly hoped we were being discreet about it, and nobody would notice.

I don't pull my hand away from hers, though. Neither does she.

"We're friends, Z."

Friends. We're friends. Friends can hold hands. Leo even approved a friendship between us. He only told me I couldn't be alone with her, and technically I've broken that rule twice already, but I'm not breaking it right now, so I have nothing to worry about, right?

"Right . . . anyway, I came to see if you know where Allie is?" Zander asks, changing the subject. "Her . . . surprise is waiting in the garage and becoming impatient with me."

"She should be out here," Willow says, dipping her free hand into the back pocket of her shorts and pulling out her phone. "Let me call her."

Based on Willow's end of the conversation, Allie was inside the house putting together a dessert she made for the party before

Willow asked her to meet us outside. A few minutes later, Allie comes skipping down the porch steps, tugging on the arm of a man who trails behind her.

Allie's wearing almost the exact same outfit Willow is—same shirt and cutoff shorts, though she's donning a pair of sandals and brightly colored toes. Her curly hair is thrown into a bun on her head, face framed by dark ringlets. The man beside her looks more dressed for a golf outing than a backyard barbeque, and I'd guess his gold watch costs more than I'll make in a year working at the surf shop.

"What's up?" Allie asks, joining us. "Oh, and Weston, this is Declan. My boyfriend."

I shake his hand, and he tosses me a judgmental once-over before taking a step back from the rest of the group. Lou smiles at him, but it's unconvincing. Livia and Zander openly scowl in his direction.

Willow shoots me a glance that says *we don't like Declan* before her gaze finds Allie again. "We have a surprise birthday gift for you."

"I thought your birthday was on Monday?" Declan asks, frowning.

"Well, we love Allie a whole lot, so we don't confine celebrating to one day," Zander sneers.

"I wasn't suggesting—" Declan begins, but Willow cuts him off.

"I'm going to blindfold you, okay? Then Lou is going to get your gift."

She lets go of my hand, pulling a silk scarf from her back pocket before gently grasping Allie's shoulder and spinning her around, forcing her to unlock hands with Declan. He appears uncomfortable, creating more space as he watches the scene unfold.

Lou begins walking toward the garage, and Liv heads toward the porch, lowering the music on the speakers set up in front of it. The rest of the party gets quieter, most guests turning their attention in our direction.

"I am like . . . not really into a blindfold kink so this better be good," Allie says. Declan scoffs as if offended.

Willow laughs. "It's worth it, I promise."

Lou exits the garage, a beaming man beside her who closely resembles Zander. They have the same build and similar features, though his eyes are lighter and his hair darker than his twin's.

Willow's standing beside me, holding both of Allie's hands as Allie faces us. Archer sneaks up behind her, and as Willow whips the blindfold off her eyes, he places his hands over them, leaning into her. "Happy Birthday, Allie Cat."

Allie gasps as a visible tremble shakes through her body at the sound of his voice. She steps forward, and Archer's hands fall off her face as she spins around, freezing when she takes him in. She's damn near trembling, like she can't believe he's standing in front of her.

When the realization sets in, Allie squeals. Literally *squeals*. Launching herself into his arms, Archer grabs her effortlessly, holding her legs at his waist and twirling her around as she sobs into his neck. It's difficult to make out the words, but I'm pretty sure she's crying something like, "You're here. You're home," against his skin.

I can't help but glance at Declan, who stares after them with a clenched jaw and flared nostrils, mouth flattened in an expression that's more disgusted than a simple frown.

"So . . . Archer *isn't* Allie's boyfriend?"

"Nope." Willow snorts. "They're *best friends*." She holds up her fingers, making air quotes. "Except, they were each other's first kiss, first time, first love, and they still have an active marriage pact."

"Oh." I nod, attempting to sound nonchalant, but . . . what the fuck. "That's . . . interesting."

"It's messy as hell, but I don't know . . . Archer plays football in Texas and has a great chance of going pro, and Allie wants to be a world-renowned pastry chef and eventually own my aunt's bakery. She didn't want to follow him to Texas when her life was here in California." Willow shrugs. "So, they went their separate ways."

"How long is Archer home for?" I ask.

"About a month. I'd place a bet that Allie's relationship with Declan doesn't make it that long, though. Archer eclipses Allie's life when he's in it, and she eclipses his even when she's not."

"Yep," I say, popping the p. "That's definitely messy."

Willow hums in agreement, but when my gaze darts to her, she's smiling misty-eyed as she watches them hold each other.

CHAPTER EIGHTEEN

WILLOW

"C'MON. IT'S FUN, I swear." I tug Weston's outstretched hand as I take a step down the stairs that lead to the beach.

Every year since we were teenagers, after the party at my parents' house, us kids come down to the cove, have a bonfire, and camp overnight. In high school we'd smuggle weed and alcohol in our sleeping bags, but once we hit college, our parents stopped caring as much. Now, we're all almost legal. Allie will be twenty-one on Monday, and the twins in November. Weston mentioned his birthday is in a couple of months, not that it matters in terms of drinking.

I admire the fact that he's choosing to be proactive in his sobriety, though. Most people are willing to take the risk for the sake of fitting in. Weston doesn't mind standing out in the spirit of protecting himself, and I think that's a lesson I could use too. I've always felt like a bit of an oddball, especially once I moved to Berkeley and away from my family. Parker and his friends were preppy cool kids, and I was always his weird, artsy girlfriend.

"Just for a little while, Wills. I do have to get up in . . ." I don't look back at him as we descend the cliffside, but I imagine he's checking the time on his phone. "Six hours."

"Dad will go easy on you tomorrow, I promise. He was definitely stoned when we left the house, and he's eaten about his weight in Allie's frosted brownies. I bet you he'll oversleep."

"I don't want to take any chances by oversleeping myself," Wes grumbles.

When we reach the beach, the fire is roaring, our tents already set up by Archer and Zander while the rest of us watched fireworks from the top of the cliffside. One tent each for the twins, and one for Allie and me to share. Declan apparently mentioned he doesn't camp, so Allie uninvited him from our sleepover.

Other people our age sit around the bonfire. Former high school classmates that know about the party and attend year after year, a few coworkers from the boardwalk, and kids of our parents' friends. I quickly find my cousins sitting side by side against a piece of driftwood, so I plop down next to them and pull Weston beside me.

"Where's Allie?" I ask.

"She hasn't come down yet," Archer murmurs.

"Declan was *pissed* when Archer showed up." Zander laughs. "I hope she's sending his ass right home."

"I don't appreciate the way he speaks to her," Archer mutters, poking the fire with a stick.

"Let her handle it. She's okay," I promise.

He only grunts in response, pulling a wine cooler out of the ice chest beside him and Zander and handing it to me. I twist the cap off, tossing it back in the chest before taking a sip. Sickly sweet watermelon fizz floods my mouth.

"Do you want one, Weston?" Archer asks. I realize I never formally introduced them to each other, but neither seems to mind.

Archer is a little timid, a little quiet and reserved, like Weston. My aunt and uncle joke that Zander stole all the noise when he came out first, screaming. Archer followed after, and has always been the calm to Zander's storm.

"I'm okay. Thanks."

Archer studies Wes for a moment, tilting his head before adding, "Water?"

Wes smiles. "That would be cool. Thanks."

He passes a bottle to me, and I hand it to Weston, who nudges my shoulder as he takes it.

"Do you want water too? That's your fourth drink."

"Please," I scoff. "I don't need a babysitter, Weston. I'm great."

I'm tipsy, for sure. I don't drink often to begin with, so it doesn't take much for me. This is the first time in months that I've wanted to get loose, though. The first time I've wanted to spend an evening being social and staying up late. I've been so afraid of feeling out of control, I haven't felt safe. Not since before that last night with Parker.

Finally, with my family close by and Weston's warmth beside me, I'm free enough to let my mind rest, and it feels *good.* I take another sip, smiling at Weston with my mouth full as I swallow.

He laughs, rolling his eyes.

When my eyes catch a figure walking in our direction, the alcohol slithering down my throat suddenly begins to burn. Tall, slim build, brown eyes, sandy brown hair that I know far too well.

Camden.

"Willow! Hey." He smiles, jogging to close the distance between us, and I stand to greet him, mostly because I don't want him to sit down and get comfortable next to me.

Camden isn't a bad guy, and our breakup was amicable, but I wouldn't say I trust him. I don't have much desire to spend time around anyone I can't trust these days, especially when there are substances floating in my body that make me less equipped at protecting myself. Plus, the messages he still sends me every time he's drunk are clear indications that he's not over our breakup, and I don't feel like getting into that tonight.

Fuck. Maybe I shouldn't have decided to drink.

I didn't expect that he'd be here. He didn't show up last year because I had Parker with me, and I figured it was still too raw for him.

I'm suddenly swaying on my feet, and as Camden reaches me, his arm shoots out, grabbing my hip to steady me. I tense at the contact, going rigid. Suddenly, Weston's presence enters my periphery as he stands too.

"I'm so happy to see you," Camden continues, pulling me in for a hug.

I'm stiff against him, unable to return it. He slides a hand around my waist, curling at my lower back, way too close to my ass for comfort. Alarm shoots down my spine, and my body flinches on instinct.

It's too familiar to the reaction I had that night. After I found out what Parker did, I was too paralyzed with fear and self-doubt to do anything about it in the moment. He fell asleep quickly, and when he turned over, throwing an arm over my stomach, my entire body seized.

I'd lain there, staring at the ceiling, silent tears streaming down my face. I was completely frozen, allowing him to touch me, lying in the bed where he'd made me hate myself.

I know . . . I know this moment isn't that, but my body is having the same reaction.

I'm trembling, unshed tears swimming in my eyes. I glance at Weston, who's watching me with concern. All it takes is one look for him to recognize it—whatever this feeling I can't describe is—and he's pressing on Camden's shoulder, shoving him off me, gentle but firm.

"You don't need to touch her."

Cam stumbles back, brows pinched as his eyes dart between Wes and me. "Sorry, who are you?" Keeping one arm on my hip, he tugs me closer to him. "Willow and I are . . . familiar. I think you can calm down."

"I don't really care what you two used to be, if she's not comfortable with you touching her in *this* moment, you need to take your fucking hands off her. I'm not going to ask you again." His gaze darts to where Cam still holds me.

"Cam, man. If Willow doesn't want you to touch her just take a fucking step back," Archer says, entering the conversation as he stands beside me.

Zander rises next to him, and when I'm surrounded by the

three men, Cam finally removes his hands.

"Willow," he says, brown eyes soft with sadness. "I'm sorry, babe. I didn't think . . ."

Guilt rushes over me, because Cam isn't like Parker, and he didn't mean any harm. He wasn't lying when he said we were familiar with each other, and though I have no doubt his intentions with me are more than friendly, the hug just now was nothing but a greeting.

"I'm sorry," I whisper, spinning on my heel and stumbling away from the bonfire.

CHAPTER NINETEEN
WESTON

"LET ME, PLEASE," I plead when Archer moves to go after Willow, who is now disappearing into the darkness of the beach beyond the fire's light.

The guy who touched her attempts to go after her too, but Zander plants a firm hand on his shoulder, holding him back despite his effort to shake out of it. I level both twins with a look I hope conveys my sincerity, a message that I have knowledge they don't. I understand Willow's reaction, and I'm most equipped to help her right now.

I wouldn't call Archer's expression trusting, with the way his jaw ticks, and apprehension flashes in his eyes as the light of the bonfire flickers over his face, but he nods.

I stalk into the night, barely able to make out Willow's silhouette ahead of me as she walks along the beach before stopping and throwing herself down onto the sand. I jog to catch up to her, coming to a stop and squatting in front of where she sits with her knees pulled to her chest and her head dropped on top of them.

"Wills," I say softly.

She sniffles, curling in on herself further—hiding from me.

"I can leave if you want me to, but I'd like to sit here with you—if that's okay." When she nods, I add, "Can I hold your hand?"

She nods again, and I gently place my palm over her hand on her knee, curling my fingers under hers and squeezing four times. The same gesture she gave me last week.

"It's okay," I whisper, sitting down in front of her and crossing my legs. "You're safe."

"I don't know why I reacted like that. I don't know what happened to me," she murmurs, the broken sound of her voice clawing at my flesh like the teeth of a rake.

"I think that was the first time you were touched since . . . The first time you were touched without consent or by someone other than your family. Even a casual, innocent embrace like a hug can feel overwhelming, can lead to a trauma response. You didn't do anything wrong."

She finally lifts her head, and though I can barely make out her features in the darkness, the moon illuminates her face enough for me to note the tears swimming in her eyes.

"That wasn't . . . that wasn't him was it?" I ask. "I assume not, I don't think your parents would've let him within a mile of this beach if it were."

She snorts a wretched laugh, throat full of emotion. "No, that's not him. Camden is my high-school boyfriend. The hug wasn't out of line. I've hugged him in the years since our breakup, when we've seen each other briefly during the holidays or on spring break. We are . . . familiar."

"It doesn't matter." I shake my head, tightening my hold on her hand. "Your body language told him everything he needed to know. It was clear to me. Clear to your cousins. You weren't comfortable, and he didn't let go. You had every right to walk away from an encounter that made you feel unsafe. You don't owe him anything."

"Sure." She nods. "But how fucking broken does that make me? How fucked up am I that I can't get through an awkward interaction with my ex without a complete fucking break down? I froze, Weston. I was paralyzed, and I just let him . . ." She wipes a shaking hand over her cheeks as tears fall again. "He ruined me.

Parker *ruined* me." Willow's eyes land on me, and the raw anguish swirling within them cuts me to my core. "What if I'm damaged beyond repair? What if I can't handle ever be touched again?"

With that, her face falls into her knees as a sob racks her body.

I hush her, crawling around her body so that her back faces me. "I'm going to touch you, okay, Willow? I need you to shake your head or tell me if you want me to stop."

I move slowly to avoid causing her distress, but I think she needs to be held right now, even if she's not capable of voicing it. I grasp both of her shoulders, gently tugging her against my chest, tucking her head beneath my chin, and holding her arms with my own, swaying us side to side.

I sit like that for a while, allowing her to cry in comfortable silence. It's the way my mom used to hold me late at night after my father had drunk himself to sleep. She'd hush me into silence for fear my tears would wake up and bring his wrath upon us again.

"Can I tell you a truth?" I whisper against the side of her head after her crying has ceased.

"Yes," she murmurs, a broken rasp accenting her soft voice.

"I have the same fear. That I'll never be able to handle being touched at all."

She sniffles. "What do you mean?"

"This . . . right now? This is the most I've touched another person since my mother died. *You* are the person I've touched most consistently in my entire life. I am terrified I'll never experience the full range of human emotion—of love and intimacy. I'm even more terrified that if I do, I'll do it wrong." I let out a shuddering breath against the top of her head, my heart thrashing against my chest with enough force there is no doubt she feels it where our bodies press together. "I've never told anyone this before, but I'm afraid I'm damaged beyond repair too."

"You're not doing this wrong," she says, voice shallow as she draws circles over the top of my hand with her thumb. "Whatever is happening right now . . ." Her cheek brushes mine as she tilts her head, gazing up at me with glistening eyes. "It feels right."

"Yeah," I breathe. "It does."

"Can I tell you a truth now?"

My lips quirk. "I thought that was the trade."

She huffs a laugh, dropping her eyes back to our hands. "I haven't even been able to . . . touch myself. Since that night. It's like . . . every time I close my eyes, I only see that last encounter. I only see his face. The feeling of afterward and . . ." She sighs. "I don't know how to make it go away. It's like . . . I don't even feel desire anymore." She glances at me, eyes blazing. "Unless I'm . . ."

"Unless what, Wills?" I ask, desperate beyond words to know the completion of that thought.

"Nothing. I'm drunk."

I sigh, knowing it's not right to push her if she's not feeling one hundred percent in control of her words. Instead, I continue holding her, watching the sky and the stars, listening to the waves crash against the shore, the crackle of fire and distant laughter beyond us.

"We should go back," Willow whispers after a while.

"Whatever you want to do. I'm here for you."

She tucks her face into the crook of my arm, and her lips tilt against my skin. With a long, soft sigh, she wiggles out of my hold, and I let her go, watching as she stands and reaches out to help me up.

We walk in silence back to the bonfire.

"Ohmygosh," Allie slurs, throwing herself into Willow's arms. "I'm so happy I found you. Guys!" She throws an arm around Willow's shoulders, spinning her in the direction of Archer and Zander before wagging her finger between them. "This is my best friend."

Zander tosses us a bewildered smirk before addressing his twin. "Is she talking to us? Does she think we don't know?"

Archer shakes his head, laughing softly. "We're aware, Allie Cat."

Willow chuckles, turning toward me to hide her face as she wipes away the last of her tears. Her eyes meet mine briefly, and I mouth *okay?* She nods, offering me a reassuring smile before she lets Allie take her hand and pull her toward the fire.

"Wait, were you two fucking?" Allie asks in what I assume she believes is a whisper, though it's definitely not.

"Jesus, Allie," Willow hisses. "*No.*"

"Oh, good. Yeah. Sex on the beach is fun in theory but it's also like begging the universe for a yeast infection."

Willow glances at me over her shoulder, eyes wide. *Sorry.*

I shrug, huffing a laugh.

I can't pretend it's not a little uncomfortable being around a group of people who are so unashamedly open about sex when I feel like I have nothing to add to the conversation. It's a reiteration that I don't fit in, that I'm too broken to be considered normal.

Though, talking with Willow just then was like looking into a pool of rippling water and seeing my own reflection. Not identical. Not a mirror. Different undulations, but a similarity so stark it's jarring. Our pasts couldn't be more opposite, and yet we somehow ended up with the same fears.

I wanted so badly to tell her all my truths, to tell her I struggle with the same obstacles. Touching myself is only ever about physical release, never desire—and I'm constantly wondering what the fuck is wrong with me because of it. I wanted to tell her the only time I can remember feeling any kind of arousal for another person is when she had my finger in her mouth last week. But when she admitted she was drunk, that she hadn't intended to disclose those secrets to me, I decided it best to keep mine to myself too.

Allie grabs two more wine coolers out of the ice chest, shoving one into Willow's chest. I expect Willow to turn it down, but she doesn't.

"Allie, you sure you wanna keep going, *amor*?" Archer asks, peering up at her from where he sits.

She only stares down at him, maintaining eye contact as she pops the cap on the bottle, tilts it to her lips, and takes several massive gulps.

Archer merely blinks. "Message received."

Allie pats his head. "Good boy."

She throws herself into the sand between Archer's legs, leaning back against his chest before whining at Willow to sit down beside her. I take a place next to Zander on Willow's other side.

"Is she okay?" he asks.

"Yeah," I say, clasping my hands between my legs. "She'll be all right, I think. Is Allie okay?"

"Yeah. Her boyfriend is a fucking asshole. I don't know what he said, but he upset her pretty badly. Her parents tried to convince her to go home with them, but she wanted to stay with Archer." Zander nods to his twin. "He'll take care of her, though. He always does."

I nod, gaze snagging on Willow as she stands, pulling another drink from the cooler, and takes a swig before she stumbles around the fire. My eyes follow her as she approaches her ex, Cam—or whatever the fuck his name is. Some conversation I can't hear passes between them, and he stands up.

I shuffle my feet uncomfortably, some kind of sticky, nauseating, red-hot sensation rattling my bones.

"Don't worry about Cam, by the way." Zander nudges me when he notices I'm staring. "I don't doubt he cared for Willow, but the only person he's ever been *in love* with is her dad. He always hoped Leo would invite him into the training program, but Cam never had the skill. I think he thought dating Willow would secure him a place, and he's still chasing that hope." He shrugs. "She never loved him either, though."

After a moment, they embrace, and a surge of panic shoots through me, that nausea rising up my throat. Willow doesn't appear afraid, she's not rigid as she was earlier. When she pulls back, she's smiling. It's not the shimmering ray of sunlight I've seen on her face when she's genuinely happy. It's polite and guarded, the kind of smile she'd offer a customer at work or a stranger on the street.

Cam motions to the ground beside him, I assume offering

to let her sit with him and his friends. Willow shakes her head, and he nods, taking a step back. She waves before turning and walking back in my direction, swaying with every step. I expect her to return to Allie, but she doesn't, she comes to me instead.

My chest expands with something warm—soft and gooey and filling—as she sits beside me, throwing her legs over one of my thighs and tucking her feet beneath my other leg's knee. She loops her arm through mine, resting her head on my shoulder. "Can I touch you like this?"

"Yeah, Wills. You can touch me."

Please touch me, in fact. I've never wanted another's touch quite so much. That all-consuming hunger envelops me again. An unrelenting need. A fire that only burns when she's near.

"Can you touch me too?"

I answer by grabbing her outer knee with my free hand, tugging her closer, and resting my head atop hers. I draw circles over her lower thigh with my thumb. A long exhale leaves her lips, warming my jaw, sending a chill down my spine.

Her breathing grows heavier, mixing with the buzz of soft conversation floating in the air around us. When I lift my eyes, I catch Cam's across the fire, narrowed and blazing. A sick satisfaction rushes through me, and I can't fight the smile I send his way.

Time passes, and the crowd around the fire begins to diminish until only a few unfamiliar faces remain when Allie groans, "I want to go to sleep."

"C'mon. I'll put you to bed," Archer says. But when he helps her up and leads her toward one of the tents, she pulls back.

"No. With you."

"Allie—"

She breaks into tears.

"How drunk *is* she?" I mutter to Zander under my breath.

"She's wasted." He laughs, rubbing his jaw.

I lift my head, glancing down at Willow, fast asleep on my shoulder. That warmth in my chest blazes brighter at her peaceful face.

Archer turns toward us, eyes wide with a helpless expression.

"Just let her sleep in your tent, Arch. It's not going to change anything with that asshole at this point, anyway."

He lets out a long sigh, nodding in agreement before he walks Allie to one of the tents set up on the other side of the fire.

"Wills?" I gently nudge her. "You want to go to bed?"

"Mm-hmm," she groans, but doesn't wake.

"Do you want me to help put her to bed?" Cam calls from across the fire. I can't help but notice he's lingered, even though the group he came with has all dissipated.

I glance at Zander, who gives me a curt nod before responding, "No, Weston's got her. Can you help me carry this ice chest over to my tent, though?"

Cam grumbles an agreement, rising with Zander. I gently unlink mine and Willow's arms before wrapping one around her back and the other beneath her legs, carrying her toward her tent. She stirs when I shift her weight to one side and bend awkwardly to catch the zipper, rising to open the tent.

"All right, Willow. C'mon." I duck inside with her still in my arms, squatting to lay her as gently as I can onto the sleeping bag. "Do you have pajamas you want to change into?"

"No." She rolls onto her stomach, groaning. "Wipe."

"Um . . . what?"

"My face." She lifts an arm, pointing at her head. I'm not sure she realizes she's lying face down. "Makeup. Off."

"Makeup remover?" I ask in a poor attempt to decipher her slurred words.

She nods into the pillow. "Backpack."

I glance around, locating a black bag in the corner of the tent. Rummaging through it, I find a small, blue pouch. Tearing it open, I pull out one of the wipes.

"Roll over for me, Wills."

Thankfully, she complies, and I crouch over her. She keeps her eyes closed as I run the cool cloth over her skin, swiping beneath her eyes and over her cheeks, taking off as much of the makeup as I can manage. "All right. I think that's good enough."

She hums, eyes fluttering open as a drunken smile overtakes her beautiful face. She blinks at me, lifting a hand to pat my cheek. "You were written by a woman, methinks."

I smile, completely mystified by her. I have no idea what that means, but I don't think it was an insult. I reach down to touch her face, brushing a thumb over her cheek. Her skin is soft and smooth, still damp and chilled.

"Good night, Willow," I whisper.

"You can stay, Wes," she whispers back, giving me her signature pout and batting her wild eyes.

"No, baby." I shake my head. "Ask me again when you're sober."

She sighs, nodding, before turning on her side.

I back out of the tent, the only people left on the beach are Zander and Willow's ex, talking outside his tent. Cam steals a glance in my direction, and a bite of unease pinches at my nerves. I don't fucking care how well Willow knows him. I don't care if he's friends with her cousins. I don't trust him.

There is no way I'm going back up this cliffside if he's still at the base of it. No way I'm crawling in my bed while he's so close to hers. No. Fucking. Way.

I find the piece of wood the twins were sitting on earlier—the same driftwood Willow leans against on peaceful mornings when she paints the sunrise—and drag it through the sand, sliding it in front of her tent's opening.

I feel Zander and Cam's gaze burning a hole through my back, but I pay them no mind. I pull my hoodie over my head, cinch the drawstrings, and settle in the sand with my back propped against the wood. Blocking Willow's tent, I close my eyes, allowing the sound of crashing waves and her heavy breathing from the other side of the nylon lull me to sleep.

A GASPED, "OH fuck," lurches me into consciousness.

Forcing my eyes open, I'm assaulted by daylight as I blink around, my mind registering my surroundings, remembering I'm still on the beach. As I adjust to the brightness, the first vision to come into focus is the plump crease where Willow's ass meets her thighs as she lays on the over top of my lap, the shorts she wore yesterday riding high on her hips.

The second thing I notice is that I'm rock fucking hard, and her stomach is making contact with my cock.

"If you stopped staring at my ass, it'd probably go down."

"Honestly, Willow, it kind of feels like your ass is the one staring at me."

She rolls over, propping herself onto her elbows, tossing me an eye roll. "Can you help me understand why I tripped over your big ass body leaving my tent this morning?"

"I slept here." I yawn, stretching my arms over my head.

Her brows knit, and her eyes go soft. "You did? All night?"

I nod. "Wanted to be around in case you needed me. Wanted to make sure you stayed safe."

"Wes—" She begins to sit up, but a stern voice calls from behind us, making her pause.

"You two look cozy."

Dread slices my spine as Leo rounds the back side of Willow's tent, towering above us with his hands on his hips. The smile he shoots my way is sickly sweet. Reminiscent of how a lion bares its teeth before tearing through its prey.

"I got drunk last night," Willow says, shading her eyes with her hand as she looks up at her dad. "Weston slept outside my tent all night just in case I needed him. I didn't know this, on account of being passed out, so I tripped over him when I tried to leave this morning."

"Outside?" Leo asks, raising a brow.

"Yep. Even though I totally invited him to sleep with me." Willow winks at me. "You should reward him for being such a gentleman. Give him the day off."

Leo flashes his dimples at his daughter. "How about I reward him with my undivided attention?" He turns to me. "Does that work for you, Weston? Would training with myself and a two-time gold medalist be sufficient for you today?"

"Yes, sir. That'd be lovely. Thank you."

He softens when he looks at me. It's almost imperceptible, and I know he and Willow are being playful, but I catch the sincerity on his face. "Good. Liv should be here in about fifteen minutes so why don't you run up to the house, get changed, and bring your board back down. It's time to start training for your first competition."

"Competition?" I ask, choking on the word.

"You said you wanted to be an Olympian." He shrugs. "Better start competing like one."

"Which competition?" Willow asks.

"I registered you for a Challenger in San Diego two weeks from today."

"I don't have a membership for the World Surf League. I never paid the fees," I admit, bashful.

"I took care of that," Leo says. "Don't worry about it."

"Oh. Th—Thank you."

Leo nods, turning toward his daughter. "Sugar, Lou, Dahlia, and Mom are going paddleboarding this morning while Liv is training with us—if you want to join them."

Willow wipes a hand down her face. "I am so hungover," she groans. "But maybe the saltwater would feel good. Yeah . . ." She yawns as she finally lifts herself off me, though I'm grateful she covered me long enough for the evidence of my . . . excitement to go down. Willow sits on her knees, leaning in to plant a kiss on my cheek. "Thank you," she whispers before standing, giving her dad a hug and walking off in the direction of the other tents.

Leo and I are quiet for a moment as I stand and dust the

sand off my shorts, watching as Willow rouses Allie and the twins, demanding Allie come paddling with the rest of them since it's her fault Willow's so hungover. Once the four of them amble down the beach on tired legs, Leo turns back to me.

"I appreciate you taking care of her last night." He rubs his jaw. "You know how I feel about you two being alone together, though."

"I respect that," I say, gruff. Either sand or apprehension is stuck in my throat. Maybe both. "I didn't go inside her tent. Not only because she was drunk, but because I knew it'd make you uncomfortable. We were never alone, but . . . I know about her ex. Why she left Berkeley." Leo's jaw ticks, and I hold up my hands. "I know what she's struggling with, and I wanted to make sure if she woke up in the middle of the night and felt unsafe, I'd be nearby."

"That it?" he asks.

"No." I swallow the frog in my throat, running a hand through my hair, forcing myself to meet Leo's eyes—he needs to see the conviction in them. "I am enamored with your daughter. I couldn't be more serious when I tell you I've never felt something like this before. I don't know if she feels the same about me, but I can't keep hiding it.

"I respect the boundaries you've set, but I want you to know that if they have anything to do with Willow's past, with what Parker did to her . . . I'm not that guy. I know where I come from, and I know why you feel the way you do, but I also know I'd be a fool not to take the chance if Willow offered it to me. I won't apologize for that. I won't apologize for seeing how incredible she is."

His lips quirk up in the corner, the most of a smile he's going to offer me, but it's a look of approval, nonetheless. A soaring sensation spreads through my chest.

"I won't argue with you about any of that, Weston. I appreciate your honesty. I appreciate that my daughter has found some comfort and solace with you, but I'll need you both to remember how fragile you are. I asked you to keep your distance because

I didn't want her rushing into something new and getting hurt worse. I'm not the kind of man that's going to lock my daughter in her room and dictate every choice she makes." He frowns, eyes going unfocused before he shakes his head and directs his gaze to me again. "And I don't give a fuck about your background. I care about your actions. Who *you* are. Parker comes from a family of doctors, speaks three languages, and went on mission trips every summer as a kid—and look at what a piece of shit he turned out to be."

I bite down a laugh.

"I like you, Weston, but I can't watch her . . ." His voice cracks on the words. Clearing the emotion from his throat, Leo continues, "I can't watch her break again. I'm happy she's found a friend in you, but I can't get on board with anything more than that right now."

It's clear that Willow's trauma didn't just affect her, it's shaken her entire family. I'm disappointed that I haven't earned Leo's favor, and I don't think I have the strength to stay away from Willow at this point, but I have too much respect for him to fight back on it right now.

I'll just have to earn his approval.

"I understand." I nod, turning to head toward the house so I can change and grab my board before Liv arrives.

"And Wes?" Leo calls as I pass him. "If you *do* hurt my daughter—in any sense of the word—this opportunity is over for you. There will be no second chances. Understood?"

I turn back at him, anchoring his gaze, keeping my voice even as I respond, "I'll never hurt Willow, but this opportunity is the least of my reasons why."

CHAPTER TWENTY

WILLOW

"THAT FUCKING SUCKED." Allie braces her hands on her knees, sucking in gulps of air.

"Allie, my love, you've gotta move your body more," Dahlia says, rubbing her back. "No way are two old birds like Darby and I in better shape than you."

"I'm in shape," she pants. "I'm just filled to the brim with watermelon wine coolers and Malibu lemonade. The water was way too choppy for my stomach to handle this morning."

I cover a snort with my hand. My mom shoots me a warning glare a moment before Allie lifts her head, brown eyes narrowed at me. "I will vomit all over you."

"Wouldn't be the first time." I smile.

She groans, holding her stomach as she stands up. "I've got to go lie in bed for three days."

My aunt pulls her shoulder-length blond hair from her face, tying it back before placing her hand on Allie's shoulder again, guiding her down the beach. "I'll have Archer come by a little later with dinner for you, okay?"

"Hey!" I call out after her. "You need to ignore Declan's calls for at least forty-eight hours."

She tosses me a thumbs up, my mom and aunt both nodding in agreement.

I wasn't a witness to their blowout last night, but apparently

Declan really drove into her after Archer arrived, accusing her of having an affair with him in front of most of the party. It wasn't until Allie's dad, Dom, and my uncle Everett essentially threw him out that things finally calmed down.

I think, at this point, we'd all prefer she never speak to Declan again, but Allie has a penchant for toxic relationships, and it typically takes several breakups with the same guy before she calls it quits for good. She never becomes emotionally invested in any of them—in anyone besides Archer. Personally, I think she's self-sabotaging, buying time until she and my cousin figure their weird fucking relationship out.

In a way, I feel for Declan. I imagine it'd be difficult to date someone and realize that they're irrevocably in love with someone else, but regardless, the way he speaks to her is despicable and I still hate the guy.

"How are you feeling, baby?" Mom asks as she and I trail Dahlia and Allie, hauling our deflated paddleboards back toward the house.

The morning sun shines down on the mountains to the east, the whipping ocean breeze and beaded saltwater cooling my already heated skin. Though, I think the sun is only a fraction of the cause for the flames erupting over my flesh after that moment with Wes this morning.

I could *feel* him against my thigh. He was hard. Throbbing. And I have no business thinking about how much I liked it while my mother is standing right beside me.

"I'm feeling fine," I say as we reach the stairs.

I glance over my shoulder, finding my dad, Liv, and Wes huddled together, talking with their arms crossed. Likely discussing strategy for his first competition. Though, when Wes's eyes flash to mine, molten and deep blue in the daylight, that heat inside my body surges.

Truthfully, I feel like I could throw up.

I don't think the alcohol or last night's breakdown have anything to do with it. I think it has everything to do with the fact that Weston slept outside my tent. On the ground, in the elements, knowing he'd have to wake up this morning and push his body to the brink. Still, he chose me—my safety and comfort over his own. Weston held me while I cried. He didn't question me, didn't doubt my feelings or my fears. His touch never made me flinch or freeze.

My chest is so full of butterflies, I fear they may begin spilling from my mouth, showing everyone on this beach how infatuated I'm becoming with that boy.

He looks at me like he may be feeling the same way. Those storms that always seem to be clouding his eyes have become clear. When he studies me now, I could swear there is a desire as potent as my own written in his features.

His stare burns into me the entire ascent up the cliffside.

"I can put these away for you, Mama," I say when we reach the garage, plucking the strap of her paddleboard from her shoulder. I notice both Allie's and Dahlia's are also propped outside the back door.

"You sure?" she asks.

"Yeah." I grab the door handle, pushing it open with my shoulder. "I'm going to wait for Weston."

"Ah." Mom nods, hazel eyes sparkling mischievously. "Okay."

"We're friends," I snap.

"Mm-hmm." She smiles, peeling off her wetsuit and shimmying down to the yellow one-piece she's wearing beneath it. "I used to be *friends* with the bad boy surfer too."

Am I that transparent?

"Just be careful, okay?" Mom asks. "I like Weston a lot, but I don't want you to jump into anything too fast, before you've had time to process everything you've been through this summer—and all that he's gone through too." At my frown, she pulls me in for a hug, pressing her lips to my forehead. "Give the both of you some grace, some time to grow into this friendship." Pulling back, she smiles at me with sparkling eyes. "Because falling in love with your best friend is the greatest feeling in the world."

I respond with a resigned nod before my mom spins and

strides off toward the house. Stripping out of my wetsuit and adjusting the straps of my green bikini before I gather it up, along with the rest of them, I toss them in the corner of the garage to be washed later. Next, I drag each of the heavy bags that contain the inflatable paddleboards inside and prop them up in the corner where my dad stores them, dusting off the dried sand.

I begin a load of laundry—mostly beach towels—and empty out the ice chests my cousins lugged up here earlier this morning.

I know my mom means well, and while my dad and I haven't discussed it, I have high doubts he'd disagree with anything she says. Plus, Weston mentioned my father told him to stay away from me. That pissed me off, and the familiar vexation surges in me now. I understand they're protective of me, especially after what I've gone through, but their misplaced concern ignites a defensive flame in me.

Despite only knowing him a few weeks, Weston has proven time and again to be nothing but respectful and kind. He's also funny. He constantly makes me laugh, and his aura is addicting. I crave his presence because I feel good around him. Less broken, and more like me.

We both tried to fight that at first—him because he needs to focus on his future, and me because I need to get mine back on track, but I think we've both realized now that we're better when we're together, and I can't see how it could be wrong to lean into that feeling.

Then there is the aspect of Weston that I nearly made a fool of myself by admitting last night when I was drunk: the *desire*. For months, I've struggled to look in the mirror, struggled to feel anything other than disgust and disappointment with my own body. Not to mention the physical side effects of my abortion—I woke up this morning to find that I was spotting. *Again.*

My libido has not only been nonexistent, but fighting against me. That is, until Weston entered the picture. Now he's the image behind my eyes every time they're closed. He's the spark between my thighs, and the touch reigniting my dormant desire.

I want him, and while I want to nurture this budding friendship between us at the same time, I don't know how much longer I can go without his touch.

As I'm organizing the extra drinks in the garage fridge, I hear the hum of distant voices growing louder.

"You did well today. I think it's time to take you out of the cove and have you begin practicing on larger waves. There are a couple spots up the coastline I'd like to take you to, so we'll start on Monday," my dad's voice echoes outside the garage.

"Okay," Weston replies. "That sounds great."

"Can you put the boards away for me? The house is a fucking mess, and I don't want Darby having to clean up inside alone."

"Absolutely. I'll take care of it."

Dad's Crocs squeak with each step he makes against the concrete outside before the garage door creaks open, and Weston enters, wetsuit folded at his hips as he holds a board in each hand.

He's beautiful.

Wet, dark hair falls at the center of his forehead, thick brows hover over those gray-blue eyes, widening when he notices me. He licks his lips, swallowing as a bead of water runs down the center of his bare chest. I watch until it disappears.

"Hey," he says, breaking my trance, stripping out of his wetsuit and down to the pair of swim shorts he's wearing beneath it.

"Hi. I waited for you."

"Did you?"

My eyes are still locked on his waist, and I take a slow perusal of his chest, raking them back up his body, catching his gaze again. "I did. I have a question for you."

"I suppose I must have an answer for you." He grins, walking the boards over to the corner of the garage and sliding one into the stands before propping the other onto the shaping board. "Don't let me forget to wax those later."

I nod as he leans against the wall, crossing his arms, settling in. Nerves prick my stomach, and I'm suddenly filled with apprehension. I breathe deep, summoning all my courage. "You said last night you're afraid. Of never experiencing the full range of emotion. Love and intimacy."

His brows draw together in surprise, before he huffs a laugh, rubbing his jaw and dropping his gaze to his feet. "You remember?"

"Yes," I whisper.

"Yeah, Wills. I'm afraid of that."

"You've never felt anything like that before?" I take a step toward him.

He lifts his head, eyes blazing. "I've never felt anything even close."

"You've never been in love? Not even a crush?"

His lips part, and he looks me up and down before his mouth snaps shut. He shakes his head. "I don't think I've ever known someone well enough to want them like that. I don't think I've ever felt safe enough to feel anything at all."

Nodding, I say, "I can understand that. I'm not sure I could've a few months ago, but I understand it now." I feel his stare in every atom of my body when I ask, "So you've never . . . daydreamed about someone? Fantasized? Even when you . . ." My eyes drop to his hips of their own accord.

He laughs softly, and my gaze snaps back to his face. "Uh, no. Not really. I don't think my brain works like that. I don't see anything or anybody when I'm . . ." He chews the inside of his cheek, crossing his arms. "I think even inside my own mind, I have to feel like I know someone. I have to feel some kind of connection."

I tilt my head. "Do you feel like you know me?"

His breath hitches, eyes sparking. "Yeah, Wills." Weston's voice is low. Rough. Fervent. "I feel like I know you."

"Do you feel safe with me?" Allowing the heat inside my core to radiate with every word, I ask, "Connected to me?"

He doesn't answer, but I don't miss the way his fingers flex where they rest on his bicep, like he wishes he were gripping me instead. We're close enough now that the heat of his exhale lands on my skin. His pupils dilate when I reach behind my neck and slowly untie my bathing suit.

"Because I do. I feel safe. Connected," I whisper, drawing the string until the knot pops and it untangles. I catch the fabric, placing my palms over my breasts before they become exposed. "I'm going to take a shower."

I step back, keeping my eyes on him a moment longer before I spin and walk toward the back door.

"Willow," he rasps, the sound so anguished it sears my flesh. "I need you to tell me what you want from me right now. I can't be guessing with you. I can't risk getting it wrong."

My chest floods with liquid warmth—a rush of blood my heart only pumps at his command.

I keep my back turned to him as I whisper, "I want you to follow me, Weston—but only if you want that too."

That warmth spreads when I hear the sound of his footsteps moving in my direction.

I exit and round the side of the garage, heading toward the shower stall built against it on the farthest end of my parents' property. I nudge the swinging door open with my hip, stepping inside the changing area. I spin around in time to watch Weston enter, closing the door behind him. He leans back against it, keeping space between us.

I cover my chest with one hand as I reach behind my back, tugging the string of my bikini, unraveling the top entirely. I drop my arms as it falls away, baring myself to him. My nipples tighten against the sea breeze and his stare.

Weston's eyes are fixed on my breasts, lips parted, breath heavy. I slip my thumbs under the hem of the bottoms on each side of my hips before pushing them over my thighs. They drop past my knees, hitting the ground as I step out and kick them aside.

His gaze drags down my body, slow and purposeful, as if memorizing every inch of exposed skin.

When he reaches the apex of my thighs, a noise crawls from his throat, some kind of whimper. His eyes glaze over, half-lidded and swimming with passion. Utter devastation.

All that desire I'd thought I'd lost comes barreling back when Weston's gaze is locked on me like this. Even without his touch, without his words, I feel him all over me.

I turn, offering him a view of my backside as I step into the shower.

A shuddered breath and a tortured, "*Fuck*," follows me inside.

I turn the handle, and water cascades around me. Weston remains at the edge of the small stall, watching me with that same tormented and beguiled expression as I drench myself, spinning around to tilt my face toward the stream and push my hair behind my head.

"You're so beautiful, Willow," he whispers brokenly. "I've struggled to find beauty in most things for most of my life, but you . . ." The words trail off, like he's lost them, and when I open my eyes through the hazy steam, he's shaking his head and rubbing his jaw, looking at me like all those lost words are written on my skin.

My body screams with need. *Touch. Feel. Savor.* Heat coils tightly in my core as my ribs ache and expand, like my heart is outgrowing the space they confine it in.

"I won't touch you unless you ask me to. Even then, I . . . I'm no good at any of this."

I step out of the water, just enough to see him clearly, but it still beats at my back.

"I don't think that's true, Wes." I smile softly. "But right now, I don't want to be touched. I want to be desired."

"Baby, I'm desiring you so hard it fucking hurts."

My eyes drop again, cheeks heating at the sight of the impressive bulge beneath his shorts. "Show me?"

His hands shake as they reach for the tie at his waistband. He unravels it, slowly pulling apart the Velcro that holds them together before his shorts drop to the floor, and I'm met with his strong, powerful body. Despite being covered in water, my mouth goes completely dry at the sight of his cock. Thick, hard, *huge*.

"No way is that fitting inside me." The words come out choked. My eyes snap to his, horror sluicing through me because I had zero intention of voicing that aloud. "I . . . I didn't mean to suggest—"

He smirks. "I think we could make it work."

I swallow my traitorous tongue, continuing to soak in the raw perfection that is his body. When my eyes find his cock again, he pulses, and though his palm remains on his thigh, the tendons in his hand flex with need.

"You can touch it," I whisper.

God, I want to watch him. He's so big, so rugged. Yet tender and deep and soft and rough. A delicious contradiction. I want to see him when I close my eyes. I want to imagine his hand is mine. My mouth. My body. I've been starved for sensation, for yearning, for an ache like this.

"Touch yourself," he begs. "Show me."

It's all rushing back to me, everything I've been suppressing for months, terrified I'd never feel again. I've not been seen naked by another person in so long, but I haven't been *looked* at like this ever.

After losing so much of myself, I thought I'd never find my way back. Safe vulnerability, comfortable exposure. Yet somehow, in a matter of weeks, the man in front of me plucked every jagged edge of my shattered pieces, and created something new.

My pulse pounds in my ears as I skate a hand down my chest, gripping one breast and rolling my peaked nipple between my fingers. The other slides over my hips, fingers dipping between my legs to tease my clit. The self-disgust that typically begins to rip at my flesh when I reach this point doesn't appear. All I see is my own desire reflected back at me through his eyes, all I feel is the expression on his face—desperate and devastated.

Weston grabs his cock, swiping a thumb over his tip, spreading the moisture beaded there down to his base before pumping hard. A rough groan escapes his lips at the movement.

My lids flutter, eyes fighting to stay open as I brush over my swollen bud. I'm fucking drenched, and it has nothing to do with the water pouring down around me, "Wes—"

A door slams nearby, voices echo, floating through the open sky above our heads.

We both freeze, and when his eyes widen with shock, I know mine are mirroring them.

"It's like . . . the dick doesn't suddenly taste like whipped cream, the whipped cream just now tastes like a dick. You know?"

I grimace at the sound of my aunt's undeniably recognizable voice.

Wes snorts, and I lurch forward, removing all distance between us as I clamp my hand over his mouth. A muffled groan vibrates against my palm, and my entire body flushes when I realize my bare chest is pressed against his. His hard cock throbs at my stomach.

"Yeah, I can get behind most kinks, but I've never understood food play." *That would be my mother.* It's quiet for a tick before I hear, "Is the outdoor shower running?"

Fuck.

"Yeah, Mom. It's me!" I call.

"Why are you showering out here?" Her voice is *right* outside the stall.

"Uh . . . I didn't want to track sand inside the house?" I say it like a question.

"Oh." She hums. "Well, I appreciate that. I should make your father start doing that."

Weston's eyes flare with panic.

"Where is Dad?" I ask, attempting nonchalance.

"Dishes," she responds. Wes and I both breathe a sigh of relief. "I'm doing a load of laundry. I was going to grab some beach towels."

"I threw some in earlier!" I call back.

"Oh, right. Because you were waiting for *Weston*," she sings, snickering. "Okay, love you."

"Love you," I grumble, feeling Wes smile against my palm as

he slowly raises a brow.

"Bye, Willow!" Dahlia calls as their voices fade away.

I drop my head to his shoulder, sighing with relief. He cups the back of my head, and if I'm not mistaken, he plants a kiss into my hair.

"We should probably go before we're caught," Wes whispers.

I whine, the sound muffled against his collarbone, nodding in agreement.

CHAPTER TWENTY-ONE

WESTON

RAIN PELTS THE windshield as we turn down Oceanside Boulevard. A summer storm rolled in just as we finished training earlier this afternoon, though the wind was howling since the early morning, making for choppy conditions. I surfed through it, because I knew it'd make me stronger. Plus, completing an almost-decent rodeo flip and an effortless snap given the unpredictability of the waves and rough waters had me feeling more ready than ever for the Challenger next week.

The weather got significantly worse as we were leaving, and the thirty-mile drive back to Pacific Shores made me thankful I hadn't driven my truck today. It still only starts up about half the time, and even though Leo has suggested I take it into the auto repair shop his family owns, I know the maintenance is going to be significant, and I don't want to accept handouts. I'm hoping by the time my summer here is over, I'll have saved enough from working at Heathen's to afford a proper tune up and at least get myself back to Santa Monica.

Leo pulls his car into the driveway and kills the engine before looking at me. "You did good today, I think you're ready. I want to take the rest of the week and go a little slower. Focus on conditioning and form, not injuring yourself."

"So, you want to stay in the cove from now on?"

"Nah." He shakes his head. "We'll stay here tomorrow in case the weather is shit, and then I'll take you back up north the last few days before the competition—we'll focus on perfecting your basics and save the tricks for the Challenger."

I nod. "All right."

Leo unlocks the door, patting my shoulder before he leaps out into the rain and jogs up his porch. I do the same, passing through the gate that separates the main house and the garage. I move quickly to get under the cover of my porch before I pause to look out at the horizon. The clouds are menacing, sheets of mist showering over the endless ocean, hardly visible through the density of the storm. The sun descends over the Pacific, fighting to peek through, clashing with the violent sky. Like two old gods at war.

I'm not a fan of storms. I don't like the screaming of wind or the rumbling of thunder. It reminds me of wrath and anger and hatred. The night is darker, loneliness somehow deeper because a mist of discomfort isolates humanity. We're all drawn indoors, hiding from the world and each other. I spend my whole life in hiding, but bad weather serves as some kind of sick reminder of it.

I used to cower beneath a thunderhead, and that kind of living made me a storm cloud. Now I'm always in fear others are hiding from me.

I turn from the cliffside, entering Willow's birthday into the keypad and unlocking the door. I head straight into the bathroom, stripping out of my wet clothes and stepping into the shower, allowing the hot water to soak my frigid bones and sore muscles.

Now that I've been training away from the cove and up the coast—meeting with Liv halfway between where she's located and Pacific Shores—I've hardly seen Willow. We've been working opposite schedules at the boardwalk, her opening Honeysuckle in the morning, and me closing Heathen's at night. We text almost constantly, but we haven't discussed that moment in the shower last weekend. It doesn't feel right to address it over the phone, and I haven't had any time alone with her, though I'm desperate for it.

I want to ask her, had we not been interrupted, how far we

might've gone. The possibilities have played on a loop inside my head every time I'm in the shower, or when I lie down at night—my cock in my hand and her face on my mind. I've never experienced a desire so potent before. I was sure this type of feeling just simply didn't exist for me.

I remind myself constantly that Willow's been through the worst kind of false love, and while she's slowly coming out the other side, I can't risk pushing things too far or too fast. I need to move at her pace, remind her I'm just as infatuated with her brain as I am her body, that I want her heart and soul just as badly as I want her physical being. I also remind myself that I need to move slowly for me too. Every aspect of this is new to me, and as much as I want to explore everything with Willow, I'm fucking terrified of being unable to give her what she deserves.

I'm terrified of disobeying her father's wishes and losing my future because of it.

Terrified of fucking up and losing Willow and surfing both.

So, not seeing her has been hard, but I also think it's exactly what we needed. Nine days of space to breathe, confirming that it's a hell of a lot easier to do so when we're together than when we're apart.

That's what Willow feels like to me. Being underwater, pushing toward the surface, watching the sun's rays dance beneath the waves, everything quiet and muted. Then, breaking through, taking that first deep, all-consuming breath of salt air. Daylight explodes, brightening the entire world. The roar of crashing waves rush through your ears. You're reminded what life feels like, and that no matter how peaceful the stillness beneath the water is, it's not living.

I'm not sure I've ever been living, not really. Not until I met her.

While I'm doing my damnedest to respect Leo's wishes, I can't stay away from her anymore, and I'm more determined than ever to prove to him, to Willow, that I can be what she needs.

After I'm finished with my shower and toweled off, I throw

one of my prepared dinners in the microwave and head into the bedroom to change. I slip on a pair of joggers and a tee before tossing my towel in the basket next to the closet door. My eye catches on the bookshelf and vanity in the corner. I've never paid much attention to either of them before, but a memory filters through my mind.

All women should read romance so they have a bar to set their standards, all men should read romance so they can learn how to properly please a woman.

Curiosity over Willow's comment pricks at my skin, and I approach the shelf, thumbing through the spines in search of any romance titles. I know Darby and Leo have a home library in the main house, so I assume these are leftovers that wouldn't fit. Mostly travel guides to Southern California. None of them seem to be romantic fiction.

The microwave chimes, and as I stride into the kitchen, I pull out my phone, typing a message to Willow.

Can you send me that list of your favorite romance books?

I bite my lip, thumb hovering over the send button, before I backspace the entire message. I navigate to my contact list and pull up Allie's number instead.

Can you send me a list of Willow's favorite books?

Romances, specifically.

I lean over the counter, digging into dinner when light flashes outside the window in front of me just a second before a rumble of thunder rattles the walls, and the lights flicker.

I fucking hate storms like this.

Unease washes through me, reminders of a turbulent past life, where every second inside my house was full of fury like this.

I finish eating quickly, putting my dishes in the sink before heading back into the bedroom. I flip on the television and open the blinds beside the bed. Though the sun wouldn't be completely set yet, it's nearly dark outside due to the severity of the storm, and the rain pounding against the glass makes it hard to see across the yard, but I can tell Willow's bedroom light isn't on.

From our texts earlier, I gathered she was having dinner with her parents tonight and then would be working on some grading for Penelope's class she's assisting. She must still be eating, but I shoot her a message anyway.

Truth: I'm not a fan of the dark, but I fucking hate a thunderstorm.

Leave the light on for me tonight?

I peek out the window again, hoping to see her lamp flicker on, but the room remains shadowed. I sigh, checking the response I received from Allie a few minutes ago. Sure enough, she provided a list of book titles and authors with no further explanation requested. I pull a notepad and a pen from the bedside table and scribble them down before shoving the paper back inside the drawer.

I check the window again, but her light is still off, and that unease inside me deepens.

I settle into bed, and when thunder rumbles louder, I increase the volume on the television, knowing I'm unlikely to find much sleep tonight.

It's nearly impossible to hear over the howling of the storm, but the knock on the front door is unmistakable. I scramble out of bed and rush to the living room, throwing the door open to find Willow standing in front of it. Her hair is damp, and she's hugging her arms to her chest. Eyes bright, even in the deepening darkness, she's so beautiful that all my breath gets caught inside my lungs.

"The light isn't enough tonight," she whispers. "I miss you too much."

I have a tendency to overthink every move I make, and the few times in my life that I've run on pure instinct have backfired on me in the worst possible ways. I'm extremely aware of the odds that I'll fuck this up, but I don't give my mind the chance to question my impulse when my arm shoots out, wrapping around Willow's waist and pulling her past the threshold of my doorway.

She inhales sharply, and the world warps as time pauses—long enough for me to watch her lips part, and her gaze dart from my eyes to my mouth before she tilts her chin upward. I skim my arm up her side and over her shoulder, taking her face between both of my hands. She blinks at me, long lashes fluttering with captivating temptation as she nods, and those immersive blue eyes fall closed.

I drop my mouth to hers, capturing her lips. The touch sends shockwaves rattling my bones as heat rushes through my veins when she sighs, melting into me. Her nails dig into my forearms, and I'm hyperaware of the warmth at each place our skin brushes.

I'm kissing Willow. *Willow is kissing me.*

It's that familiar sensation—breaking the surface, inhaling salt air, light and bright and bursts of color. The sun peeking through clouds. It's all amplified tenfold when she gasps against my lips, offering me the gift of her breath.

After a lifetime of being numb, she tears me open, flooding me with feeling—filling every void inside me with her light.

I move slowly, a languid feathering of my lips over hers, but Willow is hungrier. Moaning into my mouth, her tongue slips over my teeth, and I groan when I open to allow her in. With long, sultry strokes, we explore each other fiercely. A mess of tangled tongues and muffled whimpers.

I spin her, slamming the door shut with my foot. Never breaking the kiss, I scoop under her thighs and haul her around my waist, walking her back into the bedroom. She locks her arms around my neck, devouring me with teeth and tongue as I gently set her on the bed. Willow takes me with her as she falls back on the mattress, moaning when my weight envelops her.

She moves her mouth from mine, dragging her lips over my jaw and down my throat as she bucks her hips against me. My cock is fucking raging, and I can't help but grind down on her. She cries out at the friction, and it spurs me on further. It takes everything in me to lift my head and gulp for air—because I'd be all too happy to drown inside her instead.

"Willow," I rasp, pinning a hand against her stomach to still her movement. "Baby, I . . ."

"I'm sorry." She unlocks her hold around my neck, sliding her palms down my chest as I sit back on my heels, towering over her. She's an angel beneath me, gold hair splayed across my pillows, face flushed from my touch, lips swollen from my kiss.

Mine, some internal, animalistic, baser form of myself snaps.

"Don't be sorry. Never be sorry." I shake my head, panting. "I just . . . I need to go slow. I'm . . . I don't have a lot of experience," I admit.

Her brows draw together, breasts spilling over her tank top as her chest heaves. My cock throbs.

"You've never kissed anyone before?"

"I have, but that's about it." I laugh roughly, rubbing my jaw. "My lab partner in eleventh-grade chemistry. We were friends, I guess. I thought I wanted something more—tried to force myself to want something more because I felt like I *should*. But after it happened . . ." I shrugged. "I didn't think I was experiencing what I should have when kissing someone, so I . . . I never really tried again."

Willow props herself onto her elbows, hair spilling over her shoulder as she tilts her head.

"Nothing at all?"

"Well, Willow," I deadpan. "I did spend nearly two years in jail starting at the ripe young age of seventeen, so I'm not sure when I would've had time to explore sexually."

She snorts a laugh. "You know that's not what I meant."

"I know." I smile softly. "But I meant it when I said I can't risk fucking this up with you."

"I think you're doing great," she mewls, lips curling into the kind of salacious smirk that has my cock pulsing. "We don't have to go any further than this tonight. I just want to be close to you."

I fall forward, bracketing her head with my arms as I press into the mattress, smiling down at her. "I want that too."

She slides a palm beneath my shirt, dragging her hand up my bare chest. By the way my skin heats at her touch, I'm sure if I looked at my flesh right now, there'd be a trail of flame left in her wake. "We can still . . ." She sighs heavily, eyes tracking the movement of her hand as my shirt raises with her movement, bunching beneath my shoulders. "We can make each other feel good without going too far." Her glowing eyes flutter upward, and I'm drowning in them. "I can show you."

I whimper in response.

Willow Graham fucking owns me.

All I want is to sink into her embrace and let her heal every wound I never believed could stop bleeding.

"Show me, Wills."

She tosses me a sultry grin, pressing against my chest. "Sit up."

I obey, and she grabs the hem of my shirt, motioning for me to remove it. As I do, she lifts her hips, slipping off the cotton shorts she's wearing, kicking them to the floor and leaving her in nothing more than pale pink panties and a tempting white tank.

Her legs fall open, and I desperately want to pull those panties to the side and see how wet she is beneath them. I want to ask her if it's all for me and beg her to let me taste her. I've never experienced a carnal urge like this, as if my body knows exactly what it wants even if my mind can't be sure.

Until all of me is aligned, I'll follow her lead.

"Come here," she whispers.

I fall over her again, cupping her face and tangling my fingers in the hair at her nape as I drop into the cradle between her legs, allowing my mouth to hover over hers. "Like this?"

I press into her, and she moans. "Yeah, like that. Roll your hips, Wes. Like you're carving a gentle wave. My body is your tide."

"Fuck," I groan, kissing her hard.

She speaks in terms I can understand, painting an image I can envision. I pump against her, channeling all of the flow and fluidity I've gained in my years as an athlete. Grinding hard enough that I can feel the friction of our bodies, but not enough that I'm crushing her, I begin a steady rhythm.

She groans louder as I kiss down her jaw and over her neck, nipping her collarbones and suckling the skin of her breasts. Tasting and teasing and savoring every inch of her I can access with my mouth.

One of her hands tangles in my hair, while the other holds my hip, increasing the pressure as she begins lifting her body to meet me halfway. I'm so fucking hard it hurts, a pleasure more primal and powerful than anything I've known begins to gather at the base of my spine.

I've experienced release, but never like this. Never like *her.*

"Willow, I—" I lift my head, finding her eyes searing through me.

"I know. Me too. Keep going," she pants, begging. "Please, baby. Please."

"Fuck." My body reacts on instinct, bucking faster, harder. "Keep calling me that."

She cries out, and both our bodies enter a craze of flushed limbs and desperate need. That pleasure in my spine grows unbearably hot, coiling into something I'm struggling to hold back. My mind scatters, my pace becoming chaotic.

"Yes, baby," Willow cries. "Yes. I'm—"

When Willow's entire body tightens, legs locking around my

waist and drawing me into her, tying us together as her hands tug at my hair, and the softest, sweetest, ". . . coming," falls from her lips, I fucking unravel.

Burying my head in her neck, the power of my release flies from my lips and lands upon her skin. Light flashes behind my eyes, white and blinding. My cock pulsates as I spill a seemingly never-ending climax into my pants. I'm gripping the sheets so hard they may tear, and Willow claws into my shoulder with what I imagine must be the same intensity. Her locked legs tremble around my hips, her heart pounding fiercely against my chest.

"Willow," I whisper against her jaw. "Willow."

I can't stop saying her name, I think I need the reminder she's here. She's real. I'm tasting her skin and touching her body. It's her breath against my ear, her thighs I just lost myself between. Even with the barrier of clothing, it's the most soul-baring experience of my life.

I'm fucking raw—undone. Ruined.

It takes an embarrassing amount of time for me to regain my strength before I finally rise onto my arms and pull back to gaze down at her. She blinks at me, pupils blown and eyes half-lidded. She slips a swollen lip between her teeth before she bursts with a giggle and hides her face in the pillow.

I sit back on my knees. "What? Did I do something wrong?"

Her gaze snaps to me, brows drawn in concern. "No, Wes . . . No." She props onto her forearms, smiling wistfully. "You're incredible. I'm sorry. That reaction was all me."

"Why?" I ask, running a hand through my hair, chest still heaving as I attempt to catch my breath.

"I just . . ." She lifts her head toward the ceiling. "I can't believe I orgasmed from dry humping." Willow laughs, covering her eyes. "I feel like I'm in high school."

"That . . . um . . ." I clear my throat. "That wasn't a normal thing for you?"

"No, Wes. That is the first time that's ever happened to me. I was assuming we'd have to do a little hand stuff to get all the way there, but . . ." She sighs, face flushing. "It's been a while, and you make me feel so . . ." She swallows, shaking her head with a sheepish grin. "You made it easier."

"You made me less afraid." I bite down a grin of my own.

I track her body, watching as she relaxes, turning from lust-hazed to sleepy and sated. Her legs are still open, and my neck heats when I realize there is a wet spot at the center of her panties that I can't tell is from her or me.

"Yes, Weston. You made me come."

My cock stirs at her velvet voice, and I'm damn-near ready to do exactly that again. I drop my head, noticing the much larger display of wetness across the front of my pants. "Well . . ." I swallow. "You did the same to me."

She giggles, hiding her face again. I want to pull her hands away so I can see it, because in all my time on earth, nothing has felt quite so triumphant as being the reason for her laughter.

"I think that's hot," she murmurs.

"You do?" I ask, just as another rumble of thunder rocks the roof, startling me.

Willow remains calm, head tilted as she studies my reaction. "You really do hate storms."

"It's the noise, mostly. I don't like abrupt, menacing sounds. The lack of control and feeling of chaos, I think." I close my eyes, breathing deep. "You've been a phenomenal distraction. Thank you."

"Happy to be of service." She turns on her side, nuzzling her face into her palm against my pillow. "Why don't you change and then come lie down beside me?"

I nod, darting into the closet and throwing on a fresh pair of underwear before crawling into bed next to her. She lifts up, and I assume it's a cue for me to extend my arm over her pillow. Sure enough, she curls into me, placing her head against my chest.

Willow's body fits into mine perfectly, like it was made to be right here. I don't question myself as I run my fingers through her hair, or circle my thumb over the soft skin of the thigh she has slung over my hips. Nothing about it feels forced. Only warm—safe.

"I like holding you," I whisper. "It's easy."

"I know you struggle with touch," she whispers back. "How does touching me right now feel?"

I sigh, staring at the ceiling. "Touch often feels like a manipulation tactic to me. I spent so much of my childhood studying my father's body language, trying to gauge when he was going to scream or leave or throw a punch. No touch of his was ever soft or tender. There was no care or warmth or compassion. It was always a threat, a force. A way to ensure we conformed to his demands." Memories flood my mind, racking me to my core.

I swallow, pushing them down, and continue, "My mother's touch was supposed to be soothing. I know she intended to hold me with love, but every hug she gave me felt like an apology. A futile attempt to shield me from the pain she knew he was causing and could never quite save us from. When she slept beside me at night, it wasn't for my comfort, but for hers. It was an excuse to stay away from him. But when he came hunting for her, I got caught in the crossfire." Emotion pricks at my eyes, and my throat grows heavy. "She'd scream, 'Not in front of him! Don't let Weston see this!' knowing he didn't care what I witnessed. So . . . when my mother held me at night, even though I know she loved me, that was manipulation too."

Willow doesn't respond immediately, and apprehension swirls in my bones that I've gone too far. Shared too much. Shown her my ugliest of truths, unaware that it would be farther than she was willing to walk with me. A rattled breath echoes over my bare chest, and I peer down at her, gripping her chin and tilting it in my direction. Tears shimmer in her eyes, one spilling over her cheek and cascading down her beautiful face.

"I'm sorry," she says, lip trembling. "I don't want to invalidate your experience by reacting this way. I know I have no reason to cry. I know I can't even begin to understand—"

"It's okay, Willow." I smile, wiping her tears. "Not many

people make me feel safe enough to share like that—let alone care enough to cry for me. No one has ever made me feel like you do."

"How do I make you feel?" she asks.

"Like the word manipulation ceases to exist." I cup her face, dragging my thumb over her bottom lip to quell its shaking. "You're so pure. The kindest person I've ever met. When you touch me, I don't feel like I owe you something in return or need to be anticipating your intentions. I only feel your empathy. Your warmth. Like all I have to do is simply be beside you, and I'll be providing you everything you give to me." I bring her to me, kissing away the tears that dot her cheeks. "I think I'm explaining myself poorly, but my point is that you make it feel effortless. You make me understand why human beings are better in pairs than they are alone."

She brackets my jaw with her hand, brushing her lips over mine. "You make me feel that way too."

Willow kisses me, and it's different from earlier. Unhurried and tender. A soft exploration of one another. I could drown in it—this sensation. Willow's eyes and sounds and presence.

She pulls away slightly, but her mouth remains on mine as she asks, "Can I ask you something?"

"Always."

She plants her lips on my nose before settling back down against my chest. "Is your past the reason you've had such a hard time experiencing desire?"

I kiss the top of her head, running my fingers through her hair again. As if now that I've begun touching her, that I've given myself the permission, I'll never be able to stop. "I don't think so. I think my past is the reason I have trouble trusting people. I think it's why even casual embraces can be distressing, but I don't think it has as much to do with the connection I make between emotion and intimacy. At least, not according to one of my therapists." I laugh. "I became quite hyperfixated on it during my time in county. I'd always assumed the reason I never crushed on girls at school, never had an urge to watch porn, and felt absolutely nothing after my first kiss was because of what I went through as a kid, but when I was locked up, I met other inmates who'd gone through far more horrific things than I had, and they didn't feel the way I did. In fact, it seemed that a lot of people from abusive backgrounds lean toward casual intimacy, not away from it.

"I asked my counselor at the time about my feelings, and she said it was probably just who I am. Something written in my DNA. That sexuality is a wide spectrum, and some people can't experience physical desire without an emotional connection first. If I'd never known anyone well enough to nurture an emotional relationship, I couldn't desire them physically, either." I shrug, glancing down at her. "Does that make sense?"

"Absolutely." She nods, smiling. "Like you said, sexuality is a spectrum. I've grown up around lesbian cousins and bisexual uncles and Zander, who prefers not to use labels but would most align with pansexuality. I come from a . . . 'Whatever Fits Your Fancy' kind of family?" Willow laughs. "I guess I just want to understand where it started for you . . . with me."

"It's like . . ." I sigh, twirling her silky hair between my fingers. "I know how beautiful you are, Willow. You're striking, honestly, but beauty doesn't make me *feel* anything. Knowing you . . . that made me feel *everything*." I drop my chin as she lifts her head. Our gazes clash, her eyes boring through me with relentless anticipation, as if my words could make or break her soul. "It's like looking into a shadowed piece of stained glass. I know what I'm seeing is art. I know what I'm looking at is beautiful, but it's not until it's held up to the sun that the true colors become visible. Your kindness—compassion and intelligence and wild spirit—that is the sunlight."

All the kaleidoscope shades of blue in her ocean eyes burst, flaring as her puffy lips part in astonishment. "Weston . . ."

"Shh." I hush her, covering her mouth with mine, swallowing the soft gasp that leaves it.

Her palm lands on my neck, holding my body as she stakes claim to my soul. I'm entirely breathless as she pulls away, emotion shimmering in her eyes, like she's ravished and sated and contented. She smiles at me, nuzzling against my chest.

I press my lips to the top of her head, clearing my throat. "Speaking of labels . . . I don't like them either. I've been labeled enough, and now I just want to be me, and I want to be with you."

"Okay," she whispers, rolling onto her elbow and dipping her head to kiss me again. "You be you, and you be with me."

I brush a fallen strand of hair from her face as she gazes down at me. "Will you sleep here tonight?"

"I thought you'd never ask." She swats my chest playfully before settling back against my side.

We don't fall asleep immediately. Instead, we talk late into the night about my childhood and hers. My memories are shrouded in shades of gray, while hers burst with color. She tells me about her favorite movies, and the places she's traveled. I share what it was like to enter the foster care system, and the way Carter and Penelope saved my life.

The storm rolls on beyond the walls, but I hardly hear it anymore. It's drowned out by her voice and her laugh, and when Willow becomes quiet, the rain outside is nothing more than a background to her breathing. The night nothing more than a blank canvas for her light to shine upon. Because when she falls asleep next to me, I have no fear of the darkness and no dread for the storm.

When Willow sleeps beside me, I know only peace.

CHAPTER TWENTY-TWO

WESTON

THE BUZZING IS *incessant.*

I groan, reaching across the mattress to find the source of the obnoxious vibration coming from my bedside table. Forcing my heavy eyes open, I blink at the daylight, turning my phone in my palm to see who the fuck would be calling me at this hour—*fuck.*

Leo's calling.

It's six thirty, and I'm already a half-hour late.

I sit up too quickly, and the sheets slip over her hips, revealing her perfect fucking ass. I groan, sliding my thumb across the screen, answering my coach's call when his daughter mutters at the disturbance as she rolls to her side.

Oh, I'm fucked. I'm so fucked.

"Hello?" My voice is gravel.

"I'm not coming in there because I'm afraid of what I'll find," he grumbles. "But you have thirty fucking seconds to get your ass outside or I'm pulling you from that Challenger."

"Coming," I choke.

Willow giggles into her pillow. Leo grunts as he hangs up.

"You're trouble," I murmur, pressing a kiss into her mess of hair. She turns, peering up at me with those soul-crushing blue eyes, an amused smile playing at her lips. Brushing her cheek, I whisper, "I have to go. I'm sorry."

Her brows furrow, and she shakes her head. "Don't be.

Surfing is a priority, Weston. I won't ever ask you to change that. I'm sorry I kept you up so late you overslept."

"Don't be," I whisper, kissing her slowly, savoring the moment. "You're a priority too—it's not your fault I didn't set my alarm."

I peck her lips once more before leaping from the bed. As quickly as possible, I change into a pair of swim bottoms and brush my teeth, grabbing my wetsuit from the basket of clean laundry outside my bedroom before pausing in the doorway to get one last look at Willow.

She's still in bed, no rush to move, surrounded by pillows and scrolling through her phone. She must feel my stare, because she stops before glancing in my direction. "You better get out there, Killer."

"You look good in my bed, Trouble." An effortless smile spreads over my cheeks. "Wish I had a photo of it."

"You're late," she sing-songs with a laugh, blowing me a kiss.

I'm grinning like a goddamn fool as I step out of the house and shuffle down the porch steps, though it falls when I round the railing and find Leo Graham standing at the edge of the staircase that leads down to the cove, frowning at me.

"I'm sorry."

His nostrils flare. "I know."

Without another word, he begins descending the cliffside with both of our boards in hand. The morning passes much the same way. Curt direction from Leo, demand to complete specific maneuvers or pay better attention to my form, hard encouragement to try again when I fail.

At the end of our session, we wade out of the waves, and he hands me a water bottle as I toss my board into the sand.

"I think you have about the best reason on the planet to be distracted right now, which makes what I'm about to say difficult," he mutters, gaze fixed on the blue horizon. "My concerns over this budding relationship go farther than just being protective over my daughter. I asked you weeks ago if you were serious about this, and you promised me you were. You promised me focus. This isn't focused, Weston."

"I—"

He holds up a hand. "I can't tell you that you're too good to be distracted by some girl, because that girl deserves dedication. I can't allow her to settle for less than that. I can't even tell you that I blame you, because I think she's worth far more than surfing or titles or gold medals ever could be, and I don't want her to be with someone who wouldn't agree with me."

"She is." I nod rapidly. "She is worth more than that."

"Do you see what position you've put me in?" He rubs the tension out of his jaw, sighing. "I don't want to waste my time on an athlete who isn't serious about their craft, and I sure as fuck do not want my daughter wasting her time on a man who isn't serious about her."

"I can be both." The words rush from my mouth before he has the chance to question them. "Today was a slip up, and you've got every right to be concerned, but it won't happen again. Willow won't let it happen again, either. She's as invested in my surfing as I am."

"And who's invested in her, Weston?"

"Me." I tap my chest. "I swear to you, I can do both. I can do surfing and I can do Wi—" He shoots me a glare. "I can be there for Willow too."

"What happens when she goes back to college? When you go on tour? What do you plan on then?"

I huff, dropping my gaze to my feet as a hand comes to my neck, rubbing out the tension there. "We haven't exactly discussed that yet."

This is new—especially for me, I've never even been on a date—and it's scary for both Willow and me, and I wish I didn't have to explain that to her fucking *dad*.

"Willow's been through . . ." He pauses, and I look up to find him shaking his head, pacing the sand in front of me. "It's been hard. She's still going through it, and . . ."

"I know. I know what she's going through."

Leo chews on his inner cheek, and there is a distance in his eyes that has the unease pricking at my spine.

"I told you I'm not going to lock my daughter away, and last night when she took one look at her phone, leaped from the dinner table, went out the back door, and didn't return, I realized how invested she is too. So . . ." He holds his hands out, as if he's surrendering. "But if you are late one more time, if you stop giving this your all, then there is no need for me to continue."

"I won't. I'm focused, I swear."

"If Willow decides that she's no longer comfortable with you here, you're done. The ball is always in her court, and if she says the word, this is over."

"I agree." I nod. "I'm not going to fuck this up with her *or* with you, but if she asks me to leave, I'll go."

He swallows, dipping his chin in acknowledgment.

I bend down to grab my board before turning toward the cliffside when Leo calls from behind me, "And Weston?"

"Yeah?"

He catches up to me, and we ascend the stairs slowly. "If you two are going to be . . . whatever this is between you, you need to know that Parker has been trying to get in contact with her for some time now."

"I know. I overheard a conversation at Honeysuckle a few—"

"There have been more." His tone is so low, it's nearly a growl. A wave of apprehension crashes over me. "He's sent mail to the house. Called the other boardwalk businesses. Even tracked down Willow's ex-boyfriend, Camden. Messaged him and asked if they'd been together, and even after Cam told him no, Parker left threats, said she *belonged* to him."

Leo's jaw quivers, squeezing his fists at his sides. The rage now shooting through my veins has my body reacting in much the same way.

"Before or after the Fourth of July?"

His eyes snap to mine. "After."

Fuck. So Parker might know about me, then.

"You didn't tell Willow any of this?"

He shakes his head. "I don't want to burden her unless absolutely necessary. I told Parker when he called the surf shop that I had cameras on every piece of property I own, and that if he's caught on any of them, I'll ruin his fucking life. I also told him Willow was out of state for the summer, and if we heard from him again, I'd get a restraining order filed." He sighs, running a hand through his blond hair. "Then, Parker found some photos on social media of our party on the Fourth, and must've assumed Willow was home after all. That's when he contacted Cam. Left a nasty voicemail." He barks a laugh. "Fucking idiot. I had Cam file a restraining order against him. It's only been a few days, but we haven't heard from him again. I'm hoping it's over now, and Willow never has to stress about this."

"I think she deserves to know," I murmur as we reach the top of the stairs, tucking ourselves into a corner beside the guesthouse porch.

"She's . . . facing a lot of guilt." Leo chews his lip again, and I wonder if it's a nervous habit, or if he's not sure what to say. "The last thing I want is for her to internalize any of this harassment as a reason to feel guilty. I'd prefer she not know unless she absolutely has to."

I don't love the idea of this, but I nod. He knows her better than I do, and I have to respect that.

"I'm telling you because, if you're going to be part of her life, this is what comes with it right now. Do you understand?" I nod, and he continues, "If you receive any sort of weird message, phone call, see anyone around the boardwalk who looks like they shouldn't be there . . . you come straight to me, okay?"

"I will," I promise. "I'll take care of her."

Leo sighs, pinning me with haunted blue eyes, offering only a shallow nod. "Prove it."

He leaves me on the porch as he stalks away. I pull out my phone as I climb the porch stairs to the guesthouse, finding a notification from Willow. No message, just a photo. Her eyes are bright, lips playfully quirked as she spreads out in my bed, hair splayed over my pillow. She holds her phone with both hands, elbows squeezing her chest to accentuate her breasts, evidence of last night's marking from my mouth on display above the neckline of her tank. It rides up at her midsection, showcasing a band of tan skin between her shirt and her panties.

I set the photo as my lock screen and slip my phone back into my pocket, grinning like a fool once again.

"Hi, can I help you?" A cute brunette asks in a mousy voice from behind the counter as the bell on the door chimes, signaling my entrance.

Sugar And Vice is completely different from the other shops. Once you step inside, you're transported from the beach town boardwalk to a cozy bookshop. Painted in warm earth tones and wood furnishings, it almost feels as if I'm transported to a rustic New England village, with cobblestone streets, autumn leaves, and crisp, cold weather.

The smell of the bakery next door floats through the walls, offering an aroma of cinnamon and vanilla, and the low lighting is easy on the eyes. Soft instrumental music floats quietly through the space, creating a comforting ambiance.

Shelves line the store, categorized by sub-genres like "Sports" and "Cowboys" and "Touch Her And Die."

What the hell?

I shake my head, pulling my gaze back to the girl behind the counter. She smiles at me, closing the book in front of her. She must be damn-near a foot shorter than me, and is forced to crane her neck to look in my direction, shoulder-length hair swaying with the movement.

"Um . . . hi." I clear my throat awkwardly, reaching into my back pocket for the folded piece of paper. "I'm looking for these books."

I hand it to her, and as she unfolds it, reading through the list, an eyebrow shoots up above her round, metal-framed glasses. When she raises her brown eyes to me, the freckles smattered across her nose dance as she scrunches it in amusement. "Okay . . ." She chuckles under her breath. "These three are in the dark romance section." She points to the first few titles on the list before extending her arm toward the labeled corner of the store. "The others will be in small-town, and that last one at the bottom is shelved under fantasy. They're alphabetized by author."

I force a grin, feeling flustered and out of place. "Thank you."

"You're welcome," she chimes. "Let me know if you can't find any of them and I can come assist."

As I'm thumbing through the dark romance section, searching for the name "Violet Rose" a door opens and closes in the distance, before a low yet feminine voice says, "Hi, Zoe. How are things today?"

"Good." The girl from the front desk—Zoe—yawns. "It's slow."

"Yeah." The other woman laughs. "It's always slow."

I finished locating the stack of books Allie recommended—Willow's favorites. I hold seven in total as I walk back to the register, setting them down on the counter. The other voice belonged to Elena—the store owner and Leo's sister—who sits behind Zoe on a counter, swinging her legs as she scrolls through her phone.

Her dark eyes lift to me, and a cherry-red smile spreads across her lips. "Hey, Weston."

"Hey." I awkwardly shuffle the books into one arm, raising a hand to wave.

Her gaze darts to my collection as Zoe takes them from me and scans the barcode on each book. Elena studies the titles, tilting her head before hopping off the counter to get a closer look. She picks up one of the dark-colored covers, inspecting the novel. "Are you buying all of Willow's favorite books?"

"How do you know these are Willow's favorites?"

She smirks. "Because I introduced her to all of them—and I

wrote three myself."

My jaw drops. "You did?"

"Of course." Elena motions around the bookstore. "Does it look like this place is paying my bills?"

I swivel my head, realizing I'm the only person in here.

"Are you buying these for her or for yourself?"

"Myself," I admit, biting my lip. "Willow said every man should read romance, so I figured I'd start with her favorites."

Zoe pauses, giving me a once-over before her eyes dart to Elena. She purses her lips, nodding, as if she approves. Elena returns the expression.

"Forgive me if this question is crossing a line, but how comfortable are you with primal play?" Elena asks, leaning onto the counter and propping her chin in her hand.

"What is primal play?"

"Yeah." She sighs, nodding. "That's what I assumed." She slides three of the books in my direction and gathers up the other four herself. "I'd start with those."

"I . . ." I point to the books in her hands. "What if I decide I want to read those too?"

"Oh, I have no doubt you'll be back." She grins. "But you should ease into it."

I chew the inside of my cheek, shrugging. "You're the expert, I guess."

"You're off to a good start, Weston." Elena winks, bagging up the three books I ended up buying. "Good luck."

I thank them both, exiting the store and making my way a few doors down to Heathen's. I avoid passing by the front doors of Honeysuckle, since I know Willow is still working and I don't want her to see the bag in my hand just yet.

I slip through the back door of the surf shop and dart up the stairs to the office above it that doubles as a break room. Pulling my phone from my pocket, I hold the paper bag up next to my face, showing the Sugar And Vice logo stamped onto the front, smiling at the camera as I snap a photo and send it to Willow.

My journey has begun.

She responds almost immediately, which tells me the boardwalk must be slow for everyone today.

Willow

Oh? What did you get? Give me a haul.

I take each book out of the bag, sending her photos.

Willow

Very good choices.

They came recommended.

What am I supposed to be looking for in here, exactly?

Willow

Inspiration. New outlooks on life. Grand gestures. Swoon-worthy banter. Tear-inducing love confessions.

Willow

Lessons in pillow talk.

My stomach flips at that last message.

Really?

Willow

Oh, yeah. Some women like to be praised. Told they're a good girl. Others want to be choked and spanked and called a whore. There is a whole world of possibilities between those pages.

Honestly, I could give a fuck what anyone else is into, Willow.

I want to know what you like.

Willow

Why don't I come over tomorrow and tag my favorite chapters? I'm having lunch with a friend, but I'll be there when you're done with your shift?

Sounds like a date, Trouble.

CHAPTER TWENTY-THREE

WILLOW

"WILLOW, IS IT too much to ask that you cover your hickeys while at the dining table?" Dad frowns at me over his bowl of cereal.

"Sorry." My hand flies to my collarbone, having forgotten about the marks left by Weston that haven't quite disappeared yet. "Honestly, though, I'd feel more inclined about covering up if you'd go a little easier on him."

Dad raises his brow. "Did he say I *wasn't* going easy on him?"

"No," I drawl. "But I heard your tone when you called him the other morning."

"He was late."

I set my coffee mug down in front of me. "Did he tell you why?"

"I'd prefer he didn't."

I roll my eyes. "He has a trauma response to storms, Dad. You know a summer storm like that is rare too. It wasn't expected, and he struggles." I sigh. "You know what he's been through, and yet he continues showing up every day with more determination than any surfer you've trained since Liv. Give him some grace."

My father pouts as he holds his hands out, palms up. "I have all the respect and empathy for what he's been through, Sugar, but he works harder when he's reminded he has something to lose."

I toss him a resigned nod. I won't argue with him about his

methods when he has a track record of producing champions, but I'm certainly more defensive over Weston than I have been with any of his previous athletes.

"I'll do my best to be nice to him, Willow." Dad chuckles as I raise my coffee to my lips. "You're being safe, right?"

I scoff, shooting him a look of disbelief over my mug. "Are you asking if I'm using condoms?"

"I'm asking if you are *safe*. With your body. Your mind. Every piece of yourself."

That pulls a soft smile from me. "He makes me feel safer than anyone else ever has."

Dad chews on his inner cheek, glancing toward my mom in the kitchen before his eyes find mine again. "I don't want to tell you what to do . . . but I think you should take things slow."

"Oh, we are," I murmur.

I dip my head to hide my blush when I remember that Weston went out of his way to ask Allie for a list of my favorite books, ventured into my aunt's store, and bought them. I was ready to beg for him at that moment, but he doesn't seem ready to take the next step yet, and deep down, I know I'm not either.

"I just want to make sure you're being mindful about what you've gone through," Dad says gently, reaching across the table to take my hand. "And considering how things are going to change at the end of the summer . . ." He pauses, and I lift my head to find him biting his lip, as if he's considering what to say next. As if I'm fragile—glass—and he's afraid to shatter me. "I don't want you to get hurt again."

I offer him a closed-lip smile that I hope portrays reassurance. "We're taking it slow. Friendship first. Mostly. I promise."

"I get the feeling Weston is a little inexperienced," Mom chimes from inside the kitchen. "I think that's good for you, though."

"What gives you that feeling?" Dad mutters.

She shrugs, mixing a bowl at the counter with a smirk on her face. "Mother's intuition."

"Yeah, well . . ." I laugh beneath my breath. "His natural born talents extend beyond surfing."

"Willow, don't traumatize your father before nine a.m., please."

I grin broadly, knowing my dimples pop when I smile like this. The ones my parents say I inherited from him.

He frowns, eyes narrowing in a crestfallen expression. "That is heathen behavior, Willow Maeve."

I shrug, blowing them both dramatic kisses.

"I'm actually glad you're eating with us this morning." My mom laughs, floating into the dining room and taking a seat next to Dad. "I wanted to see if you have made a decision on schools yet?" she asks, mixing up her bowl of oatmeal—blueberries and peanut butter. The same way she's eaten it my entire life. My favorite way to have it too. "No pressure if not, but I thought it was a good time for a family check-in."

Dad reaches across the table, grasping my hand again. "We're so proud of you for not giving up on yourself, Willow."

"Thanks." I squeeze back. "I . . . I haven't made a decision yet, but I'm figuring it out, and I'll make sure to respond before the deadline."

Mom nods, smiling softly. "If you wanted to take another semester off and stay home, we'd support that too. Whatever you need."

"If you wanted to live with us and be my baby forever, that would be more than okay with me." My dad grins, dimples popping.

A laugh bursts from me, and I slide out of my chair to stand behind his, wrapping my arms around his neck and hugging him hard. "I'm definitely not doing that, but I love you. I'm going back to school. I want to go back to school, I won't let my education be taken from me." I sigh. "I just haven't figured out where yet."

Dad tilts his head, kissing my cheek as Mom extends her arm to brush her hand along mine in a tender caress. "How are you feeling? About . . . everything?"

My parents have done a phenomenal job giving me the space I've needed to process things on my own. When it happened, there was no question in my mind about where I'd run to. I wanted to be home with them, but as the memories settled over me, it became harder to voice my feelings to them.

We don't talk about it outside the reminders that they're here for me, they'll support any decision I make, and the somewhat vexing yet gentle nudge to seek therapy.

"I'm feeling better." I grin. "I promise."

"And . . ." Dad clears his throat, shuffling in his seat. "Does Weston know about . . ."

I shake my head, lifting off him and stepping into the doorway that leads toward the stairs. "Not about the pregnancy. I . . . I'm going to tell him. I just . . ."

"For what it's worth, I think he'll understand, and I don't think he'll judge you in the slightest," my dad says softly, my mother nodding in agreement. "I also think it's okay to take your time, and wait until you're ready."

I bite my lip as a smile clusters in the corner of my mouth. "Thanks," I murmur before heading up the stairs.

My palms sweat as I wipe them down the front of my thighs, taking a seat in the corner of the cafe. I wish Allie were here, but she's taking the week off to stay with her parents up in Pacific Palisades. I know it's not normal to be this nervous for lunch with a friend, but Chelsea has never exactly felt like my other friends.

We grew somewhat close due to the sheer number of group dates Parker and Chelsea's boyfriend, Hayden, would drag us on, but deep down, it never felt like she and I had much in common. Yet, she's always seemed to enjoy being around me. My first year of college when I met Parker, Chelsea knew all the best study spots, and was eager to help me find my classes. She advised me which professors to avoid and saved me seats at football games.

Sometimes it felt as if I were a pet project for her. Someone to take under her wing and help her feel more elevated. Then, I would feel guilty about thinking that way of her, because she's so damn nice. The kind of perfect that made me constantly question her motives—and the sort of kind that proved me wrong time and time again.

She's intimidating. A year older than me, and seemingly *always* put together. Chelsea has perfect skin, never misses a blow out or a manicure. I have a terrible habit of shopping for jewelry but forgetting to wear it. Chelsea never fails to dawn earrings, necklaces, rings, and bracelets—she's never not sparkling. Plus, she always smells like vanilla.

I honestly don't know why she's taken such an interest in getting together after I left Berkeley. She's been checking in on me a couple times a week ever since I came home. I avoided talking about our breakup and told her I wasn't coming back. She vowed that she didn't care to know, she just wanted to ensure I was okay. In the months since, she hasn't even brought up Parker's name.

We chat about our summer plans, my job at Honeysuckle, assisting Penelope, and which schools I submitted transfer applications to. Apparently, Chelsea is attending University of Southern California for grad school, and hopes that if I stick nearby, we can get together often.

It's been a pleasant surprise to know her interest in me went beyond her friendship with my ex, but I'm nervous to see her nonetheless.

Despite her kindness, I've never felt like I held a candle to her. Never felt like I could measure up to her effortless perfection.

I comb my fingers through my long, blond hair that I forgot to brush this morning, still half-crimped from the loose braid I slept in last night, ensuring my strands cover the hickey on my collarbone because I don't trust the concealer I covered it with to hold up. When I pull my hands away, my eyes snag on the grown-out, chipped nail polish on my fingers, and the wrinkles in my sundress. I'm suddenly questioning whether or not I should've worn sneakers with this outfit.

My stomach lurches as the front door swings open and Chelsea floats inside. Sure enough, she's glowing. Almost levitating around the patrons and tables, as if carried by clouds as she makes her way toward me. I stand, feeling microscopic as she beams, squealing with delight and pulling me into her arms. She towers above me, because she wore a pair of wedges that likely have her pushing six feet tall.

She smells like vanilla and some kind of delicious hair oil—the likely reason why her brunette strands are so silky when they brush over my knuckles locked around her back.

"Willow." She squeezes me. "I am so happy to see you."

"Me too." A mousey sheen coats my voice, and I'm suddenly reminded why I never quite felt myself up there in Berkeley.

She pulls back, offering a glistening smile as she peers down at me. "You look beautiful. So sun-kissed and tan. You can't even pay for a tan like this." She runs her fingers down my arm. "I'm so jealous."

"Please." I snort. She's wearing a pale pink babydoll top and a white denim skirt that perfectly hugs her hips. "You're perfect."

"Oh." She playfully smacks my arm. "You're too sweet." Glancing around the cafe, she asks, "Have you ordered already?"

"No, I was waiting for you."

I walk toward the front counter, beckoning her to follow. I order my regular from Stella, one of the baristas, while Chelsea requests something much more complicated that has me questioning my decision to drink whole milk.

After our coffee is ready, we take a seat back at my table as we wait. "This is the most adorable little beach town. I had no idea you were from a place so quaint."

"Oh, yeah." I laugh awkwardly, shuffling in my seat. "I love it here, especially in the summer."

"And your parents own this whole thing?" She swirls her finger in the air, referencing the boardwalk, I assume.

"Well, my dad owns the boardwalk itself, but my aunt owns

the cafe. My other aunt owns the bookshop next door, and my uncle owns the tattoo parlor at the end. My parents own the surf shop and the florist." I nod to my left, in the direction of Honeysuckle.

"That is *so* cool." She smiles, and it seems nothing but genuine. "I'm so happy I was able to stop by on my way down to visit my grandmother." She grabs my hands across the table, squeezing gently. "Parker will be happy to hear you're alive and thriving."

All of my internal organs lurch into my throat, and I erupt into a coughing fit.

Why the fuck would she say that?

Her eyes widen, face flushing. "Oh, God, Willow. I'm so sorry." She hands me a napkin. "I was just making a joke. Perhaps that was in poor taste. I won't tell Parker anything you're not comfortable with me sharing."

Heat creeps up my neck as I take the napkin and wipe my mouth. I should've expected Parker would come up in conversation. I'm such a fucking idiot for thinking I could get away with ignoring his existence. I'm going to have to tell her *something*. Maybe if we get it out of the way now, we can put the topic to bed and leave it alone. If I avoid it, it'll just make her more curious.

I open my mouth, searching for a placated response that will shut down any further discussion of my ex, while offering her some kind of update to report back to him.

"Tell me about your summer instead." Her lips quirk apologetically as she crosses one leg over the other, settling into her seat.

Fuck.

I swallow, shooting her a forced grin instead.

"Are you seeing anyone new?" She raises a brow playfully.

I hide a smile, biting down the urge to speak of Weston. He still feels like a secret that's all mine. "Um . . . no. I've been so busy."

"Oh, stop that." She flicks her wrist at me. "I see you getting bashful now. Tell me all about him."

"It's nothing, really," I lie, tucking a strand of hair behind my ear. "I've been spending time with one of my dad's surfers, but we're just friends."

"*Friends.*" She winks. "Right. Sure."

I quickly change the subject, diving into details about my cousins and Allie instead. Working together at the boardwalk and Allie's relationship drama from her birthday a couple of weeks ago. I talk about Penelope's lectures, and some of the paintings I've been working on. She tells me about an internship she completed in Berkeley, and how she's spending the rest of the summer in San Diego at her grandmother's home before starting school at USC in the fall. Hayden is still working in the Bay Area, apparently, so he'll fly down to see her on the weekends before they move in together in Los Angeles at the end of the summer.

I don't ask about Parker. I don't want to know his plans, but I hope he stays as far away from Southern California as possible. It's not big enough for the two of us.

My mind drifts to Wes, and I wonder if he feels the same about his father. I can't imagine living with the knowledge that someone who caused so much harm is not only walking free—but could be lurking around any corner.

A chill nips at my spine, sending a tremor through my body, but I cover it quickly by taking a sip of my s'mores latte.

"So, clearly you don't want me to bring it up . . ." Chelsea sighs, and my stomach sinks. "But I'm hoping, now that we're together, face-to-face, and enough time has passed . . . you could tell me what happened with Parker? He's lost without you, Willow." She lifts her eyes to me, and so much sadness swirls in her gaze. I get the gut feeling it's not empathy for me. "I hate the idea that you don't trust me enough to open up, but I understand if that's the case. Like I said, anything you share is safe with me. I guess . . . I just want to know if there is any hope for you two at all?"

"There isn't." The words rush from me all too quickly.

Chelsea rears back, blinking. "You seem so sure about that."

"I am." I nod. "And, honestly, I'd prefer not to talk about Parker. It's . . . painful." My voice breaks on the sentence—disdain masked as heartbreak. I shrug, smiling wistfully as I take another sip, hoping this'll be where we let the conversation regarding my past die.

She tosses me an unconvinced once-over, gaze narrowing as she picks at her cuticles. "I guess I'm just confused, Willow. Parker was completely blindsided." Straightening her spine, she tosses her hair behind her shoulder before leaning over the table. "He said you two were perfectly fine. That you went to bed together, he woke up the next morning, went to class, and when he returned you were . . ." She flicks her fingers. "Poof. Gone." Her brows furrow before she continues, "A few days later, he received a letter from the management office of your apartment building saying you'd paid out your end of the lease. You never even came back for your things."

Her tone is growing increasingly frustrated, and the despair inside my chest rises with each word she spews. My skin itches with the urge to become defensive. Yet, emotion pricks behind my eyes at the confirmation that Parker truly has no idea why I left him. Not because I feel guilty, or because I harbor any sense of responsibility for his feelings—I want to fucking cry because he irreparably damaged me, and it's so inconsequential to him that he doesn't even realize it.

"Chelsea," I huff, rubbing my temples, willing the tears to pause before they fall. "I have my reasons, I promise. Please . . ." I swallow the lump in my throat, blinking rapidly as I drop my gaze to my lap.

She's going to expect some kind of explanation, and from her perspective, I can understand why. I can't tell her he assaulted me. He's her friend, and I don't want to speak to the details, I don't want to explain how my live-in boyfriend of two years, whom I had an infinite amount of consensual sex, could've also been responsible for my assault. Not out of protection for Parker, but for myself. I can't bear the thought of spilling my deepest pain, only to witness the picture of doubt in her gaze after I finish. A gut feeling so potent I sway in my chair rushes through me—she won't believe me, even if I tell her everything. She's always belonged to Parker—everyone in my life at Berkeley belonged to Parker first.

I don't think Chelsea could support my decisions, even if she believed the reasons behind them. She presents herself as the kind of person whose life is without flaw or failure, and she's never shown me any reason to believe she'd be capable of understanding my actions if they weren't ones she'd take herself.

Bile rises in my throat when I recall the words he'd said about my body. I won't share those with her, either. I'm not sure I'll ever share them with anyone—the shame is too soul-deep. It's too humiliating, because I still wonder if they were true.

"Willow, I just want to know why. You have no idea how heartbroken he's been." She grabs my hands again. "I know you have your reasons, I just want to understand. I need to know why you're not going back so I can help him move on. He still thinks you're coming home."

My eyes squeeze shut in some kind of attempt to shield myself from the spears of guilt she's hurling in my direction. Whatever narrative Parker is feeding her can't be right. I know he must have some inkling of why I left, even if he's too fucking stupid to fully comprehend it. He was there that night, he knows exactly what he did—what he said—and my reaction to it.

That night—Parker's face, his words—float through my mind again, grinding my teeth to hold back the scream I want to hurl in Chelsea's face. I bite my tongue to swallow the wail.

Tension builds in my temples—the buzz of conversation around the cafe, the clinking of mugs and the chime of the register overwhelming my senses until a throbbing haze erupts behind my eyelids.

"Willow, can you please just—"

"I had an abortion," I say on a hurried breath, the words flying from my mouth so rapidly I can't catch them before they're gone, floating in the air between us.

Chelsea rears back, pulling her hands from mine, as if my skin is poisoned—as if I'm diseased. I raise a trembling palm to my mouth, opening my eyes to find her withdrawn from the table, clutching her chest, watching me with a curled lip and a disbelieving gaze.

Her jaw drops, gaping for several long seconds before finally whispering, "You were pregnant?"

I don't know why I said that.

She was too persistent, there was too much noise, and I think my subconscious decided it would be the easiest reason to throw at her—even though her reaction is a clear indication that I would've been better off saying nothing at all.

I've been open about my decision with my family, but Chelsea's response is a stark reminder why I don't share it with anyone outside of those who love me most. It's why I haven't told Weston, and now, I can't imagine how I ever could.

I won't allow her, or anyone else, to shame me for this.

I straighten, schooling my features. "I don't think I'm comfortable talking about this with you. I shouldn't have blurted that out, and I apologize, but the fact of the matter is, I made the decision to leave Berkeley and move home. I had my reasons, and there is no future left for Parker and me. I would appreciate it if you told him to let it go and move on."

She scoffs. "You never told Parker? You just . . . abandoned him? You didn't think he deserved to know, to be part of that decision?"

"No, Chelsea." I sigh. "He doesn't deserve to know anything about me ever again."

Her lips form a line as she blinks in shock before tucking a strand of hair behind her ear. "Honestly, Willow. I'm disgusted right now. You are . . . You're kind of an awful person."

The first tear that spills over my cheek is hot, my hand trembling as I lift it to my face and wipe the moisture away. The light inside me that just began to reignite in the weeks since I returned home snuffed out by the chill of her reaction.

I'm not sure I can blame her. Without the full context, I do sound terrible. Though, I realize now that the truth wouldn't matter to Chelsea. She was never my friend, she was always his first, and no matter the truth behind my decision to keep my abortion from Parker, she'd choose him anyway. Perhaps she'd accuse me of lying, or she'd believe my choice outweighs his assault—regardless, I don't want to know. I refuse to sit here and give her the opportunity to explain her contempt.

"I think I should go." I quickly wipe my eyes, pushing back my chair to stand. "Like I said, I'd appreciate it if you kept this between us. Parker needs to move on. I don't want to hear from him again."

Chelsea only stares after me, mouth gaping and eyes wide—appalled and dumbfounded, as I leave the cafe on shaky legs. I stumble through the back, vision blurred by my heavy tears. My chest tightens as a sob rips from my throat. I clutch my ribs, gulping for oxygen, choking on my anguish. The world tilts, and I'm not entirely sure how I even make it to Heathen's without collapsing.

The bell chimes when I swing the back door open, and the first inhale I've been capable of taking rushes through my nose when I find Weston standing behind the register next to Rob, Heathen's shift manager. His head whips in my direction, his beautiful face losing all its color when he soaks me in—a crying, trembling mess.

"Willow, baby," he gasps, closing the distance between us as he takes my face between his hands. "What happened? Who did this?"

"I need you," I murmur, voice fractured as the words spill from my mouth in shattered pieces, and I break down in his arms.

CHAPTER TWENTY-FOUR

WESTON

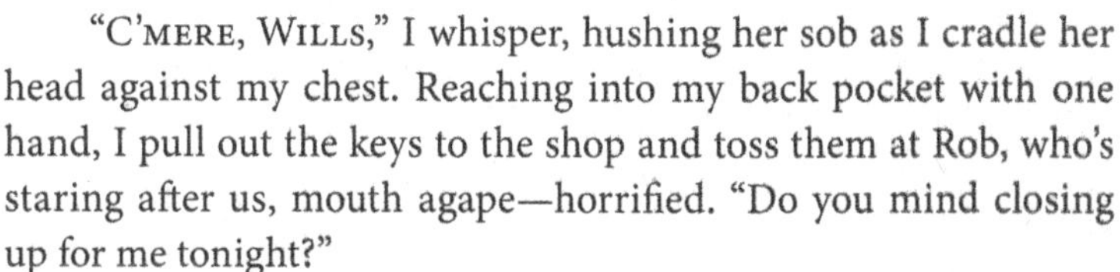

"C'mere, Wills," I whisper, hushing her sob as I cradle her head against my chest. Reaching into my back pocket with one hand, I pull out the keys to the shop and toss them at Rob, who's staring after us, mouth agape—horrified. "Do you mind closing up for me tonight?"

A quiver rushes through Willow as she turns her head into my chest, seemingly hiding from him. Luckily, the shop is otherwise empty, but I'm sure she doesn't like the idea of anyone seeing her this way—let alone one of her dad's staff members.

I'm damn-near shaking myself, desperate to know what happened. I need to know who made her feel this way, then I need to figure out how to fix it.

"Don't you think we should call her—"

Willow shakes her head against my chest. "Please don't."

"I'd appreciate if you could close up for me so I can take my girl home," I snap. "Can you do that or not?"

He recoils. "Um . . . yeah, man. I can do that for you."

"Thank you." I turn Willow toward the door, guiding her out of the building. "Where are your keys, Wills?"

She pauses, trembling as she pulls them from the purse slung around her shoulder. I lead her to where her car is parked behind Honeysuckle, unlocking it and opening the passenger door. "Let's get you home, love." I kiss the top of her head as she sinks into the seat before helping buckle her in.

Rounding to the driver's side, I start up the engine and back out of the spot, leaving the boardwalk. We don't speak on the short drive back to her parents' house. Willow only quietly cries beside me, and all I can do is brush my thumb across her thigh, drawing soothing circles.

I need to know every detail of what, or who, upset her, but more importantly, I need to get her home. Help calm her and ensure she's safe. My only instinct is to cease her tears, and all the adrenaline in my body is surging through my veins, wholly focused on it.

I pull into her spot in the driveway, next to where my truck is parked in the gravel. Killing the engine, I turn to her and ask, "Do you want me to take you to your room, or mine?"

She looks at me, bottom lip quivering, tears swimming in her glistening eyes. "Yours."

"Okay, baby." I smile softly.

I hop out of her car, but she exits before I can round the side and help her out. I reach around her, closing the passenger door before wrapping my arm over her shoulder, tucking her in close as we walk through the gate separating the main house and the garage. Willow sniffles when we reach the door of the guesthouse, and I plug her birthday into the keypad, unlocking the door.

"Do you want anything to eat? Water?" I ask, guiding her toward the bedroom.

"No," she whispers, beelining for my bed. She sits against the headboard, pulling her knees to her chest. "I'm sorry for making you leave work. I shouldn't have done that." She lifts her head, tears streaming down her beautiful, flushed cheeks, the sight gutting me completely. "I just didn't know where else to go."

I crawl across the mattress, taking her face between my hands. "You're always my top priority, Wills. It doesn't matter where I am or what I'm doing, you need me? I'm yours." She only cries harder, but offers me a subtle nod, dropping her head to her knees. I plant a kiss to her hair. "Can you tell me what happened, baby? Tell me how to fix it."

"There is nothing to fix," she murmurs. "I met up with a friend from Berkeley today, and she . . . She made me feel fucking awful about the way I left things there. The way I left him."

I rub circles into her back. "You have nothing to feel guilty about, love. You did what was best for you, and you don't owe her anything. You have no obligation to explain yourself to anyone, Willow."

"It felt like I did. It felt like she deserved a reason." She exhales a shuddered breath before burying her head against my shoulder. I swing her legs over my thigh, nestling them between my knees and cradling her head against my chest, wrapping her in me. "I didn't want to tell her about . . . About what he did to me. I was afraid she wouldn't believe me."

"She may not have," I whisper, pressing my lips into her hair again. "That's not a reflection on you, though. Those who matter believe you, Willow. Those who matter support you."

She sighs heavily, but nods. "I . . . I told her something else, though. I don't know why." Willow's voice shakes with every word. "I didn't want to, but she made me feel as if I *had* to. Now, I'm just . . . I feel as if I've been stolen from all over again. My truth. Another thing taken from me."

"Were you friends with her for a while?" I ask softly.

"Yeah." She sniffles. "For a couple of years. Ever since I met Parker."

"You're a trusting person." I brush my thumb back and forth over her bare shoulder. "You look for the best in people, always. That's a strength, not a weakness. It's telling of the person *she* is, not you, she manipulated your strength to gather that information from you."

"I feel stupid," she whispers.

"You're not stupid, Willow," I rasp, grasping her chin and tilting her head toward me. "You're never stupid for leading with your heart. It is one of the qualities I adore most about you."

She blinks, tears shimmering in her wide, ocean eyes, pert

red nose scrunching when she sniffles, pouty lips glistening when her tongue drags over them.

The devastation on her face now could kill me. I swipe my thumb over her cheek, wiping the moisture away, astonished by her beauty, even when she's washed in pain.

"How do I stop myself from getting hurt?" she asks.

"None of us are exempt from pain," I murmur, smiling gently. "Choosing to remain yourself, to keep that beautiful heart on your sleeve, is a show of courage, Willow. If you do that, you'll persevere those who harm you, every single time."

"How did you get so wise?" she murmurs, dropping her head against my chest. "You're like twenty."

"Lived through a lot of shit. I have the soul of a very old man." I snort, shrugging. "You'll learn with each mistake and every heartache. You'll know when to trust, when to show that heart on your sleeve, and you'll recognize those who are undeserving of it. Until then, I'll do my best to protect you too, okay?"

Her fingers flex over my ribcage, drawing me in closer as she nods against my body. I kiss the top of her head, running my fingers through her hair, hoping every touch is as soothing as I intend it to be. I've never craved companionship the way I do with Willow—it's all new to me, driven by instinct. It wasn't until knowing her that I began to understand how comforting the touch of another person can be. It's all I can do to try and give the same feeling back to her.

"Do you want to talk about it, love?" I ask gently. "What you said to her? What she said back?"

She's quiet for a moment, body tensing in my arms, as if she's contemplating her response. After a minute, she untangles herself from my body, and my soul goes cold at the absence. She sits up in my bed, wiping her eyes as she tucks her legs beneath her.

"Honestly, Wes . . ." She breathes heavily, voice trembling. "What she said wasn't kind, and I . . . I cannot risk you having the same reaction right now." Her tone cracks, and my heart breaks with it. "It's . . . I'm . . ." She sighs, as if lost for words. "I still have a lot of things I need to make sense of, and it's hard to explain, and—"

"You don't have to, Wills," I cut her off. "I'm confident there is nothing you could do or think or say or feel that would cause me to make you feel the kind of pain you're experiencing now, but I also know your trust is something I need to earn. Some wounds cut deep enough that no amount of bandaging is going to stop the bleed." I sit up, matching her position, grasping her face and forcing her to face the conviction in my eyes. "I'm not just a bandage, but I know that's something you need to be shown. I know it, because I need to see it too. You don't owe me your truth right now, but I'm still going to hold you until you're no longer bleeding out."

I can't blame Willow for holding onto secrets—to a past she weathered alone before she knew me. I'm doing the same to her. There is plenty I haven't told her about, so much I struggle to say aloud. I'd never hold that against her, it would never stop me from soothing her wounds or being the safe place for her to land, because the truth is, no matter how dark Willow thinks her past is—mine is darker. No matter how dark Willow thinks her past is, she's still my light.

Her brows draw together, astonishment overtaking her beautiful face. She shakes her head, lips parting and closing several times, before she finally decides there's nothing left to say, grabbing my jaw and drawing my mouth to hers.

She kisses me thoroughly, as if everything she doesn't know how to say is communicated through the soft brush of her mouth over mine. I groan, savoring the taste of her tongue and heat of her breath. Kissing Willow is a soul-deep experience, an all-consuming sensation—gratitude and grace. Care and comfort. Longing and lust.

"I think you're healing me, Weston," she whispers against my lips, and I'm not sure a more beautiful sentence has ever been uttered.

"You're healing me too, Wills." I kiss her again. "Can I cook dinner for you?"

Willow pulls back, her eyes still tear-stained, but they sparkle playfully with her smile. "Really?"

"Yeah." I shrug. "I'm good in the kitchen, and I think you could use a comfort meal right now."

"You really were written by a woman."

My lips quirk. "What does that even mean?"

"You should read those books you bought and figure it out." She winks, stepping off my bed and sauntering out of the room.

"I'll be starting right away," I say, following her into the kitchen. "How about I get you fed, showered, and then you can tab your favorite chapters for me like you promised before we go to sleep?"

She opens the fridge, raising a brow at me over the door. "Asking me to spend the night, Wes?"

"Unashamedly so." I grin.

"We'll see how good this meal is first." She bends down, rummaging through the shelves despite having no idea what I plan on making.

"Great. Grab the heavy cream, bone broth, cheddar cheese, and bread in there while you're at it," I say as I gather the tomatoes, onion, basil, and olive oil from the counter. Opening the spice cupboard, I take out oregano, salt, pepper, and red chili flakes.

She spins a moment later, hands full of the items I requested. "Who the hell keeps bread in the fridge?"

"People who don't like mold." I wink. "Now sit that ass on the counter and look pretty for me while I make you dinner."

"Yes, sir." She mock-salutes as she drops the ingredients on the counter. "What are you making?"

"I told you—comfort food. Tomato soup and grilled cheese."

"From *scratch*?"

"Yes, baby." I laugh. "From scratch."

"Wow," she breathes, unwrapping the cheese and nibbling straight from the block. "I'm a lucky gal. Your mom taught you to cook, right?"

"Yeah." I smile to myself, pulling out a baking sheet before cutting the tomatoes into cubes. "She worked for a cancer treatment center and ran the onsite restaurant for patient housing." Willow tilts her head, brows softening in perplexity. "It's where the families of the patients live during treatment. It's a nonprofit, so the families don't pay anything. Meals are included, and they deliver to the housing units, but also have a restaurant to maintain a sense of normalcy for the families."

"That's incredible," she whispers.

"Yeah." I nod, swallowing. "My mom ran operations, but she started as a line cook when she was a teenager. She worked there for fifteen years—until she passed." I clear the burn of emotion from my throat. "Anyway, we didn't have a lot of money, so she had to get creative at home. Using simple ingredients to make good meals. She taught me to cook. She thought it was an important skill for me to have."

"She sounds amazing, Wes. I mean . . . she must've been. Look at you."

I raise my head, meeting her gaze. "I just don't want it to have been for nothing, you know? Losing her, I mean. I want to be someone she would've been proud to have raised, because I think that would have helped her feel like her life, though short, wasn't wasted. I failed those first few years, but . . ." I want to say I'm doing better now, but sometimes I'm not sure.

"You didn't fail her. I don't think she would've ever seen you as a failure," Willow whispers.

"I have a criminal record and spent almost two years in a cell."

"I'm not saying she would've encouraged your actions, but I have no doubt she would've understood them. You were fighting for her."

I drop my head in shame. While Willow may be right—I was fighting for my mother—she doesn't know the full range of my intentions. The initial impact may have been without premeditation and driven on emotion, but it only took seconds for the realization of what I was doing to set in, and only I know how far I would've gone had I not been pulled off him.

"And her life wasn't wasted, Wes," Willow continues, reaching across the counter and grasping my shirt. I drop my knife to the cutting board, allowing her to drag me between her legs. "She made you, and you are *wonderful*." She kisses my nose, and I brace my arms against the counter on either side of her hips, leaning into her warmth. "But beside being a mother, raising the most tender and kind man I've ever known, she sounds like *she* was wonderful too. Talented and driven and doing amazing things in her community. She lived a life to be proud of, and I'm sorry it was robbed from her the way it was, but it wasn't wasted."

"You speak of her as if you know her," I whisper, voice cracking.

"I know you. Makes me feel like I know her a little too, I guess."

My nose stings, throat heavy, breath shallow as I rasp, "It's nice to have someone else in the world who knows her. Someone I can share her with."

Willow's eyes are misty, and she blinks hard, clearing emotion of her own. "I'd be honored if you shared her with me."

She kisses me softly, and I want so badly to disclose all my truths to Willow Graham. To split myself open and reveal every dark burden that haunts me in the middle of night. Every detail of the day I almost killed my own father, and the turn my life took after. I've never shared those deep pits of my mind with anyone, but for the first time, I feel I may have found the one who could understand. See me past the darkness, shroud me in all her light.

For the first time in my life, I feel like I could be light for someone else too.

The oven chimes, indicating it's pre-heated, breaking our moment. I decide today isn't the day, and now isn't the time, because Willow is finally looking at me like she'd rather smile than cry—such a contrast to how hurt she appeared earlier. I want to give her the comfort and calm she's craving right now. My baggage can wait.

"I've got to roast these vegetables for about forty-five minutes," I say, stepping back to the baking sheet I've laid the tomatoes, garlic cloves, and onion on. I drizzle with olive oil and sprinkle the spices over the sheet before popping them in the oven.

"Do you want to watch the sunset while we wait?" she asks. "It looks like a good one tonight."

"I'd love that, Wills." I smile.

I lift her off the counter, keeping her hand in mine as I lead her toward the door. When I step outside, I sink into one of the rocking chairs on the porch, and Willow lowers herself into my lap. Resting her head against my shoulder, I wrap my arm around her hip, gripping her thigh.

We watch the sun sink into the Pacific, a peaceful silence blanketing us. The sway of palms, the call of seagulls, and the distant crash of waves the soundtrack to our evening. It's a quiet comfort I'm not used to, but wouldn't mind spending the rest of my life wrapped inside with her.

After the world fades from light to dark, we head back inside, and I finish making dinner. We talk more about my mother—her favorite recipes and which of them I make best. Willow tells me about the schools she's applied to, and my chest soars when I realize every single one of them is within an hour drive of here. Even when the summer ends and I return to Santa Monica, she won't be far from me. Close enough for a weekend trip or a late-night drive.

After we clean the kitchen and take showers—separately, because both of us are garnering all of our strength to take this slowly, though the way she looks in nothing but one of my tees makes me weak in the legs—I crawl into bed beside her, asking, "Have you thought anymore about finding a therapist?"

She turns onto her side, raising a brow at me. "Have *you*?"

"Hey." I nip her nose playfully. "Don't snipe at me. I'm not judging you. Ever. Just asking . . . because yeah, I think I'm going to start searching again. I think it might be time for me to go back."

"Really?"

I nod, settling in beside her. "I stopped going because I wasn't seeing any hope for myself—I couldn't see the point. Now, I think it could help *us*. Whatever future we may have together, I want to be the best version of myself for it—for you. So . . . I'm going to start looking again."

Her bottom lip trembles as she takes it between her teeth. "I want to be the best version of myself for you too, Wes. I don't know if I'm ready to sort through . . . everything yet." She cups my face, smiling softly. "But I can promise I'll be open, and that I'll keep doing my best for us, and whatever that future looks like."

I kiss her palm before snaking my arm over her shoulder and tugging her against me, tangling us together. I won't push the conversation further—I know firsthand how important it is to go at your own pace when it comes to addressing trauma.

Admitting to the future I see with her was fucking terrifying, but the confirmation that she sees one too made my heart beat at a rhythm that should be studied by cardiologists, because this woman might be killing me slowly, and fuck, I'm going to enjoy every second of it.

If I thought I was falling for Willow Graham before, I was dead wrong. I never fell, I fucking leaped, and her body against mine right now feels like a soft landing among clouds.

We settle into bed, and I watch her with rapt allure as she sorts through the books I bought, speaking animatedly of her favorite moments as she sticks color-coded tabs on the pages.

Eventually, she falls asleep against my shoulder, and I reach over to flick off the lamp on her side of the bed. *Her side of the bed.*

The sound of her breathing lulls me to sleep.

WILLOW'S STILL ASLEEP when my alarm chimes, faint daylight peeking through the window behind my bed. I silence it quickly, moving softly so as not to disturb her. I keep the lights off, stumbling through darkness into the bathroom and my closet as I get ready for training.

I take the notepad from my bedside table and scribble down a message for her before sneaking out of the house.

You snore like a chainsaw.

Look real pretty when you do it, though.

— Wes

I'm grinning like a fool as I mosey down to the beach, feeling rested and well-prepared to train today. When I surf now, all I hear is Willow's laugh bouncing off the waves. A gentle encouragement, a reminder that someone out there is always rooting for me, no matter the circumstance.

Her father claims it's dedication, structured training, and a range of environment that's resulted in the improvement I've had over the last month, but I know it's her.

She makes me better—a better athlete, a better man. I want to repay her for it tenfold. I want to remind her that I support her dreams as intensely as she does mine.

I shoot Penelope a text as I shuffle down the stairs that lead to the beach.

Can I use your classroom after you finish your lecture today?

It's a surprise for Willow.

Penelope

As long as it doesn't involve any naked body parts on any of my desks, yes.

Scout's honor.

I reach the sand before Leo, completing a series of stretches while I wait for him to arrive. As I move through my flow, my mind reels with ideas as a plan begins to form. I'm practically vibrating with excitement when he shows up, asking far too enthusiastically, "What are Willow's favorite flowers?"

He frowns, crossing his arms. "Awfully focused this morning, are we?"

"You'll have my undivided attention as soon as you answer."

"Sunflowers." He rolls his eyes, but his lips twitch upward. "Because they follow the sun. They're always drawn to light. She loved that fact when she was a little girl."

"That sounds like something she'd love." I smile. "Do you think it would be possible for me to take the afternoon off from Heathen's?"

"I suppose," Leo drawls, raising a brow slowly. "What for?"

"Was gonna drive over to Golden State and see Penelope. She's teaching her lecture there today." I rock back and forth on my heels.

"The same lecture my daughter assists?"

"Oh, is that . . ." I cough a laugh, rubbing the back of my neck. "I completely forgot she'd be there."

"I'm sure." He deadpans. "Impress me today, and we'll see."

Hours later, I'm panting, dripping with saltwater, and high off one of the best training sessions of the summer, smiling like a goddamn fool as I wade out of the waves beside Leo. The swell is choppy today, the conditions less than ideal, and yet I performed damn near flawlessly.

"So..." I plop my board into the stand, tilting my head at Leo as a shit-eating grin splits my face. "How about that afternoon off?"

He scoffs, rolling his eyes, though I don't miss the twitch of his lips. "I suppose I could find someone to cover for you, but—"

A chiming erupts from the bag at my feet where we keep our phones and towels. I squat to check, and find it's my phone ringing with a number I don't recognize, and several previously missed calls from the same number. When I silence it, Leo asks, "Who is it?"

"Dunno." I shrug. "No ID."

He nods toward my screen, jaw hard set and strained. "Answer it."

His tone leaves no room for question, so I swipe my thumb across the screen and raise my phone to my ear. "Hello?"

"Is this Weston?" The voice on the other side of the line is deep and stern.

"Yeah? Who's this?"

"Are you dating Willow Graham?"

I glance at Leo before muting myself. "He asked if I'm dating Willow."

Leo puts his hands on his hips, raising his head toward the sky as he lets out a long sigh. "Fuck."

I unmute myself. "Why don't you tell me who I'm talking to and maybe I'll answer your question."

"Speaker," Leo barks, and I tap the speaker phone button.

"Is that Daddy?" The rough laugh echoed on the other side grates every nerve ending in my body. "He know that his daughter is fucking a criminal? Attempted murder, if the article I read from after you were stripped of your title is correct."

Shame mists over me, and I flick my gaze away from Leo. Of course, he knows everything. He accepted me and my past, but that was before I got involved with his daughter, and the truth of who I am—who I come from—is a sucker punch for both of us, I'm sure.

"Fuck you," I grit, masking the humiliation in my voice with rage.

He laughs again. "I guess I shouldn't be surprised, though. Really, Weston, I'm a friend. I'm offering you a warning, man. You should be aware of the kinda girl you're with now. Did you know she—"

"Parker," Leo snaps, ripping the phone from my hand. I stumble back, feeling helpless as I watch him bring my phone to his mouth. "I thought I told you to stay the fuck away from us?"

I don't know the right way to respond to this situation, and it almost feels as if my incompetence radiates off me, catching onto Leo's frustrations.

Parker scoffs, and there is a long, silent pause before the lines goes dead. Leo's jaw is clenched, chin quivering as he raises his eyes to mine—they're aflame with rage. The way they flare when he studies my face tells me I'm giving off a similar expression.

"We need to tell Willow this is happening."

Leo inhales deeply, eyes falling shut as he hands my phone back to me. He runs a hand down his face, but nods. "Just . . . I need to talk to a friend of mine at the police department and figure out what our options are. Please wait until I have plan, all right?"

I chew on my cheek. "I don't feel right about keeping this from her."

"You think I do?" He throws his hands up. "I'm at a fucking loss here, Weston. I need some time to figure out a plan, because I can't sit my daughter down and tell her he's doing this when I'm fucking helpless to fix it!"

Nodding, I swallow. "You're right. I'll . . ." I have no idea how to fix this, either. If Parker were standing in front of me right now, I'd fucking pummel him. I know well that the only resources I have against men like that are my fists. I can't offer Willow much protection outside of that, but Leo has connections. He has money and status. He can do something to make Parker leave her alone for good, and I need to give him the chance to set something in place.

It'll be better for Willow in the long run.

"You know what he said wasn't true, right?" Leo asks, tone softer now than before. He gently places a hand on my shoulder as he guides us toward the stairs that lead back to the main house. "I don't think that way of you, and neither does Willow."

Yet, I can't help but think that way of myself.

"Factually, he's not wrong. I was charged with attempted murder and stripped of my title. That information is floating around in the world for anyone to find." Information—a reputation—that will undoubtedly affect Willow just because she's choosing to be with me, and that guilt slices deep.

"You think nobody ever unearthed my mistakes, my past, and printed them too?" Leo pauses halfway up the cliff, glancing back at me with quirked lips. "Comes with the territory when you're the best of the best at something. Those who could never live up to your achievements in their wildest dreams will always look for ways to bring you down to their level, so they can feel more secure about themselves. You gotta learn to block out the noise. You've got to stop letting your history define who you are today, and who you want to become tomorrow."

I nod, wordlessly following him back to the garage so we can return our boards.

"With all that being said," Leo continues, holding the door open for me. "I think it would be in Willow's best interest that nothing about your . . . relations be public until this shit with Parker is resolved for good. I'd prefer you hold off on posting about each other online. Even with Parker being blocked, he's clearly still finding ways to dig up whatever information he can to use against her, and unfortunately, you're not exempt from that."

I chew on my lip, stripping out of my wetsuit. I hadn't thought too deeply about where our relationship stands publicly until this moment. She hadn't seemed eager to post any photos of us online, and while it's possible I could be interviewed after the Challenger this weekend, it's not often that athletes are questioned about their relationship status. Though, if I ever were to be asked, I probably would've bragged about Willow.

"I understand," I murmur as I place my board on the rack and Leo's on the wax bench.

"Please let me know if you hear from him again," he says sternly as he heads toward the exit of the garage while I get busy sorting through the duffle bag we keep the waxing kits in. "And go ahead and take the afternoon off. I'll handle the surf shop."

"I will," I promise. "And thank you."

His footsteps shuffle over the cement floor as he moves to leave.

"Leo," I call back after him. "Let me know if there is something I can do to help. Please. Give me a chance to show you I can take care of her." I can't stop Willow from having a shitty ex, and I can't take back the mistakes of my past or the toxic blood that runs through my veins, but I can fight like hell to ensure that she remains as untouched by as much of that darkness as possible.

He looks at me over his shoulder, offering a shallow dip of his chin before he wordlessly stalks away.

CHAPTER TWENTY-FIVE

WILLOW

"WILLOW, WOULD YOU mind staying a little later this afternoon to help me organize some files?" Penelope asks, digging through her desk as students begin shuffling in for her lecture.

"Sure. How long?"

She perks up, green eyes whipping to meet my gaze. "Uh . . . not sure yet. Do you have plans?"

"No." I shrug. "Just curious."

I miss Weston is what I want to say, but that seems ridiculously needy, so I keep my mouth shut. Plus, Wes works until seven, and I can't imagine Penelope keeping me here past then.

"I'm presenting that PowerPoint you made last week. If you can manage the slides while I'm speaking, that would be amazing," she chimes, gathering a clipboard from inside her desk and walking toward the podium at the front of the room.

I take a seat in her desk chair, mirror her desktop to the large screen at the front of class, and place the document in presentation mode. The moment Penelope flicks off the lights, the entire room goes silent. Students settle into their seats, eager for every word that leaves her mouth—just as I am.

Today she's lecturing on how Pompeii influenced the way modern archeologists understand ancient art, since the ash from the eruption of Mt. Vesuvius preserved so much of Pompeii that, when uncovered thousands of years later, much of the architecture and art was nearly untouched.

The PowerPoint showcases photos from a summer that Penelope spent in Italy with a research group, analyzing mosaics recovered from Pompeii. Images of her at the still-active dig sites—taken by Carter, no doubt—are accompanied by photos of her in the lab, restoring the pieces they discovered in the field. As she describes the experience, she talks through her theories on what each piece of art represented at its time, who may have created it, and where it could've belonged.

I'm so enthralled by her speech that by the time she finishes, I'm practically buzzing to get back to school full-time. Penelope's focus is set on archaeology, and the way art shapes human history, while mine is on how art shapes the human soul. Though, the foundation of both is similar—the interpretation of art and how the same piece can be seen and studied in endless ways, for eternity. I want to channel creativity like that into something that soothes people, multitudes of healing they can carry, repurpose, and reevaluate throughout the duration of their life.

As the class comes to a close and students filter out the door, I shut down the presentation and click off Penelope's monitor. "That was incredible. I never knew you spent time in Pompeii like that."

"It was a crazy time." She smiles to herself, packing her things into her briefcase. "The first few years Carter and I were together—while I was in the full-time graduate program at UCLA—we were both constantly on the go. He came with me as much as he could, developing his contracts around my travel, but it was a tumultuous time. I wouldn't have wanted to do it with anyone else, though." She checks a notification on her phone before tossing it into her bag and lifting her gaze to me. "Oh, I forgot something I printed and need to take home with me. It's in the copy room upstairs. Can you go check?"

"Sure." I meander out of the lecture hall and up to the second floor where the copy room is located. After spending what feels like half an hour searching every printer, counter space, trash can, and crevice of the room, I can't find any document that appears to be left by Penelope—and she doesn't answer her phone when I call.

Defeated, I return to the room to let her know I couldn't find what she's looking for, but I'm struck speechless when I push open the classroom door and find the room dimmed, lit only by dozens of flickering faux candles.

My breath catches in my throat as I freeze—Weston is leaned back against Penelope's desk, bracing his arms against the wood with his legs crossed at the ankles. He smiles at me when his eyes greedily soak in my body—my reaction.

He looks delectable in a pair of dark-wash jeans, sneakers, and a black tee that hugs his biceps. His dark hair is mussed, like he'd been running his hands through it.

It's a struggle to pull my gaze from him, but as I glance around the room, I take note of more than just the candles. There is a blanket laid out in the center of the room with a basket at its center, and in the corner are two easels set up with blank canvases, and paint littered atop a table beside them.

"What's this?" I ask.

He smirks. "Thought we could paint together."

A giggle bursts from my throat, and I clamp a hand over it, dumbfounded. I can't respond, can't move. I only stare at him in awe. No one I've dated has ever expressed interest in painting with me before, let alone gone to such lengths to make it happen.

I have a whole room upstairs in my parents' house filled with art supplies. We could've easily painted there together, and it would've required very little effort on Weston's part, but he did all of this.

"None of that." He tsks. "If I make you laugh, I want to see your pretty face light up." He presses off Penelope's desk, bounding up the stairs that lead toward the top of the lecture hall, extending his arm when he reaches me.

I remove my hand from my mouth, taking his as he leads me to the front of the room. "I don't know what to say," I whisper.

"You don't have to say anything, Wills, but I hope you like it."

"I love it," I say on an astonished breath. "This is . . ." I'm at a loss for words, blurting the only question that comes to mind. "Where is Penelope?"

He laughs. "She helped me set up and then she left. We'll lock up behind ourselves." When we reach the blanket on the floor, Weston motions for me to sit. He plops down across from me, crossing his legs and pulling the basket in front of him, flipping it open. "Figured we can eat first, and then you'll teach me how to paint something, I'll do a terrible job, but you'll lie and say it's great." He bites his lip, grinning when I laugh. "And if I'm lucky, maybe you'll kiss me a little when we're done."

"You don't have to do all this for me to kiss you, Wes." I shake my head, laughing again. "I'm probably more desperate for it than you are at this point."

"I like to earn it." He winks, pulling two wrapped sandwiches out of the basket and handing one to me. "Italian grinder—no tomato. Your mom said they're your favorite."

He asked my mom about my favorite sandwiches.

He then takes out two Tupperware containers, popping the lids. "I made a cucumber watermelon salad and roasted sweet potatoes. I also brought dill pickle spears because Darby mentioned you like those with sandwiches. And . . ." He reaches behind himself, drags a backpack from underneath the table, and unzips it before reaching inside. "Your dad said these were your favorite too. Asked your mom about the sandwiches when I picked them up from her."

He sets a wrapped bouquet of sunflowers between us.

He asked my dad about my favorite flowers.

"Wes, my God," I gasp, gathering them into my hands. "They're beautiful."

"He said they follow the sun, so I imagine they'll always be pointing in your direction."

I lift my eyes, his hopeful gaze clashing with my astounded one. Gently placing the flowers on the blanket beside me, I crawl over him, throwing my arms around his neck and forcing him flat on his back as I align our bodies and press my lips to his.

"Nobody has ever done something like this for me," I whisper between the kisses I pepper across his cheeks and jaw.

I feel the movement of his throat beneath my mouth as he whispers back, "Nobody has ever made me feel the way you do."

I raise my head so I can peer down at him. Raw conviction shimmers in his eyes as they study mine. He slowly raises a hand to my face, tucking loose hair behind my ear. I drop my mouth to his again, feathering my lips between his. He deepens the kiss, grasping my hip and rolling me against him, removing any semblance of space between us. I moan, and he takes advantage, slipping his tongue into my mouth, tangling it with mine. Unable to help it, I grind down harder, and when he follows it with a hiss, I swallow his sound.

"Fuck, Wills," he nips at my lips. "Don't make me get carried away and break Penelope's one rule, baby."

"What's the rule?" I laugh into his mouth.

"Not to get naked in here."

I snort, pulling away and sitting up, straddling his hips. "I wouldn't take your virginity on a dirty floor like this."

"Isn't that kind of a rite of passage?" He lifts onto his elbows, raising a brow.

I scoff, playfully smacking his chest as I lift off him. I toss a sandwich at him, and he catches it with one hand, smirking at me as he unwraps it. "You know I'm not sentimental about that, right?" he asks, taking a bite. "I'm a virgin because I've never had the urge before, not because of any moral value I place upon it. I'm not like . . . waiting until marriage."

I choke on a laugh, swallowing down my own bite. "I didn't think you were. Are you saying you have urges now?"

He slows his chewing, tossing me a deadpan expression. "Willow, you made me come in my pants."

I blush, dipping my head to hide the reaction.

"I have filthy, deplorable, nonsensical fucking urges when it comes to you, Trouble." His hand darts out to grasp my chin, lifting my gaze to his. "I'm a mess for you."

"What kind of urges?" I whisper.

He licks his lips, fighting a smile. "Today after training, I got off in the shower fantasizing about fucking you on a surfboard." He leans back on his elbows, shaking his head as he stares up at the ceiling. "I'm not even sure that's plausible. I'm certain it wouldn't even be possible out on the water, and yet that's exactly what I envisioned until I lost it all over the shower door."

Heat floods my veins at his admission, and I cross my legs to ease the ache he's created between my thighs. "I thought you didn't see anything, or anyone, when you . . ."

His eyes flick to mine, smoldering blue flames. "That was before I knew you. Now, Willow? I know what your skin feels like, what your mouth tastes like, what you sound like when you're coming. I don't imagine I'll see anything but you ever again."

"Fuck," I mutter. "Remind me again why we're taking things so slow?"

This man is driving me mad.

He tosses me an amused smile. "Because we've both been through a lot, and I'm terrified of fucking it up." Weston's face softens as he continues. "I know the last time for you was . . . I don't want to risk . . . I just want to make sure you're ready too."

I nod. Frustrating as it is, he's right. We both need to be absolutely ready to take that step, because I don't want to risk screwing us up either. "How about I tell you when I feel ready, and if it's before you do, I'll wait until you're ready too?"

"That sounds like a plan, Trouble." He grins, sitting up to take my face between his hands before pressing his lips to mine. "Now eat your food so we can get to painting those canvases."

"Oh . . ." I laugh, bringing my sandwich to my mouth. "We're not using those canvases, I have a much better use for all that paint."

He tilts his head, confusion overtaking his features. I flash him a mischievous smile.

"So . . . do I get to paint your body too?"

"Yes, when I'm finished," I chime. "Now roll over like I told you to."

Weston exhales a resigned sigh, tossing his shirt to the side before lying face down on the blanket. We traded our food for art supplies, and I hold a palette in one hand and a brush in the other as I straddle his hips.

"I've always wanted to do this," I say, swiping the brush through the blue dollop of paint on my palette.

I saw the trend—painting someone's bare back—online years ago, but Parker refused to try it with me. When I asked Weston if he would take his shirt off and let me paint his skin instead of the canvas he brought, he didn't even question it.

Inspired by Penelope's presentation earlier, I use an angle brush to begin crafting small squares starting at Weston's hip and working up toward his spine.

"I got some news today." I smile, swirling blue and green to create a new shade.

"What's that?" Wes asks sleepily.

"I was accepted to UC Irvine." The giddiness in my tone apparent. "I'm still waiting to hear from a few other universities, but Lou and Liv own a house in Costa Mesa, and they'll be spending the second half of the year in Central America with Liv's family, so they offered to let me stay there while they're gone. I can't imagine how I'd choose any other school."

"Willow that's—" He begins to turn over, but I grip his shoulder.

"Don't fuck up my paint!"

He pauses, craning his neck toward me. "I'm trying to look you in the eye when I tell you how incredible I find you, dammit!" he mock-growls, before bursting into a chuckle. "Willow, that is amazing. I'm so happy for you."

Pride ricochets off the walls of my chest. "Thank you."

"I plan on heading back to Santa Monica after the summer, so I won't be horribly far from you." His body shakes with laughter, nearly causing me to smear the mosaic wave that's forming over his spine. "I'll finally be convinced to get my truck tuned up enough to make the drive back and forth."

"First of all, didn't you drive here?" I muse. "Second, why would you go back to Santa Monica? You're not going to keep working with my dad?"

"Dunno," he says, the sound muffled into the blanket. "The agreement was only for the summer, but I imagine as I compete more, I'll need to be out on the real breaks. The cove is less ideal for competitive strategy."

I hum in contemplation, but Wes goes on, "Liv said she has some connections closer to L.A. that she's going to introduce to me to. And," he continues, "I did drive here, but there is no promise my truck is going to start up again when we leave, so I may be hitching a ride home."

"Okay," I drawl. "But I control the music."

"Of course, Wills. Whatever you want. It's your night, baby."

I want to be yours. Irrevocably.

"You know, nobody has ever done this for me before. Gone to such lengths to . . . What was the purpose of all this?" I wave my brush around, referencing the candlelit room, homemade meal, and idealistic art-date setup, though Weston can't see the motion.

"To make you smile."

I *audibly* swoon. "Nobody has ever gone to such lengths to make me smile."

Weston turns over this time, lifting himself and rolling beneath me, bracing on his forearms before his skin can touch the ground—so I don't disturb the paint. I rock backward with the movement of his hips, nearly tumbling off him before I curl an arm around his neck, drawing us together.

"I'm sorry you've never been seen the way you deserve, Willow. I wish I had an explanation for it, but honestly, I'm completely dumbfounded. All I can drum up is that most men are fucking stupid, perhaps myself included . . ." He cups my jaw, raw fervor in his eyes. "But I won't be stupid about you. I see you, and I'll never let you forget that."

A twinge of guilt pinches my nerves when I remember the secret I'm keeping from him. Weston deserves to know about the decision I made earlier this summer, and eventually, the further and deeper we fall, I'm going to have to tell him. It's an effort to remind myself that I have the freedom to navigate this on my own timeline, that Weston promised he'd give me the space to heal, to re-open my wounds and share my past at the pace I need.

I remind myself that I promised him the same, that he's still keeping things from me too.

That's why we're moving slowly. We're creating a foundation, bearing our souls little-by-little, until nothing is left unsaid and untouched, and we'll be stronger for it.

"Maybe the boys before were stupid, and there will always be things I wish never happened," I whisper, hand grazing his jaw, thumb dancing over his bottom lip. "But I'm grateful that it brought me you."

"It's like you stole the thought directly from my head."

His smile spreads beneath my skin, and he lifts his chin, forcing my hand to drop as he surges forward to replace my touch with my lips.

CHAPTER TWENTY-SIX

WESTON

"WESTON." HER VOICE floats through my subconscious like a siren song—ethereal and unearthly in a way that reminds me I'm surely dreaming. "Weston," she continues, her soft laugh like liquid warmth, curling around me in a gentle embrace. "Wake up, Wes."

I'm snapped into consciousness when there is a light pressure on my shoulder, and I groan as I slowly force my eyes open.

My blurred vision clears as I blink, and in the near-darkness, I make out Willow's silhouette above me. Golden hair frames her face like a halo as she peers down at me from where she straddles my waist.

I am absolutely still dreaming.

"Good morning," she coos, planting a hand at the center of my chest, settling her body atop mine.

My cock is hard enough to throb, and it's aligned perfectly with the center of her thighs. "Yep," I groan. "Definitely dreaming."

She laughs again, the sound a melody to my lust. I pulse, and she folds forward, her hair tickling my cheeks as she presses her lips to mine. "Not dreaming, but it is time to wake up."

"I'm up," I grumble, wiping a hand down my face.

Willow's been sleeping at home, stating she's determined I get plenty of rest this week leading up to my competition. Little does she know, I sleep much better with her beside me. She must've snuck into the house this morning to wake me before the event.

"Oh, I know," she rasps. "I can feel it."

She wiggles her ass, and I grip her hip, halting her. If she moves too many times like that in a row, I'll fucking embarrass myself.

"Your fault," I mutter, nipping at her jaw.

"Hmm," she muses, rocking her body again. "It's just morning."

I pin her with both hands, rolling us over so I'm hovering above her. "No, Willow," I scold, pumping against her just once before forcing myself away. "It's all fucking you, baby."

I leap off the bed, facing Willow as she sprawls across it, propped onto an elbow, resting her face in her hand. Her eyes track my body—ravenous in the dim lit. When she reaches the base of my torso, one of her brows raises slowly, tongue darting out to lick her lips. I follow her gaze, finding that my boxers are tented by my dick, before looking at her again.

That lip slips between her teeth, nostrils flaring before she flicks her eyes to my face. "I could help with that."

My cock jumps, and a salacious smile spreads across her fuckable mouth. *Goddammit.*

"I . . . I . . ." Christ, I'm stuttering like a fucking idiot. I don't know what to say.

I can't tell her we don't have enough time, because I'll no doubt blow within thirty seconds. I want to say yes. *So bad.*

What if she's just trying to please me because she thinks it's what I want? What if it activates her trauma? What if it's too early in our relationship?

Not to mention . . . what if *I* fuck up and embarrass myself? I'm confident that no matter how she plays with it, I'll thoroughly enjoy myself, but what role do *I* have in it all?

I don't want to ask.

"Willow, you don't have—"

"Do you like to . . . release? Before competitions? Does it help with your performance?" She tilts her head, blinking at me with those sultry, curious, innocent blue eyes.

My knees buckle. "I mean . . . I don't know if . . . scientifically it helps, but yeah. When I was surfing competitively as a teen, I would normally . . . find release before."

"And you planned to do it this morning?"

"Honestly, hadn't thought about it," I say breathlessly. "Probably, though. Yeah."

She rises to her knees in the center of my bed, clad in nothing but a tiny pair of cotton shorts and a tank top that looks painted on. Her nipples are pebbled, peeking through the thin fabric, driving me in-fucking-sane.

She tilts her head, long, lush hair falling over a shoulder. "So, why don't you do it in my mouth?"

The red-hot ache in my core is begging for release. Willow is so goddamn beautiful, the intensity of her stare radiates inside my chest, turning my entire being into liquid warmth. She *looks* at me like she wants this too, like she's as desperate as I am, but I need her ready. I need to ensure that I'll never be something she regrets.

I swallow the gravel in my throat, though my voice still sounds as if it's full of rocks when I say, "Are you sure you . . . want to?"

"If I didn't want to suck your cock, Weston, I wouldn't ask."

I'm *pulsing.*

She swings her legs out from under her, slipping off my bed and lowering to her knees right in front of me. Peering up through her lashes, the personification of heavenly sin, Willow asks, "Can I make you feel good? Please?"

"Fuck," I mutter. "I think I should be the one begging."

She smirks. "You will."

No. Fucking. Doubt.

She reaches for my waistband, tugging my underwear down my thighs. As they drop to the floor and my cock springs free, I step out of them and kick them aside. Willow gulps as she runs a palm up my length, and a blaze ignites at the base of my spine.

"So big," she whispers.

"I'm not going to last long," I admit.

She exhales through a playful smile, glancing up at me as she pumps my length once. Then twice. "That's okay, baby. Just relax for me, okay?"

That fucking name.

She's ruining me.

My head kicks back as a moan works its way from my throat, morphing into a pathetic whimper as the first wet, warm glide of her tongue covers me from base to tip. My body trembles when she slips my cock into her mouth, enclosing her lips around it and hollowing out her cheeks.

Pulling away with a pop, she rasps, "Tell me if I do something you don't like, okay?"

"I cannot imagine any reality where that's possible," I say in a broken breath. "Tell me if there is something you *would like*, okay?"

"Run your fingers through my hair." She pumps me again. "Form a ponytail with your fist."

I reach down, grasping her beautiful face before sliding my fingers across her scalp, gathering her locks at the crown of her head and holding them together. "Like this?"

"Yes." She nods. "That's good. Now guide me toward you. Move me at a pace you enjoy."

Unsure how I'm even fucking standing, a quiver rips through me, and I know this is going to be a short-lived event as I bring her mouth over my cock. She drops her jaw, and it slides in effortlessly. I inch into her slowly, deep enough that I hit resistance at the back of her throat, and she sputters around me.

I halt, but when I attempt to retreat, Willow's hands fly to my hips, holding me in place. She makes a noise of protest, so I tug gently at her hair, pulling her head back before sliding it over my cock once more. She moans in approval this time.

"Fuck, Willow," I murmur. "Can I see your eyes, love?"

That transcendent gaze flutters upward, glistening with tears as I press deep into her throat. Her eyes flare, pupils blowing before her lids droop—hooded and hazed with passion.

She's fucking enjoying this.

She chokes, saliva dripping from the corners of her lips and down my length. When she swirls her tongue around my tip before sucking it toward the roof of her mouth, my vision begins to blur. White light sparks in my periphery, that blaze in my spine shattering into an all-consuming pleasure that sparks inside my veins.

"Willow." Her name tears from my throat, drenched in fierce fervency. "Willow . . . Willow . . ." I pant through heaving breaths as she works my cock, pleasure surging viciously. "I'm going to—"

She hums, clamping her lips around me tighter. My mind scatters to oblivion—to some far-off dimension where nothing but my body, her mouth, her soft hair around my fist, and the infinite expanse of pleasure she's drawn from my being exists.

Spilling into her mouth, I *feel* the way she consumes it, her throat working with a swallow as she hums around my length. I become hyperaware of the fact that I am *inside* her. I'm inside Willow's mouth, the essence of me now moving through her. I've never known a connection like this, and it's ruining me—tearing me open and piecing me back together as someone new.

Someone that belongs to her.

I realize I'm still whispering her name—a scratched record—as reality mists over me once again. Drawing whatever is left of my strength, I force my eyes open, finding hers boring through me with satisfaction as she sucks the remainder of my release from my cock before pulling back and licking her lips—revealing a triumphant smile.

I'm devastated. Obliterated. Devoid of all composure—I only stare at her. Mouth gaping, legs shaking, mind reeling.

She stands, grinning as she places her hands on my shoulder, guiding me to sit at the edge of the bed. Bringing her face to mine, she kisses me softly—the lingering taste of my climax still on her lips. As if I'd claimed her, or maybe she claimed me. We claimed each other, and the taste is addictive.

"You seem like you need a minute," she murmurs against my lips before pulling back, winking. "I'll go make us some coffee. We need to meet my dad at the big house in about an hour."

"I'm sorry," I sputter. "I . . . I can't even remember my own name right now, honestly."

She saunters toward my bedroom door, smirking over her shoulder. "Sure remembered mine. You moaned it about a million times."

Fuck me.

My body is satiated and boneless, but my mind is far from satisfied. I need the claiming between us to expand beyond my release—I want to taste her too.

I spring from bed, checking the clock to ensure Willow was right and we have plenty of time, before I tug on a pair of sweatpants and stalk into the kitchen. Her back is turned to me, a warm glow illuminates the space from a lamp she flicked on in the living room. Willow sways her hips to some tune she's humming as she presses start on the espresso maker—the picture of perfection. The sight I'd very much like to wake to every morning for the rest of my life.

I grasp her hips, hauling her backward and spinning her in my arms. She shrieks with laughter as I grip beneath her arms and lift her, setting her on the counter and stepping between her legs. Her eyes widen, a baffled grin spreading over her cheeks. She must clock the seriousness on my face though, because her features morph into bemused curiosity when she tilts her head, honeyed hair swaying with the movement.

It's still dark outside, only the faint crest of indigo sky peeking through the window on the front door, but it's enough to brighten her beautiful face. Mixed with the warm light in the room, she's shrouded in gold. She's the definition of golden, in fact.

Her swollen lips purse, parting on a questioned whisper of my name, "Wes—"

"I want my turn now."

"Oh." Her eyes flare, mouth popping open with the word.

"You really don't have to do that. It wasn't a tit for tat kind of thing."

"I'm aware." I press a kiss to her nose. "The thing is . . ." I drag my lips down to her jaw, pressing our bodies closer as I run my tongue down the column of her throat, earning a gasp from her. "I'm starving, love." I peer upward, mouth on her chest, her heart drumming against me. "I'm in desperate need to taste you too."

When Willow darts her gaze away, a rush of defeat funnels through me. I thought I was doing a fairly good job of being seductive here, but when Willow sighs deeply, rearing back from me and closing her arms around her middle, caging herself in, I know something is wrong.

"What has you so hesitant, baby?" I ask, not stepping away from her entirely, but retreating enough to allow her to breathe.

"Nobody has touched—seen—me . . ." She bites her lip, eyes cast downward. "Since, um . . . Since Parker, and he had . . . thoughts about my body. I've never been insecure about what I look like, and for the most part, I could shake off his comments, but when he'd speak of the pieces of me that only he was looking at . . . I don't know. They hit harder, I guess. It wasn't as if I could go to Allie or my parents for reassurance, it wasn't as if I had many other opinions to compare it to. Those things he said about me are kind of the only thing I see about myself now." Her gaze flutters up, so timid and unsure. So unlike her it shreds me to my core. "I'm afraid you'll feel the same way."

I'm fucking gutted.

Annihilated by the broken look on her face, the fractured tone in her voice.

"That's why I have trouble . . ." she continues, exhaling heavily. "It's just hard to touch or look at myself without remembering what he said—what he saw when he looked at me there. It's hard to imagine anyone else seeing me differently."

"That day in the shower . . . you were . . ."

She snorts. "I was feeling bold. Plus, I knew you likely weren't going to touch me that way. I knew I wasn't going to be spread-eagle and directly at your eye line."

A soft laugh escapes me, and I tilt her head up. "Willow, baby. I'm so sorry some insecure, limp-dick piece of shit made you feel otherwise, but you are fucking perfect." I kiss her lightly, she leans into my touch. "I'm a patient man, I know it'll take time for you to forget his words. Luckily for you, I'm also a determined man, and right now, I'm pretty fucking determined to replace memories of him with memories of me instead."

She moans, head kicking back as I glide my lips down her neck again, continuing my pursuit of her body. "Move slow."

"You set the pace, Wills," I rasp against her flesh. "You need me to stop, just say that word, okay?"

She nods, and I inch my fingers beneath the hem of her shorts, crawling toward the center of her thighs. She whimpers when I reach the crease of her thigh and my hand makes contact with her panties.

"This okay?" I ask, nipping at the neckline of her tank.

She nods, hips bucking. Using my teeth and my free hand, I pull down her top, exposing her breasts. I palm one, and she arches into the touch as I slip a finger beneath her underwear.

The last thing I wanted when Willow and I reached this point was to be unable to please her the way she deserved, so I'd researched a few diagrams of the female body and its erogenous zones. I've been reading her romance books too, so I know that the stimulation of the clit is essential.

When I slip my finger along her slit, I feel her bud roll under the pad of it. The deep exhale she lets out confirms everything her books have been saying. I move in small, rhythmic circles, keeping a solid pace and not adding too much pressure.

"Is this good, Wills? Tell me if it's not."

"Good." She pants, moving her hips in sync with me. "So good."

I continue stroking her as I swipe my tongue across her breast, taking one of her peaked nipples into my mouth and flicking it. The sound she elicits soaks into my bones, spurring me further.

I continue my pursual of her chest as my finger slips

downward, teasing her center. "How about this? Can I go inside? I'm desperate to know what you feel like."

A needy whine falls from her lips, and she nods rapidly.

I curl my finger inside her, just to the knuckle. My cock springs to attention when she clenches around me. She's soft and warm and . . . "So fucking wet."

"Hmm." She hums in response, lifting her hips to force me deeper.

"Fucking tight too, Willow. A perfect little pussy."

"Wes," she cries as I press my palm against her clit.

She thrusts against my arm, head thrown back, eyes closed, breath stuttered as she chases pleasure. She's so fucking beautiful like this—unraveling just for me.

"Will you let me taste it, Wills?"

Her eyes snap open, lust-laced gaze landing on me. "Are . . . Are you sure?"

I pull out of her and drop to my knees. I grip the waistband of her shorts in both hands, peering up at her. She nods shallowly, lifting her hips to help me slip her clothing off, tossing it to the floor behind me. Her thighs tremble against my palms as I spread her wide. Willow bites her lip, and a blush crawls up her neck.

My gaze darts to the center of her thighs, and just as I imagined, her pink pussy is perfect. I'm fucking salivating at the sight—gleaming with her arousal.

"You are beyond words, Willow," I rasp, breathless—thoroughly ruined. "Perfection."

Raising my eyes to hers once more, I plead, "I'm so hungry, love. Please?"

She whimpers, and all I need is her soft nod of approval before I dive between her legs.

I dip my tongue into her, desperate for the first taste. Sliding up the length of her, I blow over her clit, kissing it gently before pulling back.

"You know I'm not experienced, baby, but I'm a quick learner," I murmur against her skin. "And fuck, I'm eager to please.

I wanna be real good to you, so . . ." I reach up and grasp her wrist, dragging her hand from the counter and into my hair, she immediately grabs hold of my strands. "Guide me where you want me. Tell me if I do something wrong and *please*, tell me when I'm doing something right."

She nods, chest heaving, eyes screwed shut. I keep my gaze fixed on her face as I slowly descend, gliding my tongue through her pussy again. I move over her in long, languid strokes, noting the trembling of her each time I reach her clit, and how she tightens around my tongue when I pierce her core.

She's so wet—her arousal tastes like her skin, but headier. Deeper—more primal. Pure desire melting on my tongue. She's fucking delectable. I take back everything I've ever claimed about lacking a sweet tooth, because Willow's pussy is the sweetest thing I've ever tasted, and I'll be needing it every day for the rest of my existence.

I press deeper, burying my nose in her scent as I lap, groaning when she rocks her hips and forces me even closer. She drips into my mouth, and I swallow it hungrily—my mind reeling at the fact that it's all for me. That I've done this to her. I've never been more determined about anything in my goddamn life than I am to get Willow to this finish line.

My entire purpose is narrowed to the center of her body—to giving her every ounce of pleasure she deserves.

She groans, nearly sounding frustrated, and my cock stands to full attention when she pulls my hair—forcing my mouth over her clit again. She's taking control, demanding the rapture she's chasing, and it's the hottest fucking experience of my life.

I'll gladly oblige.

I sweep my tongue over her bud, setting a rhythm that—by the way she repeatedly moans my name while fucking herself into my face—seems to be working for her. I don't let up, even when I'm struggling to breathe. Even when her thighs tighten around my neck and begin to suffocate me.

Fuck. I'd love to die just like this.

I tease her entrance with my finger, dipping just inside. She arches into it, attempting to force me deeper as she whimpers, "Yes—*that*. Right there."

"You want me to finger-fuck you too, Wills?" I ask, grinning up at her.

She only responds with a needy mewl, bucking against me.

I slip inside her, thrusting twice before adding a second finger. Sliding deep, I hold them there, curling slightly as I begin massaging her with a beckoning motion.

"*Fuck.*" A quiver shoots through her body. "Yes. Keep going."

"Am I doing good, love?"

"So good," she whimpers.

"Give me those eyes and tell me that again."

Her head snaps down, and I see the way she struggles to open her eyes. It has my cock pulsing. If I hadn't just come, I'd be coming now. Willow could make me blow on eye contact alone, I think. Half-lidded and swimming with desire, her gaze is a shimmering display—reflective blue pools, our shared need rippling back at me.

"Good." She pants, pink lips parted. "So good, baby."

I groan deeply, the sound of it vibrating against her perfect pussy. "I'm going to make you come now, Willow."

I set a new pace with my tongue, matching my fingers, as I close my lips around her clit. We both become a mess as I suck her into my mouth with conviction, mixing my saliva with her arousal. The sound of it is obscene—purely erotic. She thrashes against my face and hand, chanting a rapid string of unintelligible words, only one ringing through the quiet house with clarity.

Weston.

Her fingers twist in my hair, tugging hard as her legs lock around my neck and she writhes against my face. I feel the very moment she breaks—her entire body goes taut before becoming boneless as she falls flat against the counter, and her release floods past my hand.

I don't stop, though. I haven't had my fill.

I slow my movements, coaxing her down from her high before removing my fingers and dragging my mouth to her entrance, lapping every last drop of her climax until her breathing becomes shallow, her moaning dims, and she presses against my forehead, pushing me away.

"Hyper," she breathes, "sensitive."

I laugh against her core before rising from my knees. Her legs hang off the counter limply as she lies on her back with an arm thrown over her eyes. The picture of flawless satiation.

I brace my arms against the marble, hovering over her. She slowly blinks one eye open, studying me intently before murmuring, "You weren't supposed to be so good at that."

"I'm a determined man, Wills."

"Achingly aware." She sighs.

"Can I tell you something?" I ask, my tone less playful than before. The way she lowers her arm, both eyes fluttering open as her brows draw together tells me she heard it too. "You are unbelievably beautiful, and that experience was far superior to anything I've ever dreamed up in my head. I know I can't erase your insecurities instantly, but I hope in time, you'll let me continue breaking them away—brick by brick. I hope, someday, you'll tell me why they exist too."

"Wes," she whispers, lifting to her elbows. Her eyes glow with hazed fervor. She opens her mouth before closing it, several times, and I realize she's at a loss for words.

So, I continue on a lighter note, "I think I've become addicted to the way your pussy tastes, Wills. I'm not sure I can live without it now. I should be able to survive on a once-per-day fix." I smirk when it pulls a smile from her. "If I have a real hankering though, I might need to double up. I know it's a little high maintenance, but if you could accommodate, I'd really appreciate—"

"Shut up." She laughs, surging forward to kiss me.

Grasping my face between her hands, Willow's lips move over mine—a delicate claim. When her tongue swipes over mine, and she exhales a soft moan into my mouth, I swallow it—imagining she's addicted to the taste of us too.

"I know there is a lot I haven't shared, and I promise I want to . . . with you," she murmurs, peppering kisses over my jaw and neck. Lifting her head to meet my gaze, she continues, "I told you—I think you're healing me, Wes, but sometimes it's slower than I wish it would be."

"Don't apologize for mending on your own timeline, Wills. I'll be right here with you the entire time, no matter how long it takes." I kiss her nose gently. "You're healing me too, and I have things I haven't shared either. We'll get there. I promise. In the meantime, I'm just enjoying the journey with you."

"Me too." Her face lights with a subtle smile—like sunrise over the Pacific. "I trust you implicitly, I hope you know that. I have trouble sharing details of that night because it hurts me to speak them aloud—not because I'm afraid to speak them to *you*."

"I know, love. I understand." I grasp her chin with one hand as the other sprawls over her back and tug her against me. Our hearts pound in sync—a current that tethers our beings. "I have memories that hurt to speak aloud too. We'll get there."

My mind drifts to my mother—the day I lost her. The aftermath. The smirk on my father's face when he realized he'd evaded consequences. My memory flashes years later, when I saw him again. The depths of rage that hummed beneath my skin, the killer instincts that bled from me that day. My life on trial, clusters of lawyers and isolation—the way I had to lie about just how badly I wanted to kill him to escape punishment myself.

Part of me wants to tell Willow I've been researching options for counseling. It's a little tricky—being in Pacific Shores now but knowing I'll return to Santa Monica at the end of the summer. I've found a few closer to Santa Monica that offer virtual sessions, so I could start while I'm still living here.

I don't know how either of us can fall completely if we don't figure out a way to disclose the depths of our pain. I think that might be the entire point of love—finding someone who helps carry it with us, who walks beside us as we mend our broken pieces, healing wounds they never caused.

More than I've ever been sure of anything, I am sure I want Willow to be that person for me.

I don't know if I believe in soulmates or fate or meant to be, but I think I might believe in earning love like that. In creating them ourselves, and each day spent with her, I'm more confident that Willow is the person I'd fight like hell to have forever.

But I know it doesn't help to pressure someone into therapy if they're not ready. It's counterproductive—drives them away from healing. So, for now, I simply smile at her before kissing her once more.

She grins against my mouth, murmuring, "We should probably get ready to go."

"Yeah," I breathe. "Fantastic wake-up call, though. I'll be requesting this service every morning."

She laughs, pulling back and landing a playful slap on my chest. She tucks a piece of hair behind her ear as she slides off the counter, cheeks flushed, eyes fluttering bashfully as she bends to pick her panties up off the floor, slipping them over her sun-kissed legs. "So, my dad and I are going with you this morning, since you need to arrive early for check-in. Everyone else will come a little later, closer to the start of the competition. Dad reserved a private tent, so we don't need to worry about finding good spots."

I cock my head. "Everyone?"

"Yeah," she says nonchalantly, continuing to redress. "Liv and Lou are driving down. So are Carter and Penelope, with Allie and her parents. Pretty sure the twins are coming. Oh, and my mom, Everett, and Dahlia." She straightens, smiling at me casually. "August and Elena won't make it. They're in Greece . . . or Turkey? Somewhere like that, but I spoke to Elena before they left on Thursday, and she told me they wish you luck."

I only blink, disbelief rushing through me. "Everyone is coming? Your entire family? To watch me?"

"Of course, Wes." She glances up at me, and my face must be giving away my shock, because hers softens. "Your parents will be there too. You'll have the loudest cheering section on the beach, and I don't even just mean by the number of people. My family loves to holler."

An amused breath filters from my lips. "I didn't think everyone would come to watch me."

Willow's lips quirk up into a wistful smile. "Well, I can't say it's the norm for us when it comes to Dad's mentees. You're just special, I guess." She brushes her lips over my jaw as she wraps her arms around my waist. "You leave a mark on people, Wes. Even if you don't notice it."

I tuck her head beneath my chin, swaying us back and forth. "I guess I assume people want to keep me at arms-length, considering my history—my rap sheet."

"Carter and Penelope stood by you, they've never given anyone any reason to believe we shouldn't do the same." Willow kisses me lightly. "Now we know you too. We see what they always have."

My gaze drops to the floor, the emotion itching my throat too strong to face her head-on. "I've been so used to isolation, it's strange to realize how alone I truly felt."

My mother, Carter, and Penelope are the only people who've ever come to watch me surf before. I expected Leo today, as my coach, and knew Carter and Penelope would drive down for it. I hoped Willow would come too. I'd never expected this much support, though.

It's an entirely new concept to me. Growing up, the only person I had in my corner was my mother. The few competitions I competed in before she died, my cheering section consisted of exactly one: her.

"Not anymore," she murmurs. "You'll be sick of us soon enough."

"I'll never be sick of you, Willow. I may be infected by you, but I'll never be sick."

"Damn." She sighs. "That was smooth."

"Mm-hmm," I murmur into her hair as she pulls herself back.

"I need to go get ready," Willow whispers, kissing me one final time. "I'll see you soon, okay?"

"Okay, love."

I lean against the countertop, head and heart floating as I watch her walk to the door. She grasps the handle, peeking over her shoulder as she pops a brow. "For real, though, how did you get so good at . . . *that*?"

"You mean making you come on my face?" I smirk.

"Yes," she hisses, rolling her eyes playfully. "If you want to be vulgar about it."

"You know that trick about spelling the ABC's with your tongue?" I bite my lip, fighting back a grin. "I just wrote my name on your pussy instead."

"Oh." The sweetest gasp puffs from her lips, and a blush creeps up her cheeks as her eyes widen. "Well . . ." She swallows, tucking a strand of hair behind her ear. So goddamn beautiful when she's caught off guard like this. "Keep up the good work, then."

I stand straight, saluting her. "Yes, ma'am."

CHAPTER TWENTY-SEVEN

WILLOW

"He was awfully chipper this morning, Willow," Liv chimes. "That spring in his step?" She whistles. "I bet he's going to perform well today."

"Whatever morning routine you've got him on, it's doing wonders." Lou winks.

My face heats, and I dip my head to hide it. "He's just excited to compete again."

"Yeah, I'm sure that's what it is," Zander adds. "I bet there is absolutely no chance he had his dick played with this morning."

"I'm in earshot," my mother snaps from across the tent.

"Who raised these feral people?" Dahlia asks, sidling up beside her at the breakfast table my dad catered.

"They've got you written all over them, Wildflower." Everett laughs, wrapping his arms around her waist as she pours a cup of coffee.

"You look awfully post-orgasm glowy this morning," Allie whispers in my ear, leaning into me from her seat. "And I don't mean the kind you give yourself. Which is strange, considering you've told me nothing is happening between you and the hot surfer next door."

I snort. "You've been gone."

"For a week!" she exclaims, drawing the attention of those around us. "Don't tell me you went zero to a hundred in just seven days."

I tug her arm, pulling our heads together as I hiss, "We haven't gone to a hundred. We only kissed for the first time earlier this week."

"And . . ." She tilts her face toward me, slowly raising a brow. "What happened this morning?"

"We had . . . meals," I say, blushing at my own innuendo.

"Oh?" she drawls. "And how was your *meal*?"

At least she's going along with it. Honestly, Allie has the filthiest mouth I've ever encountered, with zero qualms about who's listening.

"Best I've *ever* had," I rasp, biting back a squeal of excitement.

I'm still mind-blown, hours later, at the way Weston devoured me. The way he praised me—fucking cherished me. I know it's all instinctual to him. He's not practiced, he hasn't learned the right things to say or do when he's with a woman. He moved entirely off his desires and my response, and it led to the best orgasm of my life.

Allie looks at me unconvinced, with quirked lips and a raised brow. "Really?"

I nod rapidly, knowing the grin on my flushed cheeks is all the confirmation needed.

"Wow." She hums. "Good for him." Allie is quiet for a moment before she adds, "And does he know . . . everything?"

A pinch of guilt bites my gut. "He knows why I came home—the gist of it, anyway." I sigh. "He doesn't know what happened once I was back."

She must hear the contrition in my voice, because Allie rests her head against my shoulder and pats my thigh. "That's okay. You've only known him a couple months, everything that happened to you is so fresh. It'll take time to get there. If he's really the person you think he is, he'll understand."

"He will," I murmur. "I just don't know what's wrong with me. I'm having such a hard time opening up about it. He's been so honest about his life."

I have few doubts that Weston would be unwilling to accept the choice I made a few months ago, especially considering the circumstances that led me to it. Though, there is a pesky prick of fear that has its teeth sunk into the back of my neck—stopping the words from leaving my mouth each time I think I'm ready to open up about it with him.

"It takes time," Allie whispers, kissing my temple before snuggling back into my shoulder.

It's still pretty early, and Weston's session doesn't start for another forty-five minutes. Despite it being late-July, the sun hasn't yet crested over the mountains in the east, and with our tent facing the Pacific to the west, we're completely shadowed.

My dad is still with Weston warming up—or whatever it is they do before a competition—and Carter is with them, taking photos. I've never been to one for my dad's other athletes. I attended a few junior contests with Camden in high school, but none of them were this extensive. And outside a handful of charity exhibitions my dad participated in when I was a child, he's been retired all my life.

Liv competed in the last Olympics three years ago, but we weren't able to fly the entire family out with mine and the twins' sports schedules. Lou and her parents attended the games in Portugal, while the twins stayed back with my parents and me, and we watched her compete on television.

Despite living a life that practically revolves around surfing, this is the first competition I've ever attended like this. There are far more people than I had anticipated, and nerves nip at my stomach as I impatiently wait to watch Weston on the waves.

I wonder what he thinks of it—if it's thrilling to him, or an added pressure. I know he doesn't like crowds or too much noise, but I imagine the roar of the waves drowns it all out. When he's beyond the break, I wonder if the audience makes a difference, or if he's able to tap into the tides and connect with them the same way he does when he's alone.

I can only hope for the latter, because I know how determined he is to perform well today. Not only to place, but to exceed everyone's expectations—most of all his own.

"How are things with Declan?" I ask Allie.

I assume they haven't broken up—she would've told me if they had, but she hasn't mentioned him since the fiasco on her birthday two weeks ago. I'm curious as to why she'd continue giving him the time of day after that.

Archer perks up from Allie's other side. She straightens, tossing him an incredulous eye roll before turning to me. "He tried to ultimatum me. Said I had to choose him or Archer." She snorts. "I ignored him for a week. Then, before I left to see my parents, I explained to him that I get Archer for one month before he goes back to Texas, and Declan can have me the rest of the year." She shrugs. "I gave him a hall pass. He has the remainder of July to do what—and who—ever he wants, and I won't ask any questions. But," she continues, "he can't ever again question my friendship with Archer or ask me to stay away from him when he's home."

Archer rears back so far in his chair he nearly falls out. "Are you fucking kidding me, Allie?"

He's loud enough that it pulls the attention of our parents. I turn my head in time to watch Dom's snap sideways, dark eyes narrowing, gaze set on my cousin. "You wanna rephrase that?"

"Not really," he scoffs, crossing his arms. "Did she tell you about her little arrangement with *Declan*?" The name drips off Archer's tongue with disgust.

"Yeah." Dom sighs, wiping a hand down his face. "Don't fucking cuss, but . . ." He nods. "Talk some sense into her if you can."

"Sorry," Archer murmurs, turning back to face the horizon with a grimace.

"I don't need any sense!" Allie throws her hands up, shooting daggers between Archer and her dad. "I'm dropping this conversation now." She tosses me a withering look. "Don't bring him up around the two of them—or my mother, for that matter—they're all insane."

"*You're* insane," I shoot back.

She rolls her eyes, settling back into her seat. "Anyway . . . how big is Weston's dick?"

There she is.

Dropping the conversation regarding her shitty boyfriend, I lean closer, ensuring we're out of anyone's ear shot. "You have no *fucking* idea."

"How many inches?" she whispers.

"I didn't measure it." I laugh, smacking her arm as the announcer's voice booms over the intercom, informing us the next heat—Weston's session—will start in thirty minutes.

"Well . . . take an educated guess," Allie calls over the sound of the speaker.

I extend my arm out in front of me, asking, "How long do you think my forearm is?" just as the announcement ends, and stark silence blankets us.

Every head inside our tent turns in my direction, and my skin sears under their horrified expressions. I'm frozen, still holding my arm in front of me, attempting to stretch my thumb and middle finger from the crease of my elbow to my wrist.

Zander bursts with laughter, and Lou hides a snicker of her own.

"Damn." Allie wheezes. "Good for you, babe."

I glance at Liv, whose mouth is gaping, eyes wide as she studies me before she cranes her head behind us, in the direction of where our parents stand. "You all raised some feral little weirdos."

When my dad finds us fifteen minutes later, he asks why we're all so quiet. I'm grateful nobody has the gall to explain.

JUST BEFORE THE start of Wes's heat, he finally comes into my line of sight as he walks onto the beach with his white and blue board in hand. He's wearing a red dry-fit shirt over his wetsuit with the number twenty-eight on the back, and his last name, Ashford, over the shoulders.

There are two other surfers in his heat, but Weston is the only thing I focus on. Like I'm staring through a camera lens, and everything around him is blurred. Watching him wade into the water is reminiscent of slowly climbing the peak of a roller coaster. Every movement he makes tugs at my chest in an ascending tempo.

"Did he seem ready to go?" I ask Dad. "Was he nervous?"

"Oh, no. He was confident as ever." He chuckles. "It's windy today, though. Choppier than anticipated, that's the only thing I worry about."

I swallow, unease swirling inside my bones.

Dad turns to me, his features softening into a reassuring smile as he grabs my hand. "He knows when to avoid a rogue wave, Sugar. He'll be all right."

I nod, squeezing his palm as we turn back to the beach. Dad has the timer for this session on his phone—the objective is to drop in as many times as he can during the heat, completing as many tricks with as much precision as possible. He'll be judged not only on performance, but on his form too.

I pull binoculars out of my bag, fixing them over my eyes and relocating him through the pin-pointed vision. He's paddling—the muscles in his arms and back pronounced through the clinging fabric of his shirt. Once he's passed the break, Weston slows down, sitting upright on his board, gaze narrowed on the Pacific, brow furrowed with concentration.

He's fucking beautiful.

Utterly focused, and while entirely determined, he's also at ease. Simply a boy who's most himself inside the tides, and today, he's choosing to share that connection with the rest of the world. It's as if nothing can touch him out there—not his past, not his fear, not his future. I can see that peace on his face—the only other time he houses that look of convicted determination and fulfilled contentment is when he's looking at me.

I realize Weston studies me the way he studies the ocean, the way he counts the swells.

One wave rolls toward him—powerful and fierce. A murmured, "Go," leaves my dad's lips, and as if the word is echoed through the wind, Weston lays flat against his board and spins toward the shore.

As the wave drifts beneath him, Weston begins paddling with perfect form, muscles in his arms straining with every glide he makes through the water. When the wave crests, he's in the perfect position, and as he pops up and drops in, my stomach sinks. I'm falling over the edge of that coaster, giving myself to gravity right along with him.

I pull the binoculars from my eyes, he's moving too quickly to follow with the close-up sight. He glides over the face of the wave with effortless ease, carving up toward the crest as the barrel crashes behind him. The waves today are likely too small to complete a successful tunnel, though in the back of every surfer's mind, every time they're on the water, it's a coveted goal.

Weston makes a flawless off-the-lip, stirring cheers from the crowd along the beach. He continues down the wave, carving deep, nearly losing his balance before he makes a tight cut, springing toward the top of the whitecap and completing an aerial spin. My stomach launches into my throat as he goes airborne, and I'm still choking on oxygen when he lands back down—somehow steady as he drifts through the wave, slowing himself when it begins crashing around him, floating atop it until he sinks into the foam.

The crowd goes absolutely wild—it was by far the best run of the morning. Wes turns toward the horizon, throwing his arms in the air triumphantly. A deafening whistle that only could belong to my uncle Everett nearly blows out my eardrums as he sends it Wes's way.

All of the other surfers in his session are yards away, near their starting places. Wes must've been the only one to drop in on that wave, though the others attempt to follow his lead as Wes slowly paddles back in their direction.

He drops in two more times during his session, completing another successful aerial and even an alley-oop, along with several basic tricks—his form near-perfect on each of those too.

"I've never seen him surf like this," my dad murmurs, leaning forward on his knees as he rubs a hand over his jaw in astonishment. "If he keeps this up, he's going to place first today."

"No doubt," Liv says beside him.

My cheeks hurt from the ache of my prideful grin, my throat is hoarse from the force of my cheers. It takes everything to rein in my excitement—to stop myself from jumping up and running down the beach, screaming in the face of every spectator, "See that one? He's mine!"

Weston places first in his heat, and advances to the next round. The Challenger has a total of six, with eliminations in each one. Since Wes won his heat, he advances straight into the top sixteen, where he'll face off head-to-head with the remaining competitors.

There is a lull between Weston's sessions. Allie and I take a walk down the beach—where I try, and fail, to convince her to end her relationship with Declan. We eat breakfast with our families before my dad and Carter go to check on Wes. Both Penelope and I tried to convince them to take us too, but Dad doesn't want to risk breaking his focus.

As much as I want to see him—touch him and kiss him and share in the excitement with him, because he deserves to know he's not in this alone—I know it makes the most sense to wait until the Challenger is completely over.

The nerves from earlier stir inside me again as Weston paddles out for his second heat. This time, he's head-to-head, the competition growing fiercer with each round. The wind has picked up, the waves rougher than they were this morning, meaning the number of opportunities to perform become fewer as the afternoon goes on. Not only does he have to choose each swell carefully, but each run has to be perfect to avoid elimination.

Weston passes several swells, and anticipation surges with each one that rolls near him. I'm antsy for him to drop in—not miss a single opportunity this session—but when his competitor takes a bad swell and is swallowed up by the tide, I remind myself to trust Weston's instincts.

When he finally takes a wave, the other surfer is still recovering from his wipeout and misses the opportunity. Weston drops in, completing another near-perfect run. It locks him in as a clear crowd favorite, because the entire beach is drowned out by the sound of cheers.

"He got lucky," Dad says on a breath. "That was a choppy one."

"You said he knows what he's doing."

He only huffs in response, tapping his fingers against his knee.

Weston paddles beyond the break, the time in his session is rapidly running down. I use the binoculars again to get a closer look at him—to try and gauge the expression on his face. The determination from earlier is still present, more fierce now.

"God-fucking-dammit," my father mutters, just as Weston spins his board.

I lower the binoculars to find the largest swell I've seen all day barreling toward Weston as he paddles away from it, the power in his arms almost palpable with every swift, hard stroke through the water. When it crests, the wave is at least twice the size of any other we've seen today. It's rushing toward the shore at an angle with the force of the wind.

Weston is fast, but not fast enough. By the time he springs up, the wave is already crashing. One second he's there, haloed by whitecaps. The next, he's wrecked by them, tumbling beneath their weight, swallowed by their impact.

CHAPTER TWENTY-EIGHT

WESTON

That sucked.

"And how does that feel?" the medic asks as she presses down on my ribs.

It fucking hurts.

I suck in a breath, wincing at the pressure and the way it spreads a flame throughout my body. "It's . . . mildly uncomfortable."

"Mm-hmm." She hums, unconvinced. She lowers my shirt, and I hear her riffling around beside the table she has me laid out on, though I can't see it with the way I'm covering my face. "All right, I need to see your eyes."

I groan, dropping my palms and cracking one eye open. The red top of the medical tent appears neon orange with the way the sun blazes overhead. I'm lying on an examination table inside as the medic sits on a stool beside me, craning over my body with a flashlight in her hand.

The crow's-feet at the corners of her eyes widen when she smiles at me softly, a strand of mostly-gray hair falling out of her low bun when she drops her head over mine and holds the light to my face. She shines it into each of my eyes, before nodding to herself and rolling to the end of the table and scribbling something down on a clipboard.

"Well, you're not concussed, possibly a bruised—"

"He's in here?" The rushed, distressed words filter in from

just outside the medic tent.

Willow. She sounds so fucking scared.

Shame rains down on me in rivulets. I knew I shouldn't have taken that swell. It was the idea that if I pulled it off, I'd undoubtedly move onto the semifinals, the taste of total victory so fucking potent, the vision of making her proud crystal clear—that's what made me chase that wave.

Even after I free-fell down the face of it, was swallowed up by the tide, and tossed around beneath the barrel, I only saw her face. It's what had me fighting past the fire in my chest and the ache in my limbs as I battled to the surface.

Though with each break into fresh air, I was immediately slammed with another wave, dragged into the depths again. It wasn't until a standby rescue team hauled me into a raft and took me back to shore that I became conscious enough to find awareness in my surroundings, and only now—at the sound of her voice—is the true weight of my stupid decision pressing down on me.

She bursts through the flap of the tent, my gaze immediately locked on her glistening blue eyes—red-rimmed and swollen with tears. She's gulping in breaths as if the air itself is choking her.

"Wes." Chest heaving, she holds a palm to it as she studies me, her face crumbling into a broken whimper, "You scared me."

"My love." I sit up on the table as she rushes into my arms, her tears soaking into my neck. "I'm so sorry, Willow."

I hush her, pressing my lips into her wild, wind-whipped hair, cradling her against me. My ribs are fucking burning, but it would be far more painful to let her go right now.

Just as I lift my head, I find Leo following her through the tent, and that debilitating burn radiates far beyond my torso as his heated gaze sears through me—simmering with anger.

"You . . . were u—underwater . . ." Willow breathes between her tears. "For so long."

"No. No." I grasp her face, lifting her head so it's level with mine. "I was coming up for air. I just had trouble finding my bearings. That's all. I'm completely fine, love. I promise."

"Actually, he'll be quite sore for a few days, and may potentially experience whiplash or vertigo. No concussion symptoms, though I'd get evaluated by a physician for possible bruising on the ribs, and any other contusions that may become more noticeable as the adrenaline wears off," the medic explains, looking over her notes before directing her attention to me. "You're lucky you only got the wind knocked outta ya."

"You're telling me," Leo mutters.

"Are you his coach?" she asks. When Leo nods, the medic continues, "Like I said, he needs to see a doctor before he gets back on a board, but he's good to go home today. Doesn't need a hospital visit. I'd recommend at least twenty-four hours of rest, then take him in and get him cleared." Her gaze darts to Willow and me, raising a brow. "No . . . rigorous activity."

I avoid eye contact with Leo.

Willow bursts with a fractured laugh—the most hauntingly beautiful sound I've ever heard.

She glances at me, those misty eyes now swimming with mischief, an amused smile spreading over her tear-stained cheeks. Suddenly, all my pain ceases. I'm healed.

I could drink her laugh. Bathe in her smile. If my heart stopped right now, all I'd need was the sound of her voice to defibrillate me.

I offer her a grin, though it doesn't last long, because hers still appears broken. "I'm sorry, Wills. I shouldn't have been so reckless, especially with you watching. I never should've scared you like that. I'll be more careful. That was a stupid fucking decision."

"At least you're aware of it," Leo murmurs, turning toward the exit flap of the tent. "Lessens the amount of lecturing I'll be doing Monday morning. Let's go."

I blow out a long exhale, hissing as Willow helps me off the table. I may be bruised, but it's minor. I've experienced broken ribs before, and this pain is nothing in comparison to that, though each inhale is met with a flare of discomfort.

I'm somewhat dizzy, but the kind that feels as if I'm merely treading water. The sensation when you've spent too much time out on the waves, or in a boat, and your legs sway with each step—convinced they're not on even ground.

"Leo," I call as he stalks ahead of us. "I'd prefer not to see anyone right now, if that's all right? I feel bad that I had a disappointing performance today and—"

"Nobody is disappointed in you, Wes. Just worried," Willow responds, looping her arm through mine as she peers up at me with sad, soft eyes.

"Don't speak for everyone, Sugar," her dad says, turning around. "I'm certainly disappointed, but she's right about the rest of them. I told them to disperse, and we'd let them know how you're doing later. Carter and Penelope are waiting for you, though."

Willow sighs, resting her head against my shoulder as we make our way down the beach, finding Carter and Penelope near the pier. Penelope hugs me so tight it hurts, but I don't tell her that—the guilt of causing her to worry is far more painful.

Carter's eyes flash with concern, though he makes a joke about capturing my rag-doll on camera—to which Leo requests printed copies of. Carter then asks if I want to spend the weekend with them until I'm cleared for training.

Willow's eyes flutter to me, and the pleading on her beautiful, devastated face is all the answer needed. *I'm going wherever she goes*. I politely decline, and Leo leaves Willow and me with the keys to Darby's car.

"What do you want for dinner?" Willow asks softly as she merges onto the interstate that'll take us back to Pacific Shores.

"I have chicken and vegetables at home."

She scoffs before making a gagging noise. "No. Absolutely not." She glances at me, frowning. "Don't you have a comfort meal? Something you ate as a kid when you had a bad day or when you were sick? A favorite restaurant?"

"Not really. We didn't have a lot of money so we didn't eat out much, especially considering how well my mom could cook.

There was no point." I shrug. "My mom made great meals with the resources she had, but we mostly ate what my dad demanded. And by the time I moved in with Carter and Penelope, I was so focused on surfing, I stuck to a meal plan. Then, well . . . I went to jail. When I was released, I was mainly focused on getting back on track so I could compete again."

She releases a shuddered breath. "Well . . . is there any place you've ever wanted to try but never had the chance?"

"Eh. I guess I've always wondered what all the fuss with In-N-Out was about."

"Excuse me?" she gasps, nearly swerving the car off the goddamn road. "You've never had In-N-Out? In your whole life? Where the hell were you born?"

"Never going to have the chance if you crash the car, Trouble." I chuckle. "I was born in Long Beach."

"Excuse my language, but what the fuck, Weston?" Willow flips on her blinker, merging into the exit lane. "That's it. We're going."

"I'm still on a meal plan, love. I can't fuck it up just because I surfed like shit today."

"You did not," she snaps. "You performed better than you have in your entire life. You made one, overly confident mistake that led to an injury and made you unable to complete the competition. And that sucks. But it does not diminish everything you accomplished before it. You deserve a fucking milkshake."

I glance at her from the passenger seat, a grin spreading over my face as her brows furrow in concentration, her pert nose scrunched. Her eyes dart to mine, simmering with determination. I can only laugh, surrendering. "Okay, baby."

"THIS IS WAY too much food, Wills." I stare down at the open boxes of burgers and fries spread across my bed, each with a different array of toppings.

"I didn't know what you were going to like," she says between bites of cheeseburger. "One of those is animal-style, the other is just a regular Double-Double."

"What do these things mean?"

She snorts. "Double-Double is a burger with two patties. Animal-style means it has grilled onions and pickles." Willow points to the fries. "That's why I also got plain fries, cheese fries, and animal-style fries, with the grilled onions and spread."

"Spread." I gag. "Terrible name for sauce. And animal-style? I feel like I'm on a porn set."

"Mmm." She hums. "We could make it one later, if you want."

My brows shoot up, right along with my cock.

The silk of her sultry laugh runs along my skin, eliciting flames along my flesh. "Weird names aside, it's fucking good though." She holds a white cup with red palm trees dotted along the top to my lips. "Neapolitan shake. Fucking good too."

"I stand by the fact that I'm only a sweet tooth when it comes to your pussy," I rasp, pinning her with my eyes as I lean in and wrap my lips around the straw. "But the shake is all right."

She rolls her eyes, but I don't miss the blush that tints her cheeks.

She's not wrong about the food. I devour my burger and fries—the animal-style version of both. Once we're done, Willow gathers the remainder of the food and darts to the big house to pass them off to her parents, as well as shower and change.

I showered too while she was gone and am pulling my legs into sweats when she re-enters my bedroom, leaning against the door—bare feet, sun-kissed skin on full display beneath a pair of tight, athletic shorts and a long tee. She's fresh faced and glowing—fucking beautiful as she tilts her head and smiles at me. "Are you feeling any better?"

"Physically or mentally?" I ask with a rough laugh, pressing a kiss to her lips as I pass her on the way to the bed. "Better on both fronts. It doesn't hurt to breathe anymore, so I think my rib is fine. I've had bruised and broken ribs before, I'd know if it was bad. My muscles are a little sore—and will probably feel worse tomorrow, but for now I'm fine. Would feel a lot better with you in bed beside me, though."

I expect her to blush or grin, but instead, Willow's face falls, expression becoming crestfallen. Still, she pushes off the wall and crawls onto the foot of the bed. "Your father? He did that to you?"

I swallow, nodding as she slowly comes up beside me, running her hand along my torso with a cautious touch. "I wish I could erase it, Wes," she says softly. "All the pain he caused you."

"When you touch me," I breathe, "it kind of feels like that."

"Really?" she asks before leaning over, pressing her lips to my ribs. "Where else did he hurt you, baby?"

"Fuck," I hiss, the sound of her words and the feel of her mouth spreading heat to every corner of my being. "Umm . . . mostly places that couldn't be seen. He'd kick me in the stomach, shove me into walls. Grab my arms hard enough to bruise—but only my biceps or shoulders."

She drags her mouth over my sternum, tongue darting out to lick my chest as she continues to my shoulder. "Here?"

I nod, and she moves down my arm, kissing it.

"Here?"

I nod once more, and she lifts her gaze to mine—those aquamarine pools bursting with emotion. Some war between rage for my father, sorrow for my childhood, and desire for my body.

She rises to her knees, gently lifting her leg over my hips, but doesn't drop her weight. "Is this going to be okay?"

"Yeah, love. It's more than okay." I grip her waist, guiding her down atop me.

"Are you still in pain?"

"No," I whisper. I'm sore, yes, but nowhere near enough to not be touching her right now.

Willow plants a palm on the center of my chest, dragging it down until it reaches the place where her body meets mine, fingers whispering over the hard length tenting my bottoms. "Is this okay?"

"Always, love." I whimper when she squeezes my cock before I grasp her wrist. "But I don't want you to feel pressured into touching me out of pity for my past."

Her brows draw together, full lips pouting, soft eyes flaring. "No, Wes," she murmurs, reaching into the collar of her tee and pulling something from the strap of her bra. Gold foil flashes between her fingers as she holds up a condom. "I'm ready. I've *been* ready, and after watching you disappear beneath the waves today..." Her breath halts, and she dips her head before continuing in a soft murmur, "I don't want to wait anymore. I want to feel *everything* with you."

My chest tightens at the realization she's been planning this. That she's thought through this step in our relationship enough to prepare this way. I search into the depths of myself for some ounce of hesitation, some sign that I want to keep waiting, that we aren't ready, but all I find is eagerness and raw *need.*

I lift up in bed, pain slashing over my left side, but I ignore it. Grasping her chin, I lift her gaze to mine. "I want to feel everything with you too, Wills." I laugh gruffly. "But I'm so damn afraid I'm going to make a fool of myself."

The corner of her lips tilts, her eyes morphing from hesitant and unsure to heated and utterly devastating. "I'll take care of you, baby."

My cock pulses, and those tilted lips spread wider when she feels it. I spread my fingers wide, gliding my hands up her waist, lifting her shirt with them. She grabs the hem, pulling it off and tossing it to the floor. Her gaze stays locked on mine as she reaches behind her back and unclasps her bra, the fabric loosening around her chest as the straps fall off her shoulders.

My calloused fingers brush over her smooth skin as I pull the straps down, removing her bra completely. Her peaked, rosy-pink nipples move with each expansion of her heaving chest—my tongue flicks over my lips, desperate to taste them.

"You sure you want this with me, Wes?"

I soak in her body, cataloging every inch of exposed,

delectable skin. Her golden hair tumbles over her shoulders in thick waves, freckled flesh glowing and flushed from the heat of my gaze, eyes blazing—pleading for confirmation. I'm at a loss for how to show her just how badly I want her. How I've never needed anything more.

"I'm so in awe of you that my tongue is sticking to my mouth. I'm speechless, Willow, so I'm having a bit of trouble expressing myself, honestly." I rub my jaw. "That's what looking at you does to me. That is how desperately I crave you." I buck my hips slightly, pressing my cock against her core. "Does that clear anything up?"

She tosses her head back with a laugh, and somehow, she's even more beautiful like this. Willow falls forward, aligning her face with mine, studying me with a flare of adoration. She brushes her mouth over my lips, kissing me gently before pulling back and lifting off the bed.

She slips out of her shorts and panties as I tug off my sweats and underwear. I lie back, propping an elbow beneath my head so I can watch her crawl between my legs again—entirely bare this time. My mind short-circuits when she slides a palm up my length, grasping my cock and pumping it once.

She bites her lip, and I lick mine, confident she can hear the drumming of my heart. I fear the force of its pounding may bring this entire house down. Every atom in my body rushes to my core as Willow straddles me again, the heat of her center radiating against my cock.

"I've been tested recently. After . . . everything. I also had an IUD inserted, so I'm clear on all fronts, but I'd still feel best if we used—"

I nod rapidly. "Of course, Willow. You don't need to explain yourself."

Her brows knit, eyes blazing with gratitude that she doesn't need to be expressing as she nods.

Willow takes the condom wrapper between her teeth and tears it open, eyes locked on mine—it is by far the most erotic thing I've ever seen. That is, until she takes it out and begins rolling it down my aching cock. I'm grateful she didn't ask me to do it, I wouldn't have known how.

She doesn't make me feel inadequate, in fact, Willow looks at me like I'm gifting her with the experience of owning me this way. Like I'm the one giving her something, when in reality, she's offering me *everything.*

She rises to her knees, hovering over my hips as she positions my cock at her entrance. The room is pin-drop silent outside the mingled sound of our heavy breath when Willow slowly sinks down on me.

The moment I'm enveloped by her soft warmth and mind-melting wetness, a foreign, electric sensation rushes over every inch of my heated skin. My blood catches flame brighter than anything I've known before. My entire being explodes, expanding into multitudes before snapping back together like a band—all of me narrowed on my connection with Willow. The joining of our bodies.

Some kind of animalistic noise crawls from my throat, begging for escape when she drops another inch. My hands claw at the sheets, a bead of sweat forms on my brow as I reach deep inside myself for some sense of composure, willing myself not to come before I'm even fully inside her.

"You're so big, Wes," she moans, tossing her head back as she slides down farther, until she's nearly seated on me completely.

I whimper—fucking pathetically, though I'm uncaring. I'd weep for her, crawl to her, fucking obliterate myself. For her soul, her mind, her body. The way she welcomes me, binding our beings with the mingling of flesh. Being inside Willow is beyond erotic—it's fucking spiritual. I *feel* the altering of my very composition. The imprint of her upon my skin. As if she's completing me wholly.

She tightens. I unravel.

Her body molds to mine. My soul takes shape around hers.

"Fuck, Wills," I say through gritted teeth, hands flying to her hips—desperate to feel her body tremble alongside mine. "You're taking it, love." My gaze locked on where we're flushed together, the way she's stretching around me, adjusting to accommodate my body taking space in hers. "Look at you. God, Willow. You're unreal. You're perfect."

Her voice shakes with every word when she huffs a whispered laugh, "I could be terrible. You have nothing to compare it to."

"No," I growl. Sliding a hand to knot in her hair, forcing her face to meet mine when I sit up and drag our joined bodies to the top of the bed until I'm in a seated position. "It's perfect because it's *you*, Willow. You." I kiss her forehead. "This is perfect." I kiss her lips. "These are perfect." Tugging her hair again so that her back arches and her head snaps back, I press my mouth to her chest. "This right here?" I murmur over her heart. "Does me in, baby. This is all encompassing. All consuming." I lift my hips, mind reeling at the slick, tight feel of her wrapped around me. The way she pulses with every word I speak. "There isn't one part of you that isn't beautiful, Willow. There isn't a single thing I'd ever change. Do you get that? You are more than a dream. Far beyond any expectation I could've set, any future I could've envisioned for myself. You are superior to every fantasy my mind could've ever drummed up. I don't need to experience anything else. All I need—all I want—is you."

CHAPTER TWENTY-NINE

WILLOW

I'M DROWNING IN the storm-blue eyes that tether my gaze, his words cascading across my heated skin, sinking into the depths of my bones. I don't have words for it—any of it. The conviction in his voice strikes a chord inside my chest, the current between us echoing with a transcendent hum. There is no description in existence for the way he feels inside me, filling every hollow gap my past tore open.

"Wes," I whisper, folding forward to align our faces. "I—"

He hushes me, understanding it too—this sensation beyond language. One hand glides up my spine while the other finds my face, brushing away the loose hair stuck to my sweat-slicked skin before bracketing my jaw. He feathers his lips over mine, swallowing the moan he pulls from me when he rolls his hips, inching deeper.

We trade breath—Wes sighing into my mouth when I rock against him. I slide my tongue over his, eagerly tasting his sounds of desire. He drags that hand down my back, grasping my ass as he flushes us closer.

"You feel so good, love," he rasps against my flesh, pulling my bottom lip between his teeth. "You're ruining me."

"I know," I moan, his bite slicing through me as I break free from his hold, pressing against his chest and flattening him against the pillows. "Let me ride it."

His eyes roll back, the hand on my ass gripping hard enough to bruise. "I'm not going to last long."

"That's okay," I whisper as I lift up before slamming back down. "I'm going to take care of you, baby."

"Fuck." A fractured sound catches in his throat, his entire body bowing as he pulses inside me.

I set a punishing pace, bouncing on his cock while rotating my hips in a circular motion. Weston's head sinks into the pillows, the tendons in his neck flexing with each aching groan that leaves his mouth. His skin glistens, eyes shut tight, jaw clenched—face twisted with pure ecstasy.

His hips begin snapping, meeting each grind of mine down on him, the salacious slap of our joining mingles with the echoes of our impassioned panting through the otherwise quiet house.

"Willow," he murmurs brokenly, like he can hardly find the words. His eyes open, half-lidded and swimming in bliss. "I need it to feel good for you too."

"It does," I promise. I don't know how he doesn't realize it—I'm trembling with every movement we make, he's so deep I'm certain he can feel the hammering of my pulse from the inside of my body.

"I need you to *come*," he rasps. "With me. Please. Fuck. I'm so close. I need—"

I don't slow my movements, I don't pause, because I'm close too. I grasp the hand splayed around my waist and drag it between my legs. Covering his fingers with my own, I slide them down until we're both pressed against the place our bodies join—feeling the way I move atop him, the way he thrusts into me.

"Feel that." I flex our fingers, forcing them to brush against my clit, a whimper clawing at the roof of my mouth from the pressure. I set a rhythm—soft, languid strokes of his hand over my swollen and sensitive bud. "Feel us," I whisper.

"We're so good together," he growls.

I'm quivering uncontrollably, my moans crescendoing to a height that could rattle the foundation of the house itself. Weston's fingers work at me with precision, my pace becoming chaotic as he swells inside me, chasing his own release.

"Willow," he murmurs through clenched teeth, nails digging into my hips as his eyes flare—a thousand shades of blue shattering like glass when his body goes taut, stomach tightening before his cock surges with the weight of his climax.

He continues bucking—fucking me through it, nothing if not determined to get me there too. The coiled heat in my core and the pressure of his hand against my clit bursts, sparks blanketing my vision as an orgasm rips me apart. My back arches, hands raking at his sweat-slicked chest as his name flies from my mouth.

We rock against each other fervently, wringing every last drop of the pleasure coursing through our veins, before slowing our movements as we float down from the stars together. I collapse onto his chest, the sound of our mixed staccato breathing filtering through the lust-hazed air.

Weston's heart pounds against my ear, matching the drumming of my own—as if our joining synched us together, creating a symbiotic force all its own.

We lie in stunned silence for what could be hours—I've lost the ability to tell time. Weston's knuckles drift up and down my spine until my breathing evens out and our heartbeats regulate. He's still inside me, but I don't have the strength to separate from him quite yet.

"Willow," he whispers into the darkness.

"Yeah?"

"That was the best sex of my life."

The most obnoxious snort tears from my nose, and I turn my head to rest my chin on his chest, peering up at him. He tosses me a crooked smile that forces a laugh from me. "I hate you."

He brushes the wild hair from my face. "No, you don't."

I scrunch my nose, unable to even mock a frown when he's looking at me like this—studying me with rapt adoration, tilting his head and touching my skin like he's not sure I'm even real. When I'm post-orgasm high, and safe in the arms of a partner for what may truly be the first time. "No. I don't."

I lift off him, both of us sighing as he leaves me empty. He rises out of bed, disposing of the condom before returning and pulling me onto his chest. "Does it always feel like that?"

"It's never felt like that for me before," I whisper against his skin.

He dips his chin, peering down at me through his lashes. "Really?"

I nod. "It felt like . . . more. I can't explain it." I sigh softly. "Like you weren't just inside me, you were *all over* me. Like my breath was your source of oxygen and my touch was bringing you to life." I laugh breathlessly. "I'm struggling to find the words, but you made me feel . . . essential, Weston. Every other time made me feel like my body was better than their hand, but you make me feel like your entire soul rests in the palm of mine."

"It does, I think," he admits on a rough exhale, lips drifting over my temple. "I was serious, Wills. You are devastatingly perfect. I don't need all the experience in the world to know it'll never feel like this with someone else."

I hum in agreement, nodding against him. "Do you feel okay? No regrets?"

He laughs from deep in his chest, and it rumbles against my ear, mixing with his heartbeat. "No regrets, Wills. Not a single one." His hand splays over my spine, fingers gliding over my back. "I think you unraveled me entirely, and I'll be craving you every second of the day for the rest of my existence, but . . . fuck. I'm not complaining about it." His eyes flash to mine, crinkling in the corners with the smile he offers me. "You're everything."

I cup his cheek, brushing my thumb over his bottom lip. "You're everything too."

I'M STIRRED TO consciousness the following morning by the rock hard rod digging relentlessly into my lower back. I press against it, earning a groan from Weston as he stretches his limbs and begins to wake. "It's too early to be brandishing a weapon like that."

His thick laugh skates across the nape of my neck, dripping down my spine warm and slow. His lips brush against my shoulder before I roll to face him, finding a sleepy, sated smile on his handsome face. His deep blue eyes are brighter than they've ever been, catching on the morning light filtering through the window above us.

"Your fault," he rasps, arching his hips and pressing his cock into my stomach.

I respond with a small moan as I lift my hand to his face, brushing back the hair on his forehead. "How'd you sleep?"

"Same as I always do beside you. Perfectly."

My lips quirk, chest filling with honey at the sound of his voice. "You still feel okay? About everything?"

"Yeah, Wills." His brows draw together, lips pursing—a contemplative look, like he's trying to solve a puzzle. "I feel perfect. *This* is perfect."

Perhaps I'm checking in too much, but I want to ensure he's okay with this. With us. With *me*. I tilt my head, peering up at him, uncertainty swirling inside me. "It felt good for you, though? I . . ." I swallow. "My . . . It felt okay?"

He draws circles over my shoulder with his thumb. "*Okay* would be a terribly inaccurate word to describe what you felt like to me. *Good* and even *great* would also be inferior. *Otherworldly*, perhaps? *Earth-shattering*? Fucking *mind-altering*? Those would be fitting descriptions for the experience of being inside your body." Weston's brows knit. "I want to understand where these insecurities stem from, Willow, because I want to know how to reassure you the right way."

I muffle a smile against his skin, and he grips my chin to reveal it. I bite my lip, dropping my gaze as I run a finger down the center of his chest. "When Parker assaulted me . . ." I sigh. "It started consensual, but he removed the condom without asking me. I didn't realize until after he'd finished." I swallow hard, that familiar yet suppressed bite of shame resurfacing. "I battled with whether I could call it that at first, honestly. Whether I could say he assaulted me, because I know so many women experience much worse."

"It doesn't lessen the reality of what happened to you. You have the right to call it what it is," he says softly.

"I know." I nod. "When I confronted him about it, asked why he did it and explained that it made me uncomfortable . . ." Emotion pricks behind my eyes. "He told me that he didn't even enjoy sex with me. That he couldn't feel anything when he used a condom. That I was too . . ." I shake my head, hiding my face as white-hot shame rushes over me. "Loose."

Weston's body tenses beside me. He rears back, creating distance between us—recoiling. Like he's been slapped.

I'm terrified to look at him.

"Willow," he breathes, sighing deeply, as if gathering his composure. Weston adds, "I'm so sorry. I'm sorry he put you through that. I'm sorry that—Can you look at me?"

I shake my head, burying my face in his side. "Not yet," I murmur. "That was the most humiliating thing that's ever happened to me, and I've never spoken those words aloud. Not to anyone. Not even Allie. I'm too afraid they're true. I'm afraid of anyone else knowing something like that about me."

"I understand." His chest moves as he nods. "I need you to know it's not true, though. Farthest thing from it." He plants his lips in my hair, running his arm down the bare skin of my back. "I know I'm not an expert, but even with high school level biology and basic sex education, I know that's not how the female body works. And . . ." He huffs a laugh. "I can now speak from experience that sex with a condom can absolutely feel good. Perhaps Parker was overcompensating for his own issues." He shrugs. "Regardless, those things he said were a poor attempt at deflecting from what he did to you because he'd been caught. They were an abhorrent effort to justify his actions. That does not make them true."

"He was so quick to say them. Like he didn't even need to

think about it. The words naturally fell from his mouth."

"Honestly, Willow. He probably considered the chance you'd realize what he'd done—first hoping that you would choose not to address it, and second, having a perfect excuse on hand in case you did. The kind of reasoning that would create the very insecurities you're struggling with now, so that he could continue assaulting you that way and even coerce you further without your consent. Ensuring you were too humiliated to confront him. Too insecure to leave."

I finally lift my head, emotion pooling behind my eyes when I look at him.

Weston's face is twisted in devastation, but he cups my cheeks with both hands, tipping my chin upward. "You're so strong, though. My brave, resilient girl. You broke free, and soon, you'll heal too."

"I don't want to let it define me anymore," I murmur, tilting my head and kissing his palm as one tear spills over.

"We won't let it." Weston catches my tear with a thumb and swipes it away, taking my shame with it. "I want to erase your pain too," he whispers, echoing my words from last night.

"When you touch me, it kind of feels like that." I smile softly, mimicking his.

Weston guides my mouth to him, kissing me languidly. Like he's got his entire life to do it. Those long, slow kisses morph into fervent exploration of each other's body. My tongue tasting his jaw, his teeth nipping my neck. My hands on his chest and tangled in the strands of his hair. His sliding over my breasts, grazing my nipples and teasing my skin.

Weston ends up hovering over me, nestled between my legs. His blazing eyes study me like I'm his next meal, gaze sparking heat in my veins. His hard cock throbs against my lower belly, lighting a fire in my core.

"You heard the medic," I say on a breath. "No rigorous activity. Plus, I only had one condom."

He laughs, dipping his head to kiss me tenderly. "I just wanted a taste of what it'll be like."

"What?" I ask.

"The next time we fuck," he says roughly, the words filtering from his lips and into mine. "I want it just like this. I want to see you writhe beneath me while I cage you in. Watch your pretty tits bounce with every thrust inside your perfect fucking body. I'm going to revel in the way I make those big blue eyes roll back as you claw at my shoulders. That's how I'm going to take you, Willow."

Heat rushes over me like a fucking tidal wave, breath hitching with a splintered gasp. "I think I'd like that."

"Oh, love. I'll guarantee it," he rasps, kissing me again.

CHAPTER THIRTY

WESTON

I AM ADDICTED to Willow Graham.

After getting cleared on Monday morning to return to light work, I gradually resumed my regular training schedule over the remainder of the week. Monday evening, I fucked Willow exactly as I promised I would, and the days that followed have become a flurried frenzy of our mingling bodies.

I woke early this morning, but since it's Sunday, I didn't have training. Deciding to surprise Willow with pancakes, I threw on a pair of joggers when I hopped out of bed and strode directly into the kitchen. Just as I pour the first dollop of batter onto the griddle, she saunters into the kitchen in nothing but my T-shirt.

Pride and possession flood my veins, and my atoms buzz with need at the long, tanned legs that seem to go on for miles beneath the hem. The way her nipples are just visible through the fabric, and the fact that I *know* she smells like me.

It's intoxicating—watching her sleep in my bed, seeing her face when I open my eyes for the first time each morning, her voice the last thing I hear each night.

"That smells good," she croons, hiking herself onto the counter before plucking a strawberry from the bowl beside her and popping it into her mouth.

"Are you wearing panties, Trouble?" I ask, cock achingly hard at the sight of her.

"I don't know. Why don't you check?" Her sultry voice is smooth like silk, shattering my composure as I pour the pancake batter onto the skillet.

I spin from the stove, finding her across from me, atop the island, leaning back on her elbows. She bats her eyes innocently, tongue darting out to lick her lush lips, and as my gaze rakes down her body, she opens her thighs, revealing her pretty, pink pussy. Wet and glistening.

"Oh, you are fucking trouble," I growl.

She grins, spreading her legs wider. I drop the spatula on the counter, stalking to her, leaning close as I reach around and snatch my wallet from the far end of the counter, fishing out a condom.

"Do you need to be fucked this morning, love? Is that how you'd like to start the day?"

She only whimpers, nodding rapidly.

"You'll need to use your words, Wills," I say, though I'm already dropping my joggers and rolling the condom over my length.

"I want you to fuck me, Wes," she rasps. "Right here. Now."

I snatch her waist with one hand, sliding her to the edge of the counter as the other hand positions my cock at her entrance. She locks her legs around my hips, her arms around my neck, and I slide home.

We moan into each other's mouths as I seat myself inside her, coating my length in her arousal before retreating and gliding back in effortlessly. "Look at you." I bite her neck. "Already so fucking wet. So primed for me."

Her head drops back, baring her throat as she bucks her hips, meeting me thrust for thrust. It's frantic and fervent. We're a mess of wild chaos, joining together with desperation.

"Slip a hand between those thighs and touch your pretty pussy for me, Trouble."

She moans, falling back against the counter, back arching as her fingers drift toward her clit, brushing over the bud. I slide my hands down her thighs, gripping beneath her knees and hiking them higher so I can fuck her deeper. The sight of her wrapped so tightly around me, her beckoning heat welcoming me in with each pump, the cascade of cries falling from her beautiful mouth—it's enough for me to lose my mind entirely.

The smell of burning batter permeates the air, but I'm too lost inside her to care.

"LOOK AT THE stars, Wes." The trembled whisper leaves her mouth between each thrust.

I could give one fuck about the stars, honestly. I'm peering down at Willow's flushed cheeks, golden hair a wild mess, her eyes bursting with passion.

She looks at the sky, but I find every constellation swimming in her gaze—brighter than the Milky Way itself. Her breasts spill from the top of her milkmaid dress with every rapid heave of her chest. The skirt hikes around her hips as I hold one of her legs in the air, fucking her from the side. Her head is nestled into the crook of my arm, her body flushed to mine.

"Don't need the stars." I pant. "Whole universe is staring directly at me right now."

Willow whimpers, lashes fluttering as a moan floats from her throat.

I halt my movement, cock still buried deep inside her. "Eyes, baby. Eyes. Gotta look at me when you come."

They pop open, reflective pools of starlight rippling in her irises. The power of their tides draws me in, and suddenly I'm swimming in the night sky.

I fuck her again, slow and deep, ensuring she feels every goddamn inch. Reminding her that her body was made to wrap around mine. The bed of my truck rocks with every snap of my hips, Willow's cries ricocheting off the coastal cliffs surrounding the Pacific Shores back road she took me out to tonight.

"Say my name, love," I command, exhaling over the shell of

her ear as I bury my face in her neck. "Remind the stars who it is that's making them collide for you."

"Weston!" The sound that leaves her throat is fucking delicious, floating through the air just a fraction of a second before she shatters entirely.

I follow right behind her, sinking into the depths of ecstasy.

"GOD, I FUCKING missed you." I kiss Willow hard the moment she opens the door to the guesthouse, walking us inside as I slam it behind me with a foot.

"I missed you," she says on a breath as my mouth drags along her jaw and down to her collarbone. "It's been the world's longest day."

Willow had an early shift this morning before driving out to Golden State for Penelope's lecture. I traveled north for a good swell that came in unexpectedly this evening, and am only now arriving home. It's nearly dark outside, the house warmly lit by two lamps in the corners and Willow's candle warmer that makes the entire room smell like vanilla, though the scent of garlic and herbs lingers in the air.

"I made dinner," Willow says into my mouth as I back her into the couch.

"Thank you, love," I murmur. "Need you first, though."

"Yes," she breathes. "You do."

I spin her around, cock pulsing when I realize she's wearing my competition shirt. My entry number and *Ashford* plastered across her back. The sight has my chest expanding—a primal, biological response to seeing my name written on her. It's possessive and instinctual.

Mine, that piece of me screams.

I place a palm between her shoulder blades, pressing her over the arm of the couch. Her perfect ass hiked in the air, I bend, tugging Willow's leggings down her thighs and allowing them to bind around her ankles. "Sending a message with this, Trouble?" I ask, plucking at the shirt. "You want to be owned by me tonight?"

"Yes," she whimpers into the cushions.

"Fuck." I make quick work of unzipping my shorts and slipping them down my legs, bending down to fish a condom from my wallet. After rolling it over my aching cock, I position myself behind her, scooping an arm around her waist and tugging her up so she's flush with my chest. Hand sliding up her waist and over her breasts, I cup her neck, tilting her head back.

Kissing her gently, I rasp, "I'm going to fuck you like I own you. I'm going to fuck you like the name across your back is yours too."

Her eyes roll, falling closed as she nods. I drop my hold on her throat, bending her over the couch again. I grip the back of the shirt, twisting my fingers in the fabric for leverage as I slide inside her.

I CLAMP MY palm over her mouth as another moan clatters off the walls of the room. I halt my hips, pausing deep inside her. The leg she has wrapped around my thigh presses into me, urging me to continue moving.

"What did I say, Wills?" I tsk. "Quiet girls get to come."

Willow's pussy tightens as she whimpers, the sound muffled beneath my hand. Her ocean eyes flare before rolling back as her head tips against the door. She nods, but I keep her lips covered anyway, shifting my weight onto the arm I have pressed against the door beside her head. I drive my hips upward again, hitting the deepest spot inside her. She pants into my palm but keeps quiet this time.

Her legs lock behind my back, fingers twined in the hair at the base of my neck as I pump into her. I'm trembling nearly as violently as she is, struggling to hold us both up—every clench of her around me sending an explosion of stars in my periphery and heat surging down my spine.

"Fuck, love. You're going to come, aren't you?" I groan. A strangled sound catches in Willow's throat, and she flexes her hips against me, meeting my thrusts, causing the shelves beside us to shake. "Is that what you need, baby?" I pull back enough to meet her eyes, grinning down at her. "I'm going to send you back to work with that pretty pussy dripping down your thighs."

She bites down on my palm, eyes half-lidded and narrowed as a growl reverberates against my skin. She thrashes against me, the drumming of her heart matching the pulse in her core, gripping my cock like she'll leave a permanent impression of me inside her.

I remove my hand from her mouth, slapping it against the door, needing the leverage to fuck her harder. Sliding it across the wood, I cup the back of her head, folding her face over my neck. "Need to bite down, do it here, Wills." I tap the crease of my shoulder.

She latches on immediately, a stifled cry vibrating against my skin. I drag my arm down, gliding over her chest and the dip of her waist, before reaching around to slide it under the hem of the dress hiked around her hips to grasp her ass. Kneading her soft flesh, I rock her over me, the frantic movement of our bodies slamming against the door.

I'm hoping that behind the racks of clothes in the farthest back corner of the surf shop, the rumbling behind this door will go unnoticed by shopping patrons and—God forbid—one of the owners if they were to walk in.

I told Willow to meet me here for lunch today, and since I'm working with Zander, it was easy to convince him to turn a blind eye when I grabbed her as she slipped through the front door earlier. I'd only planned on kissing her outside the range of her dad's cameras for a few dark, perfect moments before taking her down the pier to eat, but when Willow's fingers brushed my cock as I pinned her against the door, we both lost all composure. It's been two weeks since our first time, and I can't get enough.

Every second I'm not surfing or sleeping, I'm diving between

Willow's legs, greedily and eagerly owning every piece of herself she offers.

It's more than the sex, though. It's sleeping together and waking up together too. It's every deep conversation and sated smile we share when tangled together in those breathless moments after finishing. It's the way she lets me into her soul by the touch she allows me to place on her skin.

She's engrained in me now, and I feel a little less complete when I'm not with her.

I feel more than hear my name cascading from her lips as she keeps them locked in the crease of my neck. She's shaking wildly, body wound tight before going taut, a climax ripping through her. She writhes against me, and I hold her through it as she rides it out.

The flood of her release over my cock, the tight hold she has on my hair, and the sharp sting of her teeth sinking into my skin has me chasing her orgasm with my own, the heat coiled in my spine exploding into a burst of all-consuming ecstasy.

"So good, love. So fucking good," I rasp, lips tangled in her sex-mused hair as I coax her down from her release.

Her forehead rests on my shoulder, parted lips panting heavily against my arm. Once her breathing evens out, I slowly lower her legs, holding her steady as she regains the strength to stand on her own. I slide my hand out from under her dress, bending to help her smooth it down.

When I stand, I do the same to her hair, running the long strands through my fingers before adjusting the straps on her dress. Willow looks up at me from beneath her lashes, the sated heat in her gaze enough to make my cock stir again. Her tanned skin glistens under the low light, cheeks flushed the prettiest shade of rosy pink, pillow-soft lips swollen from my kiss.

"That was unexpected," she says in a breath as I make quick work of pulling up my jeans and disposing of the condom.

"I don't know." I shrug, a slow grin spreading over my face. "I guess you were just desperate to have your way with me, Willow."

"Yeah, I'm sure." She rolls her eyes, smoothing down her hair one final time before throwing open the stockroom door. "Now I'm hungry." Throwing her arm behind her, reaching for my hand, she adds, "Buy me a burger."

"Whatever you want, love." I grin, weaving my fingers through hers.

"WILLOW, BABY, I don't think this is going to work."

"Engage your core, Weston." She flips her hair over her shoulder, peeking back at me. "Brace your weight on your arms, spread your legs, and don't lose your balance."

The sun crests over the mountains to the east, the water in the deep corner of the cove like glass on this quiet Sunday morning. The sky explodes in pastels, thick clouds like puffs of floating cotton candy, but it's the sight of Willow rising on her knees as she pulls the bottoms of her bathing suit aside, revealing the slightest glimpse of her plump, pink pussy that takes my breath away.

She insisted we share a paddleboard this morning, and I was a little taken aback when we reached beyond the break of the low-tide waves and Willow demanded I take my cock out. She tugged my shorts down just enough for it to spring free, pulled a condom out from the waistband of her bathing suit bottoms, and then demanded I put it on as she turned around, balancing herself on all fours.

Her eyes shimmer mischievously in the morning light as she grins at me, bracing her weight on her knees and slipping her ankles beneath my thighs. The board sways as she settles between my legs, her plush and perfect fucking ass nestling itself right up against my aching cock.

A tortured groan leaves my throat as she balances on one arm—like she's doing fucking yoga or something, the incredible goddamn woman—and reaches back with her free hand, grasping my length. She pumps me twice, sending a rush of sparks through my veins. Swiping the moisture gathered at my tip, she coats my base before lifting her hips and swiping my cock through her slit, then notching me at her entrance.

"God-fucking-dammit, Willow," I growl through gritted teeth as she sinks down on me, her ass flushing with my hips, flesh bouncing with the movement of the board beneath us. "You're killing me, baby."

"No," she rasps, flashing me her dimples. "I'm bringing your fantasies to life."

She lifts before dropping back down at a rhythm slow enough that it doesn't send us tumbling into the ocean, but with enough force that I feel every flawless flutter of her perfect pussy when she throws herself back on me. I grip her ass, spreading wide as I rock her faster.

The view is fucking unreal. Willow's hair sways down her back, skin rippling with every bounce of her hips, the slap of our skin echoing over the waves that lap against the board. The Pacific stretches forever in front of me, sky streaked with shades of fuchsia and periwinkle as her beautiful moan cuts through the salt air.

"You are every fantasy, love."

"Wes . . ." Her breath hitches. "You're going to be late."

"Wills, I gotta eat it before I go surfing. You know that, baby." I lift my chin, smiling at her through the sheets of water that blur my vision. Even beneath the stream, I can see just how pretty and flushed her skin is, the way her breasts bounce with each heave of her chest. "It's part of my routine now. I perform better when I can taste your pussy on my lips."

"Fuck," she mutters, slamming her head back against the wall of the outdoor shower.

It's been a month-long addiction to Willow Graham, and I've come to realize that my days are undoubtedly better when they've started with her coming on my face.

Leo's offering a youth camp this week, which means I get a break from the level of training I'm used to. My responsibility is to assist with the kids instead. The first session starts late enough that I had time to paddle with Willow in the harbor. She wanted to wash the saltwater off before she went home to prepare for her shift at Honeysuckle, and while I had no need to do the same, considering I'll be spending all day on the beach, I wasn't going to say no when she invited me in with her.

I dive back between Willow's thighs, running my tongue along her slit and spreading her open, coating myself in the sweet taste of her arousal before settling over her clit. My fingers dance along her thighs, teasing the sensitive skin and putting her on edge.

I kneel before her—worshipping at her altar. Leg draped over my shoulder, hands twisted in my hair, she rocks herself against my face. Sweet, soft whimpers float from her mouth, muffled beneath the water that pounds against the concrete floor.

"Wes," she moans, voice rising above the veil of noise, my name a jumbled, nearly unintelligible mess of impassioned breath.

"Willow?" someone calls from beyond the walls.

I freeze, mouth still buried in her pussy.

She tenses, breath hitching in shock. "Umm . . . yeah?"

"Are you okay?"

Recognition flashes across her eyes as an irritated grumble of, "He must be helping out with the camp," leaves her mouth. "Yeah, Camden." There's a bite in her raised tone. "I'm fine."

"Absolutely fucking not," I rasp, slipping my finger inside her, causing a gasp to spring from her lips. "You don't say anyone else's name when I'm between these thighs."

"Wes," she hisses. "God."

"Yeah, baby. More like that."

I crook my finger, pumping once before adding a second and flicking my tongue over her clit. She hums, rolling her pussy over my mouth, setting the pace she needs.

"What'd you say?" Camden calls again.

Before Willow can speak, I pull back and snap, "She's busy and uninterested."

"Excuse—"

"You've been dismissed," I bark, glancing up at Willow.

Eyes wide, brows raised, and jaw dropped, she's stunned silent. An amused smirk plays at the corner of her mouth, and I don't wait for him to respond as I return to devouring her pussy, reveling in the hard crunch of gravel beneath her ex's retreating footsteps.

Flattening my tongue, I wrap my lips around her clit, lapping at her relentlessly while matching the tempo of my fingers inside her. Applying pressure to her favorite place, sucking on her bud, I consume her entirely—until she's shattering all around me.

Her release soaks my face, cascading down my chin along with the shower stream. Willow's boneless, body slumping as I slowly pull my fingers from her, ensuring her gaze locks on mine as I lick her taste from my skin.

She snatches my wrist, raising my hand to her own mouth. I drown in the multitudes of her eyes, swallowed entirely by her lust-laced irises as she slips my two fingers into her mouth, sucking herself away.

"Fuck, Willow," I mutter, adjusting myself when I stand, attempting to relieve any ounce of the pressure in my raging cock. "I'm going to be thinking about this all day. You have any fucking clue what you do to me, Trouble?"

"Fantasize about me," she murmurs, rising on her toes to brush her lips over mine. "Then come home tonight and show me what it is I do to you."

She kisses me once, tongue darting out to taste her essence on my lips before she spins, taunting her flawless ass as she leaves me in the shower—hard and aching.

Thankfully, I'm not late to camp, even if I didn't beat her prick of an ex down here. He glares at me when I step onto the sand. I grin because we both know I'm the one with the taste of her inside my mouth.

I run my tongue over my top lip, the gesture clear as the blue sky above us: *mine.*

LATER THAT NIGHT, after I've shown her exactly how she makes me feel, we lie tangled in my bed. She's on her side, flush against my chest as I pepper strategic kisses over her spine.

"What are you doing?" she asks sleepily—contented. My chest expands at the sound.

"Counting your freckles," I whisper, dragging my lips along her back.

She hums, laughing softly. "I read once that the placement of your freckles are all the spots your soulmate kissed you in a past life."

"Hmm." I muse, gliding my mouth over her soft, smooth skin. "I must've been hungry back then."

"Weston." Willow's breath hitches, lips parting as I gently roll atop her. Her heart pounds erratically against my chest, matching the beat of my own. She's the picture of pristine beauty, utter perfection—golden hair a halo around her glowing face, crystalline eyes bursting with awe.

I dip my head, murmuring against her lips, "But love, in this lifetime, I'm starving."

CHAPTER THIRTY-ONE
WILLOW

HALF-WAY THROUGH my afternoon shift at the flower shop, I stare out the window, mindlessly watching tourists meander around the boardwalk. Weston's words from last night are the soundtrack in my mind, playing on a loop—etched into my bones, imprinted on my ears, written beneath my eyelids.

In this lifetime, I'm starving.

I was so stunned, I merely whispered his name, all other words lost to me. He hadn't seemed bothered, though. He smiled as if he understood it—the exact, indescribable feeling floating in the center of my being. I fell asleep wrapped up in him, wondering how the sensation he elicited in me was even possible.

It's a slow August day, but Mom asked me to come in and help out since she's swamped with preparing arrangements for a beach wedding tomorrow. She's in the back, music blasting through her earbuds, organizing an array of seasonal blooms.

I'm dragged from my thoughts when a buzzing erupts in my back pocket. I pull out my phone to find a call from an unknown number with an unrecognizable area code. I press ignore, sending them to voicemail.

Last thing I'd be caught dead doing is answering the phone for someone I don't know.

A moment later, it vibrates again with a text. My stomach leaps up my throat, splattering onto the floor at my feet when I read it.

Unknown Number

It's Parker.

Unkown Number

I spoke to Chelsea. We need to talk.

My trembling hand nearly drops my phone as my thumb hovers over the screen. Anxiety slithers through my chest, seizing my lungs and constricting my breathing. My vision blurs as my mind loses focus—like I'm outside my body, watching this happen to some other girl. The screen is fuzzy as I immediately block the number he contacted me from.

My eyes dart around the shop, glance out the windows, the skin on the back of my neck prickling as if he'll be lurking around any corner.

I swallow the knot in my throat, slipping my phone back into my pocket and composing myself enough to hope my mother doesn't notice when I peek my head into her work room and say, "I'm going to go grab a coffee. Are you in a spot to take a break and watch the counter?"

She pulls out an earbud and drops the scissors in her hand. "Yeah, I'm about finished. Can you get me a Honeysuckle latte while you're over there?"

I nod, lips twitching with a smile when I'm reminded how my aunt named her coffee shop's five signature drinks after the boardwalk businesses—each inspired by the family who owns them. My mom's is her favorite cold brew with vanilla cream and honey.

I push open the doors to Honeysuckle and turn left, taking five steps before I reach the front of The Wicked Wildflower and swing it open. The cafe is buzzing with patrons littered at the tables, sipping on coffee and nibbling baked goods, but it's otherwise slow.

Allie has her back turned, boxing up what appears to be a number of custom orders—variously decorated cakes and pies.

"Allie?" I ask quietly as I reach the counter.

"One sec, babe." She finishes packaging the last of the orders before spinning toward me. Her brows knit as she studies my face, and the composure I'd garnered on my way over here begins to unravel. "What's going on?"

"Can you take a break?" I ask, my tone hollow.

She nods, features softening into a solemn expression. "Hold on." She stacks the orders, backing through the swinging doors that lead to the kitchen. She calls to Dahlia, who must be in her office, informing her she'll be taking her break.

Returning to the front, Allie loops her arm through mine, patting my hand as she says, "Let's take a walk down the pier."

"Don't let me forget to order my mom a coffee when we get back."

"Okay." She leads me out the front doors before we take a left, heading for the pier that expands beyond the boardwalk, stretching out into the endless blue Pacific. "Tell me what has you all knotted up."

It's a flawless, breezy summer day—not one cloud obstructing the infinite azure of the sky above us. Seagulls circle our heads as waves crash against the pillars below, the roar dulling the hum of beachgoers around us.

These types of days are my favorite. The reminder of how far and wide people travel to experience this kind of easy living, and how lucky I was to have grown up inside it my entire life.

I'm disappointed in myself for having a raging storm cloud hovering over my head on an afternoon like this.

"Parker called me."

Allie pauses, head whipping in my direction. "I thought you blocked him."

"I did. I guess he got a new number or called from someone else's phone. I don't know."

"Did you answer?" she asks hesitantly as we continue our walk.

I shake my head. "I ignored it, and then he texted me, telling me we needed to talk. I blocked the number after that."

"Good."

"I think . . ." I swallow. "I think he knows about the abortion."

"That doesn't mean you owe him a conversation, Willow."

I nod, but some kind of trepidation slithers down my spine as we make a loop around the pier, walking in comfortable silence. It's been months since the day I left him, and to learn it's all still eating at him enough to go to such lengths to contact me—the guilt lingers.

He may have broken me, but what does that matter if I did the same in return?

"Do you think I did the wrong thing?" I ask Allie.

"Assuming you're referring to offering Parker closure, no." She stops as we reach the boardwalk again, grasping my hands to halt me walking. "He *knows*, Willow. He can ignore it, he can justify it, he can pretend, but he knows what he did. You made a clean break, your message rang clear. He doesn't deserve closure, and the only reason he's chasing it now is to attempt to manipulate you into absolving him of his own deep-seated shame."

"You think he feels shame?" I laugh incredulously.

"Not on the surface—not in a way he's aware of, but deep down? Yeah." She nods, shrugging. "Men like that always do. He may not be capable of comprehending it, but it'll eat at him little by little every day for the rest of his life. Eventually, it'll wither him down until there is nothing left of him at all. Meanwhile . . ." She grins, grasping my face and lifting my chin, forcing my eyes to meet her convicted gaze. "You'll be soaring."

I muster the most genuine smile I can manage, and Allie's eyes roam upward, taking in the sign above the door of the building we stopped in front of. Her grin spreads wider—mischievous. "Wanna get tattoos?"

I snort. "We're both in the middle of a shift."

Her nose scrunches, eyes narrowing, gaze unfocused as she thinks through a plan. "I can talk the sisters into letting us go early."

"Doubt it." I roll my eyes.

"Let me make your mom her coffee and bring it to her myself, she can't say no to me. Dahlia owes me an afternoon off anyway." She takes my hand, pulling me with her as she skips toward the coffee shop. "Should we get pussy willows?"

"What the fuck are you saying?" I laugh as I follow her back to the bakery.

"I HAVE THREE other highly qualified artists who are more than capable of tattooing this . . . branch on you." August eyes the image Allie has pulled up on her phone over his glasses.

"It's a pussy willow, actually," she says matter-of-factly.

His lip curls as his gaze darts between her and me.

"We want you to do it," I drawl, rocking on my heels.

"Because you know I won't charge you."

I blink innocently.

He huffs, rolling his eyes, though a smile hides in the corner of his mouth. "Give me ten minutes to draw these up. Go wait on the back bench."

I grin. I love both of my uncles equally, but I've always been closest with August. Something about us having artist's souls, I think.

Allie and I meander through Ultraviolet, past the black chalk wall covered in decades-worth of doodles left by clients and staff, and the neon light in the center of the shop that reads: *You are the artist and the art.*

I hop onto the bench first, while Allie sits on a black leather couch against the wall beside me. "So . . . you know how I gave Declan that hall pass and told him we'd talk next month?"

"Yes . . ." I eye her suspiciously.

"Do you think it's bad if I . . . maybe took a hall pass for myself too?" She winces, anticipating my reaction.

Rightfully so, because I toss her an exasperated sigh. "Really, Allie? You and Archer hooked up?"

I don't know why I'm surprised. I don't know why this summer would be any different.

Allie and Archer have had a tumultuous relationship since the first summer Allie spent here when we were teens. It got more intense after they began hooking up in high school—refusing to commit to each other because they attended different schools in different cities hours apart, but refusing to be with anyone else, either.

When Archer moved to Texas to play football, they promised to spend their college years separately, dating and falling in love with other people, with the hope that if they were truly meant to be, they'd end up together someday anyway.

Dumb in theory—far worse in real life.

Allie dates the worst men on the planet, and Archer doesn't date at all, supposedly opting to entertain himself with meaningless hookups instead. But when summer and holiday breaks roll around, Allie coincidentally finds herself single, and they rekindle their lingering flame until Archer leaves again.

It's a toxic cycle that breaks their hearts time after time—one that's proven impossible to break.

"It was just once . . ." Her voice becomes rough and emotion filled. "The night before he left."

Archer went back to Texas two mornings ago, and I know Allie's been eaten up over it. Regardless of their physical slip-ups, they've always been best friends first. It's never easy for any of us to watch him leave—he's the only one who has ventured so far from home—but it's especially hard on Allie.

"I don't think you're a bad person for it, Alls. I just think you should end things with Declan. Period. He sucks, and you deserve to be with the person you actually love."

"She's not wrong," August chimes, returning from his office

with printed stencils of our tattoos. "Time is too precious to waste on anything other than the people you want to spend it with most."

She groans, dramatically throwing herself back on the couch and covering her eyes with her hands, pouting. "Leave me alone. I didn't want to be sad today."

August laughs, taking a seat on a rolling stool beside the bench I'm on before pulling a tray from the corner and placing my arm across it. As he's sanitizing me, my phone buzzes in my pocket, and I pull it out with my freehand, sliding my thumb over the screen.

"Hi, Wes."

"Hey, baby. I came down to the boardwalk early so I could see you before my shift, but your mom said you left already."

"I'm at Ultraviolet getting a tattoo. Come over here."

"We're getting pussy willows!" Allie shouts into my phone, pulling the attention of the other patrons in the studio.

"Sorry . . . what?" Wes asks into the phone.

"Just come here." I laugh before hanging up.

He glides through the doors thirty seconds later, looking fucking delectable in a pair of light-wash jeans, a white Heathen's tee, and a navy blue baseball cap turned backward.

"What is Allie shouting about your pussy?" he asks, striding directly to me and planting a kiss on my lips before pulling back with a playful grin.

"Jesus Christ," August mutters.

"Pussy willow," Allie corrects. "It's a type of tree, and we're getting matching tattoos of its branch."

Weston leans over, eyeing the stencil August placed at the center of my forearm, outlining the bundle of branches and the small, furry catkins blooming at the ends. "I mean . . . it's cute. The name is awful, though."

"Well, that's the point. We call her Allie Cat"—I nod to my best friend—"and a pussy is the same thing, right? Then, you know, I'm Willow. So . . ." I shrug. "It works."

"It's fitting." He smiles. "Can I watch?"

"Yeah." August nods toward a row of chairs at the front of the studio. "Grab one and drag it over here."

Weston does, twirling the chair and straddling it backward as he sits between August and me, watching intently as the tattoo gun buzzes to life and my uncle presses the needle into my skin. I bite back a hiss at the sting, but it only takes me a moment to adjust to the discomfort.

I'm still tense, and Weston's hand finds my leg, squeezing gently. "Does it hurt?"

"Not terribly. You should get one and find out for yourself, though." I wink.

"I told you I'm afraid of needles." He deadpans.

"This is kind of like immersion therapy, then. Isn't it?" August smiles, gaze focused on my arm behind his black-rimmed glasses. Chestnut curls fall against his forehead, pierced brow furrowed in concentration as his tattooed hand glides the needle over my skin with precision. "If you were to get one, what would it be?"

"I don't know. I've never thought too deeply about it, on account of the trypanophobia, but I always assumed I'd get something in my mom's memory."

"He actually looked up the name for fear of needles," Allie murmurs from the corner of her mouth, scrolling through her phone as she sprawls across the couch.

Ignoring her, Weston continues with a bemused smile, "I mean . . . I don't think it's actually that serious, but it seems unpleasant enough that I've never had the urge. Plus, I think if I were to actually get a tattoo for my mom, it would make her feel more . . . permanently gone? I don't know if that makes sense."

I know the question was directed at me, but my uncle answers, "It does. It's been twenty-five years for me, and sometimes I still have trouble convincing myself it's permanent too."

"You lost your mom?" Wes asks him softly.

"Brother."

Wes swallows hard, clearing his throat. His stormy eyes dart to me, swirling with sorrow. I place my hand over his, squeezing it four times.

"I'm sorry," he tells August.

My uncle pauses, lifting his head, eyes locked on Wes. "Me too." He smiles softly. "I've found that inking myself with the things that make me feel most alive is a type of healing all on its own. Maybe that's what you should consider, if you ever find you want to get tattooed."

Weston nods, eyes becoming unfocused—deep in thought—as August finishes my pussy willow, covering it in Saniderm before starting on Allie's. Wes and I sit together on the couch as Allie prattles on about a book we are both reading. Weston has an arm wrapped around me, drawing circles over my shoulders, but that thoughtful haze doesn't leave him through the remainder of Allie's tattoo.

When she's finished, she pops up, smiling down at her forearm—her piece a perfect twin to my own. "They look amazing." She looks up at me. "Don't you feel so much better now?"

"Better?" Wes asks. "What happened?"

"Oops." Allie winces, stepping back before hitching a thumb behind her. "I guess I'll wait for you outside . . ."

"Actually, I have lunch for Elena, but I need to relieve one of my workers, so I won't be able to bring it next door. Can you drop it by for me?" August asks, eyeing Weston and me curiously.

"I can do that!" Allie says too excitedly, striding toward his office behind the front desk.

I give him a side hug, thanking my uncle for the tattoo before he disappears with Allie down the back hallway. I turn back to Weston, who is watching me, eyes shadowed with unsettled apprehension.

"I got a call from some weird number today. I didn't answer it, so they sent a text. It was from Parker." I swallow the brick in my throat. "He asked to talk to me."

"Are you okay?" Wes asks, the words rushed. "What did you do?"

"I blocked the number, and I am okay." I gently grasp his

forearms. "You were still at the camp, and Allie was right next door, so I went to her. We walked around the pier until I calmed down and then came to get tattoos. I planned on telling you tonight . . . I wasn't keeping—"

"I know, love. I'm not worried about that. I'm worried about you." He sighs, stepping back from me, running a hand through his hair. "Can we talk outside for a minute?"

Trepidation trickles down my spine at this tone, uneasy with the newfound concern etched into his face as he bites his lip, and his eyes dart around the tattoo studio as if he's searching for something.

I nod, silent as he places a hand at the small of my back and guides me out the front doors. There is a bench across the sidewalk, beneath the palms and overlooking the Pacific. Weston leads us to it, taking a seat and gently pulling me down beside him.

"Your dad didn't want me to tell you this." His knee shakes as his gaze drifts out to the horizon—he's nervous. That trepidation in my spine morphs to pure fear, swirling in the depths of me. "But I think after today . . . you need to know what's been going on."

"Wes . . . what's going on?" I grasp his wrist, squeezing, the gesture pulling his gaze back to my face.

"Parker's been trying to contact you for weeks. He . . . He called more than just the flower shop that one time. He called your ex, Camden, who filed a restraining order. Your dad threatened him, and . . ." He turns, facing me head-on as he takes my hands in his. "He called me too. He never said his name, and he called from a blocked number, but he asked if I was dating you. Your dad was there, he took my phone from me, and the minute he addressed Parker by name, the line went dead. He's been trying to protect you from all this, but if Parker is contacting you directly now, you need to know."

I pull my hands from Weston's, turning away, directing my gaze toward the ocean as the information filters through me. I wonder if I'm supposed to scream, or cry, or be afraid. Perhaps I am, and may later on, when I'm alone, I'll rage and sob, but in this moment, I'm numb.

I'm shocked to my core, and somehow completely numb.

"I'm sorry, Wills. You should've known this entire time. I'm so fucking sorry, baby."

Weston doesn't touch me, but sits silently beside me, giving me time and space to process. I'm sure I have reason to be upset with him and with my father for keeping this from me. I'm disappointed that they didn't believe I had the strength to handle this, to be left in the loop when it came to my own safety.

I'm not angry with them for it, though. I can understand their reasons.

More than anything, I'm upset that it's happening at all. That Parker has not only put me through this, but that it seems as if every person in my life is getting dragged down with me. That in my effort to ignore him until he goes away, he's turned to harassing my loved ones in my place.

I'm fucking over it.

I pull my phone out of my back pocket, navigating to the text message he sent me earlier, and unblocking the number. I place my finger over the call button before my nerves can catch up with me and convince me to change my mind.

"What're you doing?" Weston asks.

"Calling Parker."

"Whoa, Willow," Wes gasps, gently placing his hand on my arm. "I don't know if that's such a good idea."

I hush him as Parker's phone goes to voicemail. A blanket of relief settles over me at the realization that I won't actually have to hear his voice or address him directly. I take a deep breath as the answering tone chimes, hoping what I say next will be enough to make him leave me alone for good.

"Stop calling my family. Stop calling my boyfriend. Stop calling *me*," I hiss into my phone. "You know exactly what you did, and nothing you say is going to make me regret my decisions, nor will it replace your actions. There is no conversation to be had between us." Emotion thickens my voice, but I refuse to let it crack for him. "You cannot manipulate me anymore, you can't make me hate myself, and I will not placate the deep-seated shame you refuse to acknowledge and relentlessly attempt to cover up by victimizing yourself." I pause, closing my eyes and allowing every ounce of pent up pain to wash through me, letting it cascade from my body and crash to the ground at my feet. When I walk away from this bench, I'll be leaving Parker behind too. I refuse to carry him with me anymore. "Be grateful I haven't reported you to the Board at Berkeley. If you contact me, my parents, or Weston one more time, I will do exactly that. Forget I exist, Parker, because I've already forgotten you."

I exhale, expelling all the oxygen in my lungs as I re-block the number and pocket my phone before turning to Weston. His eyes are a deep blue flame, blazing through me. It's his gaze that has reality pummeling into me, and suddenly, I'm falling against his chest, wrapping my arms around his waist.

"Incredible, Willow," he whispers against the top of my head. "You're incredible. My brave, strong girl."

I nuzzle into him, soaking up his warmth and scent. Being pressed against Weston is like falling into bed after a long day. Even in public, beneath the blazing sun, with the anguish of my past floating all around me, I'm nothing but comfortable when wrapped in him.

He kisses my forehead as I pull back, raising my chin to look up at him. "Did you not tell me because my dad told you not to, or because you thought I couldn't handle it?"

"I wanted to respect his boundaries, and I thought he knew what was best for you, and it was my place to listen to that. At the time, I don't think that was a wrong way of thinking, but now . . ." He cups my face. "I'm on your team, Wills. Always. We're in everything together, and I choose you every fucking time. I'm sorry for not telling you, and it'll never happen again."

We stand from the bench, Weston smiling down at me, eyes sparkling with so much adoration it seeps into my very bones. I rise onto my toes, kissing him gently. He surges forward, capturing my lips in a tender caress, uncaring of the setting as he takes his time thoroughly ravishing me.

"Do you want me to walk you to work?" I ask, pulling back but keeping my hands on his arms, still craving his touch.

He pulls out his phone, checking the time. "I still have a bit before my shift starts. I might hang back at the studio for a little while and see if August will continue allowing me to observe." He winks. "Immersion therapy or whatever he said."

I tilt my head, tossing him a mystified smirk. "Okay, weirdo. Allie and I were going to grab lunch, but I think I need to go talk to my parents first. About Parker."

Weston nods. "Your dad should be over at the surf shop, earlier this morning he mentioned he had a meeting today."

"Good, I'll grab him before I go find my mom at Honeysuckle."

I'm not angry with my parents, but I need them to know that I'm aware of the ongoing behavior from Parker, that I've handled it, and I'll continue handling it if my phone call wasn't enough to stop him for good.

Though, I'm confident that Parker values his reputation at Berkeley more than he ever did me, and I'm hoping my threat will be enough. I knew that reporting his assault would likely lead to nothing other than a he-said she-said argument, that I'd inevitably lose. But his repeated harassment over this summer is an entirely new claim to make—one that comes with proof.

"I'll see you tonight?" Wes asks as we walk hand-in-hand toward the tattoo shop.

"Yeah. I have a new painting idea I wanted to start on, so I'll probably be in my art room when you get done with work later."

His arm loops around my waist, tugging me into him. "Why don't you paint at the guesthouse? That way when I get home tonight you're already exactly where I need you, and you don't have to stop working."

Butterfly wings flutter in my chest so rapidly they may lift me right off the floor. My cheeks ache with the weight of my grin. "Are you sure? It's kind of a big project. It'll take up a lot of your space."

His gray-blue eyes blaze with enough conviction to bring me to my knees when he says, "Take all my space, Wills. Make it ours."

I'm falling in love with you.

The rogue thought floats across my mind on the back of one of those butterflies, yet the realization hits me with enough force to knock the wind from my lungs. I know it's happening, but part of me screams *too soon.* There is so much I haven't said. So many secrets still kept. Pieces of myself I'm still terrified to show him. I sway on my feet, but Weston's strength holds me steady.

"Okay," I breathe. Unsure of what else to say or do, I grab the back of his neck and pull him down, swallowing his gasp as I kiss him again.

CHAPTER THIRTY-TWO
WESTON

SOFT ALTERNATIVE ROCK floats through the air as I slip inside the warmly lit house. The coffee table has been pushed against the wall, and the plush, cream rug that used to accent the center of the living room floor is rolled up in the corner.

Willow's back is turned to me, she's on her knees in the middle of a canvas about three times her size, swiping a paintbrush over it. In only a white tank and a pair of black panties, her hair thrown up into a messy blond knot, stripes of color covering her sun-kissed skin—the most beautiful thing I've ever seen.

"Hey, love. I brought dinner."

She peeks over her shoulder, smiling. "Thank you."

"Wanna eat now or later?"

"In a bit. Once I wash this paint off me I won't want to come back to it."

I nod, setting the food on the counter before striding over to the couch and sprawling out, turning on my side so I can watch her as she swipes a long, thick stroke of teal across the canvas. "I have something to show you later too."

She pauses, glancing up at me. "Really?"

"Yeah." I bite my cheek, itching to show her now, but I don't want to distract her further.

"Well, I have something to tell you." She sits back on her knees, brows pinched as she studies the canvas in front of her. As of now, it's mostly untouched. Similar paint strokes to the one she just made are etched across it in varying colors. It almost looks like some kind of abstract sunset, but for fear of being entirely off base and offending her, I don't voice it.

"What's that?"

"I committed to UC Irvine," she says nonchalantly, eyes still fixed on her painting.

"Willow," I gasp. "That's huge."

Her eyes dart to me, doing a double take when she realizes I'm radiating with excitement. "It is?"

"Yes." I slink off the couch, dropping to my knees as I envelope her, laying her back on the floor beside the canvas, careful not to get wet paint on either of us. "You make me proud, Wills."

Emotion shines in her eyes as she peers up at me through long lashes, cupping my face with her hands. "You make me proud too."

I laugh roughly at that, I'm not sure what I've done to give her that feeling lately. I'll finish working with Leo through August, and he's helping me find resources once I return to Santa Monica, but he's barred me from competing anymore this season. He doesn't think I'm ready yet, and while we'll reevaluate where I stand before the Championship Qualifiers this fall, there's virtually no chance of me even attempting to reach the Olympics next summer.

Her brows pinch at my response. "I'm serious, Wes. Most people would've crumbled beneath the weight of what life handed you, but you carry it with grace. You somehow made room to carry me too, and I'll never stop being awed by you."

I'll never stop carrying you. Never stop loving you.

The words linger at the tip of my tongue, but I swallow them down, I don't know if Willow is there yet. I don't know if she's ready to hear the true depth of my feelings for her, the lengths I'd go to carry her for the rest of time. I'm new to this entire realm of existence, and part of me wants to wait until she says the words first because I'm not sure I can recognize the signs of whether she's ready.

Willow licks her lips, eyes cast downward, breaking contact as she twirls the fabric of my T-shirt between two fingers. "The university has counseling for students, so I . . . I registered to meet with someone once I begin classes next month. I'm going to start talking to someone about what happened. You inspired that."

I tip her chin up, forcing those ocean eyes to mine. "You make me so proud, Willow," I say again, ensuring each word is laced with the conviction that matches the warm expansion happening inside my chest. "My brave, strong girl."

Her lashes flutter as she draws me in, tangling her fingers with the hair at my nape, brushing her lips over mine in a tender kiss full of everything neither of us can seem to say yet. The soft beginning strums of "Iris" by Goo Goo Dolls filter through the speakers in the house.

My mouth moves over hers, tongue slipping through to taste her, drowning myself in her sweetness, swallowing her whimper as I kiss her deeper. She presses against my shoulder, and we rise together—a cohesive unit. There is no ending for her and no beginning for me, only what we become when tied together like this. Rolling me over, Willow pins me on my back, settling herself over my legs.

Her knee slides over the canvas, through the streak of wet paint, knocking over her palette and the cups of paint she had lined up along the top of the canvas.

"Shit, Wills," I murmur, though she continues to kiss me thoroughly. "We're going to ruin your painting, baby."

She sits up, straddling me, hair falling from her bun and framing her face in gold, cheeks flushed the most beautiful shade of pink, a perfect complement to her shimmering eyes. "I was lost with this piece, anyway," she breathes. "I want to create something new. With you."

Crossing her arms across her stomach, she grasps the hem of her tank and pulls it over her head, leaving her in nothing but her scrap of black panties.

Her rosy nipples, peaked and puckered, matching the blush

spreading across her chest, breasts bounce with every sharp inhale and Willow's movement as she unbuttons my jeans. She raises her eyes to mine—lust and a request for permission swirling within her gaze.

My cock springs to life at the sight of her, and I nod as I lift up and peel my shirt over my head while she tugs my jeans down my legs. She's so focused on getting them off me, she doesn't notice until she's tossed them across the floor and turns back to me.

Raking over my body, her gaze quickly snatches on my thigh, eyes expanding with shock. "Wes, what is that?" Willow points at the tattoo, covered by that transparent second-skin material August promised would help it heal faster.

"It's a . . . stained-glass window," I stutter, grinning sheepishly. "A tattoo."

She raises her eyes to me—bursting with astonishment. "You're afraid of needles."

"I think I was afraid of being afraid." I shake my head. "Your uncle said I should consider exploring art that makes me feel alive, rather than focusing on scarring myself with what I've already lost."

"Stained glass makes you feel alive?" she asks softly, tilting her head as amusement dances across her face.

"No, but you do. I told you . . . you're like the sun shining through the window. Your presence creates color. *You're* the art. To me."

Her lip trembles, gaze cast downward as she brushes her fingers over the ink with a feather-light touch, studying the design. I went with something simple. A gothic shape with basic borders and lines cut through it, creating geometric flowers within the panel. Black and white.

"Sunflowers," she says with a disbelieving laugh, an astonished smile spreading over her face.

"You seemed to like painting my skin, Willow." I bite my lip, shrugging. "Now, you'll always have a place to color in. As many times as you'd like. Any shade you want. A piece of me to make your own."

Her eyes flicker between my face and my leg, rapidly blinking away the emotion misting over them. Willow's chin quivers, head shaking rapidly, as if trying to make sense of the gesture. Trepidation plucks at the strings of my heart like I'm an instrument waiting to see how Willow's going to play me.

"This is the most beautiful thing anyone has ever done for me. I think . . . the most beautiful thing any person has done for any other person ever," she whispers, voice breaking. "Weston, I . . ." She inhales swiftly, raising her gaze, pinning it to me as a tear drips over her cheek.

"I know," I breathe. "Me too."

I don't need to make her say the words—I can taste them on her lips. I don't need to make her tell me how she feels—I can hear them with every soft breath exhaled into my mouth. It's happened, we've fallen. Bared ourselves to each other—skin and soul.

We jumped together, hand in hand—though each of us still holds pieces of our past untold. It's almost as if we can't voice the love we're feeling until we find the courage to voice our darkness too.

Though, when Willow pushes against my chest, laying me down and crawling over me again, I feel blanketed in understanding. Acceptance. When she places a hand behind my head, softening the landing as I fall back against the canvas, and brushes her lips over mine—it feels like being caught.

We jumped, and even tangled in our trauma, this moment is like crash-landing among the clouds together.

Her breasts scrape against my chest, and I'm aching as she grinds down, only the fabric of our underwear separating our flesh. The paint she spilled across the canvas seeps beneath my body. Willow pulls away, sitting up on me—half-lidded eyes radiating with need. The commanding goddess I'm worshipping.

"Can I have you like this?" she asks, a sultry silk to her tone that drips along my skin like heated honey. "Right here?"

"Yes, love," I hiss as she palms my cock. My hands slide

through the paint beneath me as I search for something to grip—coming away in shades of blush and lavender, they land on her hips, smearing prints across her skin as I drown in her touch.

She lifts, pulling my underwear down just enough to free my length before reaching between her legs and pulling her panties aside. Rocking her hips forward, Willow notches me at her entrance, gaze anchoring to mine as she slowly sinks down.

We let out a simultaneous moan at the mind-altering feel of our connection. That familiar sensation of no end and no beginning, only the cord that tethers our souls, humming fierce and glowing bright when we're joined this way.

Willow collapses over me, and I grasp the back of her head, smearing paint through her blond hair, weaving the strands with an array of color as my other hand slides down her spine. She seals her lips to mine, breathing life into my being with her whimper of pleasure as she rolls her hips.

Bracing her hands on either side of my head, she forces us closer, not a breath of space between our bodies as we writhe in color, relying on the other for oxygen, descending into the depths of ecstasy wrapped together.

It's more than sex. It's love we're making. Art we're creating.

Willow rises, arching her back as her palms drag down my chest, leaving streaks of indigo. I slide mine up her stomach, taking her breasts in each hand and grazing my thumb over each nipple, leaving her painted pink.

She rotates, lifting before dropping down, weaving her body over mine in a stunning display of colorful intimacy, ushering me deeper inside her.

"You feel so good, love," I rasp. "So beautiful."

I raise myself into a sitting position, spreading my thighs. Willow begins to fall back, but I catch her ass, holding her steady as her hands clasp behind my neck. I press her into me, flushing our chests together, my hips bracketing hers to set a new pace.

We morph into a mess of entwined limbs and fractured whispers, our rhythm chaotic and wild as our bodies slip and glide through the paint beneath us. When we come, we unravel together—a shared moment that expands beyond comprehension, into something all-consuming and uniquely ours.

Seconds, years, maybe even eons later, Willow and I lie side by side atop her canvas, staring at the ceiling, still searching for our breath.

"Didn't realize that's what you meant by art therapy, Wills," I murmur. "Now that I understand it better, I'd like to book another session as soon as possible."

She snorts. "You have a terrible habit of making bad jokes after sex."

"I do that a lot?" I ask, turning my face to hers.

She matches the movement, looking at me with a bemused smile. "Almost every time."

"Fuck." I sigh. "That's embarrassing. Maybe I should talk about it in therapy."

"God, Wes." She bursts with laughter, smiling so bright I almost wonder if the sky outside turned from night to day. "You need to shut up."

I return the laughter, and when we've both calmed, I reach for her hand. "I have a session next week, by the way. Penelope helped me find someone, and I'm going to meet with him virtually until I return to Santa Monica next month."

She squeezes my hand, whispering, "You make me proud, Wes." Her tender blue eyes melting through me. "You think you're ready to open up about it all?"

I nod. "I think so. Suppressing things exhausts me, and I guess I've realized that even if I wanted to forget it—black it out—it doesn't actually go away. Ignoring my past doesn't erase it. I'll never escape any of it, and pretending that I can only tires me out. Wading through it is debilitating too, but I have to believe it's better in the end." I laugh gruffly. "I'll never forget the fact that my father is responsible for my mother's death, and nobody cares except for me. I'll never erase the fact I almost killed him too."

"I care," she whispers immediately. "I'm so sorry. I . . . I can't imagine, Wes."

"I know. It's okay." I sigh. "I'm sorry I just dumped that on you. This was terrible timing."

"It's never bad timing if you're taking the moment to let go of something that gives you pain." She takes our joined hands off her stomach, lowering them to the canvas between us, and pressing my palm flat before laying hers atop it. "Leave it all right here. In the painting." She huffs a soft laugh. "*That* is art therapy."

Her ability to make the heaviest burdens feel light enough to carry will never stop astonishing me.

Feeling free enough to speak my thoughts aloud, I continue, "I lived in a cell for almost two years. I received my high school diploma in the recreation room at the county jail, ate my meals with strangers, grieved my mother alone and behind a steel door. That was the existence I knew, and I never talk about it. I feel this overwhelming need to be grateful I'm no longer there. That I got out. I feel obligated to forget, but it's a part of my history that's impossible to."

"You don't have to. You can talk about it with me. Always."

"I don't need to remind you that you chose a criminal, Willow."

"Weston." She rolls onto an elbow, hovering over me. "You're not a criminal, and I hold no judgment for your past. You've weathered more storms than I could ever comprehend, and when I look at the way you've held yourself through them, I'm in awe at the person you've become. I'd choose you every fucking time. Do you understand?"

Would she still feel that way if she knew I'd wanted him dead? That sometimes I still do?

The thought echoes through my mind—something I push so far down inside myself, even I forget it's there most of the time, but moments like this allow it to resurface. Perhaps that's another reason why I'm so afraid of therapy.

"You may not hold judgment for it, Willow, but it's still a fact. I was arrested and I was charged, and I had a trial that allowed people to form their own opinions, regardless of the ultimate outcome. There are public records and articles written about me, and that noise will only get louder once I'm competing professionally again. If I make it . . . If I reach the Olympics, or even the Championship Tour, it's something that will come out, and if you're with me, you'll be judged for it too."

She shakes her head, hair swaying over her face as she stares down at me, eyes misting with conviction. "I don't care about any of that. I don't care what anyone else thinks, and I still do not believe you're a criminal, no matter the opinions of others. So please don't say that about yourself."

"I'm sorry," I breathe.

Her lips tilt with a soft smile before she presses a light kiss to my nose. "I'm honored to be with you, Wes. I'll shout about it from every rooftop on the planet."

"I feel the same, Wills." I surge forward, planting my lips on hers. "But . . . your dad did ask me to avoid being public about our relationship until this shit with Parker is completely blown over, and I think that's probably a good idea."

Willow frowns, brows furrowed as she lays on her back, staring at the ceiling again. "Fuck that. I'm so over him taking up any ounce of space in my life, Wes. I love my dad, but he can't control that. That's between you and me."

I can't pretend that part of me doesn't still worry about Parker's retaliation, or how my reputation could impact Willow's, but I know that Leo has started the process of getting a restraining order against him after he contacted Willow last week. If all goes well, we'll never hear from him again, and if Willow wants to brave the storm that is my past alongside me, who the fuck am I to argue?

"I'm on your team, Wills. If you want to scream from the rooftops, I'll stand right beside you and scream too."

She nods, and I flip my palm so that it presses against hers, lacing our fingers together. She told me to leave my pain in the canvas, allow my words to soak into the paint smeared from our love, but I want to hold her instead.

"Are you ever afraid that he's going to find you? Your dad. Once you become a gold medal holding World Champion." She turns to face me, and I catch the smile she tosses my way. "Because you will."

I huff a laugh, shaking my head. "I don't think he'll ever come looking for me." I squeeze her hand. "It's the fear of running into him by accident that I feel like I can't escape. The knowledge that he's still out there, living like nothing happened. That he could be around any corner, and *if* I saw him . . . I'll never stop wondering if I could snap again."

Willow is quiet for a moment, but she tightens her fingers around mine. Four times. Finally, she speaks in the softest tone, "You may not move on from it, but I can hold you through it. I don't know if you'd snap, but if you did, I'd hold you back. I'd never judge you for craving justice for her, because I want it too. The difference between your past and your future, even with the pain that'll always linger . . ." She looks at me, ocean eyes exploding with something that looks a whole hell of a lot like love. "Now, you won't be alone."

Her gentle tenderness and unbreakable care rushes through me, a shudder biting my spine at the intensity. I feel Willow over every inch of my skin—from her lingering taste in my mouth, her body in my hands, the weight of her stare as I lose myself inside her gaze.

I'm stripped bare—emotionally raw yet unnervingly confident that her words ring true.

I'll never be alone again.

CHAPTER THIRTY-THREE

WILLOW

"I THOUGHT IT would look prettier, honestly," I say, staring down at the evidence of last night.

"It's beautiful in an . . . abstract way." Weston places his hands on his hips, tilting his head to study the canvas still taking up most of the living room floor. The paint soaked into the fabric in a blotchy mix of pastels with a sprinkle of handprints. "I mean . . . we can't throw it away."

I smirk. "No. I suppose we can't. You'll just have to hang it in your room."

"What?" His brows shoot up. "Why don't you hang it in *your* room?"

"What if my parents see it?" I ask. "Wes, there is a perfect imprint of your balls."

His eyes widen, zeroing in on the very spot I'm referencing. A delicious blush creeps up his cheek as he clears his throat. "Why don't we just put it in the bedroom for now? I'll find a good place for it—away from prying eyes."

I laugh, wrapping my arms around his waist as he throws one over my shoulder, tucking me in close. Looking at it close up, the painting is objectively and without a doubt the ugliest piece of art I've ever created. Yet, it's the most beautiful, because it's raw proof that I am capable of being cherished in every way I'd always dreamed I could be.

Weston's pocket begins vibrating against my hip, and when he pulls his phone from his sweats, his brow furrows as he reads the name flashing across the screen. "It's Livia."

"Were you supposed to practice with her today?" I ask.

"Not that I'm aware of," he murmurs as he answers the call and presses his phone to his ear. "Liv?"

His gaze goes unfocused as he listens to whatever she's saying on the other end of the line, before he pulls his phone from his face and places it on speaker.

"I have to make an appearance at the Sunrise Open tomorrow, and a spot just opened up. I'm going to register you."

"Why?" he asks.

She scoffs. "Because I spent a lot of time on you this summer, *estupido*, and I'm not in the habit of wasting my time. We're making you a goddamn surfer."

Wes's mouth pulls into a smile, though he sighs. "Leo said he doesn't want me competing anymore this season."

"Leo isn't the authority on surfing, Weston." She's quiet for a moment before adding, "Don't fuck up again, and he'll have nothing to complain about. Plus, it's local competition and doesn't count toward the Championship Tour. But, there will be sponsors there. Trainers and WSL reps. You need *good* exposure after that shit show you had a few weeks ago."

Though it's not a qualifying competition—Wes's participation won't earn him any points needed to qualify for the WSL Championship Tour, which is the ultimate path to the Olympics—it's still a perfect opportunity to get his name out there with sponsors, and reclaim his place in the league after his wipe out a few weeks ago.

Wes's gaze flickers to me, uncertainty written in his eyes. "He'll drop me if I go against his guidance."

"Not if you're capable of proving you can learn from your mistakes. Not if you're better than you were before," Liv says. "Not if you win."

Wes's throat works with a swallow. "I mean . . . I'm already dating his daughter, and he explicitly asked me not to do that either. Should I really be rocking the boat?"

"You decided Willow was a boat worth rocking. I guess now you need to determine if your future as a surfer is too." A long sigh echoes through the phone. "I need to know by noon if you want me to register you for the qualifier. If you decide to come, Lucille and I will pick you up this afternoon around two and you can ride with us. We're in San Diego right now."

"Can I come too?" I ask.

"As long as Weston is capable of not making an ass of himself in an attempt to impress you," she snickers, hanging up before either of us can answer.

Wes chews his lip, eyes cast down to his feet.

"You need to do it," I say. "She's right. We'll only be away for one night, so we won't tell my dad. You win yourself a championship, and when we bring it back to him, he won't even be able to be angry." I smile. "He'll be too proud." I grab his hand and squeeze, adding, "Like you said, you're only training with my dad for the summer anyway, and the summer is almost over. Maybe there will be a trainer at the competition who will want to work with you, or a sponsor for the Championship Tour next summer who'll be interested. You can't pass up this opportunity, Wes. People *need* to see you surf."

He lifts his gaze, stormy eyes swirling with doubt. "What if I fuck up again?"

"Then I'll hold your hand through it, but this is worth the risk."

Wes texts Livia to tell her he's on board, and we both scramble to get our bags packed. Livia is incredibly impatient and lives her entire life with an intense sense of urgency. You don't want to be on the wrong side of her overt eagerness.

I start in the bathroom, throwing our toothbrushes into my toiletry bag—both of which I keep in the guesthouse damn-near permanently now—when Wes calls from the bedroom, "Can you pack my meds too, Wills?"

"Yeah!" I open the cabinet behind the mirror, find the small prescription pill bottle, and place it with our toothbrushes and my skincare.

When I return to the bedroom, I hand the bag to him, and he tosses me a closed-lip smile as he tucks it into the carry-on suitcase he grabbed for us to share. "Thanks," he murmurs. "I might not need them, but I'd rather be safe."

"You don't have to justify it. I'm happy you have something that helps you when you're struggling. Whether you need to use them or not, I've got you."

His smile turns genuine as he leans over and plants a kiss to my forehead.

I convinced my dad to take my mother out for an afternoon drive in his classic Mustang. He keeps it covered in the garage most of the time to maintain its pristine condition, but when the weather is nice, he and Mom will take a ride down the Pacific Coast Highway together. Something about it being nostalgic for them. So, they're gone when Livia and Lou arrive. Weston and I sneak around the back gate to Liv's truck, and to my utter shock, when I swing open the back door, Zander is sprawled across the seat, grinning at me.

"You're coming?" I laugh.

He shrugs. "Why not?"

I crawl into the back beside my cousin as Weston tosses our bags into the bed, closing the canopy before getting into the truck too.

"He's trying to plan a meet-cute with this up-and-coming amateur surfer he started talking to online." Lou laughs, turning in her seat, eyeing us as her wife starts up the truck and pulls into the street. "Does your dad know about this?" she asks.

I chuckle, shaking my head. "Casually mentioned we were going out with Allie tonight."

"We already had a meet-cute," Z scoffs. "We've been talking

for weeks, I'm trying to fuck." Dramatically rolling his eyes, he faces me. "Where is Allie?"

"With Declan." I sneer, validated by the vexed groans of the entire car.

Half an hour passes in relative silence before Weston falls asleep against me. I run my hands through his hair, the silky dark strands melting beneath my fingertips. His closed lids flutter, lips parted with heavy breath.

He's beautiful like this. Peaceful.

How he'd ever think I'd want to hide him from the world is beyond me. I've never been more proud to attach myself to another person. Damn Parker, and damn my parents too, because Weston deserves to be loved loudly.

I pull out my phone, snapping a photo of him sleeping on my lap with my hand in his hair before posting it to my feed. I caption the picture, *somethin' 'bout a surfer boy,* with the hashtag for the competition we're heading to.

My parents may see the post, but by the time they do, we'll be well on our way and deal with the consequences upon our return.

"Oh, you're *in love* in love." My head snaps up, gaze landing on Zander who's flashing me a shit-eating grin.

"So is he," Lou says softly, green eyes flashing to mine in the rearview mirror.

"Yeah, well . . ." I glance at Weston again, ensuring he's still asleep. "I haven't exactly told him that yet, so if you could maybe shut the fuck up, I'd appreciate it."

Zander laughs under his breath, shaking his head.

"Better get to it, *bebé,*" Liv adds. "It's pretty fucking clear to everyone else."

Lou nods at her wife, turning in her seat and giving me a soft smile. "I've never seen you like this before, Willow."

"Like what?" I murmur, glancing back down at Weston to ensure he's not woken up.

"Blissful," Zander says, serious now. "Beyond happy. You were never like that before."

He's right, and I should admit my love to Weston. He deserves to know just how happy he's made me. How much he's healed me.

There are things I haven't told him yet, and I don't think I can say those three words until I find a way to disclose everything I've kept to myself. I think he's told me every aspect of his past, and I don't know how he'll react when he realizes I haven't given him the same.

My cousins are right though. I love him so bad, there's no hiding it now. I think Lou is accurate that he loves me too, and that love being so palpable it's seen by others strengthens my confidence that he's the person I can share my burdens with. My past. He'll accept all of it, I only need to give him the chance to show me that for himself.

Before I slide my phone back into my pocket, it buzzes with a notification. Chelsea's name flashes over my screen—an indication that she liked the photo—and my stomach sinks. I've been less active online this summer than I normally am, and I completely forgot to block Chelsea after our horrific lunch weeks ago.

Unease pricks the back of my neck as I scramble to block her, refusing to let anything ruin this weekend and Weston's second chance at winning a medal.

CHAPTER THIRTY-FOUR
WESTON

THE ROAR OF the crowd is so potent, it overpowers the crashing of the waves as I sit atop the water, dozens of yards from shore.

I close my eyes, inhaling deeply as I tilt my head toward the sky, allowing the afternoon sun to beat down on my face. Taking two more breaths, I center myself, drowning it all out until there is only mere buzzing in my ears, but my being is entirely concentrated on my board.

The current flows past my shins—my familiar friends. They'll carry me back to solid ground, and when they do, I'll be a champion.

It's the final heat in the competition, only ten of us remain. Four of them have wiped out and are unlikely to recover, and only one of them truly holds a candle to the performance I'm delivering today. He's phenomenal, but I'm doing better. I *am* better.

He just took a swell, and while he performed decently, I know the next one coming in is going to be a far superior wave. Still hoisting himself back onto his board, he'll miss the opportunity. It barrels toward me, and I spin, paddling with every ounce of strength that remains in me after this endless day, until I'm lifted by the force of nature beneath me.

My gut soars into my chest as I rise above the horizon, popping up as the wave begins to crest. Wind whips across my face, saltwater stuck in my teeth as I smile into the sea. I'm fucking weightless. Dropping in, gliding along the face of a force so ethereal—older than time and wiser than the earth. It soaks into me, embracing me, gifting me its power as I carve against it.

I'm propelled by a connection deeper than the planet itself, driven by the moon, entwining every corner of the world. I believe waves are the very fabric of the universe itself, and fate is created when I float among them. I believe I've earned the privilege to harness their fierceness, to carve my destiny from their energy.

I snap my board, shooting up the barrel and launching myself into the air, completing what feels like a flawless three-sixty before landing back down with precision.

It's Willow's face that drifts through my mind as I coast over the whitecaps.

I justified my tragic childhood by believing I was destined to find Carter and Penelope—to be discovered by Leo Graham through them. That he held the key to my future, my escape from the past that haunts me.

In the end, I was right the entire time. Like the moon and the tides, it was all connected, but I was never being led to surfing alone. I was being led to her.

Willow is the destiny I earned.

The endless vastness, the easy solace I only ever found out here has been rediscovered in the depths of her gaze.

It's her face I see as I float over the seafoam, that winning wave dissolving beneath me. Nothing is final until I'm scored by the judges and called up onto that podium, but today was the best performance of my life. I'm a shoo-in to place, if not take home first. The barrel crashes around me, and I coast back toward the shore. Sinking down on my board, I slap the water as I expel every last nerve from my lungs on a shout before breathing in fresh sea air and pure joy. I finally allow the roar of the crowd to soar through my ears, reveling in the celebration of it all as it sinks into my bones—champion.

Half an hour later, the second and third place surfers stand on the podium as we wait for the judges to announce the champion of the competition—though, we all know it's going to be me.

I've been scanning the crowd for Willow, but there are too many people, and the setting sun is blinding. I spot Liv to the left of the podium when my ears are pierced with the sound of her deafening whistle. Lou stands beside her, throwing me a thumbs-up and a beaming smile. Zander cheers, recording the ceremony on his phone.

Willow isn't with them.

My face must give away my worry, because Lou mouths *bathroom*. Disappointment sluices through me when I realize she's going to miss me placing first. I sigh, nodding. The competition is televised, there are hundreds of phones and cameras on me now so I know Willow will be able to watch the moment back later. The ceremony moved faster than even I expected, so I'm sure she thought she'd make it back in time.

The announcer declares the first-place champion of the competition, the title followed by my name. Pride surges through me as I climb onto the highest step of the podium. I'm awarded more prize money than I know what to do with—maybe fix up my truck. Since this isn't an official World Surf League event, I won't earn any points toward a spot on the Championship Tour, not that it would matter after I was disqualified from the Challenger a few weeks ago and lost those points anyway, but regardless, the win feels validating. I proved it to myself, to Liv and Willow, and when I take this win home, I'll show Leo too—that I'm worthy of his time and his daughter, that I have a future ahead of me.

Plus, Willow was right. The competition is crawling with sponsors and WSL representatives, and Liv has introductions planned with several of them.

I have something to take back with me, to prove to Leo—the world and myself—that I'm doing the right thing. I'm still destined for this, and I have what it takes to wear a gold medal around my neck someday.

I smile, holding up the oversized check the announcer thrust into my hands as the crowd cheers and lights flash in my face, though my eyes continue scanning the beach for sign of Willow, unease pummeling through me with every passing second I don't see her face.

I'm ushered off the podium and across the stage for an interview as the crowd slowly begins to disperse when I catch sight of her blond hair in front of the bathroom building about fifty yards in front of me. For a split second, my breath evens out and that apprehension alleviates, until I notice she seems to be having a conversation with a man I don't recognize.

He's taller than her but shorter than me, wide shoulders tapered into a slim build, hovering over her with his arms flailing. Like he's shouting at her. She cowers beneath him, and my blood runs cold. Willow's folded in on herself, arms crossed at her chest—and I clock the body language immediately. She's becoming smaller, hugging herself in an attempt at preservation from the threat looming above her. She's afraid, and every instinct in my body bellows at me to reach her.

As I pass where Livia, Lou, and Zander are standing in front of the stage's corner, I toss the large check to them, murmuring, "I need to go," to the announcer before leaping off the stage and heading in Willow's direction.

I walk briskly, navigating away from the crowds without drawing too much attention to myself, eyes locked on my destination. Though, when I watch Willow step back and the man snatches out and grasps her shoulder, pulling her back toward him, my frozen blood catches fire. My vision floods red, and I take off in a fucking sprint.

CHAPTER THIRTY-FIVE

WILLOW

I WAS so nervous during Weston's final heat I think I may have drank an entire gallon of water during the twenty-two minutes he was out on the waves. I don't know what I thought it was going to do to help calm my nerves—it must've been something about the lifting of the bottle to my lips and the act of swallowing. Helped my mind focus on something other than him getting injured again.

He surfed flawlessly though. According to Liv, there is no way he won't place first today.

"How long do you think this is going to take?" I ask Liv, hopping on my heels because I need to pee so goddamn bad, but I don't want to risk missing Weston's placement on the podium.

She glances around, chewing on her lip. "I think you have time to go."

I sigh in relief, slipping off my shoes so I can run through the sand easier. "All right. I'll be back."

I maneuver through the sea of people until I reach the end of the crowd gathered around the stage. The bathroom building is just down the beach, but I break into a jog so I can ensure I'm back in time to see Weston place first. When I break out from the rumbling noise of spectators, the sound of crashing waves and seagull calls take over, and just as I slip through the door of the women's restroom, I swear I hear someone call my name.

I exit a few minutes later to the muffled sound of an

announcer over the intercom near the ceremony stage. I can just make out the third-place winner stepping onto the podium. "Shit," I mutter to myself, stepping off the concrete to run back toward the competition.

Though, just as my toes sink into the sand, a chilling rasp sluices through my bones. "Willow."

His voice clatters off the walls of my chest as my organs shrink in on themselves, my blood turning frigid, my limbs freezing as I slowly turn to face him. When my eyes meet his—that soft brown gaze I thought I'd be looking into the day I got married, the eyes I envisioned my children having—a tear rips down the center of my torso, all of my innards splattering at my feet.

I'm left hollow and gaping—the emptiness quickly filled with fear.

Those soft brown eyes I once loved fiercely are simmering with loathing now. The jaw I once ran my lips along in the depths of night is now tense with contempt. Hands I once believed were made for healing—only to hurt me in the end—drag through his brunette hair with contention.

"Why are you here?" I ask, my voice so fractured it's near inaudible.

"I've been looking for you all day." His nostrils flare, gaze running the length of my body, nausea crawling up my throat as he makes his perusal. "I've been trying to reach you for weeks."

"I have nothing to say to you," I whisper, wrapping my arms around myself. I glance over my shoulder, lungs heavy with apprehension as I realize I'm so far from the safety of my family. Of Wes. I face him again, swallowing down the bile to add, "How did you even find me?"

"Found out you were attending this competition, and I was in Monterey visiting my parents so I figured I'd make the trip." A sickly-sweet smile spreads across the mouth that used to feel like home to me. "You moved on quickly, by the way. Did you start fucking him before or after the abortion?"

My breath hitches, mouth dry and coated in revulsion, like

my tongue wants to leap down my throat and hide within me, but it's stuck to my teeth.

Parker spews the words like venom-tipped daggers, slicing through my skin and coating me in acid sting. They seep into my veins, flooding me with the guilt I've fought so hard to dissolve—the humiliation I thought I'd escaped.

"I'm leaving," I say in a choked and ragged inhale, stumbling back.

"Bullshit." Parker grips my arm, and my vision blurs. Flashes of his last touches blanket my mind. His touch doesn't frighten me—I never feared him that way. Though now, it's just *wrong*. The aftermath of that night is all I feel now. The manipulation, the disgust, the lies. All the memories I've worked so hard not to see each time I close my eyes come flooding back with a vengeance. "You're going to explain why you didn't tell me. Why you didn't give me the basic fucking decency of knowing the decision you were making, let alone allowing me to have a say in it."

I almost clam up again. Like I did that night with him, like I did with Camden at the beach, but my instincts fight harder this time. They know better. Nobody is coming to save me at this moment.

I shake out of his grasp, gaze cast to the ground.

"Look at me, Willow," Parker snaps. "Look me in the fucking eye and tell me you were pregnant. Tell me to my face you had an abortion and that you kept it from me." His voice breaks, and it's enough for me to lift my chin, finding a hint of emotion glistening in his hostile gaze. "You owe me that."

Those eyes lift, focusing on something behind me as the sound of heavy breath filters through the air.

His voice is rough and low—a menacing beacon. "She doesn't owe you anything."

Weston's chest presses against my back, his fingers brushing over my knuckles where my arm hangs limply at my side—a simple reminder that he's here. The rock I can lean upon, even when there is no doubt he heard the harsh truth spewed from Parker's lips.

All the secrets I've been keeping, all the most painful pieces of my past, now lingering in the air around us. Another thing Parker has taken from me.

My jaw is tight enough I fear it may shatter, trembling with all the words I'm holding back, as silent tears slip over my eyes, cascading down my cheeks.

Parker huffs a disgusted laugh, shaking his head. "You're a horrible fucking person, Willow. I hope it eats you alive." His gaze flicks to Weston. "Watch your back with this one. She's a snake."

Shame slices through me. I hold no guilt for my choices, no sympathy for Parker. His hatred isn't landing the way he's intending it to. It's the fact that Weston is witnessing it, hearing the truth from a mouth that isn't mine. That he's experiencing the raw disdain radiating from a person who was supposed to love me—that I'm capable of being despised so excruciatingly. That, perhaps, I'm not worth loving at all.

"I'm not worried." Wes chuckles harshly. "I'd never put her in that position to begin with—by assaulting her."

Parker's jaw drops, brows shooting into his hairline with utter disbelief before he barks a laugh. "That's how you're justifying it? You told this guy I *assaulted* you?"

"You know exactly what you did," I whisper.

Recognition flashes over his eyes before he scoffs, rolling them. "We were together for two years, Willow. I didn't need to ask permission to come inside you."

"You are a *such* a piece of shit," Wes growls, moving to step past me.

I halt him with a hand on his stomach, and he doesn't fight it. He immediately stops, moving back behind me.

Parker watches the interaction, a triumphant grin on his face. "You are so stupid," he says, the jab directed at me. "Throwing away our entire future together only to end up with a damn criminal."

"Oh, good. So, you researched me then?" I hear the smile in Weston's tone. "You should know *exactly* what I'm capable of. I'd urge you not to speak to her like that again. Better yet, I wouldn't speak to her at all, if I were you."

"Threatening me?" Parker grins, baring his teeth. "That would be a probation violation, no?"

Wes laughs. "I'm not on probation, you worthless fucking—"

"He's not threatening you," I rasp, reaching behind me and pressing my palm into Weston's ribs.

Probation or not, I won't allow him to put himself at risk by having this interaction turn physical. Weston's future means too much, and Parker means nothing at all.

Lifting my chin, I channel everything I've longed to say to Parker in the past five months. Every ounce of rage and despair and anguish that I screamed into my pillows in the depths of night. Every thought of self-loathing echoed through my mind when I looked in the mirror. Every wave of nausea in my gut when I thought of him.

I look him in the eye, just like he asked. I open up the shadows I've been hiding within and offer him all the pain he's caused me.

"I won't explain to you what you did, because you know. I won't justify my reason for having an abortion because you know that too. I won't apologize for the choice I made or for keeping it to myself. You lost the right to know anything about me when you took away my right to choose how my body would be treated. *You're* the reason I had to go through that—and the reason I had to experience it alone." My voice shatters, right along with the rest of me. I don't wipe away the tears streaming freely down my face. I don't erase the hurt. "I know you can't comprehend the trauma you've caused or the way it's haunted me. I don't think you even care enough to try. But I hope, deep down, you *feel* it." I swallow down the sob clawing at my lungs, determined to have these words ring clear. "I hope you hate yourself a little more each day, even if you never understand why. I hope you have a daughter someday, and I hope she never has to experience what I have because of you, but I hope you think of me every time you look at her. I hope the guilt sinks its claws into you and refuses to let go, leaving scrapes you don't recognize the meaning of until you take your last breath."

I can no longer see his hateful eyes through my blurred vision, but I'm not sure I want to. I'd rather never know how this is affecting him. Taking a shuddering breath, I release one final thought in his direction, deciding that I'll never think of him again after this. "I hope it eats you alive too."

I don't steal a glance at Parker, and I don't have the strength to look at Weston's face as I turn, gaze planted on my feet as I whisper, "Can we go, please?"

I can't raise my eyes when Weston takes my face between his hands, unable to look at him as he presses his lips to my forehead. "Yes, love. Go find your cousins, okay? I'll be right behind you."

CHAPTER THIRTY-SIX

WESTON

I FEEL EMPTY as Willow walks away, and I want nothing more than to follow her. Comfort her. Heal her. Love her. But I know she'll need a moment to herself, to process this alone. I knew there were aspects of her past she hadn't told me yet, but this certainly wasn't one I was expecting. It wasn't difficult to decipher the wrecked expression on her face when her eyes refused to meet mine.

It's going to kill her that I found out this way, and I want to take time for the knowledge to settle within me too, so that when we talk about it, I can take care of her the way she needs.

I also want to ensure Parker does not ever come near her again.

He doesn't attempt to mask the devastation on his face as he watches her run away, but the anger in his gaze remains potent enough that I know he won't be taking accountability any time soon. It's the same expression my father used to wear when he'd make my mother bleed. Enough guilt that he knew he'd gone too far, but he'd still justify his actions. It was always her fault, and he'd never hurt her badly enough not to do it again.

"The best thing she'll do for herself is forget you ever fucking existed. The best thing you can do for yourself now is to make sure you remain forgotten." I take a step toward him, and he shuffles back, fear flashing across his eyes. My instincts tell me to obliterate him, but unlike the last time I found myself face to face with a monster like this, I don't listen. I won't be the violent person he's made me out to be in his head, but it doesn't mean I won't use his assumptions to my advantage. "Do not ever find yourself in the same vicinity as Willow Graham again."

Parker's throat bobs as he swallows, breath short and rapid, filtering through his lips like he's choking on it.

I hope he does.

I leave him in front of the bathroom, ignoring the small crowd gathered to witness the interaction. Fucking vultures.

Willow didn't make it far up the beach, I can see her a few dozen yards away sitting in the sand with her knees pulled to her chest as she stares out over the horizon. The sun is halfway drowned by the Pacific, bright orange and streaking the sky in shades of indigo.

As I stalk toward her, the rest of her family catches up to me—confusion and concern painting their faces. Lou is still holding my comically large check. "What's going on?" she asks before I cut her off.

"We need to leave. Can you three go get the car, please?"

They watch me apprehensively, and I don't know why I'm surprised. This entire family is goddamn stubborn.

"Please." I sigh, relenting. "Parker showed up. Confronted her. She's far from okay, and I just need to get her home."

Lou gasps, immediately stepping in the direction of Willow as indignation washes over Zander's features. Liv is solemn, grasping her wife's hand. "Let Weston go get her, okay?"

Lou's green eyes flick to me. "Should we go back to our hotel instead?"

I shake my head. "You can drop us off at the airport if you don't want to make the drive this late, but I need to get her home."

I need to get her off this beach and as far away from Parker as possible. I need to get her into my bed and into my arms, and I need her to be where she feels safest when she wakes up tomorrow morning. I can't explain the instinct, the urgency in it, but something in me *knows* that she won't feel okay again until she's back in Pacific Shores.

"Of course not," Lou says. "We're going to take Willow home if that's what she needs."

Liv and Zander both nod in agreement before the three of them slowly head in the direction of the parking lot.

As I make my way toward Willow, I pull off the hoodie I put on after the competition. Reaching her, I squat down behind her, gently placing the sweatshirt over her shoulders. "Willow, love. We're going to go home, baby."

She doesn't respond, but her entire body trembles beneath my touch.

"C'mon, Wills. Please." I slowly slip my hands beneath her arms, and thankfully, she works with me to lift off the ground. I tuck her beneath my shoulder, walking her toward the parking lot. "That's my girl. Let's get you home."

She's still crying, but it's a soft, continual type of sorrow rather than the violent sobs she was letting out when she ran from Parker earlier. I'm honestly not sure what's worse.

I kiss her forehead. "I have you, love."

"I ruined your competition," she whispers brokenly.

"Don't take responsibility for his actions, Willow. You didn't ask for that to happen. You didn't initiate it. You didn't ruin anything. I still won." I smile into her hair as we walk. "I'll show you the check when we get to the car. It's fucking ridiculous."

She doesn't laugh, and my chest splits open when she murmurs, "I'm sorry you had to find out that way."

"You have nothing to apologize for, Willow. You did nothing wrong."

"I . . ."

I hush her, kissing the top of her head again. "I want to get you home right now. We can talk about it tomorrow, but know that you have nothing to fear when it comes to me, all right?" Echoing what she said to me yesterday, I add, "I'm going to hold you through it."

She sighs, and I can't tell if it's in relief or devastation, but she doesn't say more as we find the rest of her family. I help her into the car, and outside of soft murmured greetings, we don't speak.

We drive through the night back to Pacific Shores in silence.

CHAPTER THIRTY-SEVEN

WILLOW

"Willow, love," Weston whispers into my hair. "We're home now." Kissing me gently, he opens the car door, and cool ocean air breezes over my skin.

I slept on him for the return back to Pacific Shores, though sleeping would put it generously. I lay with my eyes closed, biting my tongue to halt my tears, pretending I'd slipped out of consciousness to avoid anyone asking me about what happened, or how I was feeling.

I didn't want to be asked because I don't know the answer. I'm somehow numb and torn to shreds at the same time. I didn't want to talk about it because Weston is owed an explanation, and that's not a conversation that needs to happen in a group setting.

I think Weston knew I was awake. I know the difference in his breathing between sleep and wake, and I think he understands me on that level too, but he never pressed. He stroked my hair, whispered quiet reassurances against my cheeks, kept his hold solid and steady.

I slowly sit up in the middle seat as Weston reaches across to unbuckle me. Swallowing hard, I lift my head and blink, adjusting to the low light of Livia's dashboard. She watches me with curious concern in the rearview mirror as Lou spins in the front to face me head-on. Zander sleeps soundly beside me.

"We're going to stay with my parents before we head back to

Costa Mesa in the evening. We'll check in later after everyone has had some rest, okay?"

I nod, murmuring my gratitude as I slip out of the truck and shut the door behind me. Weston stumbles up onto the curb, holding both of our bags and his massive check. I wordlessly take my duffle from him, and before he can protest, I sling it around my shoulder and head up the driveway.

"Your bed or mine tonight, love?" Weston asks from behind me.

I pause, I don't know how to answer.

This moment feels painfully reminiscent of when I came home all those months ago. I'm running away from Parker and his death-tipped words once again. Climbing the stairs of my childhood home and crawling beneath the sheets of my girlhood bed is too familiar a heartbreak, but sleeping beside Weston when I have so much left to explain doesn't feel right either.

My bag falls off my shoulder, and I don't bother catching it before it plunks against the concrete with a dreary plop. My tears follow its lead as I dip my head and begin to cry.

"Willow," Wes breathes, dropping everything in his hands as he steps up behind me and wraps his arms around my middle, nuzzling his chin into the crook of my shoulder. "Tell me what to do. Tell me how to fix this."

"I don't think I can go to sleep until we talk about it." I shake my head, wiping my eyes and swallowing down the emotion choking me. "I can't go to sleep beside you until I know how you feel."

Wes moves away from me, a chill biting my spine in the absence of his warmth. I hear the sound of shuffling before he walks past me, sliding through the gate that leads toward the guesthouse. "C'mon, love," he says quietly, holding it open for me before he continues to the porch. He drops our things on the bottom step, but rather than ascending toward the door, he spins, taking my hand as he walks around the railing and toward the staircase that leads down the cliffside.

"The beach?" I ask.

"When we step back inside that house, I'm going to make sure you understand exactly the way I feel about you, Willow. I figure the sand and beneath the stars are as good a place as any to lay it all out."

He moves with purpose, fingers locked tightly around mine, shoulders flexing as he bustles down the steps, hauling me along with him. When we reach the sand, I slip off my shoes, leaving them beside the bottom stair as I follow Wes toward the waves.

The clock on Liv's dash read just after two o'clock in the morning, and the crescent moon is high above the horizon, the night barely lit by its soft white cast over the rippling expansion of the Pacific. It's dead silent outside the sway of palms and the lap of low tide crashing against the shore.

Weston finds our familiar piece of driftwood, stepping over it before sinking down in front of it. He peers up at me, patting the ground beside him. I fall into the sand, drawing my knees to my chest and clasping my arms around them.

My shoulder aligns with Weston's bicep. Warmth radiates in each place our skin touches, but he doesn't hold me. We take a quiet moment to watch the tides rise and rinse over the sand before retreating home.

"I'm not upset with you for not telling me. I want to make sure you understand that, and if you're still not ready to talk about it, that's okay, but if you'd like to . . ." He gently places one of his hands over mine. "I'm here."

I don't know if I'm ready to talk about it. If Parker hadn't shown up at the competition, if he hadn't said what he did, today wouldn't have been the one I'd have chosen to disclose this part of my past to Weston. Not because I don't trust him, and not because he doesn't deserve to know, but because I wanted to savor this happiness just a little longer.

The more time I spent with Weston, the more I confident I became that he'd accept every part of me, but that lingering fear still gnawed at the depths of me, and I couldn't force the words from my mouth, even in the moments I wanted to.

Though, now that I've seen his reaction, I feel silly for ever doubting him to begin with. I now realize that I'll likely never feel ready to talk about this, but that doesn't mean Weston doesn't deserve to know. I'll face it for him, cut myself open, because I know he'll heal my wounds.

That he'll let me heal his too.

"Part of me was scared of how you'd react to it," I admit. "Sometimes, I'd think I found the courage to tell you, and then the realization that I'd have to go through this with every new person I meet for the rest of my life would settle in, and it would become overwhelming. It's so . . . heavy. The wondering whether someone I've grown to care may actually hate me if they knew the depth of my past." Emotion pricks the back of my throat, making my voice rough and grainy. "I don't regret it, and I'm not ashamed, but sometimes those reminders are a mantra I have to keep on repeat in my mind, because I know there are people out there who desperately want me to feel both. It's exhausting." I bite my lip, nose stinging with tears as I look at Weston, who is watching me with misty eyes of his own. "You were an escape, I think."

"I'll still be that for you, Willow." He squeezes my hand, smiling softly. "It'll be easier now that I know what I'm helping you escape from."

I squeeze his back—four times. Resting my head on his shoulder, I sigh. "I'm sorry you had to find out that way."

"Don't apologize for that. It isn't your fault." His gaze drifts toward the dark horizon, and I follow suit. "I'm sorry you had to hear the things he said to you, and I'll be reminding you every fucking day how incredible you are until they're forgotten."

I love you.

The words are right there. Lingering on my lips, desperate to float into the air between us, and yet . . . I think I need to hear him say it first. I need the confirmation that every piece of me will be accepted, that I can truly let go of my past and my pain—I can hand it all to him and he'll cherish me anyway.

"Thank you," I whisper.

He nods, pressing his lips to the top of my head before we both look out the ocean again. We're quiet for a while, soaking in the warmth of each other's body heat and the crashing of the waves.

"I wanted to hurt him, Willow," Weston finally whispers, as if speaking too loudly may wake some sleeping monster beneath his skin. "Walking away from him reminded me of the moment I was hauled off my father. The sick smile on his bloodied and broken mouth when they pulled me away, because we both knew he'd won. He'd never face the consequences for his crimes, but I paid on his behalf. I haven't felt a primal urge to harm someone since I last looked into the eyes of the man who made me—but it awoke in me today when I looked into the eyes of the man who hurt you. I hated leaving Parker there, knowing he'll get to go home, go back to his life and, so long as he adheres to the restraining orders, he'll be able to pretend like nothing happened."

Disgust trickles down my spine, nipping at my nerves with a frost-bitten chill.

The restraining order I filed against Parker two days ago hasn't processed yet, but it should go through soon. I know we'll have that to protect us moving forward, especially after we add today's confrontation to the file, but it doesn't change the fact that he'll never truly be held responsible for my assault.

"I thought about reporting him for the assault, but I ultimately didn't have the strength. Not after . . . everything," I admit hoarsely. "I wasn't sure what good it would do. What difference it would make. It would be too hard to prove, and it all felt heavy. It hurt *all* the time, and I just wanted to find a way to see past it." My voice shatters when I add, "You made me see through it. Something brighter on the other side of healing. I wanted to leave it behind me."

His hand moves to my back, dancing over my spine, just a whisper of a touch. "I don't blame you. The justice system had all the evidence they needed to incarcerate my father for the lifetime of pain he caused my mom, for her death itself, and yet he walks free even now." Weston sighs, a shuddering and haunted breath that seeps into my very bones. "Your healing is the priority." Wrapping his palm over my knuckles, he squeezes. "It's my priority too."

I'm still looking at the horizon when Weston shuffles, pulling my gaze to him. He's facing me now, fierce conviction shimmering in his eyes as he studies me with thorough intensity. "I wanted to hurt Parker the same way I wanted to hurt my father. The kind of way that makes me wonder if the world wouldn't just be better off without them. I wanted to hurt them in the kind of way that feels like taking justice for myself. *That* is my deepest truth. It wasn't the snap of a band that launched me at my dad that day, it was an instinct to well and truly kill him. Sometimes . . ." He swallows, eyes drifting down. "Sometimes I wish I had." He lifts his chin, gaze clashing against mine again. "I felt that today, but unlike before, I walked away. I walked to you."

I flip my hand over, twining my fingers with his. "I don't blame you for those thoughts. I don't judge them. I think I'd have them too."

"You pulled me from a darkness I've only experienced once before. You changed me, Willow. You gave me something to run toward. You're that light," he whispers, unraveling our hands before slowly gliding his up my arms and over my shoulders, along my neck until he grasps my face, tilting my head up. I have nowhere to look but at him, his beautifully rough features and soft, fervent eyes. "Nothing I learned today—no secret kept, no burden carried, no choice you've made changes that for me. I've long thought your strength came in spades, often left speechless by the resilience you've shown, but that is amplified beyond words now, Willow." Leaning forward, Weston's eyes don't leave mine as he kisses my forehead tenderly, murmuring into my skin, "A choice like that is insurmountable, and your ability to find joy, to bring it to the world with every breath you take, is astonishing to me."

I grip his forearms with enough force to leave marks, my

way of ensuring he's real. He's holding me through it, just as he promised. I slip my arms beneath his, flushing our chests together as I bury my face into his neck—holding him too.

"You don't think differently of me?" I ask, voice muffled in his shirt.

"Only in the way that your courage extends far beyond what I'd understood before." I tilt my face against his warm neck, his throat working with a swallow against my lips. "Do you think differently of me?"

"Only in the way that your strength extends far beyond what I'd understood before," I mimic him, a smile pulling at my mouth where it rests upon his flesh.

His chest shakes with a laugh before he pulls away and gazes down at me, his eyes study mine, something unwritten and raw shimmering with the reflection of the stars above us.

"I want you to be mine, Willow," he says on a ragged breath.

"I am," I begin, but he shakes his head, cutting me off.

"Not in the form of possession. Not in the way that word is so often interpreted. I don't want to own you, I want to love you. In a way that's never been experienced by anyone else before." Hands drifting over my spine, gripping my hips with fervency, Weston drops his forehead to mine. "I want to love you in a way that's as rare and ethereal as I find you. I want you to know depth and acceptance and adoration beyond your comprehension. Something unfathomed by any book you've read, any movie you've seen, or song you've heard. A kind of love curated and endlessly existing with your soul in mind."

I choke on the potency of Weston's emotion, as if his conviction is soaking directly into the depths of my being, lighting a flame that didn't exist before he placed it there.

"Wes . . ."

He squeezes my hips, shaking his head against mine. "Please, let me get this out, Willow. I need you to understand."

I nod, closing my eyes, *feeling* him instead. His jagged breath and drumming heart, the heat in his flesh and the gravity in his veins—I submerge myself in him entirely. In all the love he's created solely for me.

"I want to love you with expertise no other could accomplish. I want to be worthy of you. I *want* to earn it, Willow. I want you to be mine, but maybe the better way of expressing myself is by saying that I want my love to be *yours*."

"It is," I whisper with rapid urgency. Brushing my lips over his, I rasp, "Weston, look at me. Please." His lashes flutter, and even in darkness, he's blazing with infinite brightness when his gaze falls on me. "My love is yours. I am yours." I smile, mist hazing my vision as his acceptance rushes through me, glowing bright and all-consuming—an eternal flame he lit inside my soul. "I love you."

He trembles, exhaling a relieved and tormented breath into my mouth before surging forward, kissing the tears that spilled from my eyes and landed on my lips—consuming my very being. Endless whisperings of "I love you" are echoed along my skin as he lays me back, hovering over me and blanketing me in his steady heat.

"Come to bed with me," he begs.

I nod as he helps me stand, leading me through the darkness and into light.

Once we're inside, he strips me bare—tortuously slow and purposeful, savoring every inch of skin exposed to him. He carries me to bed, laying me down with tender hands. He whispers sweet nothings along my flesh before aligning our bodies, twining our fingers together and pushing inside me with a breathless whimper—an answered prayer.

Our love is a living element, a potent haze in the air around us as we find healing in each other's arms.

CHAPTER THIRTY-EIGHT

WESTON

"THE FUCK IS on your leg?" my girlfriend's dad asks, eyeing us as we climb the steps of the big house's back porch hand in hand.

I glance down, realizing my tattoo—now free from second skin—is peeking out beneath the hem of my shorts. "A tattoo."

"Of what?" Darby asks, hair falling over her shoulder as she tilts her head, lifting her coffee mug to her mouth.

The couple sits on a swing, Leo rocking them back and forth lightly with his heels while his wife curls up beneath his arm, knees drawn into her chest and a book beside her. It's a picture of simple, Sunday morning peace—the kind I imagine most people dream about their whole lives.

"It's a . . ." I swallow, rubbing the back of my neck. "A stained-glass window."

"It reminds him of me," Willow says breezily, beaming at her parents.

Darby's brows rise, eyes widening before a soft, knowing smile spreads over her lips—if I'm not mistaken, I think it may be a look of approval.

Her husband, however, frowns. "A little early for dedicated ink, no?"

"Please," Willow and her mother grumble in unison.

A small laugh escapes me because I understand why. I've seen Leo's tattoos, and asked for the stories behind them. I know he was seventeen when he tattooed his wife's nickname across his chest after knowing her less than two months—years later adding a willow tree beside it.

Perhaps it is too soon, but a flash of mischief glimmers in Leo's eyes when they flick to mine—understanding that she's worth it anyway.

"I got a pussy willow!" Willow exclaims, pulling her hand from mine to extend her forearm and show her parents the tattoo. "With Allie. She's the pussy and I'm the willow."

Leo's mouth drops open, lip curling as he studies Willow's arm with widened eyes. "It's cute, Sugar, but I don't know how I feel about my daughter repeatedly saying the word *pussy*."

"Yeah, well . . . you should hear Weston say it." She winks, flashing her dimples before skipping inside the house, calling, "Is the coffee still fresh?" over her shoulder.

I stand frozen, slack-jawed and horrified. Leo flicks his gaze to me, mouth a hard line, tongue in cheek.

Darby bursts with laughter, kissing her husband's cheek before rising off the swing. "She is your karma."

She follows Willow inside and as the door clicks shut behind her, Leo nods for me to come closer. I think the gulp I swallow down is audible, my body radiating with nerves—I have no idea how Leo is going to react to my decision to compete yesterday, despite winning. Plus, the open knowledge that I'm fucking his only child always makes me uneasy around him.

I lean against the porch railing across from the swing he's still sitting on.

"I hear I should be congratulating you this morning," he rumbles, eyes fixed on the horizon.

It's still somewhat early, the sun cresting behind us in the east, casting the Pacific in a rose-colored hue. Willow and I hardly slept, too wrapped up in each other to bother. When the sun rose and we'd still not found sleep, we decided we'd come talk to Leo this morning. There was a good chance he'd already know about the competition given his connections in the industry—and sure enough, he does.

"I'm sorry for not telling you. But to be fair, Liv and Willow corrupted me."

"Yeah, I know." He huffs a laugh. "I set that rule in place for your own protection, Weston. Not because I didn't want to see you succeed."

"I know." I nod.

He's quiet for a long while, simply staring at the sea. It's not awkward silence, per se, but I can't help feeling there is more to be said between us, and I wonder if he's waiting for Willow to return.

To pass the time, I ask a question that's plagued me, "Why do you call it Celestia Cove?"

A smile lifts at the corner of Leo's mouth, but he doesn't look at me. "I've been surfing in that cove since I was a kid. This house used to be owned by a sweet woman named Diane, and I'd trespass through the yard weekly to sneak down her cliffside and catch waves. Surfing felt like the thing that I was destined for, you know?" He glances at me, and I nod. "One day, I came through the back gate and met a girl I'd never seen before. Suddenly, it was as if my destiny wasn't leading me to that cove to be a surfer—it had all been leading me to her. Fate. Kismet. Fucking . . . celestial." He shrugs. "When I bought this house for her years later, when I took that cove and built a business around it, I wanted to name it after the feeling she gave me. That sensation of *meant-to-be*."

Chills rush through me, I know exactly what he means. Months ago, I wouldn't have understood it—the sentiment wouldn't have made sense, but when Willow slips back out of the French doors with two coffee mugs in hand, an effervescent smile on her beautiful face when she passes one to me and takes a seat beside her father, I understand it perfectly.

"While I'm glad you won, and I'm proud of you for putting yourself out there, you still broke my rules this summer, Weston," Leo says, gaze flashing to me. Trepidation trickles down my spine as he continues, "I told you not to be impulsive or reckless. You've repeatedly been both. I also told you to stay away from my daughter, and you went so far in the opposite direction I'm now afraid my grandkids are going to end up with your eyes someday."

Willow's pupils blow, face flushing as she chokes on her coffee. "*Dad.*"

A laugh bubbles out of me at Willow's reaction. Embarrassment heats her cheeks, but I can only smile, because I can't imagine anything better than creating someone who is half her too.

Leo grins at his daughter, dimples flashing.

"Plus, you were supposed to work a shift at Heathen's yesterday and you didn't show up. So, you're effectively fired. I think your summer in Pacific Shores is coming to an end."

Mortification sluices through me. I thought I'd still have at least a few weeks left of training under Leo, and I never thought it'd end with him dropping me like this. "I . . ."

"Are you fucking kidding me?" Willow flies off the swing. "That's bullshit. Weston has . . . You are . . ." She growls, lost for words, before stomping her foot. "That's fucked!"

His smile spreads wider, lifting his palms in surrender. "Hold your horses, Sugar." Turning his attention to me, he adds, "I also asked you to be focused and determined, to give me nothing less than one hundred percent. You've done that. You've proven to me that you are who you claimed to be, and luckily for you, I know someone at the Huntington Surf Academy who is looking for a new professional trainee—and a new youth teacher too."

Willow's entire body goes slack as my jaw drops in disbelief. She spins to me, eyes misting over as a watery smile spreads over her face.

"You start September first." Leo laughs. "So, we'll continue working together until then. You are actually fired from Heathen's, though. That first-place prize money will need to get you by."

"Huntington Beach is only twenty minutes from UC Irvine," Willow says in an astonished breath. "Fifteen from where I'll be living at Liv and Lou's."

My eyes flash to her dad, who's offering me a knowing smile. He stands, and Willow leaps into his arms as he kisses the top of her head, murmuring something against her hair that I can't hear before lifting his gaze to me. "After breakfast, do you want to hit a swell? Just for fun?"

"Yeah." I smile. "I'd like that."

Leo nods, slipping inside the house.

She faces me again, throwing herself into my arms.

"Any chance you're looking for a roommate?" I ask, tone casual—though the grin taking over my mouth is anything but.

Tilting her head, she peers up at me through glistening, lovestruck eyes. "Wow," she breathes, chuckling playfully. "Asking to move in with me already? That's a little quick, don't you think?"

"Shut up." I nip her nose, laughing.

All the light that left her after yesterday's events is shining through again. I know she still needs to process not only what happened, but the things that were said to her last night. I know she may be partially masking her emotions at this moment, but when I asked Willow how she was feeling this morning and if she wanted to tell her parents about the interaction with Parker, she said yes but not today. For now, she wanted to redirect her focus to what makes her happy and not harbor on the darkness.

I can't say I blame her, because for all I still need to work through myself, I feel exactly the same at this moment. When the sun is this bright and the air is fresh with lingering salt water, when the woman of my dreams is nestled inside my arms, I want to savor it.

CHAPTER THIRTY-NINE

WILLOW

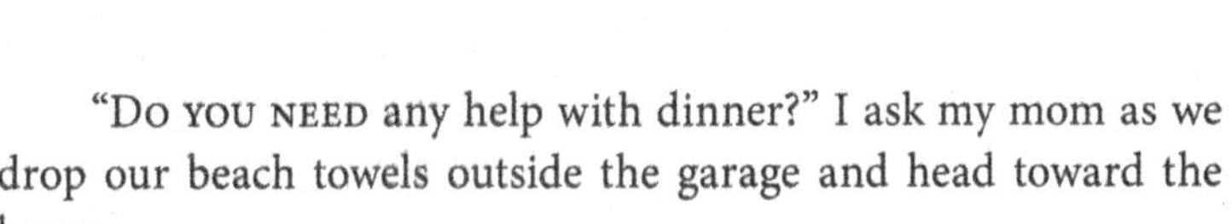

"Do you need any help with dinner?" I ask my mom as we drop our beach towels outside the garage and head toward the house.

"Monny cooked." Mom laughs, shaking her head. "Thank God. She made lasagna."

"Monny is coming for dinner?" I ask excitedly.

Monny is the nickname Lou gave my grandmother on my dad's side, Monica, when Aunt Dahlia first moved here with her when she was a kid. After the twins and I were born, she preferred that nickname to "Grandma," and it's stuck ever since.

"Oh, yeah. *Everyone* is coming over tonight. Better tell Wes to buckle up." She winks, nudging my ribs before striding into the house. I laugh, pulling out my phone to text Allie and ask her if she wants to come over for dinner too.

My parents and their siblings have had a Sunday dinner tradition for years, and there is a standing invite at my childhood home every weekend for whoever is around and can make it. It's rare that everyone is available outside of holidays and birthdays. Even today, we'll be missing Archer, but I'm excited to see my grandparents, who I haven't spent nearly enough time with while I've been home this summer.

Allie floats into my parent's house a half hour later with the ingredients to make Dahlia's famous chocolate-raspberry mousse cake—Archer's favorite. "I miss him," is all she says when I ask about it.

She buzzes around the kitchen, barking orders at me to assist with various baking tasks, and by the time the cake is in the oven, I'm covered in flour.

My family begins arriving throughout Allie's and my venture, all of them steering clear of the kitchen for fear of being roped into assisting. My grandparents arrive just as she's frosting the cake, and I'm eating leftover mousse straight from the bowl with my fingers.

"Hi, my beauty," my grandpa says as he passes me, planting a kiss against my cheek before filling the fridge with all the food they've brought.

"God, it smells good in here," Monny chimes, entering behind him. "Hi, babies." She hugs Allie before taking me into her arms too.

"Hi," I laugh, the sound muffled by my face in her neck. She smells like jasmine and citrus—the same perfume she's worn my entire childhood.

"Where are my other grandbabies? Where is your boyfriend?"

My cheeks heat. "Z, Liv, and Lou are out back. Weston was surfing with Dad, they should be done soon."

As if willing them into existence, deep, joint laughter rings through the house just a moment before Dad and Weston drift into the kitchen, my mom and aunt at their heels. Before greeting any of her children, my grandmother lights up at the sight of Weston—though his eyes are solely focused on me.

"Weston!" she exclaims, wrapping her arms around his waist. Monny is short, so her head barely reaches his chest, and his eyes widen as he stumbles back at the force of her embrace.

Sorry, I mouth.

He chuckles, shrugging with a smile as he returns it.

"I warned him, Sugar," my dad whispers, kissing the top of my head.

When we all sit down for dinner, we have to add multiple

extra chairs, and even then the lot of us hardly have enough elbow room to eat. When Archer is home, and if he were to—God forbid—someday end up with someone who *isn't* Allie, we'd have so many people at our dinner table that we'd need to add a second one. Not to mention the potential of Zander falling in love and bringing someone home too—no matter how adamantly he claims it'll never happen.

My grandmother leads our conversation, as she always does. She takes time to ask each of her grandchildren—Allie and Weston included—for updates on what's happening in their lives. Zander talks through his preparations for the start of his fourth year at Golden State University and his place on the hockey team. Allie mentions she's on track to graduate a semester early with her culinary fine arts degree at the same school. Weston speaks of his excitement to work with the Huntington Surf Academy and his high hopes of competing next year. I finally announce to everyone that I'll be attending school in Irvine and moving into Livia and Lou's house when they head to Costa Rica—though I'm not sure what Weston and I will do when they come back early next year.

Despite giving up my future at Berkeley, and losing out on an entire semester of my education, there isn't a hint of disappointment in the eyes of anyone I love. Only pride. Every person at this table knows the decision I made earlier this summer, and I know I'm a lucky one to have the freedom to be so honest without fear of judgment. To be so wholly supported when starting over. To be held while healing.

It's why I've decided not to tell my parents yet about what happened with Parker today, because the truth is, I wasn't lying to myself when I decided it would be the last time I thought of him. I refuse to continue allowing him to hold any space inside my soul, not when I have so much love to fill it instead. I know I'll have tough days, and I know there is still pain to process, but in this home, and surrounded by my family, that darkness doesn't need to exist.

Tomorrow, I'll sit down with my parents to talk about it so

we can expedite the restraining order. When I'm haunted in the middle of the night, I'll have Weston to hold me through it. I'll find a counselor at school who can help me work through the deeper gashes that haven't quite healed. At this moment, though, I feel an immense urge to be entirely present. Especially when Wes grips my knee beneath the table, holding me with tender reassurance.

We pull cards for dish duty. Wes and Zander lose, so while they go about cleaning up after dinner, Everett plays cornhole with Livia and Lou while Dahlia and Allie video call Archer. August helps my mom pick flowers from her garden, and Elena goes for a walk with my grandparents. I find myself sitting on the back porch with my dad as the sun begins to sink below the horizon.

"You know I wasn't exaggerating when I said you could live at home and be my baby forever, right?"

"You know I wasn't exaggerating when I said absolutely not, right?" I chuckle, leaning against his shoulder.

"I know." He sighs. "It's hard watching you grow up sometimes—falling in love, getting hurt, and figuring out who you are. Having you close to me this time made me feel like I could do a little more to protect you, and I guess I'm afraid to let you go now."

"You weren't this sentimental when I left for college at eighteen. Or when I moved in with Parker," I say softly.

"Maybe I should've been. Maybe that's what's scaring me now."

"You taught me how to protect myself. I'll be okay."

"I know." He nods, chin brushing over the top of my head as he holds me against him. "You can always come back home, Sugar."

"I don't think I'll need to this time," I whisper, my words laced with unbreakable confidence. "Weston is different."

"I think he is too."

That confirmation from my father settles over me like the crackling of fire on a breezy beach evening. I'm not in the habit of asking permission or seeking approval over the things or people I love, and my parents have never set that expectation themselves. I've always been given unconditional support to seek a life that is solely mine, but hearing my dad's favor of Weston from his own lips is another omen cementing my faith that this is exactly where I'm meant to be.

A throat clears, and I lift my head to find Wes standing in the doorway that leads from the house. "Hey." He smiles bashfully. "I'm not interrupting, am I?"

"No." I laugh. "I was actually just going to grab dessert. Do you want some, Dad?" I ask, lifting out of the swing.

"Yeah. Grab some for Mama too," he says, adding when I take a step forward, "Your shoe is untied, Sugar."

"Oh." I pause, glancing down to find the lace of my yellow Converse unraveled.

"I got it." Weston drops to his knees in front of me, gently grasping my ankle and setting it on his thigh as he reties my shoe. When he finishes, he presses a kiss to my calf, eyes drifting up to peer at me through his lashes—the pure adoration in his features enough to make me tremble. "There you go, love."

"Thank you," I murmur, cheeks flushing. Weston takes my hand, interlocking our fingers as he grabs the handle to the back door.

I peek over my shoulder at my dad, who watches the interaction with rapt reverence, a tender smile taking over his features when his eyes meet mine. A mutual understanding. This one is different. This one is forever.

Later, after we've had cake—well, I had cake while Allie forced Weston to try at least two bites at the threat of deep offense, even though he claims to still hate sweets—he and I sit on the back porch of my parents' house as the sun finishes sinking into the Pacific beyond us. The clouds are painted in a deep hue of rustic orange and violet, lingering daylight casting the earth in gold.

I'm shading the tattoo on his thigh with some washable markers I found in a kitchen drawer, doing my best to match the color of the sky on his skin.

"I love you, Willow," he murmurs softly.

"I love you too." I laugh, lifting my head to catch his gaze.

The fading sun pools inside his eyes, setting that gray-blue aflame. There are no longer storms within his irises—the clouds that used to haunt him seemed to have vanished entirely, leaving behind only radiance.

"Your eyes used to be so shadowed," I whisper, grabbing his face. "Dark and turbulent. That's gone now."

His full lips tick upward at the corner of his mouth. "Guess it's all the sunshine you shrouded me in. I was lost in darkness and found myself in your daylight."

When he kisses me, I realize that is perhaps the most precise way to describe this—us. Heated touch and soul-deep warmth, Weston's love is like rays of sun filtering over my face, iridescent spectrums of color dancing across my skin—like he anchored it and brought it home for me.

He sighs contentedly into my mouth, and I settle back into his chest and continue drawing over his skin. His thumb circles my shoulder, while his other hand brushes my hair behind my ear, and his lips press into the top of my head. He pulls me in tighter, tethering us together so that he's in contact with as much as my skin as possible.

He's always like this, burrowing as close to me as our bodies will allow. As if he's finally discovered the divinity of a soul-deep caress.

"You know, I think your love language might be physical touch after all," I say softly.

"No, Willow. My love language is you," he responds, voice like daylight.

EPILOGUE
WESTON

Five Years Later

"I JUST HAVE one last question for you, Weston."

I smile awkwardly, crossing my ankles as I settle back on the sofa, reminding myself it's almost over. Lou and my publicist, Chloe, *insisted* I take this interview, but I've never gotten used to the moving cameras in front of my face or the boom mic hovering above my head.

"Absolutely," I say through my teeth, hoping that the worldwide live audience isn't picking up how much I'm sweating right now.

"Any big plans for celebrating your new status as an Olympic Medalist?"

The most genuine grin I've accomplished throughout the duration of this interview spreads across my cheeks, followed by a breathless laugh. With a shake of my head, my eyes flit to Lou, whom I know for certain pre-screens every question I'm asked.

She's standing, pantsuit-clad, even in the tropics, with her arms crossed at her chest. She must be damn near six foot in the heels she has on, and as she tosses her long blond hair over her shoulder, she looks every bit the powerhouse agent I know her to be. Popping a brow, she taps a finger against her wrist.

Her not-so-subtle hint at eagerness for me to make the move

everyone has been waiting for.

I face the camera, looking directly into the lens for the first time this evening. "Oh, I have big, big plans." I turn toward the interviewer. "But you'll have to wait for that."

She laughs animatedly, thanking me for my time before closing out. Once the lights dim and the cameras shut off, I stand from the sofa and wipe my hands down my thighs. It's a make-shift studio set up in a banquet room of the hotel hosting the Olympic Surf Trials.

The podium ceremony was a couple of days ago, and Lou had us stay around for press, but I couldn't be happier to hop on a plane tomorrow morning and fly back to California. The rest of the family flew home after Liv and I received our medals. I took silver, which I'm incredibly proud of considering it is my first games. Livia took gold, for the third time, but it was the perfect way to close out her career.

With two toddlers, it's become a bit much for her and Lou to handle all the travel involved with both of their careers, and Liv is retiring so they can finally settle down—well, as settled as the two of them could be. They'll still spend half the year in Costa Rica with Liv's siblings.

"Did I do okay?" I ask as I reach Lou.

She holds up a finger, and I realize she's got an ear bud in. She scoffs, rolling her eyes before barking something about contract deadlines and not to call her about bullshit again, before pressing on the earpiece and sighing.

"Yeah, Wes, you did well. You're personable without being overindulgent, which is good enough for me."

I don't know what the fuck that means, but I shrug it off.

We walk through the hotel lobby, the sun a blazing orange orb through the paneled windows that look out toward the Tahitian coastline. I should have just enough time to make it to mine and Willow's room before the sun completely sets.

When we reach the elevators, Lou reminds me not to be late for our early flight tomorrow, then reminds me that she's done working for the evening and not to bother her.

I promise just that—because I imagine she'll want to be occupied in exactly the same way I will—as I step off at the twelfth floor. Willow and I booked a spacious suite with a private balcony, but the Costa-Ramoses have the penthouse. They claim it's because it's the only suite large enough to accommodate their kids, but I'm certain Liv's taste for luxury is the true reason.

When I reach our room at the end of the hall, I press the card against the door and push it open. "Hey, Wills. Are you cool if we just order room serv—" My words die on my tongue as I round the corner between the sitting area and the bedroom of our suite, finding Willow sitting at the end of our bed, propped back on her elbows with my medal nestled perfectly between her bare breasts.

She's completely naked, miles of smooth, tanned skin splayed out in front of me like a fucking offering. She widens her legs just enough to give me the tiniest tease of her pussy, and I now have saliva pooling on my tongue like a man starved.

My gaze selfishly eats up every inch of her, until I slowly make my way to her face—God's finest fucking masterpiece. She tilts her head, luscious long hair drifting across her collarbone as her ocean eyes blink at me innocently.

"Yeah, baby. We can order room service, but I thought you might want dessert first."

I'm shrugging off my sport coat and tossing it to the floor, rolling up the sleeves on my button-down under shirt as I stalk toward her. "Oh, you're fucking perfect, aren't you?" I fall to my knees when I reach the bed. "Wearing my medal." My fingers dance up her bare stomach, grasping the silver that hangs heavy on her chest. "But you know you're the real prize, don't you, Trouble?"

I nudge her legs open with my shoulders as I move between them, pressing a kiss to her inner thigh. Her head falls back on a moan, and she spreads wide for me.

"Mm-hmm." I spread her lips, flicking my gaze to hers as I bring my mouth to her clit. "This pretty cunt is my reward, isn't it?"

"You did so well, baby." She sighs, falling back onto the bed, arching her back as I drag my tongue the length of her slit. "Such a good surfer boy."

Willow knows I hate giving interviews. I *really* did not want to participate in the press today, so I should've known that my perfect girl would've had something special planned for when I returned. Little does she know, I've got plans too.

I don't waste time teasing her—not this time around. There is a little black box burning a hole in the drawer of the nightstand on my side of the bed, and the sun is rapidly sinking into the Pacific outside the windows behind my back.

I pull back just slightly, gathering saliva on the tip of my tongue and spreading Willow's pussy before spitting onto her.

"Fuck," she hisses, thighs trembling.

She's already glistening, but now she's completely soaked—pretty and pink as I run the pads of my fingers down the length of her, smearing my spit over her swollen clit before sliding it down and slipping inside.

I add a second finger, curling them both and massaging her as I circle her clit with my tongue, closing my lips around it and sucking hard. Setting a fervent rhythm, I have her shaking, chanting my name like a prayer, within minutes. When she unravels on my tongue, I savor every last drop of it before I move out from between her thighs.

I stand, wasting no time as I strip out of the rest of my clothes, admiring the way she looks splayed out in the bed—skin flushed, chest heaving, eyes soft and sated. She bites her lip, watching me with a half-lidded, passion laced gaze.

Those pretty blue eyes widen when I grab her hips, roughly dragging her to the end of the mattress and hauling her into my arms. She shrieks with laughter as she wraps her legs around my hips, my raging cock pressing against her abdomen.

"What're you doing?" she asks breathlessly, looping her arms around my neck as she cranes her head behind her, looking in the direction of where I'm walking.

I stride across our suite, shifting her weight into one arm as I throw open the door that leads to our balcony. It spans the length of our entire room, lush with potted palms and hibiscus creating a secluded, private paradise that blocks out the neighboring suites.

The view is phenomenal, the sun low on the horizon, shrouding the endless sky above us in shades of deep orange and bright fuchsia, reflecting on the blue water below, casting the entire world in the kind of vibrancy I often find in Willow's paintings.

She drops her feet as I set her down, her eyes bright and wide with curiosity as she studies me before her gaze bounces between our new surroundings. I spin her around, causing her breath to hitch as I press her up against the glass railing of the balcony.

"Nice and quiet for me, love, so I can let you watch the pretty sunset while I fuck you, okay?"

She nods, choking on a whimper. I wrap one arm around her hips, tugging her flush with mine before I knock her legs wider with my knee, gripping my cock and guiding it toward her soaked center.

I drag a palm up her stomach and over her breasts before I reach her neck, clasping her throat, muffling the moan that she threatens to let escape as I slide myself inside her. "I know, baby. I know." I squeeze as I rock my hips, thrusting deep. "You love wearing my necklaces."

She whimpers as I retreat before plunging back into her tight, wet warmth. Her perfect body hugs my cock like a glove made just for me. I set a fast pace, holding Willow's throat in my grip to muffle her sounds of pleasure, though the smacking of our skin echoes through air—obscene proof to anyone within earshot of what we're doing out here.

I don't give a fuck.

I want the entire world to know she's mine.

I look down, watching the way her ass ripples with every slam of my hips. I slip a hand between her thighs, putting pressure against her clit. Willow's breathing picks up, pussy tightening as I strum her bud with precision, drawing her closer to climax.

"Wes," she breathes, "I'm going to—"

"Yeah you fucking are."

I move my hand to her thigh, gripping hard as I lift her leg and adjust our angle, allowing me deeper, hitting the place that causes her entire body to tremble. I slide my palm up her neck and grasp her jaw, tilting her head to face me.

Her eyes are bursting with passion, the setting sun reflecting off her irises like the rippling crystalline waters below us. Her skin glows, cheeks flushed, pink lips parted with heavy breath.

"God, you're unbelievable, Willow."

I crash my lips against hers, swallowing her moans as she becomes unbearably tight, body going taut before her release barrels through us both.

She pants into my mouth, quivering with the force of her climax, and heat surges in my veins, coiling in my spine as it races through me. I explode, filling her entirely.

I drop her leg, falling into Willow as she collapses over the railing, the both of us floating down from the stars together. I run my tongue over her glistening spine, tasting her sweet skin, savoring the feel of her heavenly body against me—her breathing and her scent. Dipping my finger inside her, I push back in the climax that's begun seeping out.

I definitely have a breeding kink. I'm addicted to finishing inside her, watching it drip from her afterward. In my imagination, I'm filling her with babies, watching her grow with the life of my child, and blessing myself with the privilege of making her a mother.

It took about a year before Willow healed enough from her trauma to feel comfortable forgoing condoms, but once we reached that point, I realized just how addicting it is to release inside her bare. From there, my mind ran rampant. Desperate to fill her in every conceivable way.

Though, she's still on birth control. We're not there yet, and for now, we're happy exactly how things are. I travel so much for surfing, and when I'm home, I'm a trainer at a nonprofit Willow founded, Healing Tides.

It offers free therapy, art, and athletic courses to low-income and uninsured families in the Southern California area. Willow has a team of counselors that work with people of all ages, trauma, and disabilities. She teaches painting and has a team of volunteers that run youth camps, art classes, and recreational athletic leagues. I manage the youth surfing program, along with Livia when she and Lou are in California.

We bought a beautiful home in Dana Point last summer—ensuring there were plenty of extra bedrooms for whatever kind of family we may create someday. We adopted a dog, Pinto, because Willow thought she looked like a bean when she was a puppy. Hopefully, if our next conversation goes well, we'll spend the next year or so planning a wedding, and maybe I'll get lucky enough to knock her up on our honeymoon.

And even if none of that comes to fruition, even if I never win another medal, never compete again—if all I get in life is her, I'll consider myself the luckiest man on the goddamn planet.

I'm still inside her as the words, "Marry me," leave my mouth.

When Willow's spine goes rigid, the reality of it sets in.

Fuck.

Yes, I planned on proposing to her tonight. Yes, I wanted to do it at sunset on our final evening here in Tahiti. Yes, I got caught up in fucking her instead, and I may be panicking a little as the sun rapidly fades from my grasp, but the request rushing out while I've got her naked body pressed against the railing and my cock still buried inside her was a complete slip of the tongue.

"I'll ask again," I say on a breath. "In a more romantic way. I swear. I have the ring. It's in the room. I was going to take you out here and get down on one knee, but I fucked you instead, and now I'm losing daylight and—"

She straightens, and I pull out of her, stepping back to give her space as she spins around. She lifts her chin, glancing up at me through hooded eyes, my stomach leaping into my throat as I anticipate her response.

It sinks back down, butterfly wings taking its place when a

soft smile spreads across her sated face. A giggle follows it, and she clamps a hand over her mouth, nodding rapidly.

"Yes, I'd love to marry you, dork."

Thank God.

I surge forward, grasping her hips as I pull her into me, feathering my mouth over hers. She kisses me fiercely, arms looped around my neck as we remove every ounce of space between our bodies. I force myself back from her, knowing how easily it'd be for me to be caught up in her lips all night.

The sun has fallen beneath the ocean behind Willow's head, but streaks of deep orange stroke the sky, and lavender clouds float between the twilight stars just beginning to appear.

"Stay here," I rasp, kissing her once more before I turn around, running back inside our suite.

Willow laughs as I make quick work of putting underwear back on. "I'm going to keep my last name, though, just so you know," she calls from outside.

"Great," I say, sweeping her favorite silk robe off the chair beside our bed. "I'll make it my last name too." I grab the box from my nightstand drawer before heading back outside.

Her jaw is dropped, eyes misty as she watches me make my way back toward her—shocked. "You . . . You want to change your name?"

"Yeah." I help her slip the robe over her shoulders, and as she ties it at her waist, I add, "The name Ashford doesn't mean a goddamn thing to me. That was his name. The name Graham?" I smile, gently gripping her chin as I tilt her head up and hover my lips over hers. "It got me here. Gave me you. It's a good one."

"Yeah," she breathes. "It is."

I kiss her gently, and her astonished eyes only widen further when I fall to both knees in front of her.

She laughs again, shaking her head as she looks down at me. "You don't need to do that."

"Yes, I do." I nod. My hands are fucking trembling as I fiddle with the box in my hand. "You deserve a proposal worthy of your favorite romance novels, and I know this isn't that. Truthfully, I wanted to propose to you at a million different points in time over the past five years."

She wanted to wait until she finished school, and then we got caught up opening the center, and I began training for the Olympics, and it felt like life got in the way, but now I realize that none of that matters so much.

"Thousands of tiny moments when I'd watch you sleep, or the sun would catch your eyes in the perfect light. When you'd tilt your head back in laughter, and suddenly my favorite song was playing." Her misted eyes well with tears, and my throat thickens with emotion. "The day you graduated college. The pure joy on your face when you passed your licensing exam. Or that afternoon last month when I sat in on one of your classes, witnessing the patience and understanding you show those kids. The way your entire face lights up when you're working. The sound of your whistle when I'm on the waves, reminding me that you're watching. Rooting for me.

"I'm in awe of you always, and every second with you feels serendipitous and somehow destined at the same time. Every breath and laugh and smile is significant. Every moment with you is worthy of a grand gesture, including this one."

"Wes," she whispers, a tear spilling over her cheek. She bends her knees, as if she's going to meet me on the ground too, but I shake my head, squeezing her hip—an unspoken plea that she stay in place.

"When I won that medal, you're who I looked for in the crowd. When I rode that winning wave back to shore, you're who I searched for the minute my feet hit the sand. When I was asked how I felt, what it was all for, and what it meant to me by every reporter—my mind drifted to you. When I sat down for that interview today, I wanted so desperately to call you my wife, and I don't think I can go another day without seeing this on your finger . . ." I shakily open the box, and Willow gasps as her eyes fall on the ring—oval cut on a diamond band. "I can't promise every second is going to be extravagant and grandiose, but I can promise you a lifetime of tiny gestures and stolen moments—an everyday life that is worthy of the love you deserve, Willow."

She's crying now, and it's not until she bends over, wiping the tears from my own cheeks that I realize I'm crying too.

Brushing her trembling lips over mine, she whispers, "I love you so much, Weston."

"I love you," I whisper back, slipping the ring onto her finger before grasping her face and kissing her deeply—with every fiber in my being, every atom in my bones, and all of the force inside my soul.

ACKNOWLEDGMENTS

Tattered Tides is truly a labor of love. Not just mine, but so many people who've rallied around me through my journey and helped lead me here. My eighth book, my true traditional publishing debut, and a second generation to my most beloved story. The idea to continue this family came to me years ago, before I'd ever released *Heathen & Honeysuckle* into the world, and for a long time, I let it stay exactly that: an idea. Nestled into the corners of my mind, because I wasn't sure there would be an audience out there for Pacific Shores, that I'd find readers who'd fall in love enough to continue with me through the future.

So, first and foremost, I want to thank all of you, readers. For anchoring yourself to this small town right along with me, and giving me the opportunity to continue telling its stories.

Jenna, this is actually an apology. You see my ugliest sides on the most frequent basis, a feat only my husband could rival, and yet you're still here. A true saint! Thank you for allowing me to be my most unhinged, neurotic, high maintenance self, and still loving me. I've said it eight times in eight books now, but I couldn't do this without you—your resilience and support and unmatched determination. Thank you for being here with me from the beginning, please never leave.

Page, my publicist, for your unending support and the way you uplift me at every venture. You are a strategic genius, but more than that, you're the kindest soul and the most wonderful friend.

Maddy and Cassie for helping me keep this boat afloat, especially when I've got no idea how to steer this thing. I'm forever grateful for your creative expertise, admin support, and the love you have for these stories. I couldn't keep my head on my shoulders without you.

My beta readers, Cait, Catie, and Rachel. I'm so grateful to have each of you here from the earliest stages, and for knowing this world as well as I do. Your thoughtful feedback is invaluable to the crafting of this story, and your unhinged comments keep me going on the days I'm struggling most.

The independent bookstores and small businesses who have supported me and helped get my stories into the hands of countless new readers. I couldn't do it without you! Wildflower Fiction, The New Romantics, Trope Bookshop, Kiss and Tale, Love & Other Books, The Last Chapter, Heartbound Bookshop, Always Yours, Flower Crowns & Fiction, Scribbles Bookshop, Wellread Candle Co, and Jadestone Creations.

S.A.B's Soulmates, you keep me going on the hardest days. Thank you.

I have so many author friends who uplift and support this journey of mine on a daily basis, and I am endlessly grateful. Especially to Ambar Cordova, Bailey Hannah, and Tarah DeWitt, who have held my hand through every up and down of writing this book, who have rooted and celebrated every win with me and helped guide me through each loss.

Tori Ann, the president, chairman, and CEO of the Leo Graham fanclub. He wouldn't be here, in his Crocs, without your consistent bullying over the years. Thank you for that, but more, thank you for being a wonderful friend.

My agent, Katie, for your support and endless hard work in getting my stories into the hands of others. Thank you for believing in me!

My editor, Jordyn. This book was such a doozy for us, but I'm grateful for your support and dedication as we worked through it together. I'm so proud of this one, and I couldn't have done it without you!

The Page & Vine team for bringing these stories into the world.

Lexi, you're my best friend and my confidant and my number one supporter. I never feel alone in this world, because I've never known someone so much like me, and that somehow makes every obstacle feel a little less challenging. I'm forever grateful this journey brought me to you, almost like it was destined or something. Thank you for holding my hand every step of the way.

My husband, Bubs. You are what all my dreams are made of. I'll never have the words to express my gratitude to you, for the care and love and support you've given me since the very first day of this journey. Since I was seventeen and even more of a mess than I am now. You are my most favorite person in the world, and if I never did another thing but spent the rest of my life with you, it would still be the best life ever lived.

WILLOW & WESTON'S PLAYLIST

"ocean eyes" | Billie Eilish

"seven" | Taylor Swift

"Surf" | Mac Miller

"Black Friday" | Tom Odell

"willow" | Taylor Swift

"Clouds" | Børns

"Tongue Tied" | GROUPLOVE

"The blue" | Gracie Abrams

"Fallingforyou" | The 1975

"Movement" | Hozier

"Out of the Woods" | Taylor Swift

"Two Is Better Than One" | BOYS LIKE GIRLS

"Iris" | The Goo Goo Dolls

"Francesca" | Hozier

"Daylight" | Taylor Swift

ABOUT THE AUTHOR

Sarah fell in love with reading as a child. She quickly learned that books can take her to all the places she always dreamed of going, and allow her to live endless lifetimes in the one that she was given.

Sarah believes that to be seen is to be loved, and that's why romance is such an important genre. She believes romance novels offer readers reflection and relatability, ultimately helping us understand ourselves, and the world around us, a little better. She prides herself on crafting healing, raw, and uplifting stories that explore the complexities of the human spirit through the guise of love.

Sarah was born in California and raised in Southern Oregon, and still considers herself to be a Pacific Northwest gal at heart; right down to being a coffee snob, collecting hydro flasks, adamantly believing in Sasquatch, and never having owned an umbrella.

She now resides in Arizona with her husband and their pup, Rue. When she's not writing, she's reading, and if she's not reading, she's probably out searching for a decent cup of coffee or binging Vanderpump Rules for the millionth time.

Connect with Sarah on social media: @sarahabaileyauthor

Sign up for her newsletter to be the first to know about updates and announcements: sarahabaileyauthor.com/newsletter

Also by Sarah A. Bailey

Pacific Shores series

Heathen & Honeysuckle

Wicked & Wildflower

Reckless Roses

Vice & Violet

The Soulmate series

The Soulmate Theory

The Fate Philosophy

The Forever Experiment

Celestia Cove series

Tattered Tides

Sidelined Souls (coming 2026)